HE CHAIN THAT BINDS THE EARTH
I0712257
SEAN O'CONAILL

ENDORSEMENTS

I really enjoyed the book. I felt that the characters were realistic, as were the problems they faced. The plot was gripping and I didn't want to stop reading.

Cáit Passmore, 14

The Chain that Binds the Earth is a compelling novel that you feel a part of as soon as you start reading. It shows the power of friendship and love, and there is never a dull moment. You always want to keep reading on, and you are never disappointed when you do. The book is filled with strong, likeable characters whom I quickly grew to love. Unputdownable and utterly brilliant.

David Brussard, 14

REVIEWS

This is a wonderful and quite remarkable work… that will engage, provoke and inspire a wide audience from a variety of backgrounds, interests and ages…. It is much more than a novel… Echoes of the Troubles are everywhere in this work… O'Conaill does not shy away from the claim (made by those such as Archbishop Oscar Romero and those of the liberation theology position) that compromise and identification with the powerful since Constantine has undermined the mission of the Church and 'made Jesus safe' to follow. … A wonderful book, deserving of the widest audience and consideration.

Aidan Donaldson, (Review in *The Irish Catholic,* August 27th, 2015) https://www.irishcatholic.com/a-remarkable-book-with-a-vision-for-the-future/

A novel for young adults that turns out to be a must read for their parents and teachers as well…. O'Conaill does a good job of dramatizing the various and random ways in which scapegoats are chosen as we follow a series of bullying incidents. These encounters carry the threat of violence, which is often realized, and adult readers will wince at the ignorance of the teachers to what is happening on their watch. We wince because we recognize the truth of this fictional account, especially the way in which the author connects the bullying in the school to the scapegoating violence perpetrated and endured by the adults. The children are sadly victims of the sins of their parents and O'Conaill clearly intends this to be a message for all of Northern Ireland to hear. The foursome… are troubled by issues that defy easy answers, from crime to the environment to the sheer number and variety of obstacles in the way of peace. But they are united by two things: a deep desire to stop bullying in their school and their prayerful search for a solution to the world's problems.

Suzanne Ross (Review in the Bulletin of the international Colloquium on Violence and Religion (COV&R), December 2015.)
https://violenceandreligion.com

THE CHAIN THAT BINDS *the* EARTH

SEAN O'CONAILL

ARPress LLC
45 Dan Road Suite 5
Canton MA 02021
Hotline: 1(888) 821-0229
Fax: 1(508) 545-7580

Ordering Information:
Quantity sales. Special discounts are available on quantity purchases by corporations, associations, and others. For details, contact the publisher at the address above.

Printed in the United States of America.

ISBN-13:   Softcover   979-8-89356-696-3
                 eBook   979-8-89356-697-0

Library of Congress Control Number: 2024904033

I

It had all happened, Johnny realised later, because he lived on the wrong side of the bridge.

That first morning—a Friday—his stomach was in a knot. To make things worse his mother Anny was with him at the bus stop. His blue uniform was the only one in the queue of twenty or so. None of the others there would cross the bridge, or even board the bus he waited for. He was going, for the very first day, to a new school, the 'big school' on the western side of the bridge, the City side. They would stay on the side they called their own, the Waterside. They were Protestants, while his family was Catholic—and he was going to a Catholic school.

So when he saw the bus, and stuck out a hand, jeers followed him onto it. The driver waved him past on this first day. He knew Anny would be annoyed if he didn't look back, so he did, embarrassed again, and nodded. As he expected, the jeering became louder. She waved, and turned to go—already late for work. Again he saw the dark swelling on her right cheekbone, which she had tried to hide with make-up. And he tried again to forget what had made it.

As the bus pulled away, he looked down the aisle for blue uniforms like his own, and saw only ten or so. Most belonged to older pupils, who ignored him. Towards the back, also in blue, was wild-haired Mary McNevin, from the same primary school class. Only two other faces, about his own age, looked at him with any interest. One looked Oriental—strange to him—wary and anxious, holding tightly to a schoolbag on his lap. Johnny found himself staring, and then, as usual, embarrassed.

Two rows further back was a tall girl with black-rimmed glasses, sitting alone, also in blue. She had straight dark hair, tied in a too- neat ponytail. She looked at him appraisingly, without any expression. Then she took her bag from the seat beside her and he sat down. She didn't look at all embarrassed—although she too had stared.

'I'm Margaret,' she said. 'Phillips.'

'Johnny Mullan.'

He wondered if he should hold out a hand, and thought not. She seemed a little snooty, disapproving—like his Auntie Kath. He was used to that.

Soon the bus turned onto the upper deck of the older bridge linking the two sides of the city. Almost immediately he could see the morning sun glinting on the sculpture that stood at the far end of the bridge. The bus would skirt it, and he knew that for a long time now he would see this scene every morning and afternoon from Monday to Friday from almost every angle—two men in frozen metal with hands outstretched towards one another, not quite meeting. He knew what it stood for: the divided city, and the peace that people wanted but couldn't always get.

He had already visited his new school, south of the city, overlooking the river, on the open day, months earlier. But now as he approached on his first day as a pupil, he was far more keyed up. Anny expected so much—maybe too much.

As they approached the wide gates of the school, with IONA COLLEGE painted in black on the two white pillars, a large sleek silver-grey car coming from the opposite direction slowed down and signalled to turn in to the college also. As it passed in front of the bus Margaret Phillips spoke for only the second time.

'That's Maroneys' car!'

Johnny knew vaguely about the Maroneys. They were the closest thing to royalty in the city. Maroney senior was a big wheel in the business world who had returned from the USA as head of a clothing corporation. As an Irish American who had 'made it big' he was highly regarded. One of his factories employed many people east of the city and he was rumoured to be thinking of investing heavily in further expansion. Rumour had it that he often flew in and out from the city airport on his company's jet.

The car and bus descended a winding avenue through tall trees, and then drew into the forecourt of the school central block—an imposing grey stone building with a Victorian facade. As Johnny left the bus he saw the driver of the Maroneys' car, dressed in a grey suit and cap, jump out smartly to open the rear door. A tall man, elegantly dressed in a dark blue suit, white shirt and mauve tie, stepped out. From the other side of the car a boy of about Johnny's age joined his father as they walked towards the entrance. Johnny remembered him vaguely from the first trial day at the school three months earlier. There on the step to greet both of them was the school principal, Mr Ferguson, who had eyes for no one else.

'Mr Maroney, welcome … and Aidan,' he greeted both.

'Principal,' said Mr Maroney, 'I just came to check if that had been sorted out—Aidan's technology requirements?'

'Yes, of course, Mr Maroney. We cannot be lagging behind what's possible nowadays.'

'Well, Aidan,' said Maroney, turning to his son, 'here's your school. Make sure to make the most of it. You have a lot to prove!'

Then Maroney senior shook hands with the principal and turned to leave. His glance swept quickly over and then past Johnny and Margaret, who had been standing watching. In a moment he was gone.

Johnny found himself face to face with Aidan Maroney. Aidan was slightly taller. He stood confidently, his chin slightly lifted.

'Are you in Year Eight?' he asked, with an American twang.

When Johnny and Margaret nodded he held out a hand as though he had rehearsed the gesture.

'Aidan Maroney—Eight B.'

'Margaret Phillips. We're Eight B too,' said Margaret. Johnny was, as usual, slow to speak when meeting someone for the first time. He was about to give his name when Aidan went on:

'I hope they're up to speed here. Dad's expecting me to lead the class in technology with some stuff I've got here.' He pointed to his bag with his free right hand.

Johnny closed his mouth again. His name was clearly unimportant just then. How was he to compete with someone like this? He guessed that Aidan had brought at least the latest in mobile computer technology, linked to the Internet. Johnny didn't even have use of a desktop computer at home, and could count his hours of Internet experience on his fingers.

'Year Eights to the Assembly Hall!' a speaker announcement sounded. That was Johnny's year—his first year in secondary school after seven years in the primary school. The three found themselves in a flow of other Year Eights headed down a corridor towards a row of doors that opened into a large hall, smelling strongly of varnish. On a stage at the front stood Mr Ferguson with several other teachers. Most smiled in welcome.

Soon the entire new first-year group of ninety-six boys and girls was standing waiting in the hall. Some were talking in low tones, and most were looking nervous.

'Welcome, Year Eights,' said Mr Ferguson through a microphone. 'This is an important day for you and the school. Iona College is named after one of the most famous and important islands in the world—where the great Irish Saint, Columba, lived in exile. He came from these parts of Ireland, and founded a monastery on Iona, off the west coast of Scotland, in the sixth century. His monks founded other monasteries and spread out across Scotland, Northern England and then Western Europe to convert people who had never heard of, or who had forgotten, Christ.

'In the same way the pupils of Iona College leave here eventually, many of them going abroad. This school too is an island—an island of study, centred on Christian values. The school's motto is *Scopus meus excelsior est*—my goal is higher. That must be your goal too, excellence in everything you do.

'Already you have seen the rules of the school, and signed the form agreeing to keep them. You will be held to that agreement. Your form teachers will conduct you now to their rooms. First, Mr O'Kane—form teacher of Eight A.'

A tall teacher stepped forward and descended the steps leading to the floor of the hall. The pupils parted to let him through, and Eight A filed in behind him.

'Mrs Walsh—Eight B.'

A cheerful looking woman—about Anny's age, Johnny thought—with dark red hair, came forward and descended, and Eight B followed her. Johnny found himself alongside a pale freckle-faced boy who looked even more nervous than Johnny felt.

'H ... lo,' this boy said, with a stammer. 'I'm K ...Kieran L...Lowney.'

Kieran stuck with Johnny all the way to Mrs Walsh's room, which turned out to be outside the main complex of buildings, on a terrace on a lower level. It was a prefabricated classroom sited with eight others, on the outside row of three—with a view of descending lawns. Beyond was a line of trees and shrubs, and through them Johnny could see glimpses of the river below.

Mrs Walsh opened a folder.

'I'm not just your form teacher, I'm also taking you for English. I want to put your faces to these names. Now—answer when I call your name. Rosemary Allen.'

'Here,' said a plump girl in the front row.

'Say present,' said the form teacher, Mrs Walsh, 'and sit up straight.' Rosemary, whose head had been resting on her desk, shot up blinking, to giggles from the class.

'Asleep already?' Mrs Walsh asked, in mock astonishment.

'That's a bad sign.'

'I was just thinking,' said Rosemary, blushing.

'Don't let me discourage you—but do it from a vertical position, or teachers may suppose you have somnolent tendencies. Look that up for homework, and tell me what it means next class.'

Johnny was sure that 'somnolent' meant 'sleepy', and began to feel better. English was his best subject. He wondered if he would get a chance to prove this. 'Patrick Andrews.'

'Present', said a tall, fair boy at the right. Already he had placed on his desk a fancy blue leather pen and pencil case, with a gold clasp—with his name highlighted in gold also. From this he had taken a pen that could write in any colour, chosen by turning its top. He was busy practising an elaborate signature on a jotter. Show off, thought Johnny, enviously. He felt self-conscious about his own red plastic case from the discount store, and the cheap pens inside.

On it went. They were a class of twenty-four—Eight A, Eight C and Eight D had exactly the same number.

'Right,' said Mrs Walsh finally, closing the register. 'As your form teacher I'm the person other teachers will complain to—if you give them cause. And I'm also the teacher you should come to if you have any problems you can't solve yourself. We have form class once a week, and English class once every day—so you'll be seeing a lot of me. First of all today we'll work through the school rules, give bus passes to those entitled to them, and answer any questions. Then we'll do some English.'

Quickly she passed out a list of school rules and went through it. To Johnny the rules were mostly sensible, although she put a lot of stress on never speaking without putting your hand up first.

Then Mrs Walsh called out the names of those entitled to bus passes, which depended upon distance from the school. Anny had told Johnny to make sure he got one, so when his name was called he was pleased to go forward and receive his own. 'John C Mullan' it said—and his route and stop. Mrs Walsh seemed pleased when all of this was over. She closed her form teacher's file and stood up.

'Now! Who are the Jedi knights in this class, I wonder?'

Eight B looked at one another self-consciously, no-one putting up a hand.

'Hmph?' she said. 'No-one with telekinetic powers, wanting to use the light side of the Force against the dark side, flying between the stars—attacking battle stations? What a tedious lot!'

'The Jedis were long, long ago and far away,' said Johnny without thinking, and he was again embarrassed when everyone turned to look. He watched those films often.

'Yes, they were Johnny,' said Mrs Walsh, seeming pleased that someone had spoken at last. 'But that is where our imaginations can take us—and into the future too.'

'What's teleketic, Miss?' asked Mary McNevin, smaller than most, with wild crinkly straw-coloured hair.

'Tele-kin-etic—Well, anyone?' asked Mrs Walsh.

'I think it means being able to make things move without touching them,' said Aidan Maroney.

'Yes, indeed it does,' said Mrs Walsh. She explained how the parts of the word came from Greek, like 'telephone'.

'We learn new words best when we meet them in an interesting way, and by using them when we need them.

But we've got to want to do it. And that's why I'm talking about the Jedi knights. They belong to a time and a place that came into existence first in the imagination of George Lucas. It is his own made-up galaxy, yet millions of children, adults too, want to go there, even though it *was* long, long ago and far away. When we go into that world we need the words he invented to describe it—so people learn words like 'Wookie' and 'Millennium Falcon', without even trying.'

She paused then, looking at them to see if they were listening, which mostly they were. The teachers Johnny had known in primary school had never spoken in this way of an imaginary world that excited him, into which he could escape—and too often didn't want to leave.

'Where does your imagination take you? That's your first task, Eight B. Now, into groups of four and talk about that. Ten minutes only.'

Johnny found himself in a group with Mary McNevin, Patrick Andrews and Edward Li—the boy who looked Chinese.

Without asking, Patrick took the spotlight.

'It's Wembley stadium. The final of the European Cup. I'm a striker, playing for Man United. The score is two all, and there's only two minutes to go. I've had a kicking from this big defender….'

Patrick launched into a pass-by-pass commentary which went on and on, without thinking of the others. When Johnny looked at the classroom clock, almost three of the ten minutes had gone. He began nodding his head, to say 'OK, we get it' but Patrick never noticed. Johnny looked at the other two, but neither was anxious to tackle the big striker in front of goal.

'And then you score the winner!' said Johnny at last, breaking in, because someone had to.

'Oh, mind reader huh?' said Patrick, annoyed, maybe because he had planned the final score in much more detail. His big build-up had been ruined, and he might not forget who had done it.

'There's only five minutes to go,' said Johnny. 'We all need a chance. Edward now.'

The Oriental-looking boy hesitated, but Johnny said 'Go on!' He wanted to make up for his bad manners on the bus.

'It's Eddy,' the boy said in a Derry accent. 'I'm on an away team from the starship Enterprise. I'm an expert in martial arts and crime science, and I have to find out who has murdered the leader on a planet that's about to join the Federation.'

Eddy told an exciting short story that lasted no more than a minute, and then stopped. Johnny knew that Eddy had noticed that Patrick had been rolling his eyes backward and miming extreme boredom. At one point Eddy rolled his own eyes back quickly in imitation of Patrick, for Johnny's benefit, as though he was used to this.

Johnny turned to Mary. 'Right—your turn.'

'Hogwart's school. It's my first day there too. I can do magic, just a little, sometimes by accident. This big heavy pushes me over and laughs—and I say 'Grunthog!' He changes into a hedgehog that runs about squealing. He keeps slipping on the polished floor, and rolling over onto his prickles, and everyone laughs at him instead of me. I'm an Irish witch, the next great Hogwarts pupil after Harry Potter.'

She reddened, because Patrick was again rolling his eyes.

'Go on,' said Johnny. 'Why do you want to be able to do magic?'

'Because … life is so boring, often. And you can do things there... turn things upside down. You can turn bullies into frogs, and stuff. It's a bright, usually happy place, with an adventure just for you.'

'Kids' stuff!' said Patrick. 'Now you—know-all,' he said, turning to Johnny.

'I like Harry Potter too,' said Johnny, to back Mary up. 'He's like a Jedi knight in a way—he just uses a wand instead of a light sabre.'

And then he paused, and went on:

'I too imagine another place, far away, and it has solved all the things that are wrong here.'

He knew he couldn't explain this fully, because what was wrong for him was a family secret. He felt stupid about that, and grew embarrassed again. And hurried on.

'But somehow this other place turns out to be real also, and … somehow it's connected to this place, and I can travel between the two. I discover it, bit by bit. It helps me to change this place, where I am, most of the time, bit by bit. I don't know how yet. I haven't worked out the details.'

'What a dumb idea,' said Patrick. 'My story is the best, because it's real and cool.'

Only for you, Johnny thought to himself. He knew that Patrick's football world was just as unreal as all other imaginary places, but didn't want to challenge him again. He sensed that already he had made an enemy.

All three let Patrick's self-applause just sit there. They were glad when, in a moment, Mrs Walsh called them to order.

'Right, now, you've just been practising for your first English exercise for next Monday—a piece of writing called 'My Application'. You are to write an application to join some organisation, or team, or expedition, or project, something that you would like to belong to, it doesn't matter what. If you can't think of one you like, make one up. However, if you do that, make sure to include a description of the organisation. Say why you want to join, and what you think you have to offer, your talents or qualities, things that might impress them. At least eight sentences altogether. OK?' Johnny wrote the task carefully into his homework diary. He noticed Aidan Maroney working with a fancy tablet computer, using a stylus. Johnny knew this meant it had advanced character recognition. He was even more impressed—especially when Aidan finished the task in no more time than anyone else.

'Now, finally,' said Mrs Walsh, 'would anyone like to tell the class where their imagination took them?'

Only one hand shot up—Aidan Maroney's.

'Good, Aidan—let's hear!'

'It's to a place my Dad showed me once. A wide room with this big table—where all the top people in his firm make big decisions.

There are video screens half-sunk into the table for everyone, and a large screen at the top of the room for video projection. It's at the top of one of the tallest buildings in New York. My Dad's firm is run from there. But I imagine a room even bigger, where the brightest people of our age will solve all sorts of world problems—like crime and terrorism. Some of us could be there.'

Seated at one of the desks in the front row, Aidan addressed the last sentence to the class. All were impressed, including Johnny. How daft his own idea was by comparison. He was thinking only of his own problems, here and now, and flying off stupidly into space, while Aidan was thinking on a huge scale, for the future, and in the real world.

'Very impressive, Aidan,' said Mrs Walsh. 'Notice how Aidan is obviously thinking about the best kind of world to build. So you should all be—but not necessarily in the same way. Now—anyone else?'

There was a long pause as no-one dared to compete with Aidan Maroney. Johnny wanted to, but was sure that Patrick Andrews would roll his eyes again. So he sat silent.

'Margaret ... What about you?' Mrs Walsh asked—looking at Margaret Phillips, who stood up slowly.

'I imagine the world as it was before we humans came along ... with every tree and animal that we have made extinct still here.

There are no roads or overhead wires or power stations, or factories, or cities or jet planes—or people. Just wildness everywhere. Ireland is covered in forests, with bears and giant elk and wolves roaming around, and all the swallows and geese and other migrating birds that are now in danger. In the spring, thousands of salmon make their way up the river down there, and otters, bears and seals can be seen hunting them. And there's no rubbish in the river, or oil or other muck. It's much nicer than today. And safe from us humans.'

'Excellent,' said Mrs Walsh. 'You are an environmentalist, I see.'

'Miss!' said Aidan, with his hand up.

'Yes, Aidan?'

'That's all unreal to me. We belong here too—and we were meant to invent technology and build cities.'

'Maybe,' said Mrs Walsh, 'but Margaret did what she was asked to do—let her imagination take her somewhere, and describe that. Now we all know something important about her: that she loves the natural world, and is sad for it. Just as we know something important about you: that you are positive about technology and industry. These differences are what make us who we are.

'We all have a right to be different. In fact we *should* all be different. Every one of you is unique, and every one of you will write a different application over the weekend. In that way we will learn all about you next week.

'Now, we've had so much to do this morning that there's no time for your usual fifteen minute break after second period. A prefect will be here to guide you to your next class, technology.'

The school bell had gone just before Mrs Walsh had said that everyone should be different. Johnny remembered this as he packed his bag and lined up to leave. Could he be different—if that was what she expected?

Again Johnny found that Kieran Lowney was at his elbow as they left Mrs Walsh's room. An older pupil, a prefect, had come to guide them to one of the rooms in the technology block.

As they climbed the steps on the terrace to take them to the level of the main school, Kieran went ahead, with his bag strap looped over his head and resting on his left shoulder. So did another heavier boy from Eight B—Gavan Maguire, close on Kieran's heels. Gavan had been sitting beside Aidan Maroney. Johnny had already noticed Gavan kicking Kieran's bag, and wondered why Kieran let him.

'Watch this,' whispered Gavan, turning to Johnny.

He jerked hard on Kieran's bag strap, pulling him backward from the topmost of twelve steps. Kieran lost his balance, couldn't reach the rail with his left hand and came tumbling down the steps—straight into Johnny, who almost fell backwards also. Kieran's bag spilled some of its contents—including a Spiderman comic. As Kieran replaced them, Johnny raced up the steps to where Gavan was standing, leering, at the top.

'Lowney the loony can't stand up!' Gavan said with a laugh.

'Why did you do that?' Johnny asked. The steps were steep and Kieran could have been seriously hurt.

'Don't worry about him,' said Gavan—nodding towards Kieran who was making his way again up the steps. 'He's adopted, y'know.

God knows who his parents are. No-one else does. Now he lives with people who have no kids of their own.'

Johnny felt suddenly angry—so angry he lost his self- consciousness.

'Don't do that again!' he said.

'Oh—who'll stop me? Not you anyway!'

Gavan was almost half a head taller, and much heavier than Johnny. He was sneering now at both of them. Johnny's anger grew but he had been in trouble over this in his primary school, and Anny had warned him about fighting in his new school. Keep your temper, whatever happens, she had said. So he did, just.

'Come on,' he said to Kieran, and headed after the class. Kieran followed on his heels, and Gavan came behind them both, still sneering.

The next class was Johnny's first experience of technology. The teacher, Mr McKinley had a beard and a lot of enthusiasm. He told them what technology was all about and then asked if anyone could explain how a car engine worked. Again Aidan Maroney's hand went up immediately.

'There's this closed metal box called a cylinder. Inside it gas ... I mean petrol and air are mixed and then lit to make an explosion ...'

'Hang on,' said Mr McKinley, 'Let me draw that ...'

He drew a simple diagram of the engine as Aidan spoke.

'Excellent, Aidan. Very well explained.' said Mr McKinley, completing the drawing. 'You'll have no problems in this class I can see. Everything we see has an explanation.'

He then showed them some things made by older pupils. Johnny found that, despite his fears, he liked the class—because Mr McKinley was so enthusiastic about his subject. He liked the thought of working with wood and metal to make things. His Dad had once shown him how to use some simple woodworking tools, so he should have a good start there.

Kieran Lowney sat beside him through this class, and lined up with him when the bell went. Johnny felt uncomfortable about this. Gavan Maguire had sat at the next table, and again seemed more interested in kicking Kieran's bag under the table than in the lesson. Kieran had pulled it out of his reach, but Gavan lined up behind them again as the bell went, and began punching the bag again. Johnny could see that Kieran was used to this treatment, as he said nothing—merely looked away.

Maths class followed. Johnny found he could follow what the teacher said, as he took things slowly. Johnny had dreaded the thought of Maths, as it had given him problems in primary school. So he felt relieved to be given homework he thought he could do. Lunch period followed. Almost the whole class went to the dining hall, with just a few opting for a packed lunch. They ate this in a separate room. Anny had told Johnny he should take the canteen dinners, so he found himself at table in one of the noisiest rooms he had ever been in—half-full of the din of clattering plates and cutlery and people's raised voices as they shouted to be heard. The first- years had been allowed to enter first, so sat bunched together at the far end of the hall.

Johnny found himself sitting with Eddy Li and Kieran Lowney and other first-year pupils from the other three classes. When they finished their main course of sausages and mashed potato they lined up for the second course. Aidan Maroney, Patrick Andrews and Gavan Maguire were standing just behind them in the queue.

Just as Kieran reached the head of the queue Johnny noticed Gavan sidle up to Aidan and Patrick and whisper something—pointing at Kieran as he did so. Aidan looked at Kieran and grinned. Johnny guessed that Gavan was planning something stupid, and wondered what.

Kieran collected his plate of fruit and ice cream, and waited a moment for Johnny to do the same. Just as Johnny turned to follow him back along the queue he saw Gavan Maguire deliberately strike Kieran's hand from below. His plate somersaulted and fell with a crash on the tiled floor. Kieran stared aghast at the spreading mess. There was an ironic cheer from the tables—but an angry voice soon silenced everyone.

'Who did that?'

It was the supervising teacher, who had been standing close to the tail of the queue. A middle-aged, heavy-set man, he now stood glaring at the hapless trio, with the owner of the fallen plate easily identifiable.

'What happened here?'

'An ac.....cident,' said Kieran, with a great effort, firing up as the whole canteen stared.

'Is that true?' asked the teacher, looking at Johnny.

'Yes,' said Johnny quickly. 'Gavan wasn't looking and knocked Kieran's plate as he passed.' He looked straight at Gavan as he said this.

'Is that true?' the supervisor asked, turning towards the other three boys.

Gavan hesitated, and then looked at Aidan Maroney. Aidan also hesitated, looking at Johnny. Johnny knew it was important that Aidan understand that he had seen exactly what had happened, so he returned the stare. After what seemed too long a pause Aidan nodded.

'I guess..,' he said.

'Maybe,' said Gavan lamely. 'I wasn't looking and maybe I ...'

'Not looking is not good enough. You know the rule in the canteen. If you spill it you ... ?'

The teacher paused at that point, waiting for Gavan to finish the sentence.

'Clear it up,' said Gavan, without enthusiasm.

The supervisor pointed wordlessly to a bucket and mop standing in an alcove, and Gavan went to fetch them. The canteen returned to its normal hubbub as Gavan repaired some of the damage he had done—although there was nothing he could do for the plate. By this time Johnny, Eddy and Kieran were back at their table, Kieran with a new plate.

'Thanks,' said Kieran to Johnny, who shook his head.

'He did that on purpose, and he'd do it again if he got away with it.'

'What has Gavan got against you?' Eddy asked. 'I saw him kicking your bag in class.'

Kieran said nothing, just lowered his head towards his plate.

Johnny thought he knew why this was, and again felt strangely uncomfortable.

'Gavan's just a bully,' he said. 'He picks on someone he thinks is soft. He doesn't know Kieran is a karate black belt and could tear him apart.'

For the first time that day Johnny saw Kieran smile and perk up.

'Yeh,' Kieran said, and laughed.

'You're not!' said Eddy, half in admiration and half in disbelief.

'I'm learning Kung Fu myself, from this book I found.'

Just then Gavan Maguire came striding by deliberately, after finishing his self-inflicted chore.

'I'll remember that, Mullan,' he said.

'Only if you write it down and revise it every week,' said Johnny—remembering what Mrs Walsh had said about how to remember important stuff.

'Very funny,' said Gavan furiously, as the other two boys spluttered. 'We'll see who laughs last. You wouldn't be half as funny if there wasn't a teacher here.'

He strode angrily out of the dining hall. He had missed his second course and put on a clean-up show for everyone, through his own malice. But Johnny could see that in Gavan he had made another enemy.

When the three had finished, Eddy dashed off on some errand.

'Let's go and explore,' said Johnny. 'We've got fifteen minutes.'

He and Kieran soon found themselves in the school grounds, walking towards the wood that lined the descending grounds—where they began to slope down even more steeply towards the river.

Both boys knew that all of the paths through the wood to the river were usually out of bounds.

Johnny knew there was something he wanted to say to Kieran, but wasn't sure how Kieran would take it. Maybe a question would be best, now when there was no one within earshot.

'Is it true you're adopted?'

Kieran's face flushed and he looked at the ground.

'Gavan told you that!' he said, desperately.

'Yes! But who cares? What does it matter? You're just as good as he is.'

Kieran bent and lifted pebbles from the path and began hurling them into the bushes.

Johnny persisted.

'You're better! You're not vicious like him.'

'I'm nn....othing,' said Kieran. 'He's got his own family. His D... Da builds supermarkets. His Ma has her own car and thinks Gavan's t...errific. I'm just st....tupid.'

Johnny thought about this for just a moment.

'He picks on you because you let him. Why do you do that?'

He was remembering what he himself had learned in his last year in primary school. He had been insulted about his own Da until he had suddenly lost his temper. That had got him into big trouble, but the bullying had stopped. The biggest bully had got the fright of his life when Johnny had come at him in a raging fury. He had been bowled over and hit his head, and needed three stitches.

'If you were stupid you wouldn't be here,' Johnny went on, because Kieran hadn't answered his question.

'I'm only any good at Maths,' said Kieran. 'My writing is awful.'

'Well Maths is my worst subject. You could help me with that.

And if you're good at Maths you'll be good at science and technology too, probably.'

'Maybe,' said Kieran, throwing another pebble.

Soon after, as they headed towards the terrace for their first history class, the two boys noticed Gavan speaking to a much taller boy of similar build and appearance.

'That's Gavan's big brother, Conor,' said Kieran. 'Watch out for him—he's dangerous. He's in Year Thirteen.'

Just then Gavan caught sight of Johnny and Kieran, and said something to Conor, nodding towards Johnny. Conor turned and stared hard at Johnny in a meaningful way—his face dead. Johnny felt a cold chill at the top of his spine.

II

Nearly two hours later Johnny found himself on the bus again, travelling homeward. He sat alone, because he wanted to think. Three afternoon classes had failed to make him forget the two hostile faces he had seen at lunchtime—the faces of Gavan and Conor Maguire. They were warning him, but what about? He would find out, he felt sure, the following week.

But now he was heading home—where someone else might be waiting. His father, Kevy, was almost always in a bad mood these times. As the bus approached the bridge for the second time that day, Johnny remembered the bad dream he was having most nights. It was always the same dream. He turns into Inishowen Park from Inishowen Avenue. This is his street—but where is his home? There is number four, McClean's and number eight, White's—but no number six, with his small bedroom window above the door. So he knocks on McClean's door and asks Mrs McClean: 'Where's our house gone?'

But Mrs McClean just stares blankly.

'How would I know? I don't even know *you*!'

'Johnny Mullan. Number six!'

'There's no number six. Never was. Away wi ye!'

So he can't get home. So he wanders about, looking for a way back.

He talks to some boys playing football on the green, including Pete Thompson. Pete looks at him as though he's never seen him before and tells him to 'shove off, loony'.

So he goes back to the top of Inishowen Avenue, where it joins the main road through the estate, Inishowen Road. And then to where Inishowen road joins the main road into the city. And there, across the main road is Kevy, his Dad. The traffic is strangely heavy so he shouts 'Da! Da!'. But his Da seems not to hear, and turns to walk away—out towards the hospital. Johnny follows him, running along his own side, but Kevy gets further and further away, even though he's just walking. And the traffic is heavier than ever. So Johnny falls further and further behind, until Kevy goes out of sight behind a bus. And when Johnny finally gets to cross the road it is as wide as the river, and it feels as if he's wading through thick mud. And when he gets to the other side there's no one in sight.

At this point in the dream Johnny always woke up, sweating. Why is his Ma nowhere in the dream? And why is Kevy heading towards the hospital? And why doesn't he hear when Johnny calls?

Johnny didn't know how to talk to Kevy any more. Nothing he said made any difference. The more he pleased his Ma the more annoyed his Da got.

When he had got the letter to go to Iona College she had been so excited and gone on and on about it. Kevy just glared and went out, banging the door. And came in late, drunk and shouting and swearing—and slamming the cupboard doors in the kitchen as he always did when he was mad.

And when she had brought home Johnny's school uniform and fitted it on for the first time, Kevy had come in and sneered.

'Well would ye look at that! Bloody wee professor! Little Lord Bookhead! Y'r far too good for us now, Johnny, right enough.' Then he had lifted Johnny's school bag, and taken out the history book and looked at it, flicking through the pages, saying 'Much they know!' scornfully and then shoving it roughly back and throwing the bag on the floor. And then gone into the front room and turned the TV on too loud.

Why had Kevy said he was 'far too good for us now'? Johnny didn't feel any better in that uniform. In fact he sometimes felt a prat—a Mammy's boy. He knew something had happened between him and his Da, something he couldn't understand.

He could remember when things were different. Kevy would take him to the pictures, or even out to play football. Now it was as though there was a space Johnny couldn't cross, as though the air had turned into water and he couldn't swim through it. And his voice couldn't carry through it either. Kevy was always mad at him now, and mad at Anny too. And drinking too much too often. He had come home late the previous night and then picked a row with Anny and hit her—not for the first time.

Again Johnny wondered was he somehow to blame for all this? What was he supposed to do?

Now, on this first day at Iona College, it was his home bus stop. He left the bus and walked the half-mile to his home. There it was, thank goodness. Anny had given him a key, so he let himself in. There, in the kitchen, was Kevy, glowering as usual, sitting at the table with a mug of tea and the daily paper. A cigarette stub smouldered acridly in a half-full ash-tray, making Johnny's eyes smart as usual.

'Hi,' said Johnny.

'Still talkin to us then!'

As usual Johnny didn't know how to answer this. Kevy was saying, as usual, that Johnny was now somehow different, snobby. He couldn't ever think of a good way of saying he wasn't, because the words that came to him were words that Kevy would say were snobby. If he used these, Kevy would take them and pronounce them in a jeering way—as evidence against him. He waited too long to reply, as he took a bottle of milk from the fridge.

'So y'r *not* talkin' to us then!' said Kevy in the same sarcastic tone.

'Yes I am. Why wouldn't I be?'

'You've got others to talk to now. Stuck-up friends from the suburbs!'

'They're not all rich. Some are just like me.'

'But *you'll* be travellin' high, won't ye—with all y'r big words?'

That was always it—words. Words Johnny couldn't use to close whatever gap had opened up between them. Johnny knew that his father read almost nothing other than the newspaper. Kevy had got little from his schooling, for some reason. He was a good joiner, and should be in big demand, but his drinking made him unreliable.

This was why he was sitting at the kitchen table at four in the afternoon, in a bad temper.

And because Johnny liked reading he felt that maybe his father was right—that he was travelling away from Kevy. Words were a river that he wanted to explore, but his Da could not come with him.

But why should Kevy always be bringing this up? Johnny felt resentful, but he said nothing. Soon he had finished his glass of milk and biscuits, and went upstairs.

Anny had made sure Johnny had a small table and chair in his room, so that he could do his homework there. She had badgered Kevy to make them out of matching pine that she had paid for, and Johnny looked forward to using them. She had wanted a set of shelves for Johnny's books to go above the table, but Kevy had never got around to that. So his best books stood in a row at the back of the table, against the wall. Others stood in piles below the table, against the wall.

Johnny wanted to get down to the task Mrs Walsh had set, but knew he would spend ages on this. So he did his other homework first.

After five he heard the hall door, and Anny came up the stairs immediately.

'How did you get on?' she said eagerly as she opened his bedroom door.

He told her about his favourite classes, especially English.

He had also decided to tell her a bit about Gavan Maguire, as he had some foreboding over this. He had kept everything to himself at primary school when the name-calling started, so she had become angry when he had got into trouble and had to tell her why. She had made him promise never to keep anything like that secret again.

'That's *bullying*, Johnny,' she had said. 'That's dangerous. Promise me you'll always tell.'

She had taken him by the shoulders then, and looked him right in the eye.

'Promise!'

So he had, and now he told her almost everything about his first day. But he was in no way prepared for her reaction to one particular name. Her eyes widened in shock, and she took hold of his shoulder with her right hand.

'Gavan *Maguire*. No! Tell us quick—what do you know about him?'

'Nothing much. Kieran says his Da's a builder.'

At this her hand went to her mouth and she went white.

'What happened? What did he do today? Tell me again!'

So Johnny told most of the story, from Gavan pulling Kieran backward dangerously on the steps to the incident in the dining hall.

He left out Gavan's threat, and Gavan pointing him out to his older brother, Conor. When he had finished she sat still on the bed, thinking.

'Johnny,' she said at last, 'you did nothing wrong, but the Maguires and the Mullans don't get on. There's something that happened ... back years ago in the Troubles. I can't explain it to you yet. If Gavan says things ... bad things— about your Da, you mustn't believe them. Do you follow me?'

Johnny wanted to ask her 'what things' but he knew from her tone that he wasn't supposed to, so he just nodded his head.

'Don't mention Gavan to your Da yet. And keep out of Gavan's way. Promise me?'

Johnny wasn't sure how he could avoid someone in his own class, but he nodded anyway.

She went away then, and got busy making a meal. Soon she called him, and the family ate together, saying little. Anny seemed to be still brooding over what Johnny had told her. Johnny helped her wash up. Kevy went to watch the TV news in the front room. He seldom helped in the house—unless something needed fixing.

Then Johnny headed back to his room to tackle the task he had postponed—the application he had to write to join some organisation.

'Make it up if you like,' Mrs Walsh had said. He liked the thought of that, but could he risk it? He thought of Patrick Andrews rolling his eyes and pretending to fall asleep, and Gavan Maguire sneering. And of what Aidan Maroney might produce, using his computer. And then there were the bright girls as well—like Margaret and Bridget.

But still he did not want to fall back on something safe, as that would also be boring. So he tried to think of a name that would suit his imaginary organisation. He lay down on his bed and tried to make a mental picture, but nothing would come.

He found himself thinking instead of what his mother had said about Kevy and the Maguires. What was it Gavan Maguire might say, and why? What had started the quarrel between the two families? Had it something to do with Kevy's drinking and his bad temper? And why had Gavan picked on Kieran Lowney? Why did the Maguires ever pick on anybody? Some people seemed to want to do that—as Johnny had found in primary school.

Suddenly into Johnny's head floated a picture of the old Derry bridge he had crossed twice that day. Bridges let you cross things you can't cross otherwise, he realised. You were stuck here—and then, if there was a bridge, you weren't stuck any longer. Bridges could also cross railway tracks and roads.

Other things got in your way too. Johnny remembered that anything that got in the way was an obstacle—even things you couldn't see or put a name to, like whatever stood between him and his Da.

And Gavan Maguire was going to be an obstacle too—something his Mother had told him to avoid. Johnny couldn't understand that fully either, but then he realised that things you couldn't understand were obstacles too. Mr Foley had set them a problem in History, but hadn't solved it. In fact he had said that in History it was often hard to be certain.

'Get used to using words like maybe and perhaps and probably!' he had said.

And Margaret Phillips was worried about the problem of the environment—so there was another problem, another obstacle. And Aidan had mentioned other problems like crime and terrorism. And then there was Derry's old problem—people on different sides of the river who often couldn't speak to one another without arguing or fighting. Problems, obstacles were everywhere!

Suddenly Johnny had a name for his organisation: *'The Bridgers'*. They found ways of getting around all obstacles—including distance, space—so they could also be space travellers. Every problem was an obstacle, so he wouldn't need to mention his own private stuff when he wrote about the Bridgers—just things that everyone knew about. Wherever you were stuck you needed a bridge of some kind—and the Bridgers would help.

Excited, he took out a sheet of paper to make a draft before messing up his English exercise book, and began to write.

Organization: The Bridgers

What they do: Get you over obstacles, anything that gets in the way. Not just things like rivers but other problems you can't solve on your own. Like the problem of the environment, or wars, or people who don't like you. Bridgers do this by maybe giving you an idea, or teaching you something. Like the Jedi knights they can cross between the stars, and maybe even bridge time. I don't know much more yet, but I could learn if I was a member!

My Application: To the Bridgers.

Dear Sirs,

I want to join the Bridgers because I like getting over obstacles. I'm not sure what qualifications I'll need—but I'm not too bad with words, and I'm fairly bright. If Bridgers need to take risks sometimes, I'm ready for that. And I want to travel between the stars someday—and the Bridgers can take me there. I'll need some training, I suppose, but I'll be a good learner if you'll take me on as ...'

He paused at this point, trying to think of a word for someone on the lowest rung of a ladder. Then he remembered what trainee Jedis were called, checked the spelling in his dictionary, and added it at the end.

'*an apprentice.*'

Then he signed his name.

When he re-read the application he was disappointed, because it sounded cheesy.

Then he got to thinking again about Gavan and Patrick and Aidan—the boys in the class who seemed so much more confident and knowledgeable. He pictured himself reading the application in class—and then Patrick rolling his eyes for Aidan to see. Gavan would call him 'the Bridger'—and tell him to 'jump off it'—as people did in Derry sometimes.

Then Johnny remembered again what Anny had warned him of—that Gavan might come to school on Monday with some story against his father to tell the others, just as he had told Johnny himself about Kieran. Johnny felt hot and then cold at this, and completely lost faith in the whole 'Bridgers' idea. Far better to play safe—to write something ordinary that wouldn't be noticed. He could do that tomorrow.

He lifted the draft Bridgers application and crumpled it up. Anny had given him a large cream-coloured plastic emulsion paint tub for a waste paper basket. Now he aimed the ball of paper at this, and threw it hard in annoyance. It made a whuffing sound as it hit the bottom. Then it bounced, spun a few times and lay still. *That's the end of that*, he thought.

That night he had the same dream about Kevy.

—∞◦❈◦∞—

'We're going to your Auntie Kath's tomorrow,' Anny said when she woke him on Saturday morning. 'Have you got your homework done?'

'Nearly,' said Johnny. He had done almost all the work that teachers would inspect on Monday, but there was more he still had to do, like looking up the island of Iona for RE, and finding out more about evidence in history. He didn't look forward to this.

He was even more depressed when he remembered his 'Bridgers' application in the bin—and that he still had to write a boring alternative.

'Why are we going to Auntie Kath's?' he asked at breakfast. His aunt, who tended to look down her nose at him—or so he thought—lived nearly thirty miles away, near Coleraine. She was Anny's only sister, and Anny seemed always to want to talk to her directly for hours in a crisis. Was this another crisis then, he wondered—the story he had told Anny about Gavan Maguire?

'We haven't seen her in a long time. Don't you want to see Leo and the dogs?'

At this Johnny brightened. Leo, his cousin, was a year older but might let him play with his computer. And the retrievers, Jet and Ebony, were his Uncle Bernie's dogs—well trained and full of fun. Johnny would probably never have a dog of his own, he knew, as Anny insisted their house was too small. He smiled as he thought of the dogs, with their long pink tongues lolling out and their eager eyes.

So he spent Saturday morning writing an application to join the Jedi knights. As Mrs Walsh seemed to like the Jedis this would be safest, he thought.

Then he looked up 'Iona' in the Encyclopedia, where there was a map also. It looked so small. He couldn't understand why St Columba and his monks were so important either. Getting people into heaven by prayer sounded unlikely, and so did heaven too. And Johnny couldn't figure out why there was so much fuss about 'salvation' and 'redemption', or even what these words meant. It was all so long ago and far away too, and boring.

He knew he wasn't supposed to think this. Anny insisted they went to Mass every Sunday, though Kevy never went. She still checked sometimes that Johnny said his prayers, but he didn't expect them to be answered any more. He had prayed so often about Kevy, but things had just got worse. And from what he heard on the news, and from reading just a few articles in the Sunday papers, he knew that some people thought religion in Ireland caused more problems than it solved.

So that Sunday began as usual with Mass at Our Lady's chapel. The priest was old and complained again about people not praying hard enough for faith. 'You must lose your lives to save them,' he said, but Johnny couldn't make any sense of that either. His mind wandered off to Downhill where he might get to play with Leo and the dogs. When his ma went up for Communion he went too, out of habit. He had been told that the communion bread was the body of Jesus and the bread of life, but he had never noticed any difference after swallowing it.

Sunday dinner was roast chicken and peas, well cooked by Anny as usual. Kevy appeared in time to eat it—mostly in silence.

'What's up?' he asked eventually.

'What d'you mean?' Anny asked.

'That stuck-up sister of yours. You two hold a council whenever somethin's up.'

'We haven't seen them in ages, that's all. And Johnny wants to see Leo. Don't you, Johnny?'

Johnny nodded, even though he thought Kevy might be right. He didn't need to ask if Kevy would be going too. Auntie Kath disapproved of Kevy even more, and Kevy was aware of that.

The journey to Downhill in Anny's battered Fiesta took less than an hour. But when they got to his uncle's farm near Downhill, not far from Coleraine, they found that Leo was staying with a friend twenty miles away that weekend.

'I'm sorry I forgot to tell your Mum about that. Would you like to play with Leo's computer?' asked his Auntie Kath. 'Or go for a walk in the wood? You could take the pup.'

'The wood—just for an hour,' Johnny said, perking up. He guessed 'the pup' would be a young collie in training. He sensed that his ma and aunt wanted to be alone in the house, to talk out the news that Anny had brought.

The pup turned out to be an excitable handful, a half-grown border collie called Greeta, all black but for a white forehead star, and white paws. She wasn't quite broken to the lead, and tended to dash at every possible direction other than Johnny's.

The wood was the 'Bishop's Wood' just down the road. Johnny had explored it with Leo and the other dogs earlier that summer.

There was a stream through the southern half of the wood, and Johnny had loved playing along it.

It was a breezy day, with the sun coming and going as large cotton-wool clouds passed over it. Although the wood was a well- known place for a walk Johnny found it deserted that day. He found it boring at first, but soon the silence of the wood, broken occasionally only by wood pigeons and rooks, took his mind off his father, and why he hit his mother and drank too much.

So far Greeta had reluctantly followed Johnny's direction but now suddenly she began to bound forward along the path, as though with some idea of where she needed to go.

Johnny thought 'why not?', and let her lead him. He quickened his pace, breaking sometimes into a run. The dog yelped as it ran.

Johnny found himself getting excited. If ever he could own a dog of his choice, he thought, it would be this one. Some hope!

After about a minute he saw ahead a huge clump of rhododendron bushes. When Greeta reached these she darted straight underneath—into a natural cave formed by the high shrubs. Johnny knew it well, as he and Leo had often played there, using it as a hideout.

The dog pulled him towards the darkest part of the cavern. He could just make out its white parts flickering. Then it suddenly pulled him towards the blackest patch of descending foliage—and disappeared. He found himself right up against the wall of the cavern, pushing against the underside of the branches as Greeta went on pulling.

Suddenly the branches parted, and Johnny found himself in a place he had never seen before. There was a small grassy clearing surrounded by half grown trees. In the centre was a wooden seat.

Greeta went to that, and suddenly lay down, gnawing at a stick.

Out of breath and dizzy Johnny sat down too. He had always liked lonely places where he could relax and be himself. He felt suddenly at peace here, with everything forgotten that had happened or could happen. He wished that his Ma would let him take Greeta back home with them, but knew she wouldn't. Instead his unfinished homework for English waited for him there, and the thought of it made him depressed. Then he noticed that Greeta had fallen asleep, and suddenly felt sleepy himself, sitting against the backrest.

Then, without noticing, Johnny fell asleep too.

But now there was someone else in the clearing, opposite him—a man sitting on the ground with his left knee drawn up, supporting his left forearm, which in turn supported his head on his left hand.

'Hi Johnny,' said the man with a half-smile, as though he had known Johnny all his life.

Johnny looked again, but was sure he had never seen this person before. He was dressed in casual clothes, with an open-necked grey shirt, blue jeans and grey trainers. He was pale, with a thin face and blue eyes under thick dark hair.

'I don't know you,' Johnny said, warily—remembering vaguely everything his mother had ever told him about strangers.

'Mick's the name. Don't have time to mess about. Need to talk to you about this.'

The man reached for the haversack, opened it and pulled out a grey folder. From this he pulled out a sheet of paper—one that had once been crumpled. When he held it towards him Johnny was suddenly startled. It was his own draft application for his imaginary organisation, the Bridgers—the one he had thrown in the bin!

'Are you serious about this?' Mick asked.

'How did you get that?' Johnny asked.

'As you guessed, we bridgers connect space, and many other things,' said Mick. 'My job is to greet applicants in this region and look after them. I've hours of work ahead. Tell me—are you *serious*?'

Johnny knew he was staring and gulping like a fish, but couldn't help it. He didn't know what to say.

'Imagination and wishful thinking are one thing. Reality is something else. Our apprentices soon find that out. You've got a lot of obstacles just now, and you want to get past them—and this just fits as an application to our outfit. So *are* you *serious*?'

Mick was looking right through him, and Johnny wasn't sure all this was happening, but he had heard the word 'apprentice' and knew he had been asked the same question three times, and that he must answer.

'Yes.' As he said it, Johnny felt suddenly afraid—as though he had moved into a totally different space, where danger lurked. But Greeta was still there, lying with her forepaws in front of her, her head also flat on the ground between them, still asleep. He lost his fear. He was certain he didn't want to escape from this place.

'Good. You're now on probation. That means you've got to prove yourself—with some important bridging to do straight away. But first you need to know that it's not your application alone that gets you this chance. You're a natural bridger, and have already begun.'

'When? Where?' said Johnny, puzzled.

'Look here,' said Mick, pointing behind him. Straight away, against the darkest shadow among the background trees, a scene appeared that Johnny instantly recognised. It was Mrs Walsh's room at Iona College. At a table, he himself, Mary McNevin and Eddy Li were sitting listening to Patrick Andrews. He could hear no sound, but suddenly saw himself speak and Patrick getting annoyed.

'That's you, tackling Patrick on his long trek towards goal. You took a risk, for your own sake, of course—but then you let the others speak before you. Patrick was an obstacle for all of you, but instead of becoming another obstacle for the other two by hogging it yourself you made a bridge for them in that important first class.

Now look here.'

The scene against the shadow changed—to the dinner hall.

Patrick saw a close—up of Gavan's whispered comment to Aidan Maroney—and then Gavan's hand striking the plate. Then he saw himself speaking to the supervisor—and then Gavan cleaning up the mess.

'That could have been a disaster for Kieran,' Mick went on. 'He's already feeling bad about himself, and Gavan wanted to make things worse. And then you told him it was no problem to be adopted. That's a huge obstacle for Kieran. That was important.

'You'll have other obstacles next week. Maybe harder ones, are you ready?'

Johnny thought about that. He wasn't sure he could cope with harder tests than the ones he had faced on his first day at Iona.

'Do I need some special powers or something?' He was thinking of Luke's ability to use the light side of the force.

'The powers you are thinking of—powers that amaze or overpower others—can't build the best kind of bridge. They build rickety bridges that never last. There is another kind of power entirely that you will come to learn about—a power that builds stronger bridges. Often people mistake it for weakness, and sneer at those who use it. Are you ready for that as well?'

'How do I use it?'

'Just ask for the power of the bridge, thinking about nothing else—and wait until your mind is clear—and then speak or act. But be ready for what follows—it can be something you can't foresee.

Sometimes you may appear to come off worst—for the sake of the bridge. You may take some pain, I warn you—for the sake of the bridge. Are you *sure* you are still serious?'

Mick was looking intently at him, speaking to him in a way no adult had ever spoken before—as though to another adult—and Johnny knew there was danger here. He was afraid—but he knew he would never forgive himself if he backed off now.

'Yes!' He said—and all fear left him. Somehow he was sure, no matter what, that this was right. This was where he was supposed to be, and he was OK.

For an instant Mick seemed to grin, but then he was all business again.

'OK. Now—what's your first bridging test, do you think?'

'Da,' said Johnny, without stopping to think, and fearful again as he remembered what Mick had said about pain. His Ma knew about that.

'That's tougher than you can fix just yet. Your Da is troubled by an obstacle he can't get past just now. You can help by forgiving him if he is hurtful, by trusting him— most of all by looking for something he could help you with. Starting tomorrow, you yourself will face more obstacles in school, so tackle those as best you can. There are others in your class who will be tested also, and you may be able to bridge some things there.

'Pay attention,' Mick went on. 'especially to insults— and insulting behaviour. You know, bad slagging, stupid words and actions meant to put someone down. See who is doing that—and to whom? Why? And who objects? And what can follow. You must listen, watch, think and learn— and do your schoolwork too.'

Johnny nodded.

'Patrick was an obstacle there,' Mick continued. 'And you were a bridger. What's the difference?'

Johnny thought for a moment.

'He thought he was more important than us,' said Johnny.

'Right. So how might you become an obstacle rather than a bridger?'

'By thinking I'm more important than anyone else?'

'Right. That's why Bridgers should maybe be spelt with a small b.'

Mick got to his feet at this point. Johnny was surprised to see that he was not so tall—just a foot or so taller than himself. He looked at Johnny, whose mind was racing.

'Just three questions for now,' Mick said. 'I can tell you only what you need to know now—for your own sake.'

'When ... I mean, *will* I see you again?'

'When I'm needed,' Mick answered.

'Are there other bridgers—like me, I mean?'

'Yes—but most bridgers on your world are like your ma and have other ways of thinking about all this. You came up with the idea of the bridgers because you are at a particular point in time and space, and because you have special obstacles to overcome.'

Mick paused, and then went on with special emphasis.

'You'll make friends whose minds are more like yours, and some of them could also be conscious bridgers like yourself—if they express a wish for that. If that happens, the power of the bridge may help you decide if you can tell them about what's happening here.'

From the way Mick had said this Johnny knew he must not forget, so he nodded.

'Another tip: in your schoolwork look out for other bridgers of the past and the obstacles they overcame. If you look and listen hard enough you may even find out about the greatest bridger. That's most important—to help you understand. Promise?'

Johnny nodded again. He had one last question.

'What about my application? I mean tomorrow?'

'Why not copy this'—Mick held up Johnny's draft application—'into your English exercise book and hand it in with all the others.

You'll find out why soon enough.

'One last thing,' said Mick. 'In any crisis remind yourself of this: nothing can destroy or harm the deepest part of you—the part that wants to be a bridger. No threat, no insult, no jeer can destroy your real self. So try to make your mind go calm, and ask for the power of the bridge, and wait. Can you do that?'

Johnny nodded. 'I'll try.'

And then Johnny woke and found himself alone with Greeta, still sleeping. He stared around, disbelieving and feeling slightly cold.

He had never had such a vivid dream, with all the details so sharp in his mind. What had just happened? If it had been just a dream why was he feeling so unafraid?

Greeta raised her head then, climbed to her feet, yelped, yawned and pulled on the lead.

III

For hours afterwards Johnny's mind raced with doubts and questions about his dream in the Bishop's Wood, and what might happen the following day. He wanted to believe that his dozing mind hadn't just invented it all, but couldn't quite do that. This was why he heard little of Anny's early chat on the journey home from Downhill—until suddenly she mentioned Kevy and started to speak differently.

'Your Da and I were just a little older than you are now when we met, up in Creggan ... when the troubles were still bad. Awful things could happen to people back then ...'

She was speaking fearfully, hesitantly, thinking out every sentence, and looking over at him. Johnny remembered that while he had been in the wood, Anny and his Auntie Kath had been having a council—about himself. He realised that now he was hearing what they had decided to tell him, to prepare him for what might happen tomorrow.

'There was a war going on. Most people didn't want it, but it was going on anyway. A nationalist organisation, the Irish Liberation Army, wanted to take the north-east corner of Ireland, including Derry, out of British control and into a united Ireland. They were shooting and bombing the police, the RUC. The police were against a united Ireland. They were always looking for information on the organisation—the ILA. Are you with me?'

She took her eyes off the road ahead for a moment to look straight at him. He nodded vigorously. He was on the edge of the mystery, and mustn't miss a word.

'Sometimes the police would pick up teenagers along the road and bribe or threaten them to spy on the ILA. They would tell a young lad that if he didn't do this they would hold him for a few days, and then drive him back to Creggan and let him out of a marked police car—for everyone to see. They would say that they would let out word that he had spied anyway. You know what that could mean?' Johnny nodded. He had heard many stories of what could happen to 'touts'—people who gave information to the police.

'The year your Da was fifteen a lot of ILA attacks went wrong. They would find the police waiting for them when they tried to raid a post office or plant a bomb. They started looking for an informer in Creggan.'

She stopped then for a long moment. Johnny couldn't see her whole face clearly but somehow he knew she couldn't speak.

'They picked your Da....'

She stopped again for a while.

'He hadn't ever been lifted by the police, but people were ready to believe anything then. And your Granda had always been against the movement, so the family was ... suspected.

'So they came to your Granda and told him that if he didn't take your Da to be ... punished they would lift him anyway and leave him lying dead in a ditch somewhere.'

She stopped again for a long moment.

'Your Granda had no choice. So he took your Da to where they said, and they shot him.... in the knees.

'They said he was an informer, and all his friends dropped him. No one went to see him in hospital except his Da and Ma and me, and mostly people wouldn't speak to him when he got out.

'But the next ILA attack went wrong too. Two bombers were caught with their bomb, in a stolen car. So your Granda went to them—to the officer who had ordered the shooting—and faced him with it. "You made a mistake", he said. "Admit it!"

'And the ILA officer said "Yes—we made a mistake. But we won't admit it. The cause is bigger than we are, and far bigger than Kevy. We've made too many mistakes lately. People will lose faith if we admit another. So Kevy will just have to put up with it—for the cause."'

She stopped then for the longest time, until Johnny wondered if that was all. And then she said:

'But then they did the worst thing of all. Because some people weren't believing your Da was the informer, they let it out that he had been ... bullying little children in Creggan and had to be stopped.'

She stopped again and looked at him. He had never seen her so sad or so angry.

'They never took it back. And your Granda and Gran never got over it. Their health broke down when they had to leave Creggan and go to the Waterside. They didn't live long after that.'

Johnny understood in that moment why he had never known his Gran and Granda, Kevy's parents—and why Kevy seldom spoke of them. And why his family lived on the Waterside instead of the city side.

'Johnny, that ILA officer was Hugh Maguire—Gavan's Da.'

She looked at him again, to make sure he understood. Her eyes were wide, inquiring. Although he was shocked he knew she needed an answer, and nodded again.

'We were going to tell you all this, when you were older. But heaven knows what Gavan will say, or if his Da will tell him any of it—or tell him the truth. I'm telling you now, so you'll be ready for the worst, for any lie they tell.

'But I can't tell your Da what's going on for you. God knows what he would do the way he is now. So you mustn't let on to him you know all this. Not yet. D'you understand?'

Johnny nodded again, in full agreement.

'But you mustn't doubt him. You mustn't—whatever Gavan says. You *mustn't*!'

'I won't!' said Johnny, forcefully and truthfully. He was certain Anny had told him the whole truth, and Mick had said the same.

'And you mustn't start anything with Gavan over this either! If you did we couldn't keep it from your Da.'

She looked at him then sternly. He nodded again.

'If it gets too bad for you we could take you out of Iona, if you like? I could make up some excuse for your Da. He doesn't want you there anyway.'

'No,' he said, shaking his head hard. 'I'll be OK.'

Anny relaxed at that, and blew her nose with a tissue. She looked at him then again, two or three times, and suddenly smiled and tousled his hair with her left hand. He didn't mind that so much when there was no one to see.

'Nearly home,' she said.

Kevy was watching TV when they got in at about seven o'clock. Johnny had some milk and biscuits and then raced upstairs to take his bridgers application from the bin, and then unfold and copy it into his new English homework book. He read it again to see if there was anything he wanted to improve. It didn't sound so cheesy anymore, so he didn't change a word—just concentrated on his handwriting, replacing every capital B in bridger with a b. Then he signed his name at the bottom.

Then he lifted the first draft. He wondered if he should crumple it up again and throw it in the bin a second time. But then he placed it carefully in a folder he had kept from primary school—with his best stories and essays—and put this back on the top shelf of his wardrobe.

He sat on the edge of his bed then, and stared at the usual view from his window. It seemed the same, but not quite—because he himself had changed, or had he? He didn't feel much different, and this disappointed him. Maybe nothing had happened in the wood. Maybe it was all just a story his mind had made up to make him feel better.

Then he went downstairs, to where his Da and Ma were sitting on the sofa. When he looked, there was just enough room for him, beside his Da, so he sat there.

Anny sent him to bed as usual at nine. He read in bed then for a bit—from his favourite *Star Wars* book, the one with stills from the films—showing the battle stations and Luke in his x-wing fighter. For the first time it didn't make him disappointed about his own life. His own world was now somehow different after all, and he wanted to think about that instead. He closed the book, put it back on his table and turned off the light.

He didn't sleep right away, but when he did, he didn't have that usual dream about his home going missing, and Kevy disappearing. Instead he went star-hopping. On a planet with three silver moons in a lilac sky he saw Greeta again, with her lead in her mouth.

Next morning Johnny went to the bus stop on his own. He had again told Anny she mustn't come if he was to get any peace from the other school-goers. This time they weren't so interested, as he had hoped. And this time, when the bus came, he made sure to sit with Eddy.

'What did you apply to join—for English?' he asked, as soon as he was seated.

'I made up a police force in space—'Galapolice'. I want to be a detective some day, and I wanted to make it as exciting as possible. And Mrs Walsh said to make it up if we liked.'

'Why d'you want to be a detective?'

'I like the idea of solving mysteries—catching bad guys and locking them up—and martial arts and handcuffs and stuff. Did you make something up too?'

'Yes,' said Johnny. He told Eddy about the bridgers application in a matter-of-fact way—leaving out everything to do with the fact that they might exist.

'Cool,' said Eddy. 'I can't wait for English class, second period—to hear what the others have done!'

Johnny couldn't wait either, but couldn't exactly explain why. Part of him wanted to tell someone of his experience in the wood, but he knew well no one would take it seriously.

As soon as they arrived at the forecourt in Iona that Monday, all Year Eight pupils noticed a huge increase in blue uniforms and noise. Only Year Eight and Eleven, and some senior prefects, had been at school the previous Friday, to allow the newcomers get used to things, but now the whole school was together, with most pupils towering over Johnny's year-group. Concourse and corridors were thronged and hundreds of conversations competed with one another, as friends swapped news of the summer. An electronic notice board in the entrance hall transmitted the message 'General Assembly at 9.00', and soon that hour was signalled by the school bell.

Johnny and the other Year Eights—the youngest pupils in the school—soon found themselves at the front of a full Assembly Hall, with the older classes rising in tiers behind. There was a hubbub still, with so much news to be exchanged.

Soon a severe looking middle-aged woman entered the stage and rang a hand bell in front of the microphone, calling for silence. Gradually the hubbub sank to a murmur, and the principal, Mr Ferguson, entered the stage from the wings.

'Welcome back,' Mr Ferguson began. 'Congratulations to last year's examination classes for summer results—among the best ever. We expect the same of Year Twelve and Year Fourteen at the end of this school year.

'Let me remind you all of the purpose of the school—to achieve academic excellence within a framework of Christian values. As you know, the year will end with the awarding of prizes—and the greatest of these are the 'Top Year' awards—the trophies for the outstanding pupil in each year group. Here they are!'

At this, a curtain was opened on the stage, revealing a row of seven glittering trophies, each standing about eighteen inches high, on a raised platform. Highly polished wooden shields displayed in their centres silver plates inscribed with the names of winners over many years.

'These were won last June by pupils who are here today. Come up and take your places as I call your names.'

Mr Ferguson then read out seven names, and six pupils came forward and climbed the steps to the stage, each taking a place in front of one of the trophies. The winner of the seventh trophy, for Year Fourteen, was dressed in civvies, as she had left the school that summer.

'Now begins another year. Who will stand here this time next year? Seven pupils, beginning with someone in Year Eight, will answer that question by sheer hard work and dedication. And they will begin right away, leaving nothing to chance.

'For the benefit of Year Eight, these Top Year trophies are awarded on a points system. The higher your ranking in each subject, the more points you score.'

Johnny looked along the line of his own class, wondering who would stand in front of the Top Eight trophy in a year's time. Aidan Maroney's eyes were fastened on the trophy, as were Bridget McSorley's. But who knew yet what the other three Year Eight classes would produce in the way of competition. Johnny felt that he himself had little chance as he didn't have the all-round ability needed.

—∘∘∘▸◆◂∘∘∘—

Johnny didn't have long to wait to find out what Gavan Maguire might say after the weekend. Coming along the corridor to queue up for Maths in the first period he saw Gavan outside the Maths room already, with a good number of the class.

'Here's Mullan!' Gavan shouted loudly. 'How's your Da's hangover this morning, Johnny?'

Immediately the rest of the group fell silent and looked towards Johnny.

Johnny knew that Gavan wanted to provoke him, and that any denial on his part would probably be followed by lots more of the same, so what could he say? Again he felt anger rising in him—anger and shame. His Da drank too much—that was a fact, and there was no point in denying it. What *could* he say?

The first thing he thought of was an insult for Gavan— 'has *your* Da stopped lying yet'. But that would have the result that Anny had warned him about—an 'incident' that Kevy would have to be told about.

Then he remembered Mick's parting words in the wood. Nothing could harm him, Mick had said—and immediately Johnny found himself believing this was true. Silently he asked for the power of the bridge.

The group was still quiet when he got to it—waiting. Johnny faced Gavan, saying nothing, just looking at him. By then, out of nowhere, a wild idea had formed. He heard himself say:

'Morning, Gavan. I'll bet I know what's happened!'

It didn't sound like his own voice, because there was no anger in it. It was as though Gavan hadn't said anything at all annoying.

'Huh?' said Gavan.

'Yes,' Johnny continued. 'You've been thinking about what organisation you'd like to belong to—for English homework. And you've come up with a good one. It's called *The Insulters*. They go around saying rude things to everyone. That's much more fun than paying cheesy compliments, isn't it?'

Margaret Phillips giggled.

'Can I join too, Gavan?' Aidan was laughing along.

'Me too,' said Margaret.

Gavan stared for a moment, and then grinned.

'I suppose.'

'I must think up some good insults then, for future use,' said Margaret. 'Just in case.'

At that moment Aidan Maroney lifted his tablet computer from his bag, shifting the focus of interest. As Patrick Andrews and others gathered round Aidan, Gavan stared hard at Johnny for a long moment—half in warning Johnny thought, and half in puzzlement—and then followed suit.

Johnny stood back, wondering at what had happened. Often in the past he had thought of clever things to say at times like that—but always afterwards, when the opportunity had passed.

There was something else. He had bridged an obstacle—Gavan's attempt to put him down—by making a joke. This had somehow taken away the power that Gavan had tried to use—the power of knowing something about Kevy that could embarrass Johnny. Good jokes could be a bridge! They could disarm people who tried to do that to you, and put everyone back on the same level—without a fight.

Johnny noticed then that Margaret Phillips was hanging back from the group around Aidan Maroney, and looking over at him with curiosity. She came over.

'How did you think that up?' she asked.

'I don't know,' said Johnny, truthfully. 'It just came to me.'

'I was sure at first you were going to hit him. Then you came up and just stood there, looking at Gavan. Then you said something funny instead.'

'And that's given me an idea,' Margaret went on. 'That's not the first insult I've heard around here recently.

Now we know where they all come from, don't we!'

As Margaret moved away Johnny was wishing he could tell her about his strange experience in the wood, and how he had come to answer Gavan that way just now. She wasn't stuck up as he had thought, and he had liked what she had said in Mrs Walsh's class about the way the world had been before humans came along. She would surely be looking for bridges over the environmental problem. She looked as though she could keep a secret too. But he couldn't think of doing that yet.

In the class that followed Johnny and Kieran were sitting together, and, when the teacher set the class working on a problem, he asked Kieran for help at one point. Kieran was attempting to explain when the teacher, Mr Conway, looked up.

'No talking. I want you working alone on this problem!'

Just a few minutes later Johnny heard a whispered conversation to his right. The teacher looked in that direction, but said nothing. The conversation continued, growing steadily louder. When Johnny looked over he saw Gavan and Aidan talking, side by side. Mr Conway looked again and said nothing.

Some teachers made exceptions for some pupils, Johnny decided.

Break time came then—fifteen minutes of freedom in mid- morning, an opportunity for speeding to the tuck shop or playing outdoors. On his way outside Johnny came across a groups of pupils huddled round Aidan as he sat on a bench in the corridor. When Johnny looked more closely, he saw that Aidan was showing off an advanced multi-player game on his tablet.

'I'm getting one of those for Christmas,' said Patrick Andrews.

'I'll have one sooner than that,' said Gavan Maguire.

Margaret Phillips was one of the group. She looked at the two boys, and then at Johnny. She winked slyly.

This pleased him, as he was regretting again that he couldn't hope to compete with these boys in personal technology.

Then he remembered the power of the bridge, and forgot all about that.

Then it was English—with Mrs Walsh collecting homework first thing. Johnny handed up his book, wondering when Mrs Walsh would be returning it.

'One small piece of Eight B form business,' she said as she did this. 'In a fortnight's time the class will elect two prefects—one boy and one girl. Prefects report any problem to me or the office on behalf of the class, and do various small odd jobs—like collecting these books. The prefects serve for a whole term. If anyone thinks he or she, or another boy or girl, would make a good prefect, give me the name on a piece of paper next Monday. I'll put a list of these nominations on the board for next Tuesday, and we'll hold the election on Friday week.

'No homework missing!' she said as she reached the end of the last row of tables at the back of the class. 'Excellent! I hope that continues. I'll have these back, marked, on Thursday. For now, prepare to visit the school library.'

After library class came Eight B's first music class. In their 'Notes for Year Eights' they had been told that anyone with an interest in music should come prepared to show off any talent for this first class. Lining up outside the Music room Johnny noticed that Mary McNevin was carrying a battered guitar case. Arona Gilsenan, dark and dramatic, was carrying a large cardboard box—leaving her friend, Ann O'Kane, to carry her schoolbag. Aidan Maroney had what looked like a clarinet case. A few other pupils had instruments, not all identifiable, in their cases. Johnny could whistle a tune, but that was about it.

Mrs Hayes, the music teacher came then and let them into her music room, a large bright room with sound-insulated walls and a tiered platform for choirs at the back. Posters explaining musical terms such as 'falsetto' and 'nocturne' were displayed on the wall.

'Right, now!' said Mrs Hayes. 'Let's see what talent we've got here. Instruments first, please. Aidan—why don't you start us off?' Aidan had already assembled his clarinet and launched right away into a passable version of *Stranger on the Shore*. Gavan Maguire led the applause—a little bit over-enthusiastically it seemed to Johnny, though he realised he himself was jealous. Aidan's all-round ability was becoming daunting.

The other instruments followed, with Eileen Daly especially impressive on Mrs Hayes' piano.

'Vocalists now—who would like to start?'

Arona Gilsenan stepped forward then and revealed the contents of her large cardboard box—a gleaming karaoke system that flickered and flashed rhythmically as soon as she plugged it in.

'I'll do the Tina Turner number *River Deep, Mountain High*,' she announced, selecting the number from a list. Immediately the room was filled with the fast and dramatic rhythms of the Tina Turner classic, a song demanding a powerful voice of wide range.

The class was electrified by the performance that followed, complete with dance steps. Arona had a voice of great strength. She did not need a microphone but used one anyway. Mrs Hayes winced occasionally on the high notes, but didn't protest.

The class was enthralled, and tapping their feet to the rhythm throughout. When Arona finished there was a storm of applause, with some of the boys whistling, to Mrs Hayes' slight annoyance. Arona bowed dramatically, seeming well used to such appreciation, and began re-boxing her karaoke system.

'Marvellous, Arona—you have an excellent voice for that kind of music. You have still a little to learn about control on the top notes, but you have a great talent. We will all look forward to hearing more. Now—Mary.'

Mrs Hayes was speaking to Mary McNevin who came forward with her guitar already tuned.

'This is a song I wrote myself. It's called *The Dark Switch*.'

Mary's song was a complete contrast, gentle and sad.

I couldn't reach when I was small
The light switch high upon the wall.
'When I grow up,' I said to me,
'I'll reach that switch and then I'll see
The light go on and there will be
No darkness through the night.'

But now I'm big it doesn't work.
The light won't come and it stays dark,
The shadows fall; the day won't come,
And night-time just goes on and on,
And morning calls in sick.

I've changed the bulb and fixed the fuse,
But still I've got those no-light blues –
Has someone flipped a dark switch?

Please guide my feet, don't let me fall,
And guide my hands along the wall
So I can find that dark switch.
I'll flip it off and glue it tight,
So I'll be safe from any fright,
And then I'll flip the bright switch.

Then no more shadows will I fear,
No dread noises will I hear,
And light will stay forever.

The applause this time was more restrained. Mary blushed and hurried back to her place.

'Another great talent,' said Mrs Hayes. 'Song-writing takes great skill and patience, and you have an expressive voice. We will hear much more of you also.'

Johnny had liked Mary's song, and her singing, but couldn't help noticing Arona frown heavily—especially at Mrs Hayes' comments. The class bell soon sounded, and the class filed into the corridor and headed for their first PE lesson. Arona was part of the leading group, and Johnny heard her powerful voice raised bitterly in the corridor, for everyone to hear.

'*Dark* Switch? She's loopy, that one—as loopy as her mother over in Gransha!'

There was a loud clatter as Mary McNevin, following close behind, dropped her guitar case. Margaret Phillips immediately stopped to help. As Johnny came alongside he saw Margaret put her arm round Mary, and look angrily after Arona, who hadn't stopped. Mary seemed shocked.

He knew why also: 'Gransha' was the short name for the city's mental hospital.

Margaret shook her head as Johnny watched.

'That was wrong. Arona's just jealous, Mary. Don't mind her!'

Johnny could see that Mary was hurt, and didn't linger, knowing Margaret would deal with the situation better than he could. He was annoyed also, as Arona had treated Mary in much the same way that Gavan had treated Kieran and himself—perhaps worse.

Johnny was also remembering what Mick had said in the clearing:

'*Pay attention, especially to insults and insulting behaviour. You know, bad slagging—stupid words and actions meant to put someone down. See who is doing that, and to whom? Why? And who objects? You must listen, watch, think and learn.*'

Arona had certainly tried to put Mary down, and Margaret had objected. But what could Johnny do about it? And what was he supposed to learn? He made a mental note to think about that again later, and to begin some kind of record of such incidents so that he would not forget. He hadn't expected to meet two examples before lunch on Monday and wondered what the rest of the week would hold.

The class had its first period of PE then, girls and boys separately, joining with Eight A boys and girls.

As he changed into his PE gear Johnny noticed Patrick Andrews, Gavan Maguire and Aidan Maroney together close by. Further away Eddy Li was changing, facing in the other direction.

Suddenly, as Patrick finished changing, he gestured towards Eddy silently, to draw the attention of Gavan and Aidan to himself, without Eddy noticing. He then faced towards Aidan and put a finger to each of the outside corners of his own eyes—for Aidan's and Gavan's amusement.

Gavan grinned appreciatively. Aidan wasn't so amused, but didn't protest. Patrick repeated this mime until Eddy had finished changing and was on the point of turning. Then Patrick bent and began tying his shoelace, but went on grinning up at Gavan, who grinned back. Aidan looked a little uncomfortable, Johnny thought, but did nothing to show disapproval.

Johnny made another mental note. Eddy hadn't noticed anything, but if this continued he was bound to sense something soon. Johnny wasn't sure what he himself could or should do about it. Patrick had behaved as though everyone should find his mime amusing, but its purpose was to invite everyone to be rude to Eddy, including the Eight A boys.

'*Insulting behaviour,*' Johnny noted, '*intended to put someone down.*' There was certainly no shortage of such behaviour in his own year group at Iona. But what could he do about it?

Mr Slaney, the PE teacher appeared at that moment and whistled them out onto the football pitch. There the boys played their first twelve-a-side soccer match, Eight A against Eight B. Patrick Andrews proved himself the best player for Eight B, scoring a hat trick of goals. Gavan was an effective defender, using his weight aggressively to block and frustrate the Eight A forwards. Eddy Li also shone in a mid-field role, passing the ball accurately up field. Johnny concentrated on not making a fool of himself in a defensive position, and managed that at least.

The final score was 5-3 in favour of Johnny's class, who whooped it up in the shower afterwards.

Patrick Andrews was especially elated. As he changed he resumed his jeering of Eddy behind his back, to Gavan's increasing amusement. Johnny watched this with growing annoyance and frustration—especially when Patrick's mime took monkey form. To protest would only draw Eddy's attention to what was going on, but Johnny felt he should do something to separate himself from what was happening.

On an impulse he stood, went forward, and pushed Patrick's soap bar off the bench beside him onto the floor where Patrick was acting the fool. Next moment the mimer trod on the soap. Patrick fell with a crash on the tiled floor, half dressed. Eddy turned and joined in the laughter, totally unaware of what had led up to it. Patrick climbed sheepishly to his feet—to find Eddy handing him back his soap. The laughter grew louder—for reasons that puzzled Eddy. Patrick was well aware of them, and that put an end to his antics that day.

But Johnny wasn't sure he had done well. Patrick had hurt his right arm on the bench as he fell, and was now rubbing it ruefully—glowering at Johnny. One of the other boys had told him why he had slipped.

Johnny realised that he had left yet another obstacle to be overcome. He got another glower before they left the changing room—this one telling him the incident would be remembered.

IV

Later that day Johnny heard Anny climbing the stairs at home, without taking time to take off her coat.

'Well?' she said, flinging open the door of Johnny's room. He didn't need to ask what she meant, as she had reminded him again in the morning to be careful around Gavan.

'OK!' he said, and described the scene outside the maths room. She stiffened angrily when she heard of Gavan's 'hangover' taunt, but when she heard how Johnny had responded she sat on the bed and laughed longer than Johnny could understand. He didn't tell her about Patrick Andrews—that incident still bothered him.

That night after his homework Johnny began a list of 'put downs', briefly describing and dating each one. On Tuesday he was able to add to it again, when Gavan and Patrick began jeering at the biggest boy in their class, David Reynolds. He was truly wide for his age and had been the slowest boy on the pitch on Monday. He was self- conscious and didn't retaliate, and so was fair game.

So was Martin Cassidy of Eight A, who had shown himself unsuited for a contact sport like football. Although as tall as Johnny he was lightly built. He had shied away from tackles and mis-kicked several times—to hoots from the athletic types. At lunchtime on Tuesday Johnny noticed Martin eating on his own in the canteen, and then again walking on his own at the back of the school. Just then Gavan and Patrick came by.

'How's Martina?' Gavan shouted at the blonde-haired boy, who turned a strawberry colour and couldn't meet Johnny's eye as he hurried past. Johnny learned later that Martin was the cleverest pupil in Eight A, but had not yet made a friend among the boys of his class. He tended to shy away from other boys in fear, and to concentrate on his school work.

And Arona Gilsenan carried on where she had left off on Monday, jeering at Rosemary Allen for her plumpness and Catherine Canning for her visits to the school oratory. On both occasions he noticed Margaret Phillips watching grimly. He sensed that something was coming.

Sure enough, on Wednesday at break Johnny came upon Arona and Margaret squaring up outside the Art Room. The rest of the class had not yet arrived.

'Who do you think you are? I'll say what I like!' Arona shouted.

'If everyone spoke to you that way how would you feel? Doesn't everyone have a right to respect!'

By this time some other pupils had come up.

'No they don't,' shouted Arona, 'not if they're fat or stupid or loopy or thin as a hosepipe like you—you long string of misery!'

At this, Arona's friends Ann O'Kane and Deirdre Hasson laughed outright.

'Ooh!' said Margaret icily. 'So you've joined Gavan's group too—*The Insulters*. May I join too? Am I speaking to the ravishing Arona, Queen of Karaoke and diva of Eight B?'

A louder laugh followed. By this time most of the class had gathered.

Arona went pale and, for the first time, speechless. Then she rallied again.

'I'll bet you can change light bulbs without standing on a chair!'

'I'll bet they won't let you sing in church, in case all the stained glass falls out!'

At that moment the Art teacher, Mr Turley, arrived—a little breathless and overweight.

'Girls, girls, what's this, what's this? Falling out already? Over nothing I'm sure! Birds in their nests, you know?'

Margaret marched into the art room with her chin up. The class followed, highly diverted. Johnny too had been entertained, pleased to see that Margaret could hold her own. He wondered if any of the other girls had challenged Arona's taunts. Mary McNevin still seemed anxious after Monday's events, and Johnny was sure it was on her account especially that Margaret had challenged Arona. He suspected this battle was far from over.

On Thursday second period Johnny's stomach was again in a knot as Eight B trooped into Mrs Walsh's room on the terrace. Straight away he saw she had stacked their

'Application' homework open on her desk in two piles of equal height.

'There wasn't one bad homework in the whole set, and I'm pleased and impressed. Most of you wrote applications for places or organisations that we all know about—and that's great if you already have a clear idea of what you want to join. Catherine Canning—you think you might want to be an aid worker. A courageous and individual choice in these times! This carries on an old Iona tradition. Well written and well done!'

Catherine reddened. Johnny could see she was pleased also—Arona's taunts must have hurt her.

One by one Mrs Walsh passed back the books, commenting encouragingly on every one.

'Kieran Lowney's application is for an engineering firm. He took the trouble to find a real firm on the Internet and look up their educational requirements. Well done Kieran!'

Kieran was clearly delighted also. Johnny knew he felt awkward about his bad writing and spelling, and probably glad Mrs Walsh had said nothing about this. Patrick Andrews had applied for a place in Manchester United's junior squad, and Bridget McSorley to a law firm.

'Gavan Maguire's application is to join a political party. I needn't say which one. He stresses the need to progress towards a united Ireland as quickly as possible, overcoming all obstacles. A lot of effort obvious here.

'Arona Gilsenan—you have applied to a recording company asking it to listen to a recording of a band you have formed. You describe the recording in great detail, teaching me a lot I did not know about pop music.

'Edward Li has thought about the problem of policing in the far future when crime will join the space age. Very imaginative and persuasive. Well done too!

'Margaret Phillips—you have thought up an environmental organisation that links young people from all over the world on the Internet to help put climate change at the top of the political agenda everywhere. Nothing could be more valuable at this time. Well done.

'Aidan Maroney—you foresee a global think-tank advising governments and the United Nations Organisations on world problems, and apply to join. A lot of thought went into this. Very impressive indeed!'

There was only one book left now.

'John Mullan. You have thought up a multi-world organisation known as the bridgers. It helps people overcome obstacles of all kinds, including the threat to the earth environment. You suppose it may already exist. But you spell 'bridgers' with a small 'b', even though it's a proper name. Can you tell us why?'

Johnny hadn't been expecting a question, and his mind raced as he stood up.

'Because they think everyone's special—so no-one's more important than anyone else. So they're not supposed to think they're terrific either.'

'Ah,' said Mrs Walsh thoughtfully. 'That's interesting. There's a debating point there. Thank you for that Johnny— because it reminds me of something else. But that can wait until tomorrow. The bell's about to go. Take a rest tonight, Eight B. Well done everyone!'

Her eyes were bright as she said this. No-one doubted she meant it, and there was a general murmur of appreciation as the class rose to leave. No-one had been put down.

Outside on the terrace, Margaret Phillips was waiting for Johnny.

'I just love that idea, the bridgers,' she said. 'If they existed I would sign up right away! Especially after this week!'

Johnny respected Margaret's opinion, so that made up for all the knowing winks and jeers Johnny had seen Gavan and Patrick exchange as Mrs Walsh had passed back his book. He wished again that there was someone he could share his strange experience with.

He also wondered when or if he would see Mick again, as there was so much to talk about.

On Friday morning, first period, Mrs Walsh took Eight B on their first visit together to the locker cubicles. Eight B had a cubicle of their own—three sides of a rectangle. Johnny's locker was midway along the left side, beside Aidan Maroney's. Each locker was big enough to take an overcoat and other belongings that weren't needed for most classes. Mrs Walsh warned them that they could not expect total privacy for their locker contents, as 'in rare circumstances' these might need to be searched.

'So keep them respectable please,' she said. 'We want no fermentation of deadly bacteria or nerve gas from ancient sandwiches, pizzas or bananas. Nor will we appreciate a month's accumulation of odorous PE gear. Nor—worst of all—the indescribable stench of a hamster or other diminutive domestic pet that has expired in lonely neglect.'

Then, as the school bell rang, they returned to Mrs Walsh's room on the terrace for English.

'Yesterday I mentioned debating. This year I'm starting an after- school debating society especially for Year Eight. There is a senior debating society already, but it resembles the Colosseum in Rome, where sweaty barbarians cheered the chopping up of gladiators. You lot need something a little milder, where you can develop debating skills from scratch. Your homework for Monday is to compose three motions for debate. You may do this in collaboration if you wish—I mean as a team with one other person.

"What's a motion?' you may ask. Well, here are a few.'
Mrs Walsh then wrote on the board:

That war is always wrong.
That humans are destined to destroy planet Earth.
That eleven is old enough to vote.

'Notice that a good motion is always capable of being debated.

'That boys and girls are different'—that's not a good motion because any team supporting that motion has a clear advantage to start with.

The same problem exists with 'That the sky is often blue' or anything else too obvious to require an interesting exchange of arguments. Don't choose anything either that requires too much specialised knowledge—for example, 'That nuclear energy is a threat to the environment'. Stick to things you actually can debate with one another.'

She told them then that they would be bound by the rules of the World Schools Debating Competition. These required a three- person team on each side of the debate.

'Debating is a skill of particular importance for anyone thinking of law or politics as a career—but anyone can benefit. Any of you wanting to form a team should let me know next Monday.

'Now—into groups for the rest of the class, with every person to come up with one good motion. That'll start you off with your homework.'

This time Johnny found himself in a group with Catherine Canning, Bridget McAlonan and a short-sighted boy, Eamonn Heaney. No-one had any difficulty coming up with a motion that seemed OK—but the bell rang before there could be any comment from Mrs Walsh. Johnny left the class excited but wondering if the 'after school' requirement ruled him out.

On the bus home Margaret Phillips surprised him by sitting alongside.

'What about forming a debating team—the two of us and Eddy, or maybe Bridget?'

'I'm not sure. About getting home late.'

'I'll ask my Mum—she could maybe give us a lift on whatever day it is. We both live out in the same direction.'

'OK,' said Johnny, brightening. He was sure Anny would want him to take such an opportunity. 'I'll ask my Ma.'

'I live out in Glencarn,' Margaret continued. 'That's only a mile or so from where you get off. There's a bus that takes you quite close. What about meeting tomorrow to think out motions? I could meet you at the stop.'

Johnny nodded again.

'But I'll need to check with my Ma. I could phone you tonight if it's OK.'

Margaret agreed and gave him her home phone number. He reflected on the way home that she had changed a lot in that week.

On the previous Friday she had been barely speaking to him. Now she was excited and ready to talk. In the meantime a lot had happened to both of them—and they knew far more about the challenges they would both face.

———∘∘∘✺∘∘∘———

Next morning at ten, with Anny's permission, he took the bus for Glencarn. Sure enough, five stops further on Margaret was standing at the bus stop. She looked different—less stiff and formal—in sweater and jeans.

'This way,' said Margaret, pointing across the road. When they had crossed the road they walked back along it to a T junction with a smaller road and headed up the spine of the T. Soon they were crossing a bridge over the winding river Faughan.

'We'll go up through the glen,' said Margaret a minute later, turning off the road onto a quiet path that led through a public walking area alongside the river. As they walked Margaret stared about her, rapt. Johnny had never been along this path, and his eye followed it upward.

Soon they saw the remains of an old watermill. 'I love this place,' said Margaret. 'Come and see!' The mill was a ruin, but Margaret knew a safe way through it to the water side. She ducked through a narrow gap in a wall. When Johnny followed he found himself in a quiet enclosed space, opening only towards the river, flowing darkly past. Opposite, alder trees came almost to the bank.

'I come here to read sometimes.'

Margaret sat down then, on the remains of the wall that had once fronted the river. She stared at the flowing water, rapt.

'I know you'll keep this to yourself,' she said then. 'What Arona said about Mary hurt her, because her mother is seriously ill. She *is* in Gransha. She has bad depression. I'm worried about Mary. She nearly didn't come to school again on Tuesday. That's why I went for Arona on Wednesday, but she seems to have no feelings for anyone else. I'm not getting much support from the other girls either. What you said about everyone being special—that's the way I feel too. Not even Bridget McSorley dares to face Arona. Cathy Canning says she was upset at what happened after music, but even she prefers not to fight.'

She looked straight at Johnny then. 'What do you think the bridgers would do, if they existed?'

Johnny wasn't sure what to say. He remembered that Margaret had said that she would join the bridgers if they were real—but if he told her what had happened the previous Sunday she might well think that he too should be in Gransha. He tried to quieten his mind—and then did again what he was now used to doing. In another moment his mind was made up.

'When you asked me on Monday how I had come to answer Gavan that way—about The Insulters—you asked me how that had come to me.'

Margaret nodded, so Johnny gave a full account of his dream in the Bishop's Wood—saying at the end that he still wasn't sure, from one day to the next, that it had happened. He left out only the details of his own family problems. Then he went slowly through his encounter with Gavan again.

Margaret had not stopped him once to ask a question. Now she just stared hard at him, slightly pale, then at the water, and then back at him again—a long, attentive look as if to check something. He tried to stay calm, dreading what she might say next.

'So you're still not sure?' she said then.

'No—I'm still testing it out—to see what happens when I ask for the power of the bridge. Should I be locked up too?'

'No—but that's the weirdest story I've ever heard. I don't know if I should be frightened for you, or if I should believe it myself.'

She made the sign of the cross then, moving her open right hand from her forehead to her chest and then to her left and right shoulders. She closed her eyes and stayed that way for seconds.

When she opened her eyes again she seemed unafraid.

'I'm going to write my own bridgers' application tonight—to see what happens. But now would you do something? Ask for the power of the bridge—to help us think up some good debating motions for Mrs Walsh? I want us to debate what we should do about the environment.'

Relieved, Johnny was only too ready to agree, so they went out together then, through the opening in the wall and the rest of the ruined mill, to the sunlight. Soon they were close enough to see Margaret's home, a bungalow set on the sloping ground on the opposite side of the road that adjoined the Faughan walk. Inside they met Margaret's mother, also tall and thin, who gave Johnny an uncomfortably long inspection, as though looking for woodworm. She reminded Johnny of Margaret as she had been on the first Friday at school. Margaret had told him on the way that her mum was a lecturer at the University. She hadn't said anything about her father, and Johnny saw no one else there that day.

Mrs Phillips was a bit older than Anny, he decided, and spoke with a different accent. She had milk and biscuits waiting for them in the kitchen—and a few questions for Johnny. The early ones were about where he lived and his family. She did not seem to be interested in the answers to these. Then she took a new tack.

'Margaret tells me you stick up for people. Why is that?'

Johnny felt uncomfortable. He had the feeling Mrs Phillips was putting him under a microscope, as though he was something she couldn't quite identify and didn't quite believe.

'I don't know,' he said, truthfully.

'I hope it's true,' she said. 'People often start out well and turn out... differently.'

Sensing that he was 'on approval', Johnny didn't know what to say at first. Then he thought of something.

'Margaret sticks up for people too!'

'Oh? Tell me!'

So Johnny told Mrs Phillips the whole story of Mary McNevin and Arona Gilsenan and the music room and what had happened then, and the exchange outside the art room on Wednesday.

Margaret excused herself when she was first mentioned. Mrs Phillips didn't seem to notice this and listened intently as Johnny described the scenes outside the music room and the art room, repeating the whole dialogue word for word as he remembered it. Mrs Phillips expression changed to one of rapt attention—as though she was hearing something about Margaret that she didn't already know.

When he repeated Margaret's 'Queen of Karaoke' line he saw Mrs Phillips mouth open in surprise. He wasn't sure what she would think about Arona's taunts at Margaret, but told her anyway. She said nothing for about ten seconds, and then:

'*Moses!*'

She then went on staring at Johnny as though he was an even stranger specimen.

'Well!' she said at last.

She got up then and went out of the kitchen, looking for Margaret. Johnny was on his own for a while, and spent the time searching his head for debating motions. He knew Margaret would soon be asking him for those, but instead all he could come up with was more questions. One concerned a scene that was playing over and over in his head—another event from last week in school.

When the two came back Mrs Phillips had brightened up, and Margaret seemed pleased.

'I hope we can work out a lift for those debates,' said Mrs Phillips then, agreeably.

Margaret then showed Johnny the small room set aside for her homework—the walls covered with rainforest and animal pictures.

She seemed especially fond of orangutans and gorillas and lemurs—and whales. Johnny noticed a small microscope on a shelf, and a computer with a large screen on a desk in the corner.

'Now,' said Margaret, sitting at her work table and taking a notebook from her bag. 'Those motions. I've already thought of one—'that everybody is equally important'. Mrs Walsh has already said that could be debated, and we must persuade the Insulters not to be hurtful. Is that OK?'

Johnny had no problem with that, so Margaret wrote it down.

'Have you had any ideas yet?'

Johnny hadn't. Instead that scene was playing again in his head from the previous Monday—their classmates crowded around Aidan's extra-powerful tablet computer, and then the two boys boasting they would soon have one. He described this to Margaret, and she remembered.

'You winked at me then,' he went on. 'Why did you do that? I think I know, but I'm not sure.'

'Because they were copying one another. They just want one of those powerful tablets because Aidan's got one! So they can show off too!'

'Yes, that's it!' said Johnny. 'What's the word for that? It's not just wanting—it's a particular kind of wanting. It's not like wanting food when you're hungry, or like wanting shelter if it's cold and stormy. You need those things. It's wanting something that you see someone else with, something that makes them seem important, so that you can be important too. I can't think of a word for that, can you?'

Margaret shook her head. 'But why are you going on about that?'

'I'm not sure. It's just in my head a lot. And it reminds me that on the first day I was comparing Patrick's fancy all-colour pen with my own, and wishing I had that instead. And I wanted a better bike last Christmas when another boy went past our house with a new one, with the spokes all shining. Has anything like that happened to you?'

Margaret sat back to think. Suddenly she sat up with a jump.

'Jiminy! I've just remembered something. There was an expensive dining table and chairs in the furniture store—with a big photographic cut-out showing someone using the table to entertain.

And it was made of expensive solid mahogany, not veneer, probably from the rainforests. And that was just one of the things made of rare wood in the store. Everyone who came in was supposed to think that everyone else would admire them if they bought those things.' She sat silently awhile longer, and then looked up. 'You're right, Johnny, everybody does that—to make themselves feel more important.'

'But why, if no one is more important than anyone else anyway?' Margaret thought about that for just a moment.

'That kind of wanting is often silly, and it's a threat to the rain forests too. We should think up a motion about that.'

'But I can't think of a word for that kind of wanting. And a dictionary is no good—because we don't know the word we're looking for!' Johnny said.

'My Mum might know that. But give me the meaning of the word we're looking for again.'

'Wanting something that someone else has because you think it makes them better than you.'

While Margaret wrote that down Johnny went on:

'We know what we're looking for now anyway. I think there's a special kind of dictionary, a *thes*-something, that gives lists of words that mean almost the same thing. It might give us another word for

'want' that means 'wanting to copy'. Do you know what that book is?'

Margaret shook her head.

'Can't we make up a word?' she said then. 'Just for the two of us?

Just for now?'

'Yes,' he said, liking the idea. 'If we put 'wanting' and 'copy' together.'

'Wanting-copy doesn't sound right!'

'How about copy-wanting?' Johnny asked.

Margaret thought a moment. 'Yes—that sounds about right.

We'll say it means wanting to copy someone by getting something they have got, to be just as important as they are.'

'Write that down—it's the definition,' he said. 'I'm sure everybody copy-wants.'

Margaret skipped a line and wrote their new word, and its definition. She wrote more neatly than he did, Johnny could see.

'Oh my Go...!' said Margaret then. She put her hand over her mouth and began rocking back and forward and bouncing up and down on her chair, unable to speak. Johnny couldn't make out what was wrong with her.

'What is it?' he asked.

She shook her head—she needed time to recover. She was spluttering and giggling as though a big piece of biscuit had gone the wrong way. At the same time she was waving at him to say she was all right, and gradually calming down.

'Arona!' she said at last. 'Arona!'

'What about her?'

'She does it too! She copies pop-singers! She wants to be a diva!'

Johnny was startled. His mind had been focused on the example of the two boys and Aidan's computer, and his own desire for a better pen and a new bike—but instantly he could see that Margaret was right. Arona's every gesture and vocal mannerism had been copied from TV programmes or pop videos that he had seen sometime.

'But what is it she wants to get? It's not a computer, or something like that!'

Margaret put the top of her pen in her mouth and thought awhile.

'I know—it's everyone to clap! Remember the way she bowed!

She loves applause, that's what pop singers get, and being on TV.

People think they're special!'

'Could that be why she was nasty to Mary?'

'Yes—she was jealous because Mrs Hayes liked Mary's song better.

Everyone could see that!'

'Put that down quick,' he said then. 'As another example! People can want applause—and they can be spiteful if someone else gets more than they do!'

At that moment there was a knock on the door and Mrs Phillips put her head round it. 'Lunchtime you two! I hope you've got your debating motions thought out!'

They were glad then that they had made some progress. They agreed to go on thinking and exchanged phone numbers. Margaret's Mum had gone to a lot of trouble, making a thick soup that Johnny didn't recognise. It tasted vaguely oniony, but delicious. She had also made some banana sandwiches, and small chocolate eclairs, something he didn't often get and especially liked.

'We're going shopping in town this afternoon,' said Mrs Phillips then. 'We can give you a lift to your home, Johnny, and maybe meet your Mum. It will save you the bus fare.'

Johnny could only thank her, but his heart sank. The Phillips' house was much bigger and better furnished than his own. And his was on an estate where people were often roughly spoken and badly dressed. And what if Kevy was at home and glowered at Johnny's 'swanky friends'—and even smelled of drink and said something insulting? What would the Phillips think of him then—especially Margaret? Maybe they wouldn't want to know him after that.

For the first time Johnny realised he sometimes felt ashamed of his father, and immediately felt guilty over this.

He was fearful all the way in the Phillips' car, which was much newer than Anny's, and smelt nicer. He knew that Margaret sensed he was worried about something, because he wasn't interested in talking and didn't hear what she said, making do with occasional nods.

Then, as they turned into Inishowen Avenue he saw Anny walking homeward ahead of them, carrying a shopping bag. She sometimes did that if she didn't have too much to carry—'to get some exercise' she said.

'There's my Ma!' Johnny said.

Mrs Phillips pulled the car in just ahead of Anny, and got out to talk to her. Johnny and Margaret got out too and waited for their parents to finish, just out of earshot. After the usual getting-to- know-you stuff Mrs Phillips began talking confidentially to Anny, facing away from the two friends. They knew this was parents' business they weren't supposed to hear.

The two adults were soon finished. Johnny said goodbye to Margaret and her mother, and they drove off.

'Go on thinking about those debating motions,' Margaret had said on parting. 'And phone me if you think of anything.'

'Well!' said Anny then, in a pleased voice. 'They are nice people.

I hope you remembered your table manners!'

Johnny could sense that Anny and Mrs Phillips had made friends and was relieved.

It was still in his head that copy-wanting wasn't a word he would find in the dictionary, and that he couldn't think of another for the same idea. That puzzled him, because he had been sure that everything that happened had a name. As he watched TV then he saw an advertisement for a luxury car that showed a rich person driving it away from a posh hotel. Other advertisements did the same thing—linking products with a lifestyle far more glamorous than his own.

The more he watched the surer he was that copy-wanting happened all the time, and that people did it without noticing.

Johnny at the same time was bracing himself to ask Kevy something. As he was tidying up the line of books on his table he remembered the pinewood that Anny had bought to make a bookshelf to go just above his table. It was in his Da's small workshop at the back of the house, where he kept his tools. Kevy had never gotten round to it.

Now Johnny could be doing with it, as he needed all the space on his small table for working. Should he ask Kevy again? He knew his Da was downstairs, watching sport on TV. Interrupting TV was something that Johnny had stopped doing, fearful of Kevy's bad temper.

Then Johnny remembered that Mr McKinley had warned them that they would soon be starting a project to make a simple electrical switch that would be enclosed in a plywood box. He had shown them the woodworking tools they would use, and similar boxes made by last year's class. Surely Kevy could show him how to use the tools for that? He would have to ask him sometime, so why not now? Maybe that could start him off, and Johnny could mention the bookshelves at a good moment later.

Johnny did again what he was used to doing now. He asked for the power of the bridge and went downstairs. Kevy was sitting back on the couch, with his hands clasped behind his head, watching a horse race. Johnny got a glass of milk and sat down on a chair, waiting for it to end. His Da didn't usually put money on horses, so he wasn't that involved, just passing the time. He looked tired as usual, because he had been out late, drinking. His breath smelt— but there wasn't the smell of recent drink that Johnny hated. Anny was in the kitchen area, mopping the floor.

'Da?' he said when the race ended.

'Humph?' said Kevy absently.

'There's this subject in school, Technology, and ...'

'Computers and stuff! You're flyin' now!'

Kevy glanced at him sarcastically, and then turned back to the TV.

'Mr McKinley says that technology began with wooden machines like water wheels and spinning wheels. He says there wouldn't be any technology without that.'

'Does he now?' said Kevy. There was still sarcasm in his tone, but maybe something else too—just a hint of interest. He had turned now to look at Johnny, at least.

'And he says we have to learn some woodwork, to make things like plywood boxes. With saws and chisels. He says we have to learn ... to get it right!' Johnny had almost used the word 'accuracy', but stopped himself just in time.

'Does he now? Before you go on to the more important stuff, I suppose!'

'No—he likes woodworking, honest—he even showed us a spinning wheel he made himself!'

'Did he now? Well if he's that good, he can teach you too then, can't he!' Kevy had turned truculently back to the TV.

Johnny was almost at a loss. Whatever he said, his Da turned it into a reason for bitterness. Then he had another idea.

'The other boys—I'm not as good at making things.' This was just true enough. 'If I had some practice ... if you showed me again.

Just a few things ... how to saw straight, and stuff, I wouldn't fall behind.'

Anny had been listening, and was now standing looking at them both, drying her hands.

Kevy said nothing for a while, just considered morosely.

'I'll have a look outside later, and see. I don't know if there's any plywood.'

'OK,' said Johnny. His Da hadn't promised anything, and might just be putting him off, but it was the best he could do for now.

He had finished his milk, and rose to put his glass in the sink.

Anny nodded at him, and gave a small smile—one his father wouldn't see. Johnny knew that if his Da didn't raise the issue again soon, he would just have to pester him again in a few days.

Johnny had still some other homework to do, but finished it that day. He went to bed that night thinking of Margaret's decision at the river. Now he had a friend who might also become a bridger—someone he could talk to about what was going on inside his own head.

Again he tried to read, but found all his own adventure books dull in comparison to what was happening to himself now.

V

'Come on, Margaret! What's wrong with you anyway?'

Again her mother was calling Margaret in the shopping mall—when she wanted to pause, look and think about what she was seeing. This time it was a queue at one of the mobile phone shops.

The latest smartphone had arrived that same week and was here in the window, alongside a huge dazzling image of itself. It was those queueing that drew Margaret, and those leaving the same shop with small, slickly decorated plastic bags. Some of the excited new owners were stopping at the coffee shop opposite—to unpack and stare at their new phones, before they were even charged. These faces told of intense interest. It seemed that at that moment nothing could be more important to these happy owners, and some were little older than Margaret herself.

Margaret had seen that phone advertised on TV that week—and had wondered then if her own year-old basic phone wasn't past it now, not meeting her needs. Could she too not do with a phone that could search the Internet—and still last more than a day without recharging? But what were her real needs anyway, and why did she want to believe they included this phone?

'*Maargare-et!*'

Again her mother jogged her arm, this time in some exasperation, and hurried her towards the book and stationery store further along the same floor of the mall.

Copy-wanting! That was it, surely. In the mall the urge to want what others wanted seemed to increase. That was surely what brought many people who could afford to pay for the huge variety of goods on display. Yes, people had real needs too—for clothes, furniture, electrical goods, even freshly-baked bread. Maybe everything here was genuinely needed by someone—but there was an air of excitement in the mall, and in herself, that told Margaret that wanting and needing were not an exact match for many.

What was puzzling Margaret was that she had not noticed this behaviour until today. None of the adults who had taught her had ever pointed it out or given it a targeting name. And this could be happening in every shopping mall on the planet at that moment—a planet unable to cope properly with what was being thrown away. Why hadn't she heard more about those serious problems, and about copy-wanting, from those who had taught her, especially her religion teachers?

Margaret wanted to believe what she had been taught—about there being a kindly God of some kind. But she wanted to believe in the bridgers too—and it was Johnny Mullan who had told her that story, and then got her to notice and to give a name to a problem her teachers had never spoken about.

Or had they? Had they perhaps spoken about all of this in another way, using other words, without her noticing?

Now they had finally reached the book and stationery store. Margaret was glad when her mother told her to please herself for forty minutes. She went as usual towards the nature shelves, but her mind was still on the scene outside the phone shop. 'Consumerism'—that was what these books would call this behaviour—but none of them had helped her to understand what often made people almost feverish consumers. And now she had a word for that, a word that described more clearly what was going on.

It had been her undecided, busy mind that had made Margaret say a prayer at the mill on the river earlier that day. Prayer sometimes helped you not to worry—her mother had taught her that. Margaret believed it too. She had tested it out again for herself earlier in the week, when hesitating about what do about Arona's behaviour towards Mary McNevin, and about having no one to back her up. Here too in the stationery shop the fact that she was staring down on other girls older than herself made Margaret self-conscious about her height. She had been more deeply hurt by Arona's taunts than she had tried to show. Whenever she remembered how Arona had behaved towards both herself and Mary she had felt a deep anger that worried her. She knew she wasn't supposed to hate anyone, but at times she felt she wanted to do just that—to spend time thinking up some deeply cutting things to say to Arona, something that would make her cry as bitterly as Mary had. That made her uneasy, and even afraid of what she might do, and that was another reason she tried to pray.

Worried again at the river that Johnny's strangeness, and his dream, might mislead her if she put any trust in it, she had said another prayer then at the mill, making herself attentive to her deepest feelings. She had suddenly felt safe then, and made up her mind. And then, at her request, Johnny had asked for bridging help with debating motions—and then got her to notice what they had agreed to call copy-wanting.

And now she was seeing what they had named all around her. She mustn't forget that. She mustn't forget what she was now intently watching—something that was connected in so many ways with what interested her.

A diary! That was what she needed now, to note down in detail all that was going on for her. She looked about her to locate the likely shelves—and soon found herself staring at notebooks designed as special diaries, with padded covers and 'My Diary' in gold leaf on the richly-coloured front covers. But these were far more expensive than simple bound notebooks. Margaret wasn't sure she could keep up a diary either, or, even if she could, how many pages she would need from one week to the next. So she chose a simple, strong notebook with lined pages and good paper, and went to the pay desk. Whatever happened, this notebook would come in useful, and she could repeat the exercise if it got filled up quickly.

Then, as Margaret browsed idly near the entrance, where she would soon meet her mother again, there was a sudden disturbance in the general background noise. A confused shouting, and then a shriek, penetrated into the shop from outside—and then the sound of rapidly running feet. A blurred figure ran past the window.

'Stop him—stop!' This loud shout made Margaret go out quickly—to see the same figure dodging and twisting down the concourse as shoppers watched. Then the runner fell—and was held down by others, one wearing a Mickey Mouse costume. Watching teenagers cheered ironically—until a security guard and a policeman arrived.

These then walked right back toward Margaret, each gripping an arm of a boy aged about sixteen. The guard was also holding a woman's purse, showing it for identification now to a well-dressed woman who approached.

There was laughter now in the mall. Mickey Mouse was flexing his arm muscles and sticking out his chest. Cameras were flashing.

But it was the thief who drew Margaret's closer attention. Ginger- haired, he wore a light, grubby, gaudy track suit and didn't seem shocked or ashamed by his predicament. He was instead wearing an amused face, mingled with defiance.

Then, catching Margaret's eye, he grinned and shrugged—and the trio went on past. Her Mum caught her arm again. 'Are you alright?'

Margaret nodded, but was still re-running the whole afternoon in her head. She did so all the way home. Then she set out to make a detailed record of that whole day. She knew now that seemingly routine events sometimes needed to be replayed in slow motion in her head—to be fully understood—and was determined to go on doing that.

That evening something else happened that put Margaret in mind to ask some serious questions in school the following week. Before going to bed she did as she had promised earlier in the day. She wrote her application to the bridgers.

'To the bridgers

I want to understand what to do about the mess we're all making. Today I think I am beginning to understand more, but I'm still mixed up. I can't understand why most adults aren't as worried as I am, and why they don't seem to notice what Johnny and I call copy-wanting. And why some people are cruel—and what I should do about that too when it happens to me and my friends. Sometimes I feel I should hate people, and be cruel too. I don't know what else to do.

I know there could be some price to pay for asking for the power of the bridge, but I don't care so long as I can learn more and not just be useless or spiteful. Can I be an apprentice bridger—but only if I can be a Christian too?

Margaret Phillips

It took her ages to get to sleep that night. Her head was busy with the wording for questions for Miss Doherty and with the events of the day. After midnight the ginger-haired thief began running through her mind, pursued by Mickey Mouse. Both ran into a garden centre in the mall, past shelves of potted plants, and then out the back and into some fields—and then Margaret was at the mill again. When she reached her favourite place on the river side, there was no sign of the thief or Mickey Mouse—and then the mill around her disappeared too. Different trees, maybe Aspens, appeared on the opposite bank, and the water turned the colour of strong tea with milk in it, as if after heavy rain. A deer with antlers came, drank from the river and looked at her.

Then it was winter, and when Margaret looked she was wearing the skin of the deer—and four wolves were now looking from the opposite bank. One raised his head and howled, making her lonely. The trees were covered in frost—leafless and shivering in a light breeze. Night fell. Margaret sensed the wolves were still there. Then the sun came up, and the river was a darker colour, and lower. The wolves had disappeared. The frost was gone also from the trees, and new leaves appeared. She felt warmer, as if held close. And then there was a disturbance in the water in front of her.

A figure was suddenly standing in mid-stream, leaning back against the waist-high current and throwing dark hair off an eager face. This person turned toward her.

'Margaret!'

She was wearing an olive-green wetsuit, dappled with a lighter green pattern. As she waded towards Margaret, and climbed out onto the bank, Margaret could see that this pattern was formed by leaves—every one different—beech, oak, alder. There was an image of a pine cone on her left shoulder—and then, elsewhere, of a beech cupule, a hazel nut and an acorn—all in their natural colours.

'Will it matter what I do or don't do?' Margaret asked.

'Of course! Don't be afraid to ask your questions, even if sometimes that causes pain for yourself. Your teachers need good questions. The ripples you make could be important. You already know, though, what you mustn't think?'

'That everything depends on me?'

'Yes. Everyone makes ripples—be sure to take time to laugh. The greatest bridge has already been made by someone else. Be patient.

In a crisis, be still and wait for your mind to clear. There is no hurry—hurry is part of the problem.'

The girl came closer then to Margaret, who had an impression of grey eyes staring through her.

'About words and actions intended to hurt. These will happen, because everyone is free. They will cause great pain—and you cannot prevent all of this. But that pain is not the worst thing. Being alone is worse again, and you are already helping there. Try to understand where the need to hurt comes from, and go on standing with those in most need. Some of them will do the same for you.'

'When I am insulted I get angry and I want to do the same back.' The wetsuited girl raised her index finger and looked at Margaret intently.

'Wait, then, and ask for the power of the bridge. There will come a feeling that carries a deeper wisdom—a wisdom that cannot be shamed. If you wait you will come to know that feeling, and to trust it.'

Margaret heard above all the word 'wait' and nodded.

There was another much smaller splash in the river then.

Suddenly a dark, wet, sinuous shape ran over Margaret's bare foot, and stood upright, chittering—a half-grown otter, small mouth agape.

'Time for us to go, Margaret.'

'What do I call you?'

'Aleena. All will indeed be well, even if darkness falls heavily sometimes. The greatest bridge is already soundly made—and all will cross.'

In a moment Margaret was alone again. She looked for traces of Aleena and the otter in the water, but could see none. She felt content, unafraid, and went into the river herself. She let it carry her down to the Lough, and swam there till morning.

———∘∘❈∘∘———

'First, are there any nomination slips for class prefects? That election will be this day next week, remember. If not I'll just have to appoint them myself.'

Mrs Walsh was speaking, in English class, second period on Monday morning.

Johnny had forgotten completely about the elections for class prefect—one boy and one girl—announced by Mrs Walsh the previous week. He knew that there had been some vote-hunting for both Aidan Maroney and Arona Gilsenan by their friends, but that had all gone out of his head. Now he watched as Gavan Maguire, Eddy Li, Catherine Canning and Ann O'Kane handed up slips of paper. Mrs Walsh glanced at each of them, and placed them in her table drawer.

'Five nominations—three girls and two boys. I'll not announce them yet, to give an opportunity for late nominations. If anyone has forgotten, have a quick think and get one to me before Wednesday. I'll put the complete list up on Wednesday morning.

'Next—the Year Eight debating society. I've consulted with other members of staff and the best day for most is also Wednesday. I hope that suits most of you lot also?'

Johnny glanced over at Margaret. She was already looking his way, and nodding emphatically. That told him Mrs Phillips must have okayed that day for a lift.

'Now, debating teams. Any of you can form a team later at any stage, but are any teams already formed?'

Three hands went up immediately: from Aidan Maroney, Arona Gilsenan and Johnny himself.

'Marvellous!,' said Mrs Walsh. 'Give me the other team members, please. Aidan first.'

'Gavan, Patrick and myself.'

'Now Arona.'

'Ann, Deirdre and me.'

'And I. Right. Johnny?'

Johnny named Margaret, Eddy and himself. Eddy had jumped at the idea on the bus that morning, saying he was sure his mum would say yes if he could be sure of a lift home afterwards.

'Great! Three promising teams! We will have some fun on Wednesdays I can see.'

As she spoke, Johnny couldn't help noticing Gavan looking at Aidan Maroney with amused eyebrows!

'We'll see,' he thought to himself.

'Now: some ground rules for debate,' Mrs Walsh continued.

'First, marks are not awarded for abuse or insults. A debate is a disciplined exchange of arguments—carefully researched and well delivered speeches that focus on the question being debated and set out reasons for taking a particular view. Witty comment on an opponent's speech is permitted, even welcome, but good debaters never get personal. If they do they lose marks. Is that clear?'

The class expressed agreement in various ways, though Johnny thought he heard some disappointment also.

'Second, there needs to be an *exchange* of arguments. That means that neither team can rely simply on prepared speeches. Both teams need to deal with the arguments put forward by the opposing team.

'This is the most difficult part of debating—because you do not get to hear your opponents' speeches beforehand. You can try to guess what they *might* say, and to be ready for that, but you must still respond to what they *do* say. Is that clear?'

The class murmured 'yes Miss', but Johnny could see that many were thinking that debating might be beyond them.

'That's not as difficult as it sounds. Remember, whatever your career you are probably all going to have to speak in public at some stage, and to think on your feet. It's *not* too early for you to start.

At first you will prepare short speeches for your own debates—no more than two minutes long, and you'll have half a minute maximum for rebuttal. That's answering something an opposing speaker has said. So you *will* be able to do it, I promise you!

'Now this Wednesday you'll hear your first school debate, if you can arrange to stay on after school—an exhibition put on by the senior debating society, just for you. Anyone can come and listen.

The motion will be ...'

Here Mrs Walsh put up on the electronic board: *That this house would ban all TV advertising to people younger than thirteen.*

''House' means the whole audience—including you people. We chose the age of thirteen to make the debate especially relevant to you. The seniors will be giving sample speeches written to make sense to your age group. It'll give you all an idea of what's involved.

'Now homework. First, hand me up those motions you thought up over the weekend. For tomorrow everyone must think up just one argument for or against the motion, and write it down in no less than five sentences. You can pack up to go once you have made a note of that.'

As the class trooped out Gavan Maguire made a point of approaching Kieran Lowney. Johnny could almost guess what was coming. When it came it was loud enough to be heard by all.

'Why don't you try it, Lowney? It would only take you a m m m m.....onth to give a short speech!'

Kieran flushed, but didn't hang his head this time. He stared angrily back at his tormentor, and then turned away.

Johnny could see that Kieran had changed since his first day at Iona. He might not put up much longer with this goading. But what would he do? His inability to express himself easily in words meant that he might bottle up his anger until he finally couldn't, and come off badly.

As Eight B trooped into the music room Mrs Hayes was standing expectantly holding a typed letter with a dramatic purple top border.

'Good morning, Eight B. This tells me that the major TV channels have combined to organise a major school's talent competition. It's for secondary schools.

'Called *Fame School*, it will climax with a competition between ten finalists who will perform on TV on six weekends in spring. The winner will be chosen by phone-in poll. Auditions will be held in all the major cities, including Derry, beginning next month. This letter comes with a poster, so look out for a copy on the notice board in the corridor.'

Ann O'Kane, sitting in the front row, turned to Arona alongside and touched her on the elbow, nodding excited encouragement, her eyebrows arching as usual. Arona acknowledged the tribute with a toss of her dramatic black hair—as if to say 'if I can find the time!', but Johnny could see that she was excited also. She had exactly the kind of looks and talent that could succeed in such a competition. Similar events for older performers had launched dazzling pop careers in recent years.

'This class has members who could audition for this competition, as you all know. We will wish them every success,' Mrs Hayes continued.

Mary McNevin, sitting beside Margaret, didn't lift her head for either of these announcements, and the second one seemed to Margaret to cause her some distress. She thought about offering her some encouragement, but decided to wait for a better time.

'Right boys! This week's PE will be a cross-country run!'

Now it was the hour before lunchtime, a double period. Mr Slaney, ginger-haired, red-faced and almost as wide as a door, stood in the changing room in a navy blue track-suit, with a silver whistle on a white ribbon round his neck.

'We'll be using the paths and track along by the river and the wood. Much of that is usually out of bounds. Make the most of this chance to see more of the school grounds—and get fit at the same time! No lagging and no carry on, or you'll have me to deal with!'

Johnny was changing this time in the inside of a bay alongside Kieran Lowney and the heaviest boy in the year group, David Reynolds. Looking towards the neighbouring bay as he tied his laces he caught sight of Gavan Maguire. He was speaking in a conspirator's whisper to Patrick Andrews and his football sidekick Brendan Brady. Patrick turned to face the bay opposite, and grinned. When Johnny looked in that direction he saw Martin Cassidy, isolated as usual.

Certain that Gavan was up to no good, Johnny felt himself tense. He quickly closed his eyes and asked for the power of the bridge. Soon the boys were whistled out into the school grounds and down a path towards the wood fronting the river. Gavan, Patrick and Brendan waited for Martin to leave, then followed close behind, grinning at one another.

'Stick with me! Something's up!' Johnny whispered to Kieran Lowney, and elbowed his way to a position close behind Gavan, Patrick and Brendan.

When they reached the boundary path along by the trees Mr Slaney turned left and took the year group, at a trot, along the boundary path. He stopped when he reached an arrow marker pointing downward through the wood towards the river, and turned to face the Year Eight boys.

'Right now—twelve at a time! When I blow the whistle, follow the arrows. They'll take you back here. When you get here, go back to the changing rooms and shower.'

He moved back along the column of boys, counting as he came.

'Twelve!'

At that he blew a loud blast and the first group moved off. Johnny quickly calculated that Martin, Gavan and followers would probably be in the third group to set off—and that he and Kieran would probably be in the following group. Searching for sight of Martin ahead, he caught him looking apprehensively over his shoulder at Gavan.

'Twelve!' shouted Mr Slaney, and blew another blast.

As Johnny had feared, Mr Slaney ended his next count with Patrick Andrews, bringing his arm down just ahead of Johnny and Kieran.

'Twelve! Preeeep!'

At the whistle blast the third group set off. Gavan and his friends immediately fell in behind Martin, following him closely although he was trying to outrun them. The last thing Johnny saw was Patrick Andrews trying to knock Martin's heel sideways to make him trip. Nothing serious would happen for a while, Johnny hoped, until the group had gone some distance along the track.

'Twelve! Preeep!'

Johnny and Kieran set off immediately at the head of the fourth group, and turned at the marker down towards the river. Soon they caught sight of the tail end of the third group about sixty metres ahead, rounding a bend in the path as it bent once more to parallel the river.

'Gavan's planning something—against Martin!' said Johnny over his shoulder to Kieran. 'We've got to get closer!' He quickened his pace, and heard Kieran doing his best to keep up.

By now the path was beginning to straighten out again, and, when it did, the two boys had the group ahead in full view. All were well away from the school now. Tall trees lined the path on both sides, with the river glinting not far below to their right. Johnny knew that Gavan would soon be in ideal territory for whatever he might have in mind.

Suddenly Johnny heard a yell ahead, and saw a confused jumble of white forms go to the left off the path, disappearing immediately into the trees. Looking intently ahead then he could see none of the four boys he had been keeping in view.

'They've gone ... into the wood!'. He knew he was talking to himself. By this time Kieran had dropped back some thirty yards.

Johnny had tried to mark the approximate point on the path where Gavan's group had left the track—just beyond a beech tree with a sawn-off branch. When he reached this he turned sharply left, and found himself following a natural track. When he looked he thought he could see footprints in the leaf mould. Knowing that he could now easily get lost himself, and completely miss whatever Gavan was inflicting on Martin, he stopped and stared through the gaps in the surrounding trees, hoping to see, or hear, something. There was no sign of Kieran.

It was the sound of raised voices that gave him the direction he needed—not far away and directly ahead. He had gone no more than twenty paces when he came to the edge of a natural clearing—where three boys stood in a triangular formation, pushing a fourth from one to another. As he got his first clear view, Johnny saw Patrick Andrews shoving Martin Cassidy violently towards Gavan.

'Super shampoo, Martina,' shouted Gavan, wrinkling his nose and pushing Martin towards Brendan Brady.

'You're *not* worth it, Martina' said Brendan, shoving the fearful boy towards Patrick. This brought a loud laugh from Gavan.

'Let me alone!' shouted Martin, very pale.

'Oh please cry for us, dear Martina!' mocked Patrick, pushing him back towards Gavan.

'Let him alone!' Johnny heard himself say.

Startled, Gavan Maguire turned.

'Mullan the mouth! Another loser! And all on his own this time!'

Gavan was sneering. He nodded to the other two, and came towards Johnny.

'What are you trying to prove?' Johnny heard himself ask. 'What harm has he done to you?'

'You're right, Mullan—he's totally not worth it. So now *you'll* get what you deserve for interfering. Hold him!'

In a moment Johnny had his arms held by Patrick and Brendan.

Gavan bent then and lifted a dead stick as long and almost as thick as his arm. He tested it by slapping it against the nearest tree. The top snapped off, shortening the stick into a club.

'Hey—watch it!' said Brendan nervously.

'He just needs a lesson he won't forget!' Gavan said. He came towards Johnny, drawing the stick back behind his head.

At that moment a white blur came hurtling into the clearing, straight at Gavan—striking him just above the waist. He doubled up as he staggered backwards, and his club flew off into the trees. Then he was lying clutching his stomach on the leaf mould—with Kieran Lowney on top of him, hitting him in fury about the face with his fists.

'Get ... him ... off!' Gavan Maguire gasped as Brendan and Patrick stood motionless in astonishment. Kieran was making a moaning sound as he struck almost blindly, again and again.

In a moment Johnny was free as the two released him at the same moment to obey Gavan's orders. Instinctively Johnny followed close behind. He winced at a heavy blow in his ribs from Patrick Andrews, whose face was twisted in malice.

Although Gavan had been badly winded, the tide soon turned against the lighter boys. They were on the point of being overpowered when a sixth body hurtled into the scrum and began a new assault on Gavan Maguire. When Johnny, struggling with Patrick, looked round to see what had happened he found himself staring at the almost unrecognisable face of Martin Cassidy.

'You ... stupid ... pig!' shouted Martin, punctuating each word with a blow. 'You ... stupid ... stupid ... stupid ... stupid ...'

At this point he was the only person in motion, as Gavan could do no more than shield his face—and the other four boys had gone into spectator mode, totally astonished.

'OK! OK! OK!' Gavan said then, from behind his hands. 'That's... enough! *OK*! I said *OK! Right?*'

At last Martin's arms stopped whirling. He backed off and stood up, his chest heaving. Gavan slowly drew his hands away from his face, but didn't attempt as yet to get to his feet. There was fear and bewilderment in his eyes, and his nose was bleeding. He would not recover for some seconds, Johnny could see, and the others were for the moment leaderless.

'Come on!' Johnny said to Kieran and Martin, making a guess on the direction to the running track. The two took one last look at Gavan as he raised himself onto an elbow, and then turned and followed.

Mostly by luck the three found themselves back on the running track a few seconds later, panting. There was no sign of anyone ahead of them, but when Johnny looked back in the direction of the school he saw the broad figure of David Reynolds approaching, at little more than walking pace, completely on his own.

'What's up?' David asked as he came up.

Johnny looked at Kieran and Martin and grinned, his hands on his knees as he stood doubled over.

'I had to stop these two … from beating up Gavan and his friends in the wood!' he said.

Martin looked startled for a moment, and then began to grin between pants, as though experimenting with the idea. Kieran joined in, chuckling strangely. It was the first time Johnny had seen either one laugh out loud since their first day. Martin was looking at his bruised knuckles as though hypnotised.

'Go on!' said David Reynolds, eyes wide.

The four were almost the last to arrive back at the school. Mr Slaney seemed to take it that the heavier boy had been the reason for their slowness. As Johnny showered with the others he saw Gavan and friends arrive—and then saw David Reynolds' eyes widen when Gavan turned to show a bruised and red face.

Dressing, he saw that Martin Cassidy had moved his gear into the bay where he and Kieran were dressing. Martin and Kieran were looking at one another with a half-smile. He felt it best not to try to catch Gavan's eye, and wondered what he would be feeling. He also wondered what he would do next.

———◦◦◦❍◦◦◦———

As Johnny arrived for Miss Doherty's class that afternoon, Margaret caught his eye and gave a determined nod. Religion was Eight B's second-last class of the day, and the lesson followed naturally from others given the previous week—on human reproduction and the need to protect family life. The biology and religion teachers had combined for this, and today Miss Doherty—dark-haired and often seemingly scatty and absent minded—was stressing the roots of unhappiness in what Christians call 'sin', the worst mistakes that people commonly make. She had already listed the most serious causes of sin and now spent time explaining why Catholics saw Jesus' family as the example for all families to follow. She gave examples of how the third of the most serious sins could harm people's lives.

Johnny couldn't understand how Margaret would find an opportunity to ask about what they had been discussing that weekend.

'Pride, covetousness, lust, anger, gluttony, envy and sloth—the seven deadly sins, and you children are just old enough now to learn about the dangers of lust—uncontrolled sexual attraction. Too often the TV we watch shows people disregarding that danger—as if there's no problem with that....'

But now Margaret Phillips' hand was raised high, and she was urgently saying 'Miss! Miss!'

'Yes, Margaret.' Miss Doherty seemed surprised. The class had been listening without much interest, Johnny thought, and without questioning anything so far.

'Coveting, Miss—the second deadly sin. Is that when you think you need something—like a new phone—and you don't need it, but you go on and on about it until you get it?'

Miss Doherty stared for a long moment.

'Yes, I suppose that's right, but …'

'Or maybe someone thinking he should change his car every year, to keep up with his neighbour who does the same?'

'Yes, I …'

'Or wanting a much bigger new house, just because you win the lottery?'

'OK, yes…'

'Or a rich person wanting another big yacht, when he sees someone else with one?'

'I suppose, yes, but …'

'Isn't coveting a big, big problem then too, Miss? Isn't copying rich people ruining everything and helping to cause real danger—for the Earth?'

Miss Doherty stared back at her for a long moment, her mouth slightly open.

'She's barmy about all that, Miss. Don't mind her.' Arona's right index finger was making circles near her ear.

'No, Arona, that's rude.' said the teacher. 'Margaret is asking good questions that I need to think about and come back to, but is her mind with today's lesson? Have you been hearing all I've been saying, Margaret? Do you agree, for example, that great pain can be caused if parents simply follow new feelings—breaking old promises and forming new relationships—especially if children are involved?'

Johnny saw Margaret hesitate. Her gaze seemed to turn inward.

She made as if to say something, but stopped herself. Then she closed her eyes, as if wincing, opened them again and bobbed her head, twice, as if to say 'yes'.

And then she slumped into her seat, put her arms on the desk and lowered her head onto them. Her shoulders began to shake. Mary McNevin looked on in complete bafflement and dismay.

But Mary's expression was no match for the teacher's. Miss Doherty put her hands to her face, her eyes wide. She too then winced. After a moment she looked back to the clock at the front of the room. Then, banging herself twice on the back of her head with the heel of her right hand, she lifted the textbook from her desk and told the class to turn to the end of the chapter they had been working through.

'Question three there, do you see? Take that for homework, and you can start on that right away.' Then she took a box of tissues to where Margaret was still silently sobbing and put it on the desk. She put her hand for a moment on Margaret's shoulder, and then stooped to whisper to Mary McNevin. Mary nodded and began putting Margaret's books away in her bag.

'We will definitely come back to those questions of Margaret's,' the teacher said then. 'Two of the ten commandments warn us about coveting and the earth is indeed in danger. There must surely be some connection.'

Soon she had the class line up for the bell, everyone but Margaret, who was still lying on the desk. When the usual clanging came she lifted her head, and looked for her bag, but Miss Doherty was there to tell her not to worry and to wait. The last thing Johnny saw before the door swung shut was his teacher pulling her chair to Margaret's desk and sitting down beside her.

'She'll be alright,' he said to Mary, who was also hanging back. Her face was still bewildered. She looked at Johnny closely. He nodded, and accompanied her to Mr Foley's room for history.

They both looked hard at Margaret when she arrived five minutes late for the class, with a note for her history teacher. She seemed to Johnny to have recovered, but to be far away. Mr Foley read the note and nodded her to her desk. She seemed to be not always attentive to the lesson from then until final bell but she was no longer tearful. She could even manage a smile for Mary then—who seemed relieved. Those two sat together on the homeward bus. As he stood up for his own stop he caught Margaret's eye. She held up a thumb.

VI

As soon as she had taken the time to understand it, Margaret had been stunned by Miss Doherty's question. She had felt a heavy blow in her middle, leaving her breathless. A memory had come to her—of being taken out in a northerly storm when much younger, to see its full force from Malin Head. Grim, immense waves were charging at her, peak after peak, from the north-west. As these struck on the rocks below, clouds of foam and spray were shooting skyward, and then lashing onto massive ebony cliffs. Someone was bracing her from behind with both hands on her shoulders—against the buffeting, tearing wind and spray. Then he said 'well, Mag, what do you think of that'?

That was the day she had come to love being out in the worst of weather—but now that memory was overbearing her, like one of those waves. She couldn't speak. She could only dip her head to the teacher and collapse onto her seat. She put her head on the desk and let sorrow flow freely. She heard and saw nothing that happened in the class for the next ten minutes—did not feel Mary's or her teacher's hand on her shoulder, or see her class queue up at the door for the bell, or Mary and Johnny staring back. Only when the jangle sounded did she realise she too had to go. She wiped her eyes and looked around, confused, for her bag.

Miss Doherty was there beside her, pale as a ghost. She said not to worry about the bell, that Margaret could wait until she felt better.

'I didn't think! I am so sorry—can you forgive me?'

They were alone, and the classroom door was closed, shutting out the corridor hubbub. Her teacher's face was strained, almost horrified, so Margaret had to say 'yes'. She was truly feeling lighter now. 'I'll be OK. I'm sorry I went like that. I was remembering something. I couldn't hold back.'

Miss Doherty looked at her closely, and nodded. 'Sometimes we are surprised like that.' She seemed relieved. The colour was returning to her face.

'I remember your questions, Margaret. Every one. Especially the last. And I will come back to them soon—I promise.'

She gave Margaret a note then, to excuse her lateness for her next class, and opened the door for her. The corridors were silent and empty, with all classes back at work. Margaret went to the cloakroom first, as her teacher had advised, to wash her face. In History class Mary was still anxious, so Margaret gave her an 'OK' nod. She did feel better—but different too. She was trying to understand the difference.

The bus journey home wasn't a suitable time to explain. She again assured Mary that she was fine, and that she would she tell her more later, when they were alone. She changed the subject lightly. Then she went back to studying what had happened to her.

By the time her mother had come in around five, she had made progress. She felt older. She thought she understood her mother better. She made sure to be as helpful as possible in the kitchen, but did not speak of anything that had happened that day. It had occurred to her that her mother might have been overcome sometimes in the same way but wouldn't have told her about that. After homework she had time to think again of how she had changed. Some kind of tension had gone from her. She thought she understood why that was—and she felt even lighter. She remembered Mary's worried face, and began thinking of what to tell her next day.

Had she made a fool of herself? Did it matter if some who had watched would think so? 'No,' she decided. She had needed to put those questions to her teacher, and now she would get a response. It was also right to have those memories and to be sad when you had cause. She felt stronger for it, and had learnt something. She could explain, at the right time, to those who deserved any explanation. Johnny's last look on the bus had expressed no doubt of her either.

It had asked simply 'Are you OK?' She had so much to tell him, and didn't want to wait until Saturday. She slept that night without dreaming, but woke certain she should talk to Johnny on the bus if possible.

Mary's face was searching hers when she boarded. She too needed to be told something.

'That 'dark switch'. Your song. It's in my head. It says there's something wrong, but you don't know what it is, right?'

Mary nodded gravely.

'That's what I think too—all sorts of things are wrong.'

She told Mary then of all she had seen in the shopping mall on Saturday.

'People copy one another, I mean in what they want, but they don't notice that. I do it too—and I didn't notice until Johnny got me to. I asked him to help me think up some motion on the environment for the debates, but instead he reminded me of some of the boys admiring Aidan's computer—and we thought up a word for that, 'copy-wanting'. And then I kept seeing that everywhere—people watching other people with something new and suddenly thinking that they need that too. Do you see that?'

Mary considered for a moment, and then nodded eagerly.

'Whenever I see someone with a better guitar I always feel mine is no use. I see all the scratches on it, and where the varnish is worn away. And all the grey places on the case where I've bumped it. And if I see an especially good guitar, with a great sound, that picture stays in my head for days. I get to thinking people would like my songs better if I had one like that. I know that's silly too. My dad got me the best guitar he could.'

'That's it, that's it! Everybody does it. So I said to myself there must be another word for that besides copy-wanting—and I asked my mum. She said 'you need the thesaurus' and showed me that on the computer. So I typed 'want'—and up comes a list of words that have something to do with wanting. And in the list is that word 'covet'—that no-one uses any more. And when I looked that up in the dictionary, it said coveting is a kind of yearning—a wanting that you can't get rid of—especially for something belonging to *someone else*. So copying is part of it too.

'So then I remembered that the ten commandments mention coveting and looked that up to be sure. Mary, they mention it twice in two different commandments—and then they say "don't covet *anything* your neighbour owns".

'So I said to myself, why don't we hear more about coveting—at Mass and in school—if the bible goes on and on about it, and if it's supposed to be such a serious sin, and if it's all around us? It just has to be part of climate change. So I wanted to ask Miss Doherty as soon I could. Do you see?

Mary had been paying close attention, and now nodded, satisfied. She hesitated for a moment and then went on:

'Can you tell me what happened then, when she asked you that question?'

'Can I tell you that later, and can I talk to Johnny now? He doesn't know why I asked that either, and I want to ask him something else. Could you swap seats with him?'

By this time Johnny's stop had come, and he was sitting three rows ahead, chatting with Eddy Li. Mary lifted her bag and made her way forward. By the time they reached the school gate he also knew what had led up to that scene in Miss Doherty's room—but not what had happened to her then, or the full story of her dream of Aleena at the river.

'Could you do something?' she asked then. 'Could you think about other kinds of copy-wanting—where you don't want something like a computer or a phone? More like Arona wanting to be a famous pop star? I want to understand if that has anything to do with bullying.'

'I've been doing that,' said Johnny, surprised. 'Do you remember what Mr Foley was talking about yesterday, last class?'

Margaret tried to think back—she knew the lesson had been about ancient Rome, but she had been in a daze. She shook her head.

'No time now,' said Johnny. The bus had stopped in its usual place—it was now almost their turn to leave. 'Something else happened in PE too yesterday, before lunch.'

'Maybe later?' Margaret wondered about break or lunchtime—or even English class, depending upon what Mrs Walsh would tell them to do.

Johnny agreed and turned away. As he walked ahead of her towards the doors she noticed he had a slight limp.

When Margaret and Mary arrived for their first lesson that day—in the Geography room—their teacher, Mr Malone, was nowhere in sight. A third of the class had already arrived, with Arona and her friends sitting at the front. They were all staring straight at Margaret, as though they had been waiting for her.

Then, as Margaret took her seat, Arona put her hand in the air and said 'Miss! Miss! Miss!', in mock excitement. Next she stood up and went 'gabble gobble gabble, gabble gobble gabble!' She paused for a moment then, reeled backward, slumped to her seat, put her head and arms on the desk and began twitching her shoulders.

Deirdre Hasson and Ann O'Kane spluttered. In a moment Arona began this mime again, exaggerating every part of it.

A larger audience was gathering as the rest of Eight B arrived.

Some were finding Arona just as amusing as Ann and Deirdre.

Others, including Catherine Canning, were looking uneasily towards Margaret and then looking away. Mary's face was tense, and Johnny Mullan was also watching closely.

Margaret was sorely divided. On the one hand she was sure she hadn't been talking nonsense the day before, and angry that her private feelings should be made fun of. She wanted to say all of that, as sharply as she could—to make a scene and put a stop to this silly pantomime. However, something else was telling her to become lighter. When she remembered Aleena's raised finger and the word 'wait' she did that, and asked for the bridger's power. Soon there was another thought in her head. And then another feeling that was saying to her: *'Isn't this funny too?'*

And it *was* funny now. Arona's twitching had become a convulsion, threatening to topple her from her chair. Margaret suddenly found herself laughing as freely as she had wept the day before. The whole class erupted just as freely. Arona lifted her head, turning in curiosity. When her eyes met Margaret's she stared, surprised. Margaret found this even funnier, and so did the class.

'That's more than enough of that,' said Mr Malone loudly, emerging from his store adjoining the classroom. His mind was bent on ocean currents. And soon most of the class was focused there too.

Margaret found her head focused on an important Atlantic current, the one that flowed north—the Gulf Stream. It helped to give Ireland its moderate climate.

Scientists were uncertain what might happen if the Arctic ocean warmed further and the North Pole's ice cap shrank to nothing in summer. But then Margaret's mind was asking if Mr Malone had ever noticed copy-wanting.

It wasn't until he told the class to prepare for the bell that she became aware that Mary was regarding her with a puzzled frown.

She caught this look several times during the Maths class that followed, and found out what lay behind it when she and Mary were sitting in the September sun at break, on one of the seats overlooking the wood and the river.

'How did you do that?' Mary began. 'I mean first thing, in Geography? You went from, from mad to … to laughing as I watched. Arona wanted to make you look stupid. And you *were* mad—you went like this.' Mary frowned darkly, set her lips into a tight line and tensed her whole body.

'I was sure you would go for her. Instead you started looking at nothing—and then your face changed and you *laughed*. That scared me, until I was sure you were alright. What happened to you?' Margaret knew right away that she couldn't simply make light of this. Mary needed an explanation of some kind, and maybe something more. It would probably alarm her to hear the full story, but was there another way of explaining? She asked for the bridger's power and waited again, and something came.

'At first I wanted to be mad. But I knew that Arona wanted that too, or … for me to collapse again. So I … asked … prayed for something else to do. Then I waited. It came to me then that Arona doesn't know me—doesn't know what I know or what I feel. She sees only this … this nerd who doesn't admire her or bow down to her, this silly gabbler she can make fun of. Maybe she even rehearsed that at home. Do you see?'

As Mary considered this, Margaret found she wanted to say more.

'Who knows us, Mary? Who knows us through and through?'

She looked directly at her friend.

'You mean you believe?' Mary's gaze was intent.

'Yes! I do. I believe it more than ever. Arona wanted me to feel… as though I was nothing. And, when I said that prayer, something was saying to me, 'No you're not. No one is nothing.' I felt warm deep inside, and then, all of a sudden, when Arona made as if to fall off her chair, I was laughing at that silly person who doesn't exist, that nerd who isn't me. D'you see?'

Mary gave her a close look again, and then set herself to think, staring unseeing at her shoes. Suddenly she looked up at Margaret again. 'Maybe I'll try that, asking and waiting.' When the bell went she linked Margaret's arm as they walked back to class.

For third period Eight B were again in Mrs Walsh's room on the terrace. As Margaret entered she saw some of the class grouped round the notice board near the door. Johnny was one of them.

'Guess what!' he said, turning. 'Someone has nominated us for class prefects!'

When she looked she saw there were six names there. The others were Aidan, Arona, Bridget and Eamon. Aidan was one of the group also, looking pleased. Arona was holding court near the front of the class, tossing her hair as usual.

She wondered who might have nominated her, and remembered then that Eddy had handed up a nomination slip the day before. It couldn't be Gavan—he must have nominated Aidan. Who could have nominated Johnny?

'Seats now please!' said Mrs Walsh. 'I've got your motions sorted out!

'Some of these won't do,' she said 'for reasons that I've put on the sheets that you handed up. But some were good, and will lead to great debates. I'll put some of the best ones up now. In some cases I have changed a word or two, to make the meaning more clear.' She turned then and wrote five motions on the board.

That rising crime is due to the lack of punishment
That animals should have legal rights
That we shouldn't have to do chores for pocket money
That teenagers have too little freedom
That everyone is equally important

'The first one was proposed by Aidan and Gavan; the second by Catherine Canning; the third by Bridget McSorley; the fourth by David Reynolds; the fifth by Margaret and Johnny. Well done all.

I've made a list of other good ones for later. For now I just want you to look at these as good examples. They raise important questions—questions that do not have easy answers.

'But let's just take the first for a moment. Deirdre: *rising crime is due to the lack of punishment*. Do you agree?'

'Yes, Miss,' said Deirdre Hasson.

'Give us one reason you think so.'

'People wouldn't steal if they knew they would be punished!'

'Does anyone disagree?'

There was silence for a moment. Then Eddy Li's hand went up.

'Eddy?'

'Drug addicts do a lot of crime. They sometimes do anything just to get drugs. Even if they know they will be caught they will maybe still do it—because they can often get drugs in prison too!'

'Good. Notice I have not said to Eddy 'You're right' because who is to say who is right? Eddy has just raised a *counter argument*, questioning whether Deirdre is *always* right in saying that if you know you will be punished you won't steal.

'The word *crime* covers a wide range of different things that people do, things there are laws against. Eddy's mind went searching for exceptions to the general rule that Deirdre made, and came up with drug-related crime. That's an excellent example of how a debating team, faced with the task of opposing this motion, might go about it.

'Now, would it be important for *both* teams to know roughly *how much* crime is connected with drugs?'

There was a general murmur of agreement.

'And that's why, for many motions, you need to do research beforehand. You need to find out the facts about the subject. Some people who may be shy about speaking in a debate could help with research—they will still be learning that way. There are Internet sites where such facts can be found, some of them designed for just this purpose.

'Now, Aidan. Has Eddy's point changed your mind about this motion?'

'No, Miss.'

'Why not?'

'I still think there are many crimes where if people know they will be caught and punished they won't do it.'

'Can you think of an example?'

'Someone who is not an addict and who steals to become rich. He won't be rich if he's caught and sent to prison for a long time.'

'Good. I hope you are all seeing what can happen in the to-and- fro of a debate, and how you can go about attacking and defending any motion. Good motions are *controversial.*'

Here Mrs Walsh put that word up on the board.

'That means that there are good arguments for and against, and people disagree strongly. You must learn to put up with the fact that many important questions have no easy answers, and to respect one another's point of view.

'So a debate is an opportunity to hear *different* points of view. We should not see it as a competition to decide who is right, but as a test of our ability to argue effectively, in which we can learn from one another. The most important questions are never finally settled.

They will be debated over and over again, maybe forever.

'Homework! Everyone is to take just one of the other four motions and come up with one argument for it, and one argument against it. We'll look at those tomorrow, and that will prepare everyone for the debate after school.'

After lunch, Johnny met Margaret on her way to the boundary walk to meet Mary and told her what Mr Foley had said on Monday about Julius Caesar.

'He wanted always to be the greatest man in Rome—as famous as Alexander the Great. One historian says he cried once because he thought he would never be as famous as Alexander. So *he* was a copy-wanter too. He went off to Gaul, conquering, to prove how great he was. His wars maybe killed a million people there. I want to ask about other examples of that. I know someone else who wants to be first, and who doesn't care who he hurts.'

Johnny gave Margaret a brief account of the events in the wood on Monday. It left her with a chill of apprehension. Johnny didn't seem too worried but she felt sure that Gavan wouldn't let the matter rest.

VII

For the first two periods on Wednesday morning Year Eight boys went to the school swimming pool. In the changing rooms Johnny found himself again alongside Kieran Lowney, Eddy Li, Martin Cassidy and David Reynolds.

Conscious of being stared at from behind, Johnny turned at one point and saw the dark and disliking eyes of Gavan Maguire. He had a slightly black eye, and his face showed other dark bruises. Instead of turning away Gavan held his stare at Johnny and kept a hard face. Johnny knew he was being warned again, and turned away.

Johnny could already swim, and so had no difficulty doing the exercises the instructor showed them over the next half hour. Then the boys were allowed ten minutes freedom to swim and play as they wished. The pool was soon filled with yells and splashing sounds as the boys jumped and dived.

Johnny surfaced at one point alone in a corner of the pool. When he had shaken the water out of his eyes he found himself surrounded by Gavan, Patrick and Brendan.

'You were lucky on Monday in the wood,' said Gavan. 'Your two sneaky friends were lucky too. We'll be ready the next time.'

'We don't pick on people, and we're not sneaky,' Johnny said.

'You're safe enough.'

'Well *you're* not,' said Gavan. 'Especially not in places like this.

You could bump your head by accident, and even drown.'

'I'll remember that,' he said.

'Good idea,' said Gavan, swimming away.

The pool was well supervised, by the swimming instructor as well as Mr Slaney, one on either side of the pool. Even so Johnny felt a chill at Gavan's tone and words. He made a mental note to be careful, and to avoid being alone in all unsupervised areas of the school.

And again he had questions tripping over one another in a stream that had begun on Monday afternoon in Mr Foley's history class.

They surfaced again that same Wednesday afternoon, at another history lesson.

'Who was the greatest of the Romans, Sir?' asked Aidan Maroney.

By this time Eight B were aware that Mr Foley could sometimes be diverted by a question.

'Ah, Mr Maroney—and what does 'great' mean to you?'

'Famous, Sir, highly regarded.'

'So it depends more on what people think than on what may actually be true?'

'Yes ... No ... I ...'

'You're not sure—and that's where the world is these times, Aidan—not sure of what constitutes 'greatness' or of how to achieve it. In the ancient world, the world of the Alexanders, and Hannibals and Caesars, the title 'great' was usually awarded on the basis of military victory. Notice that, for example, Spartacus wasn't called 'Spartacus the Great'. So, to be defeated was a disqualification …'

But Johnny couldn't wait any longer.

'Sir!'

'Yes, Mr Mullan?' Mr Foley squinted slightly— seemingly a bit annoyed to be interrupted in mid flow.

'You said last day that Caesar had wanted to be like Alexander—as famous as him. Were there any other people in history who wanted to be like them?'

'That's called a tangent, Mr Mullan, a diversion from the earlier question, Mr Maroney's question—who was the greatest of the Romans. And from the even bigger question of what greatness means anyway. Would you care to give us your opinion on either of those?'

Johnny was stumped and embarrassed, with seemingly no time to pause and think—but he did that anyway, and something came.

'If people just copy one another, Sir, and other people later copied Caesar in making war, what's great about that? Won't there always be wars then?'

Mr Foley stared. 'I see you have learned the useful trick of answering one question with another. Can you stop doing that? Can you tell us what you think yourself?'

'I think to be great you must do something different, not be just a copier.'

'So who do *you* think was the greatest of the Romans then?'

'I don't know, Sir. It mightn't be possible to know. That person mightn't have been written about in the history books. Didn't *you* say that history is nearly always written by the winners, the people who come to power by force?'

Johnny was quaking as he said this. He had bottled it up, not knowing if it would make any sense to anyone else.

Mr Foley stared at him for a long moment, and then turned to the class.

'Does anyone else see a serious problem here?'

'Yes, Sir,' said Gavan.

'So what do you think the problem is, Mr Maguire?'

'Johnny's gone bananas, Sir.'

'That could indeed be a problem, for Johnny. However, as I see it, the problem is even more serious—because it's *my* problem. The teacher's problem is to stay ahead of the class—but in this case I was preparing you today for Friday's lesson. And in that Friday class I would have hoped that some of you would have arrived at the conclusion that History has often *no* conclusion, because the sources cannot tell us everything. Especially they cannot fully answer the deepest questions, for example about 'greatness' and what it means.

For those of you looking for absolute certainty in History class, that will be a huge disappointment. Mr Mullan, on the other hand, appears to have arrived to that point already— to have understood some of the limitations of this strange pursuit we call History. That's the problem, as I see it. I'm not sure what to do about it either. Can anyone suggest anything?'

There was silence for a moment. The teacher had said all this with an expression that was entirely serious, even a bit severe.

Then Aidan Maroney put up a hand.

'You could give him extra homework, Sir.'

Mr Foley didn't join in the laughter at that but instead raised his eyebrows.

'Aha! Sentence has been pronounced, Mr Mullan! Please wait for a moment after class. Now, the rest of you take this question: 'Why is history so often unable to reach fixed conclusions?' Remember especially what you have been told about the primary sources for

Ancient History, and those who wrote them.'

He brought that question up on the electronic board, and the bell went soon after.

Slightly quaking as he bagged his books, Johnny went forward to the teacher's desk, as the rest of the class filed out.

'Are *you* disappointed to know the limitations of history, Mr Mullan?'

'No, Sir'

'Not even if that gets you extra work?'

'That depends, Sir.'

'On what?'

'Would it be interesting—and not too much?'

'Right, let's see.' Still serious, Mr Foley thought for a moment, frowning. 'You were asking about other military heroes, and whether they may have been influenced by an urge to emulate or copy such people as Alexander and Caesar—right?'

Johnny nodded.

'Right. The detailed sources are too heavy for you still. So begin with the encyclopaedias in the library—the simpler ones. Start with Napoleon the First. Give it just one hour, even if you can't find anything. Try Adolf Hitler then, if you still have time. Report back here this time next week—to say how you got on. Have you got that?'

'Yes, Sir. Thank you, Sir.' Johnny made an entry in his homework notebook.

Mr Foley nodded and rose without further comment. Johnny made his way to French class, still undecided on whether he was being complimented or punished. It took him awhile to realise he could possibly complete Mr Foley's assignment in his library period the following day, so it mightn't even be homework at all.

At half-past three that same afternoon Johnny found himself with most of his year group for the first time in the school's lecture theatre. About two thirds of Year Eight had stayed to watch their first debate. The desked benches rose in tiers from front to back, so when he and Eddy had found a place about six tiers up they found themselves looking down at the front of the room, where a long desk stood in front of a large rolling screen and blackboard.

On the blackboard Johnny recognised Mrs Walsh's handwriting in the motion: *That this house would ban all TV advertising to people younger than thirteen.* In front of the wide desk, in a central position, was a small platform and reading stand. Johnny guessed that the debaters would speak from there.

Soon Mrs Walsh entered, with Eight B's Religion teacher Miss Doherty, and an older man whom Johnny didn't recognise. He was a good foot taller than their RE teacher. What impressed Johnny most was that he was dressed in a long dark academic gown, and carried a blue clipboard under his right arm.

Some other Year eight teachers followed, including Mr Foley and Miss Doherty. Lastly came six senior pupils, holding folders or sheets of handwritten paper. One of them was Conor Maguire. He looked up and scanned the tiers of seating until he caught sight of Gavan in the third row— who raised an arm in salute. Conor grinned confidently and waved his notes.

'Welcome everyone to this first meeting of the Year eight debating society,' said Mrs Walsh. 'Our first debate today will be an exhibition—by members of the senior debating society. They have been asked to keep their speeches short and clear, to make sure you can understand everything they say.

'Before we begin I must introduce to you someone who has kindly agreed to comment on today's debate—Dr McGinnis, head of the Religion department.'

At this Mrs Walsh bowed her head towards the tall gowned man with the piercing eyes. He stood and bowed in response, with a slight smile.

'Dr McGinnis will listen to the debate and then at the end comment on all the speeches. This will help you to understand what makes a good speech, and perhaps what mistakes to avoid. We are grateful to him for giving us his time and attention, so please thank him in the usual way.'

Dr McGinnis acknowledged the ripple of applause that followed with a dip of his head, and then sat to one side of the central desk, his clipboard at the ready. Already the six debaters had seated themselves along it, on either side of Mrs Walsh in the centre.

'The team supporting the motion is called the proposition. The leader of the proposition is Peter Cullen, who will now begin the debate. Peter!'

Peter Cullen, a tall, slim boy with glasses, seemed far less confident than Conor Maguire as he went to the reading-stand.

'Madam Chairman, Dr McGinnis, members of staff, boys and girls—my first task is to define the motion. That means saying clearly what the motion means—and what it doesn't mean.'

Peter went on to say that his team was proposing a ban on TV advertising to young children because it intruded into the home, undermined the role of parents, and harmed children by teaching them to overeat and to want things their parents couldn't afford. What he said was sensible, but he delivered his speech in a flat voice that made Johnny feel a bit bored.

Johnny found he agreed with Peter's main point, however—that children should not have to watch advertisements directed at them in their own homes. When the speaker finished by appealing for Year Eight to support the freedom of all children from commercial exploitation he was ready to applaud.

'Now the leader of the opposition, Conor Maguire,' said Mrs Walsh.

At this, there came a small commotion from the third row, where Gavan and his friends were seated. When Johnny saw Gavan punching the air he realised that for some the debate would be just another football game. They would always support a particular team—instead of waiting to hear the best argument.

Conor began in the same way but then went on:

'I'm sure you found all that very impressive. What a pity that it's mostly nonsense—as we will prove.

'If the members of the proposition had bothered to do a little research they would have discovered that there are absolutely no good reasons for banning TV advertising in the afternoons to children.

'First, there are children's channels that carry no advertising whatever. If parents keep their children's viewing to these channels there is absolutely no intrusion by TV advertising into the home.

That answers the first argument we have heard, as well as the second—that parents are being undermined.

'Second, there have been research studies which prove that children are well able to recognise an advertisement when they see it, and do not want to buy everything advertised. You people are far more intelligent than the proposition would like us to believe. The second member of the opposition will tell you more about this.

'Thirdly, advertisements on children's TV keep children up-to- date on what they can buy. They too should have a choice. Our third speaker will tell you more about this.

'I will simply list for you the TV programmes that you would no longer see if advertisers could no longer pay money to those channels. The proposition have forgotten that advertising pays for these programmes to be made and shown. If those channels could not show adverts in the afternoons, they wouldn't show children's programmes either—so children would have much less choice.'

At this, Conor began reading from a list of well known children's TV programmes. After each one he paused, waiting for the groans of the Year Eights. He miscalculated with some, Johnny could see, as some people laughed instead of groaning. Towards the end of the list, however, he listed some popular cartoons. Johnny had to admit to himself that Conor had skilfully won the support of most of the year group, as many applauded enthusiastically when he finished and walked back to his seat.

'Patricia Brolly—second speaker for the proposition,' Mrs Walsh announced.

Patricia was a tall girl with dark and long straight hair. To Johnny she seemed the one member of the proposition who had not been affected by Conor's success as he was speaking. She smiled confidently as she began.

'What a good show that was! What a pity it didn't address the points made so well by our first speaker.

'First, it simply isn't true that parents can prevent intrusive advertising by stopping their children watching commercial channels. If the leader of the opposition had done as much research as he claims he would know that many, many parents don't have time to supervise their children's viewing. Most are at work when their children turn the TV on after school, for goodness sake—as you all know.

'Isn't that so?' she asked, looking straight at her audience and waiting for a response. Many nodded.

'That last speech was a good example of playing to the gallery,' Patricia went on. 'It was full of bad information and bad logic. That's because the speaker doesn't know that you lot are now growing up, and capable of thinking for yourselves.'

Patricia paused for an awfully long time. The theatre had gone suddenly quiet. Conor Maguire's grin had disappeared. He looked a little annoyed instead. Patricia was speaking to her audience as though they were no longer primary school children, as though they wanted to be grown up. And they were listening.

'About that research we're all supposed to be impressed by—when it turns up. I'll be surprised indeed if any of it was done in this country. I'll be even more surprised if it answers the questions that need asking—such as what benefits flow from advertising to children. Listen carefully for that, would you. As this is a debate you can put up a hand and ask those questions.'

Patricia turned at that point towards Mrs Walsh, who nodded.

'I should have mentioned that, of course,' Eight B's form teacher said. 'Yes, anyone can put up a hand to ask a good question. The speaker doesn't always have to stop and answer, but today I'll allow all questions. Make sure they are good ones though—and make do also with the answers you get. You can't start an argument with the speakers. They will go on with their speeches once they have answered.'

'Our homes are important spaces,' Patricia went on. 'Places where you and your brothers and sisters grow together into the people that

God wants you to be. You are not just customers, people valued only for what you can spend.

'You are not pounds and pennies looking goggle-eyed at cartoons, waiting to throw yourselves into the pockets of chocolate salesmen or teenage cosmetics firms.

'You are instead...people. People who deserve to be respected not as consumers but as the persons your parents love.

'When *they* come home do they want to be met with 'buy me this and buy me that' or 'listen to what I learned today about poor children all over the world who never get to see TV?' What do *you* think?'

Patricia paused for a long time again, and Johnny sensed that the mood of his whole year group had now changed. They were thinking, and listening, as though they were at least a year older than they had been a few minutes before.

'A wider range of choice you were told! Between one cartoon and another, one superhero and another, one gormless teenage soap and another. What kind of choice is that for intelligent beings?

'You know well what channels teach you most about the world.

You know well what channels don't. With few exceptions they are the commercial channels—showing cartoon after cartoon or soap after soap, full of silly superheroes, daft monsters and would-be pop stars. They teach you ... what?

'About the best nail varnish, perhaps, or the most trendy overpriced chocolate bar, or which pop stars make the most money.

As though you needed to know!

'That, Year Eight, is what the opposition want you to *learn*. If that's all you expect from TV, throw out this motion as they will ask you to.'

Patricia turned and walked back to her seat. The applause wasn't as loud as Conor's—but Johnny could see that many were impressed.

There was something else about Patricia's speech that gripped Johnny. Although she had never strayed from the motion, and had completed the task she had been given, Patricia hadn't read a word of what she had said. She had not taken her notes to the reading stand, had never stopped looking at her audience, and had spoken straight to all of them as though she wanted to tell them something she fully believed.

'Fidelma Friel for the opposition,' said Mrs Walsh.

Patricia had also given Fidelma a problem, Johnny could see.

Sharp featured and almost as tall as Patricia, she brought her notes and arranged them in front of her before starting.

'My task is to tell you about the research that has been done on advertising on children's TV. As our first speaker told you it proves that children are no more likely to be influenced by TV advertising than adults.'

As Fidelma droned on, mostly reading her notes, Johnny remembered what Patricia had said—that anyone could ask a question by holding up a hand. Would anyone dare to? And what was it Mrs Walsh had said about rebuttal—about responding to the points made in a previous speech? So far Fidelma hadn't said anything about Patricia's speech, and the longer she went on the less likely it seemed that she would.

Meanwhile Johnny was noticing that Conor Maguire was looking increasingly uncomfortable. Was he worried that someone would ask about that research?

At that moment a hand went up in the second row—Catherine Canning's. Fidelma had her head down and didn't see it for a moment, until Mrs Walsh cleared her throat.

'Just a moment, Fidelma. Catherine has a question!'

'What does the research say about the benefit of advertising on children's TV? What good does it do?'

Fidelma blinked and hesitated.

'Well ... the research doesn't say about that. But it says that children learn by the age of seven that advertising doesn't always tell the truth. So I suppose that's a benefit. They are learning about advertising, and that's important.'

Fidelma was doing her best, Johnny could see. But her whole speech was low key and matter-of-fact, as though she wasn't fully behind what she was saying. She took up again where she had left off, and got a round of polite applause when she had finished. But

Patricia's speech had somehow taken the steam out of the opposition's cause, and Fidelma hadn't regained it.

And the rest of the debate didn't change things. The third speaker for the proposition, Imelda Connolly, a cheerful girl, argued that serious health problems were being caused by children eating the wrong food, and that too many children were also demanding expensive branded clothing and other goods.

'It's true that we don't know for sure whether advertising on children's TV is a cause of all this. There are other possible causes—peer pressure for instance. We don't know enough about the real impact of TV. The reason for that is that the research hasn't been thoroughly done.

'But you need to ask why that is. One reason could be that research itself costs money. Advertisers are not going to pay for research that might prove something they do not wish to hear. That is probably why so little research has been done, and why it seems to support the case for TV advertising to children.'

That again was a strong point, Johnny felt. Imelda had underlined the point made by Patricia, the point that Fidelma had failed to deal with. There was little hard information available on the proven effects of children's advertising, good or bad. The opposition had relied heavily on one piece of research they had found, not thinking about why they couldn't find any more.

The final speaker for the opposition, Niall Dempsey, tried to recover lost ground by simply repeating the strongest points already made against the motion—that children wanted a wide range of programmes to choose from, and that there was no real evidence of any harm to children coming from TV ads.

'The proposition haven't proven their case. They talk of the need for more research. OK then, let's have it, and do another debate later on.

'But you Year Eights need to vote now in this debate. Remember, banning that advertising now will stop many of the programmes you and younger children now watch— and some of them are as good as the best programmes on the non-commercial channels.'

Gavan and friends in tier three cheered enthusiastically at this, as did Arona and her court in tier four.

At that point, sitting below Johnny in the fifth row, Margaret Phillips put up a hand.

'Yes, Margaret?' said Mrs Walsh.

'Could the speaker name three good programmes for children on the commercial channels—programmes we can learn something from?'

Niall stared. He looked round at Conor for a moment, but found no help there.

'Well,' he said at last. 'I'm afraid I don't watch much children's

TV now, but there's *Celebrity Kids* still on somewhere I think. And that one where you learn how to make things out of cardboard and sticky tape. And I think there's a news programme for children somewhere too. Will that do?'

Margaret shook her head vigorously, although Niall's reply had been cheered again in the third and fourth rows. Patricia Brolly was laughing and looking toward Margaret, and nodding her head in approval.

Niall went on then for another half-minute, finishing with:

'Do yourselves a favour, save your favourite programmes and throw out this motion!'

Johnny felt that Conor had been the most effective speaker for the opposition, and that Patricia had been far better. The debate finished with a brief summary by Peter Cullen of the proposition's best points. Again this was low-key, gaining polite applause rather than cheers. Mrs Walsh stood again.

'While Dr McGinnis completes his notes we can take a vote now on the motion. Mr Foley and Miss Doherty have agreed to act as tellers. You can vote for the motion, against it, or abstain.

Abstaining means you can't decide either way—and that's fine in a controversial matter like this. Abstentions don't count, either for or against the motion. All those who think that TV advertising to children under thirteen should be banned, put your hands up now.

Johnny put his hand up immediately. He could see that a good number of other hands were up also, but not a majority.

Meanwhile Mr Foley and Miss Doherty were counting hands. Soon they were finished and put their heads together. Mr Foley then passed on the result to Mrs Walsh.

'Twenty-nine votes for the motion! Now, those opposed—hands up.'

From where he sat Johnny could see Gavan scanning the tiered audience anxiously. It wasn't clear which way the vote had gone, so there was some tension in the room. Again the tellers conferred and agreed.

'Thirty-one votes against! The motion is defeated narrowly by two votes.'

There was a loud cheer from the lowest benches, with Gavan hooting and punching the air. Conor waved his notes above his head and shook hands with his team. The proposition were a little disappointed, Johnny could see, but pleased nevertheless that the result had been so close.

'Order, order,' Mrs Walsh called. Gradually the hubbub subsided.

'I must thank all the speakers on your behalf,' said Mrs Walsh.

'They have all taken time from their studies to prepare for this day.

Research and preparation take a lot of time, and this is a difficult subject to think about. They have all given you a thrilling first experience of debating, so I hope you will show your appreciation in the usual way.'

The lecture theatre was immediately filled with appreciative cheers and applause, until Dr McGinnis suddenly rose and went to the reading desk. Immediately there was a hush of expectation for the head of the Religion department.

'Finally, Dr McGinnis will now address you, delivering his important verdict on the debate.'

'I must congratulate both teams,' the head of Religion began, in a deep and solemn voice.

'This is a most important subject, as Television is one of those forces that threatens many of the values this school holds dear. You

Year Eights will not be so aware of this at your age, but wisdom will come in time. You are all products of the television age, and so you are inclined to watch far too much of it. You are too easily swayed by arguments that tell you how marvellous it is, and will need to think harder about much of what you see, realising the dangers there.'

Dr McGinnis paused at that point, scanning the audience.

'If this debate were part of a competition, I would award marks to each speaker. Half of the marks would have gone for the content of the speech—the quality and quantity of the information it contained, and whether it made complete sense. The other half would have gone for presentation—the way in which the speech was delivered.

'As you have seen here today, it is difficult to score highly on both content and presentation. Some speeches that had a lot of content were delivered in a less interesting manner. On the other hand, one speech that had rather less content was delivered effectively—and probably gained those two extra votes for the opposition. I refer, of course, to the first speech for the opposition, by Conor Maguire.'

Dr McGinnis paused at this point, and there was a ripple of applause.

'But the best speech, I felt, was delivered by a member of the proposition. Delivered without notes it nevertheless came close to the heart of the question that we are faced with here—just what value is there in most of the programming for children on the commercial channels. It came close to winning the debate on a motion that favoured the opposition on this occasion. I refer, of course, to the speech by Patricia Brolly.'

There was more applause at this point, in which Johnny enthusiastically joined.

'I said her speech came *close* to the heart of the issue, because I was a little surprised by something that was missing from all of the proposition speeches, something of profound importance in a Catholic school.'

Dr McGinnis paused again at this point, to give his point more weight.

'I refer, of course, to something called *materialism*.

'Now it could be that the proposition was trying to avoid words of many syllables, to avoid confusing you Year Eights. However, the word materialism names one of the gravest problems of the modern era. It is, at the simplest level, the modern habit of living to acquire merely material possessions—everything that clutters up our homes and lives today—from mobile phones, TVs and computers to larger and larger houses and even swimming pools.

'At a deeper level it is the false belief that only material things exist, that there is no *spiritual* reality, no God. The mind of the modern world is often gripped by this false belief—and that is why so many people are materialistic in their own lives.

'I feel sure that if this argument had been properly made here, the result of the debate could have been different. Commercial television—and even most non-commercial television—is still gripped by materialistic views of the world. I hope that if this or another related issue is debated among you again you will remember what I have said.

'Indeed, I have found this debate so interesting that I may well attend on future occasions to hear you yourselves debate with one another. I especially commend the interest and attention you have shown. Those who asked questions today showed that real learning can happen in a debate, so I commend them also.

'Finally, I thank Mrs Walsh for inviting me, and all other members of staff for their support. They all deserve your thanks also.'

The theatre resounded once more to the sound of cheers and applause. Mrs Walsh stood to make a final announcement.

'That's all for today, Year Eight. The next debate you will attend here will be held in three weeks time—between two Year Eight teams. They will be selected before the end of the week. Look out for them—and the motion—on the main notice board in the front hall. Safe home!'

Outside the lecture theatre Johnny retrieved his bag and looked for Margaret. She was chatting animatedly with Patricia Brolly, but then came towards him, looking pleased.

'Where do we wait for your Mum?' asked Johnny.

'She'll be at the main door soon after five. We're to go to the library until then, with some others who are also waiting for lifts.

Let's get our bags.'

As they made their way towards the locker cubicle Johnny suddenly remembered something dull-sounding he had to find out about.

'Uh—*materialism*—we'll need to look that up!'

'Yes! Materialism sounds horrible. What did you think of Dr McGinnis's talk?'

'He's a bit ... heavy. As though he knows everything. And doesn't think it's exciting.'

'Maybe he does know lots. He is a doctor, after all—of theology I think. Miss Doherty says he's brainy. He has written a big book... about the last pope, I think.'

'What will he say about copy-wanting, I wonder—if he hears us talk about it sometime, in a debate?'

'I hadn't thought of that!' said Margaret, reflecting. 'We'll need to be sure of what we mean, in case he ever asks!'

That evening at the meal at home Kevy gave Johnny a surprise.

'Have ye got a design for that plywood box—the one you talked about?'

Eagerly Johnny fetched the drawing from his bag. Kevy looked over it for a while.

'That's easy enough,' he said. 'We could do it tomorrow.'

'I'm meeting Margaret in the morning—to get ready for the debates.'

'Huh! Who's Margaret then?'

'I told you,' said Anny. 'From his class. D'you not remember last week—when Johnny went out to Glencarn?'

'Oh aye! Well, in the afternoon then—if he can spare the time!'

'Yeh!' said Johnny. 'Thanks! That'll give me a head start next week!'

Saturday was going to be busy he thought.

VIII

On Thursday at lunchtime Margaret and Mary were exploring the school grounds out towards the main gate, not far from the avenue as it wound through tall beech trees and sycamores. By now they had fallen into a habit of lunching together in the canteen, and sticking together afterwards until bell time.

Suddenly, a car came through the school gates, faster than the ten- mile-an-hour limit on the sign. It was low-slung, dark red and sporty—and highly polished, with bright chrome trimmings. The engine made a deep growl as the driver revved it needlessly. As it came past them the horn sounded three times. The driver grinned and waved through the open window.

'Who's that?' Margaret asked.

'Father Phil,' said Mary. 'He was in our parish until last year. He's the school chaplain now. I'll bet he's come to say the Mass.'

That afternoon, at about two o'clock, there was to be a special Mass in the assembly hall, to open the school year. The whole school would attend, Margaret knew.

'Flashy car,' said Margaret, looking after it.

'His family bought it for him, my Dad says,' said Mary.

Cars had a lot of *matter* in them, Margaret reflected. Steel, rubber, glass, plastic—and probably lots of other things. She had been trying to make sense of *materialism*, Dr McGinnis's important word. The dictionary had told her that it had two possible related meanings—either a belief that nothing but matter existed, or a tendency to be interested in material rather than intellectual or spiritual things 'What's he like?' Margaret asked.

'He's good fun,' said Mary. 'Doesn't go on long on Sundays. Tells jokes sometimes. He's mad about motor racing. My Dad likes him.'

'Hey, we better get back,' said Margaret, looking at her watch.

'Five minutes to bell.'

They turned and headed briskly towards the main block. As they came to the concourse in front of the entrance they saw a tanned and bearded priest aged about thirty-five, dressed in casual clothes and a clerical collar, chatting to some Year Nine boys. He had parked his car nearby.

Again Margaret studied it. Fr Phil would need a car, she knew—and didn't everybody need at least some material things—food and shelter for example? What exactly was it that made a person a 'materialist'?

⸺∘∘⦅◉⦆∘∘⸺

In the assembly hall the seating had been arranged in semicircles to face an altar placed in front of the row of windows that faced out onto the central concourse. The Year Eights were allowed to sit close to the altar, as this would be their first school Mass. The seating was arranged in semi-circles facing it. As the other year groups filled the seating behind, Margaret noticed Miss Doherty and Dr McGinnis conversing at the side of the altar, where there was a vacant lectern. On the stage Mrs Hayes was organising the senior choir, while another music teacher sat at an electronic keyboard linked to the speaker system.

Margaret became aware of a sweet perfume, and then of the flowers that made it, arranged around the altar.

The whole staff entered together then and sat at the back of the hall, near the doors. Soon the organist received a signal from somewhere and a hymn began, one that Margaret hadn't heard before. Miss Doherty made a lifting gesture at the altar and everyone stood at once. Margaret knew by now that there were about seven hundred people in the hall altogether.

When she turned to look towards the doors she could see a procession approaching from the entrance. The head boy who came first was carrying a large bible. Other senior pupils following carried an assortment of items—a football, a notebook, a painting and other things Margaret couldn't make out. These pupils sat in seats reserved for them facing the altar, while the head boy arranged the bible on the lectern.

Meanwhile robed altar servers were taking up positions in front of the altar, on either side of Fr Phil, changed now into white robes. One carried a thurible, a metal container with vents, hanging from a chain. From this another pleasant scent, of burning incense, rose. They bowed together toward the altar. Fr Phil then took the thurible and went behind the altar to swing the incense over it. He waited then as the hymn came to an end, and the service began.

'Well boys and girls, and members of staff,' he began, 'here we go for another year.

'As most of you know, every mass is a celebration, a joyful occasion. It's also sad, of course, because it reminds us of Jesus' death. This death was an end of the best human life ever lived, but also a new beginning, a beginning that never ends. And that is why we say a mass at the start of every school year.

'Before we begin I remind every one of you that everyone here is dearly loved by God—no exceptions. Everyone is welcome here—no exceptions. That is the simplest and most important meaning of *Catholic*.

'Especially welcome are our newcomers, Year Eight. Not every one of you may be a believer, but you are welcome nevertheless, for no-one is unwelcome in the kingdom of heaven.

'And so we begin. The Lord be with you.'

'And with your spirit,' everyone responded. The familiar words seemed especially loud to Margaret.

From then on almost everything else was familiar to Margaret. The head boy and girl gave readings from the Old Testament and St Paul while everyone sat. Then all stood to hear Fr Phil read from the Gospel. It was about someone called Nathaniel.

All sat then again, to listen to the homily—the priest's short sermon based on the readings.

''Can anything good come out of Nazareth?' Nathaniel asked when he first heard about Jesus. What did he mean?'

Fr Phil paused there and looked about.

'Well *you* might say, can anything good come out of Muff, or the Waterside, or Drumahoe, or Creggan or Culmore—or wherever you don't come from yourself. We all have these hang-ups, these prejudices, about the places other people come from. We don't want to be surprised by other people, and so we put them in a box.

Nathaniel thinks he has seen it all, so he thinks to himself oh no, not *Nazareth*!

'And he *says* what he thinks. But he goes along anyway to meet this unlikely mystery man. And the first thing this man says to him is "I saw you standing under the fig tree!"

'Why was Nathaniel zapped by that? Why did he then say 'My Lord and my God' when a few hours before he had said 'Oh no, not Nazareth'?

'Well you see it's because Nathaniel *had* been standing under that tree when he had first heard about Jesus. Jesus had been nowhere in sight then, so how could he have seen Nathaniel? Nathaniel knows that the only one who misses nothing is God.

'But if Jesus had seen him there, he must have *heard* him too. He must have heard Nathaniel going 'Oh no not *Nazareth*!

'Nathaniel knows that. But he's zapped also by something else.

Jesus hasn't said 'I heard that crack about Nazareth!' Nathaniel knows he has been let off!

'How *did* he know? That's an interesting question, and I'm going to guess at the answer. My guess is that Jesus said it with an up- and-under look, like this:'

At this point Fr Phil put his head down and then looked round at everyone as though he was looking over the top of a pair of glasses.

'"I *saw* you—standing under the *fig* tree!"

'He was sending him up, you see. As if to say, "you didn't think I heard that dig at Nazareth, did you? Well I did, you so-and-so, and it's OK."

'The point is that Jesus wants us to be the way we are— to be absolutely honest. He doesn't want us to say 'Oh, wow! A Holy Man from Nazareth! Fantastic! Take me to him! I'll throw myself at his feet!"

'He wants us to come with all our doubts and questions—as we are. And he says "That's OK! You are an honest person, and that's what I want."

'That's the way you should all be. And that's the way many of you are. I'll give you an example.'

At this Fr Phil began scanning the ranks of the Year Eights. He saw someone then sitting over to the left of Margaret and stopped and grinned.

'I was coming in the door today, and one Year Eight boy asked me how fast my car could go. Next thing—would you believe—another one asked me if I had to confess to speeding in it!'

At this there was laughter. When Margaret looked towards the doors, she could see that most of the staff were finding that funny.

It took seconds for the din to settle. Dr McGinnis seemed to disapprove however, as he was looking about with a frown.

'Year Eights are often like that, you see. And that's the way they should be. That's the way they should *stay*— absolutely honest.

'But the serious thing about that story is this, boys and girls. It's the reward for honesty and faith. Jesus told Nathaniel what it would be. He said 'You shall see angels ascending and descending'. What did he mean by that?

'None of us knows what an angel actually looks like. You've all seen medieval paintings of them, but those artists hadn't seen angels either. Those who saw them, at the first Christmas, for example, weren't artists. So they must have described wonderful, mysterious, brilliant beings zipping about the sky. So they probably said something like 'flying creatures who made a beautiful noise' and this got translated into winged men and women playing harps.

'How would a modern artist depict that if he saw it? What would a camera show if it caught it? We simply don't know. But I'll tell you what *I* think of.

'I think of Steven Spielberg's *Close Encounters of the Third Kind*!' The hall was still. Again, when Margaert looked, Dr McGinnis was frowning.

Fr Phil raised his right hand then, and pointed behind him, up and out the tall windows.

'Many of you wonder if you will ever get to see what's out *there,* beyond everything you can see. Well, the greatest theologians tell us that heaven is more marvellous than we could ever imagine. And they tell us we will see it—if we trust this man, the man Nathaniel called Lord *and* God.

'He came from Nazareth—an unimportant place back then. Wherever *you* come from, that's a place like Nazareth. It's considered unimportant now, maybe, but tomorrow who knows? Every one of you is important too!

'So come and meet this strange man from Nazareth. He sees every one of you too from a distance, and he loves what he sees, especially when you hurt yourselves.

'That's what sin is, you know—hurting yourselves and others. He sees that, just the way he saw Nathaniel under the tree, and he forgives it, just the way he forgave Nathaniel. But he doesn't want us to go on hurting ourselves—and that's why we have the commandments.

'Stay true to him, and true to yourselves, and you too will see angels ascending and descending. This I believe.

'And now, although it's not Sunday, we'll say the Creed in hope of that.'

The school assembly rose then, and made a declaration of faith that dated back many centuries. Margaret knew the words well and said them in the usual way, without attending closely to what they might mean.

She was thinking of something else entirely throughout the ceremony that followed. There was something else she had to discuss with Johnny.

'Next, we need to make out a programme for those debates,' said Mrs Walsh in English class on Friday morning. 'Remember, the first one will be two weeks from Wednesday of next week. I've discussed this with the English teachers of the other Year Eight classes and we've drawn up a trial list of motions. Here we go!'

She turned to the board and began writing:

That the motor car was on balance a bad idea.
That rising crime is mainly due to the lack of punishment.
That we shouldn't have to work for pocket money.
That the disadvantages of the Internet outweigh the advantages.
That materialism is Earth's biggest problem today.

As soon as she saw the word 'materialism' Margaret glanced over at Johnny. Her excitement became intense when she was able to see the whole motion. 'Earth's biggest problem' just had to be the environment, and she was now sure that copy-wanting was a major cause of that!

'We're not sure about that last one,' said Mrs Walsh, turning to face the class. 'We were thinking about what Dr McGinnis said, but we're not sure any team would want to oppose. It's maybe one of those motions that favours the proposition too much. Yes, Margaret?'

'We might be able to oppose it, Miss! We'll need to discuss it first though.' Margaret looked across at Johnny, not at all sure how he would react.

'Might you indeed? That's interesting! What do the others think? Johnny?'

Johnny seemed taken aback.

'I'm not sure, Miss.'

'Eddy?'

Eddy looked inquiringly at Margaret and Johnny, and then hunched his shoulders and shook his head to indicate complete bafflement.

'Take a week to think about it. I'll put you down as a possible opposition, and give you first choice. You've lots of time to get ready, after all—over seven weeks. That'll be great if you think you can! The other teachers will be pleased.'

Margaret nodded eagerly again at Johnny. He gave a different kind of nod, which meant 'maybe', underlined three times. She could see he didn't fancy debating a motion that would give them little chance of a win, especially when Gavan and his friends would be there, jeering at all the ideas they were working on.

'Now, the second motion there is Aidan's, Gavan's and Patrick's, so they will be proposing it. The other motions come from people in the other Year Eight classes. Take them down, all of you, and think about them. If any team would like to oppose, tell me tomorrow.

'For homework everyone is to think up just one argument for or against any of those, and write it down carefully. You can begin now, if you wish. It'll be bell time soon.'

On the terrace at break Margaret came over to Johnny. She knew from his look that he wasn't enthusiastic.

'We've got all week!' she said. 'Don't make up your mind against it yet!'

'What about Eddy?' Johnny asked. 'He's never even heard of copy-wanting yet, and we need three in the team.'

'We'll explain it to him. It's just common sense, after all. Already Mary understands it. I'm sure she would make a third person, if Eddy doesn't want to.'

Then she had another thought.

'Why not ask Eddy to come to our house tomorrow, to talk about it? He lives out our way too!'

'OK,' said Johnny, still looking unconvinced.

That Friday morning Mary McNevin seemed to Margaret to have become brighter. At break she said she wanted to hear more from Margaret on what she had discovered in the shopping centre—about coveting and the environment.

'Maybe it'll give me an idea for another song!' she had said.

Margaret's own spirit had soared at this. Sooner than she had expected, Mary seemed to be putting Arona out of her head and trusting in herself.

At lunchtime, during the first course, Margaret told Mary about the expensive furniture in the shopping mall and how it was being sold.

'People are falling for all that,' said Margaret. 'Grown adults! All it takes is for one woman in a street to see that display, and then to throw a party for all her friends. She'll go to her husband and say 'Ah go on—we can afford that dining table now! *You* could bring your boss home for dinner. He'll be so impressed when he sees it!

'She'll nag him and nag him until he says 'yes'. And then she'll throw her first party and show off all that precious wood—and guess what'll happen next?'

'I see!' said Mary. 'Her friends will all get jealous, and want one too! Or maybe even a more expensive one.

'That's copy-wanting,' said Margaret. 'That's the way it works.

'That was just one shopping centre, in one city. But that store was part of a chain with stores all over. And there are other chains all over the world. And it's not just mahogany—it's every precious timber everywhere. *And* it's not just timber—it's everything!'

'It's like an infection,' said Mary then, after a pause. 'Something we catch from one another!'

'Yes!' said Margaret. 'That's exactly right! But no one's looking for a cure! People are too busy catching it and passing it on. They don't even know they've got it! And 'materialism' makes you think of something else—it's not the right name for what's going on.'

After lunch the two friends were strolling along the boundary path by the wood, Mary humming to herself and twisting a lock of her hair. It *was* frizzy and fly-away, Margaret reflected, but it was part of who she was—and she was such an interesting person.

It was a day when tiny, darting shapes littered the air and often came daringly close. When one of them passed close over Margaret's shoulder she turned:

'*Swallows*, Mary, what if they ever stop coming?'

Margaret and Mary turned then to walk back to the terrace before the bell—and saw Arona leading her trio towards them. Arona was nursing a smirk, and the other two were trying to suppress giggles behind their hands. There was no time for Margaret to think up a way of avoiding another confrontation.

'Mary!' said Arona, coming up.

'Yes?'

'We love your hair. How do you get it that way? Do you stick your finger in the dark switch?'

Margaret didn't notice Deirdre and Ann doubling over again. She was watching her friend closely. Mary's face grew troubled, and she closed her eyes. Margaret opened her mouth to complain to Arona, but then heard her friend speak first.

'Arona—will you tell me something?'

'What?'

'When you are trying hard to be nasty you can't see your own face, can you?'

'Huh?'

'You won't be looking in a mirror at that moment, will you, or posing for a photograph? So you won't know what you look like.

Well I'll show you. You go like this.'

At that Mary pulled a face that caught exactly the look Margaret had seen a moment before on Arona's usually photogenic face—a vindictive and deeply unpleasant grimace.

Mary held that face for just a moment, but just long enough.

Arona's friends had gone silent. Arona herself stared, and tried to laugh. Margaret could see she had been startled.

'Mary's right, Arona' said Margaret. 'You do yourself no favours at all in the looks department when you behave like that.'

'But you two will always be gargoyles,' Arona said then, without conviction, and walked away.

'Brilliant, Mary,' said Margaret. 'You caught her expression exactly. You may even have taught her something she didn't know.'

'I did what you said,' Mary turned to Margaret. 'I waited for something to say, and that popped out!'

They watched the departing trio for a moment, and then turned to sit on a wooden seat facing the wood and the river beyond.

'Can you tell me now what happened you last Thursday in Miss

Doherty's class?' Mary asked this shyly.

Margaret considered a moment. This was a private matter that she had never before spoken about to anyone. Could she trust this person she had only known for a few weeks? She looked closely at

Mary, and suddenly thought she should.

'My dad. He broke up with my Mum when I was eight. They had argued a lot before that, and then my Mum told me he had taken up with someone else. For a long time I thought maybe it was my fault—because they had argued over things like what I should read. And I didn't cry about it, even though I missed him a lot. When Miss Doherty asked me that question it all came back in a rush.'

She told Mary then about the day she had remembered— the day of the storm on Malin Head, and the rushing waves.

'I realised I still … miss him. He is a zoologist and taught me all about animals. I just couldn't hold back—and I didn't want to either. I just let go. And something else was happening to me too, all that day. I was realising I wasn't the reason he went away. Do you see?' Mary nodded. 'That's just like me. When my Mum got ill and couldn't stay with us I thought it was our fault, me and my brothers. My Dad didn't explain well then, and I didn't know any better. Now I've heard of other people with depression and what can cause it—like the Troubles. One of my uncles—my Mum's younger brother, got mixed up in that and spent time in the Maze. She would have seen the police coming to search and to arrest him. And after that we got broken into one night too, burgled, by druggies. One had a knife—it was horrible. My Dad says my Mum is on a journey, trying to understand it all.'

Margaret had only been living in Derry for about three years, so was only dimly aware of what Derry had gone through in the Troubles, the years of bitterest conflict. She realised that Mary herself was carrying a heavy burden from that time, passed on by those who had suffered through it.

'We've had family counselling about it all,' Mary continued. 'The counsellor guessed what I was thinking about being to blame. I like her. I sometimes think I'd like her job too, explaining those things to people like us—when they can't understand.'

Margaret realised that just as she had decided to trust Mary, her new friend had decided to trust her. An idea was building in her head, but there wasn't time now to do what she had almost decided to do.

'Why couldn't you be a counsellor *and* a singer?' she said, and rose to head towards class. Mary smiled shyly and climbed to her feet also. 'Maybe.'

'Later!' said Margaret to herself.

By the end of the day she had been given something else to think about. In Religion class Miss Doherty had begun a new chapter in their religion book.

'It's about a boy called Joseph, and his coat of many colours. His father, Jacob, gave it to him, as a sign of his special favour. But guess what—his seven brothers were jealous of him because of that coat, and even thought of killing him. Then they decided to sell him as a slave instead. Just as well for them they changed their minds! For homework you must find out *why* it was just as well. The chapter tells the whole story of Joseph, taken from the Bible. You can begin reading it now, to yourselves.'

Anxious to shorten the time spent over the weekend on homework, the class began reading quietly.

The further she read in that chapter the more excited Margaret got. As the bell went she glanced over towards Johnny. He met her glance, his eyes wide. When he nodded and raised a thumb she knew that he had seen exactly what she had.

Should she ask Miss Doherty the question that was now begging for an answer? She closed her eyes and waited. No, she decided. Time enough. Let that rest until her teacher had responded to her earlier questions, as she had promised she would.

Her mind was made up on another matter too. She must find an opportunity to speak to Mary as soon as possible, confidentially—about what had happened to Johnny and herself.

IX

'You can't be always going to Margaret's without inviting her back,' said Anny to Johnny on Saturday morning. 'So invite her here for next Saturday morning. D'you hear? It'll be OK. Your Da knows.'

'OK,' said Johnny. He had misgivings about this, but knew his Ma was right. He felt surer now that Margaret wasn't stuck-up. She would find his house different, and much smaller than her own, but she would surely get used to that. He had even heard her say that her own house was too big for just two people.

As he caught the bus that morning his mind turned straight away to Eddy, who would join him two stops further on. On the bus home the previous day he had explained to Eddy how he and Margaret understood covetousness as copy-wanting. As soon as he had given examples from his own experience, Eddy had nodded.

'I want a tablet like Aidan's too,' he had said. 'My dad's computer is slow as a snail, and he's nearly always using it himself anyway. All those gadgets Aidan brings to school make me feel useless. He brought a night-vision camera once. If I had one of those I could link it to our computer and point it at the street outside. I might even catch a burglar.'

'So you'll think about that motion—to see if we could debate against it?'

'OK' Eddy had said, and 'OK' again to meeting up in Margaret's the next day.

So now Johnny wondered what Eddy had decided, and looked eagerly toward him when he boarded the bus five minutes later. But Eddy just nodded solemnly this time and didn't speak—and wouldn't speak at all on the journey. Keeping a completely deadpan expression he just looked ahead or out the side window. When Johnny asked in exasperation 'what's up with you?' Eddy hunted in the bag he was carrying and then handed Johnny a card with the handwritten words *'I'm inscrutable'.*

'You mean you won't give anything away?' asked Johnny.

Eddy just gave him a slow impassive nod. And then turned to watch the passing scenery.

So Johnny still didn't know what he himself was going to tell Margaret when they met. Was she so caught-up in her planet- saving cause that she couldn't see anything else? He was now himself convinced that copy-wanting had often a lot to do with why some people wanted to be in charge of everyone else and came to blows, but felt he didn't know half enough yet to be sure. And Dr McGinnis had been so sure of himself too. Johnny was certain that whatever team would propose that motion was likely to be well coached in all that.

In another few minutes Johnny had another surprise. At Margaret's stop there were two people waiting instead of one. As the bus drew nearer he recognised Mary McNevin alongside Margaret.

'Great,' said Margaret as they got off. 'Well, Eddy, can we do it?'

Eddy still wouldn't say a word. He just stared around him as though he hadn't heard.

'He's being inscrutable,' Johnny explained.

'Oh,' said Margaret. And then to Mary, who was baffled:

'Chinese people are often described that way—impossible to read—in books.'

'Detectives often need a poker face too, don't they Eddy?' Johnny offered.

Eddy bowed his head again, without changing expression.

'OK. I hope he won't keep that up all day though,' said Margaret.

She turned to Johnny then. 'I should have said—I asked Mary if she could come too. She's interested in copy-wanting, coveting, and can maybe help us. I was sure you wouldn't mind—she won't be a spy.

'That's OK,' said Johnny. He liked and trusted Mary, but wondered how she could help—and why she had looked at him so intently as they met. They had known one another from primary school, but now she had peered at him as though she was seeing him for the first time.

They crossed the road then and headed for Margaret's home. This time Margaret made no detour along the river, and when they arrived at her home her Mum was waiting. She appeared to know Mary already, and laughed when Margaret explained why Eddy had just bowed his head without speaking as he shook hands.

Again Mrs Phillips had milk and plain biscuits waiting for them in the kitchen when they arrived at Margaret's. They sat on high stools in the kitchen area—Margaret had already set the dining table for their conference.

'Margaret told me about the debate on Wednesday last,' said Mrs Phillips. 'Is that the topic again today for you four?'

'Yes,' said Margaret. 'Mrs Walsh may ask us to debate when she makes out the programme for Wednesdays.'

'What did you think of Dr McGinnis?' Mrs Phillips asked.

'I'm not sure,' said Johnny. 'He went on about materialism as though it was important.'

'That's a bit strange, you know,' said Mrs Phillips. 'He's quite well off—family money. He has a holiday house in Italy somewhere. He goes there every summer, and sometimes at Easter. I have a colleague at work who knows him quite well.'

That was odd, Johnny thought. Houses too had lots of *matter* in them—cement and sand and roof timbers and metal pipes and glass.

'He also studied in Rome for his doctorate—the Gregorian University, I think. He is said to be well connected to the Vatican department that watches people who teach Religion all over the world, the CDF—so don't go preaching any heresies in your debates.'

'What are heresies?' Margaret asked. She hadn't noticed that her mother was smiling as she said this.

'A heresy is an idea the church thinks is wrong— opposite to revealed truth. For example, saying Jesus isn't God. Heresies can cause big splits in the church. The Pope said Martin Luther was preaching heresy in the early 1500s, and that's what mostly caused the split between Catholics and Protestants. It caused wars back then, and is still part of the problem between people here in Northern Ireland today.'

Johnny looked at Margaret then, and could see she was just as interested.

'Would Dr McGinnis get annoyed if we had different ideas?' asked Margaret.

'I was just joking,' said Mrs Phillips with a laugh. 'It's highly unlikely you lot would come up with a heresy, and he would hardly get worked up over it even if you did.'

Margaret nodded, but Johnny could see that she was still thinking about what her mother had said. So was he, and he had several questions in his head. They could wait until Margaret and he were alone, though.

'My friend tells me Dr McGinnis could well be the next principal of Iona,' said Mrs Phillips then. 'Mr Ferguson is retiring at the end of next year. She says Dr McGinnis is keen to get the job, and is well in with the bishop.'

This surprised Johnny, and he could see he wasn't the only one.

'Will the bishop choose the next principal?' asked Margaret.

'No—the board of governors, but the bishop is represented on that, so he will have a strong say.'

Johnny looked at Margaret again. He was thinking of Dr McGinnis as principal, speaking from the stage in the assembly hall. He didn't like the idea somehow.

'Who else might get that job?' he asked.

'Well, there might be outside applicants. Miss Considine might apply too, but has had health problems in the past.

Mr Foley's well liked, and able, but isn't far from retirement either. Some even say Mrs Walsh should be considered, if she applies.'

Johnny much preferred the thought of that final possibility.

'OK, then. Rinse your glasses when you're finished. Lunch will be at midday sharp, in time for buses. I'll leave you to it.' Mrs Phillips stood and left them to themselves.

Johnny had already noticed that Margaret had furnished the circular dining table with a jug of water and four glasses. Sheets of paper waited at each of four places. Some notes were scribbled on her own sheet, and she looked at these as she sat down. Johnny sat opposite her, with Eddy to his left and Mary to his right.

'I suppose it's up to me to say why I told Mrs Walsh we might speak against that materialism motion?'

Margaret looked around for agreement, and got it.

'Well it's because I don't think it *explains* anything. I even think it points in the wrong direction. Just look around you here, for example! What do you see?'

She paused then as her friends looked about them.

'What's that?' she said then, when no one spoke. She tapped the water jug with her pen.

'A jug?' said Johnny.

'Made of?'

'Glass, I think.'

'And the table?'

'Some kind of wood!'

'What's in the jug?'

'Water?'

'What do they all have in common?

'They're all made of *matter,* don't you see,' Margaret went on, unable to wait for an answer. 'But does that mean my Mum is *materialistic?*'

'We have those things at home too,' Mary offered.

'Everyone needs things like that,' Johnny agreed.

Eddy nodded like a robot.

'So what's a *materialist* then?'

Johnny thought back to the Wednesday debate when Dr McGinnis had gone on about materialism in such a critical way.

'Does it mean overdoing it—wanting material things you don't need?

'Do you see anything like that?' Margaret waved her hand at the rest of the room.

Johnny looked about. Neither the kitchen nor the dining area were lavishly furnished, but on shelves in front of him were delicately decorated ornaments and plates of various sizes.

'That … vase? You could live without that, couldn't you?' He pointed—to where vivid flowers had caught his eye—painted in fine detail on the base of a pure white object. It tapered upward to a strangely long thin neck. Some tiny flowers were painted on the neck as well.

'That's Meissen porcelain. It's over 200 years old. It's an heirloom, from my Grandad.'

Johnny heard a whistle. When he looked around he saw Eddy resuming his impassive appearance—but also making a note on the bare page in front of him.

'So does that make my Mum a materialist?', Margaret persisted.

'Or those other antique plates? Or that grandfather clock in the hall? Those are heirlooms too.'

Johnny wasn't sure what to say, and felt embarrassed again.

'We have ornaments in our house too,' said Mary then.

'Yes,' said Johnny, remembering his Mum's precious Beleek china teapot that never was used.

'That's what I mean. My Mum gave another of those vases for a charity auction after that last Famine in Africa—in the University where she works. So she cares about things like that. She wants to live in this house because it's quiet. She says she can't find anything smaller that's suitable just now. She might give that vase away too, if there was another bad famine. But it's a reminder of my Grandad too, do you see?'

Margaret put down her pen at that point.

'Why is it so hard to decide what *materialism* is exactly?' she asked then. 'Shouldn't a name *explain* something. Everyone needs lots of material things but I'm sure now that people aren't thinking of what anything is made from when they buy stuff they don't need. I think they do that because they are always looking at people who have more than they do, and marvelling at the different things they've got. I do that too—I have clothes in my room that I wanted because

I thought they would suit me—because I saw them on pictures of taller models, or on mannequins in shop windows. They looked special to me then but I wasn't thinking of the wool or linen or whatever. They were … *magical* to me then. Now they just look ordinary.'

She paused again, for a long moment, and then went on:

'Until people know they are doing that they won't stop doing it.

That's coveting—copy-wanting. Doesn't the word 'materialism' point to something else entirely, to what the dictionary calls a *preoccupation* with material things? I looked that up. A preoccupation is something that's in your head all the time. Now—think back all of you to when you wanted something—a bicycle or a phone or a book or whatever—were any of you thinking of what any of those things were made from: metal, plastic, glass, paper?'

She stopped and looked around. Johnny thought again of the new bicycle he had wanted—of how it had glittered in the shop window, and made his own second-hand one seem dull and dirty. Yes! That new bike *had* looked magical—and he hadn't been thinking then of what it was made from. He shook his head.

'I forgot to ask,' Margaret said then. 'Does Eddy understand what we mean by copy-wanting, and why we think that could be what the Bible calls coveting?'

Eddy nodded three times mechanically.

'Does he agree?'

Eddy didn't nod this time, but Johnny thought he saw a suspicion of a smile, for the briefest of moments. Then his face went blank again.

'Do we need to give him other examples of copy-wanting?'

Eddy shook his head.

'Well—that's me then,' said Margaret. 'People are always changing what they have got for something newer when they don't need to. I'm sure now that a lot of what we humans do to harm the earth is due to wanting what other people have, just because they have it. I'm almost certain now that coveting is the same thing. And

I want to stand up and say that. So what do you all think?'

'I don't have a vote,' said Mary. 'Unless Eddy decides he doesn't want to speak.'

She looked at Eddy then—but he was still giving nothing away.

Johnny could see from her shaking head that this was annoying Margaret. He too wanted Eddy to make up his mind for him, but it was up to himself to speak now.

'That Joseph story,' he began. 'It sticks in my head. He's wearing that special coat of many colours—and Mrs Doherty says that would have been unusual back then. Many modern dyes hadn't been invented and the most vivid colours were something only rich or powerful people could afford.

'So Joseph's brothers see that on him, and it keeps reminding them that his father likes him better. If they all had been given those coats they wouldn't have hated Joseph so much. They want it but they can't have it—there's only one of it in the whole world. And that's why they bully Joseph.'

Eddy was making another note, but still wouldn't speak.

'That reminds me of Julius Caesar,' continued Johnny. 'There could be only one dictator of Rome. Mr Foley gave us some of that speech from Shakespeare—what Cassius said about Caesar standing over Rome like a … Colossus—a giant statue looking down on everyone. What happened to Caesar was like what happened to Joseph. Joseph got thrown into a well and sold as a slave, and Caesar got assassinated—because people hated them for having something important *they* couldn't have.'

Again Eddy made an impassive note.

'So … does a lot of fighting happen because people want the same thing, and because, if they can't share it, they start hating one another and fighting? Is that why Napoleon invaded Russia also—because he wanted to be conqueror of Europe and because the Emperor of Russia wouldn't do what Napoleon wanted? Napoleon thought Caesar was the greatest ever General before himself too, so was he wanting to be like him, copying him—to be master of Europe?'

Johnny waited, but no one spoke.

'But if that's true why don't teachers say that?' Johnny went on.

'Mr Foley doesn't talk about coveting. He talks about 'Imperialism' instead: wanting to have an empire. If copy-wanting—coveting—causes wars and fighting and bullying as well as buying what you don't need and harming the environment, why don't teachers use that word, and why can't I find that in the encyclopaedia. Wouldn't that be much easier to understand?'

Margaret was agreeing. 'Miss Doherty didn't say Joseph's brothers were coveting his coat, even though I had asked her questions about coveting last week. That story says to me 'don't covet—it's dangerous!'. Why doesn't she see that?'

Johnny saw Margaret looking at Mary then, who nodded. What was going on between those two? But Eddy was more exasperating—sitting with his arms crossed and his eyes closed. Johnny knew he had to get him to speak, so he made his last big point.

'Dr McGinnis knows all about things like materialism too—and if we speak against that motion the proposing team will be talking about all that. We might just look like stupid loopers. If we have weeks to prepare I might risk that—and say that copy-wanting causes wars and fighting, and that the Bible and history give examples. But I'm just not *sure*. So now, Eddy, it's your turn.'

As he said this Johnny punched Eddy on the shoulder with his left fist. *'Say something!'*

Eddy put down his pen, splayed the fingers of both hands on the table, brought the finger tips together, and then began tapping them against each other with eyes closed—in a pantomime of the deepest contemplation.

'That's it!' said Margaret. She stood up, lifted the half-full jug of water and began tilting it just above Eddy's head. His eyes remained closed until some drops fell on his forehead. At that he opened them, rubbed his face and grinned.

'You'll get all of it, Eddy,' Margaret warned. 'My Mum will understand the mess when I tell her the whole story!' Mary giggled. At that Eddy pointed the index finger of his right hand directly upward in a 'just a moment' gesture, and went to his bag beside him on the floor. Returning with a folder he began placing sheets from it face down on the table.

'That was all my Dad's idea—to try to wind you all up! I have to tell him how it went when I get home.'

Eddy was grinning even more widely now and enjoying himself.

'He's into crime too, see. Sherlock Holmes and Inspector Morse especially. That's what I want to talk about—copy-wanting and crime.'

He turned one of the sheets over—a photo of mangled car wreckage.

'I collect crime stories on my Dad's computer. Things that happen in the news. This is a sports car that was crashed up around Dungiven, by two teenagers. They said they just wanted to be like the rich man who owned it, but couldn't ever own one themselves. They watched him and saw that sometimes on a cold morning he would start it in his driveway and then leave it to warm up. So they stole it one morning and drove it so fast they almost killed a policeman who was trying to stop them.'

He turned over another sheet. It showed a group of hanger-like buildings surrounded by fields.

'That was built to be a horse-breeding farm by one of the biggest drug bosses in Dublin—with drug money. He wanted to be like the rich people who go in for that—Arab sheiks and English lords.' Another sheet was turned, showing people in fancy morning dress, speaking to the queen.

'That could be why he wanted to make it big in horse racing—that's Ascot, where the queen goes every year.'

The next sheet showed a large old stately home with extensive gardens around it.

'The man who owned that was an Irish politician. He paid for it with money given to him secretly by rich people who wanted him to help their businesses. That's called corruption—another crime.

That house once belonged to one of the great Irish landlords long ago. Why do you think he wanted that?'

The last photo showed a brilliant large white diamond on a rich red velvet background.

'That's the Koh-i-noor, found in India centuries ago. It was the biggest ever diamond until it was cut up. Indian princes fought and killed one another for it—before it was bought by the English government. It's now in the Queen's coronation crown in the Tower of London and has to be guarded night and day against burglars.'

Johnny saw that Margaret and Mary were just as excited as he was.

'Another thing,' said Eddy. '*Crowns*. If you try to take a crown from a king, that's called treason, the biggest crime of all. People got their heads chopped off in the past for that. Murdering Caesar was probably called treason by his friends.'

'Crime!' said Margaret. 'That's a *third* big Earth problem. I should have thought of that.'

'And there are three of *us*!' said Johnny. 'Each of us would have something different to talk about—the thing we're most interested in.'

'Will you two do it then?' asked Margaret excitedly. 'Will we each give a different reason for saying copy-wanting is a bigger problem than materialism?'

Johnny paused, asked inwardly, and then felt sure. 'Yes, let's risk it. Even if we're sure to lose.'

'We won't lose, Johnny! The other team won't be ready for us!' said Eddy, and sat back triumphantly.

All four fell quiet then for a while, as they thought about what they would most want to say. Johnny was the first to break the silence.

'We'll also need to think about what the proposition will say, so we're ready for that too. Who would help us with that?' He looked at Margaret.

'Patricia Brolly would—she said so. I asked her on Wednesday, after the senior debate.'

Johnny remembered the tall senior girl who had spoken without notes, and grew more confident.

'The first thing is for each of us to make out a speech to show Patricia. She'll help us to make it better.'

Eddy and Margaret nodded agreement.

'That's great,' said Margaret—her eyes shining. She stood to put away her notes. 'Let's take a break.'

She turned towards Mary then, who immediately asked Eddy to come to see the garden at the back of the house.

'There's a pond and a swing,' she said, 'Come and give me a push, Eddy.' She left then, through the kitchen door and Eddy followed. Mary seemed to have read a signal to do this, Johnny thought. He turned toward Margaret.

'I've told Mary about the bridgers,' she said, sitting down again at the table. She was speaking softly. 'I hope you don't mind?'

He shook his head. He knew that Margaret too had probably been told to watch out for people she could speak to like that. 'I like her. What did she say?'

'She's … boggled. She doesn't know what to think. So much is happening so quickly, she says—it will take her days to catch up. She says she can't understand why we two are different … so sure about things. She says she has to … to pray about it.'

Margaret stopped then. She was looking at him closely. Then she closed her eyes for a moment, opened them again, and went on:

'Johnny—I'm sure the bridgers have something to do with the Bible, with what we're being taught in religion—what do you think?' She waited a moment, and then went on:

'"Do not covet" … the Joseph story … what Fr Phil said about angels … asking for the power of the bridge … waiting till your mind is made up … isn't that like praying?'

'I suppose … but it's not like just saying words without thinking.'

'When you had that dream in the wood—was there anything about a 'greatest bridge'?'

Johnny thought hard for a moment, making his mind go back to that strange time. Then he remembered.

'I was told to pay attention to what I was reading and hearing—to see if I could see who the greatest ever bridger was.'

'That's it!' said Margaret. 'I was told the greatest bridge had already been well made—the bridge that all would cross!'

Johnny was impressed by that, and he could see that Margaret was too. He was sure he hadn't told her before what Mick had said about the greatest bridger.

'What bridge was that?'

'I don't know.'

Johnny remembered something else then. 'Mick told me my Mum is a bridger even though she doesn't know it. She likes the Rosary and says it every night—it just sends me to sleep.'

'So you don't rule it out—that the bridgers could be connected with the bible?'

'No—I suppose not. But they're not … soppy and boring, like some priests. They don't want us to be all goody goody and useless—just singing hymns and doing what we're told.'

'I know what you mean, and I agree. Should I tell Mary what we've been told about a greatest bridger and a greatest bridge?'

'Yes, do that!'

'OK, then—that'll do us for now. Mary knows I'm telling you now what I've told her about the bridgers. Have you spoken to anyone else about that … Eddy maybe?'

'No … do you think I should?'

'No … not until you are sure.'

She got up then, and Johnny followed. As they went outside Johnny looked towards Mary, on the swing, and nodded as she met his look. He knew right away what Margaret had meant by 'boggled'. Mary's face showed deep thought, but something else also, something that made him feel good about himself.

'Give us a push, Johnny,' she said, and smiled shyly. He did that, shoving her as high as he could, and felt even better. He was almost sure he would have two strong friends now, friends he could trust.

Should he risk trying to make it three? He looked towards Eddy—jumping back and forth over the narrow end of the goldfish pond.

'What did *you* make of that Joseph story, Eddy?' asked Margaret soon after, as they were all sitting together around the patio table taking a final drink. Johnny guessed that she was wondering if he had any religious beliefs. He remembered Eddy had been one of those Year Eight pupils who hadn't gone up for Communion at the Thursday Mass.

Eddy was being the opposite of inscrutable now: 'When I told that story to my Da, and asked him about copy-wanting, he said 'Ah!' and then something else … *Why do we want what others want?*' He said that's from an old Chinese book, way before Jesus' time. It's called the *Tao Te Ching*. It's one of his favourite books.'

'What did he say then?' asked Johnny.

'He said the book doesn't answer that. He says that questions are often more important than answers. "Sit with the question," he says, "there is danger in sudden certainty". Eddy took a long sip then, before going on.

'He sent me to Iona because it is strict and will teach me about Christianity—but he told Mr Ferguson that I'm not baptised and must make up my own mind. He's annoyed about the time when your Church sometimes handed over people with different ideas to be tortured and put to death by the government. It was the Inquisition that did that, in Spain and elsewhere centuries ago.

"Too much blood in certainty!" my Dad says. "Too many certain Christians!"'

While speaking his father's words, Eddy had given these a slightly different accent—Derry mixed with something else—so Johnny formed a vague impression of Mr Li as a person who would be inscrutable too, but interesting. An idea was forming in his mind—but he wouldn't speak to Eddy about the bridgers just yet.

Midday arrived soon after and the group broke up—as soon as they had agreed to tell Mrs Walsh on Monday of their decision.

Johnny was surprised when Mary gave him a hug at the bus stop as they said goodbye. He was too surprised to be able to think if he should respond. She hugged Eddy too—but was it quite the same kind of hug?

'Does he want you to use a power saw or a hand saw?'

Kevy was asking Johnny this, soon after he got home from Margaret's. He had taken Johnny out to his workshop in the small back yard of their house. This smelt of wood and was dusty. The window hadn't been cleaned in a while, Johnny thought. Along the opposite wall stood a tall workbench. Tools of various kinds were arranged on the wall above. There was also a cupboard. In a back corner furthest from the window stood something tall that Johnny couldn't make out. An old grey dust-covered cloth had been pulled over it.

'A power saw—I think he called it a jig saw. He said some of us mightn't be able to manage a hand saw.'

'Right so,' said Kevy, and went to his cupboard. He took from this a tool like one Johnny had seen in Mr McKinley's in school, but older looking. He plugged the trailing lead into a wall socket and rested the saw on the tall bench.

'That's too high for you,' Kevy said. He fetched a smaller and lower folding bench from the back wall of the workshop. When he had arranged this to his satisfaction he lifted a piece of plywood.

'To cut a straight line in this you need to fasten it tight, with a straight edge to hold the saw against.'

He arranged the piece of plywood so that its centre covered a slot running down the centre of the small bench. Then he took a straight piece of timber and placed it on top of the plywood, with its edge to the left of where the saw blade would go. He fastened this down using clamps attached to the bench.

'I'll start it, just to show you. It'll be noisy. You must keep the foot of the saw in against the straight edge. If you don't do that the saw will wander off.'

He placed the saw so that the blade came up against the edge of the plywood. He pressed a switch on the top of the saw then and it began to whir noisily. With his left hand pressed down on top of the clamped straight edge he began slowly moving the saw forward with his right hand. As the saw blade bit into the plywood Johnny could see sawdust flying away from underneath.

When he had cut about two inches into the plywood Kevy stopped the saw.

'Now you. Make sure to stand with your weight right behind the line you want to cut.'

Johnny did as he was shown. His father grabbed him then, and made him stand with his feet exactly right.

'Now—push forward as you hold it against the straight edge, and flip the switch with your thumb.'

Johnny wasn't sure exactly what Kevy meant, but he thought he could see how Kevy had kept the saw going straight. He flipped the switch.

Immediately the saw began to vibrate powerfully and threatened to jump up from the bench. Johnny pressed down harder and the vibration lessened. He pushed forward then and the saw began to bite into the plywood.

Almost immediately the saw began to wander to the right, away from the straight edge. He realised that he had to push down and forward and to the left, all at once. He tried that. It was difficult at first, and he felt himself beginning to sweat. His shoulder soon felt sore also. But the saw came back to the left again, until its foot was back against the straight edge. Soon it was travelling true, and he was cutting a straight line slowly through the plywood.

He felt a tap on his shoulder soon, and switched the saw off. Kevy was nodding.

'Right! You're not so slow. We'll measure some pieces now.' Working from the drawing Johnny had given him, Kevy began marking a larger piece of plywood, using the straight edge to draw lines with the pencil. Then he arranged the piece carefully so that the saw blade would travel truly along the pencil line, and Johnny began sawing again.

Johnny's arm and shoulder soon ached, but he didn't mind, so long as he sawed straight. As the pieces began to collect he could see that there would soon be enough for the whole box. All four sides would be the same height, and it wouldn't need a lid.

'Now we'll cut the piece for the bottom of the box,' said Kevy. When they had done that Kevy arranged the side pieces around the edges of the base piece. He showed Johnny that they didn't sit exactly flat along their edges.

'We'll use a plane,' he said.

He carefully arranged two side pieces together, so that they exactly overlapped, and then clamped them in the bench, their two edges uppermost. He took a small plane from the cupboard then, and tested it for sharpness.

'Keep your arm straight behind the plane and push it all the way along in one go!'

Johnny again stood as he was shown and pushed. He felt the plane glide along, biting into the edges now and again. When he looked closely at the edges he could see that in places now they were perfectly smooth, where the plane blade had removed the tops of the slight bumps in the edge cut by the saw.

'A couple more goes should do it!'

Soon both edges were smooth and aligned. They did the same with all the other edges, and soon the sides of the box were sitting truly around the edges of the base.

Kevy explained that as the box was small they wouldn't need to make fancy joints where the sides met at the corners. They could just glue and pin the pieces where they met.

'That's called a butt joint,' he explained.

Soon enough the whole box was ready to be glued and pinned.

Kevy started the pinning, to make sure everything was sitting straight, and then allowed Johnny to hammer in the rest of the pins, using a special hammer with a slender head. Johnny liked the smell of the glue and cut wood together, and didn't mind getting some glue on his hands.

'We'll leave it to dry overnight,' said Kevy, setting the completed box on the taller bench. Already it felt solid and strong to Johnny—a whole box. Two hours earlier it hadn't existed, except as a drawing. Now there it was.

'Pleased with that are you?' Kevy asked, with a funny grin.

Johnny realised he had been staring for a long time at the box as it sat on the tall bench. It was the first thing he had ever made in wood almost all by himself. He had been thinking he might even soon be able to try making one without Kevy's help—measuring and sawing and planing and pinning.

'Maybe we'll do fancier joints some other time,' said Kevy.

'What's under that?' Johnny asked, pointing to the draped dusty cloth that covered something tall, standing in the corner of the workshop.

Kevy didn't answer for a long time. He just stood and looked. To Johnny it seemed he couldn't make up his mind what to do next.

Then he went over and began lifting off the cloth, pulling it from the top.

As the trailing edge of the cloth rose up, Johnny saw the base of a dark wood carving appear, and soon the feet and legs of a woman in a dress that reached below her knees. His eyes followed the cloth upward, until it revealed her whole body, then her head, slightly tilted forward and framed by shoulder-length hair. The woman was just about Anny's age he thought. She had her arms folded, with her hands visible and resting on her elbows.

'Who's that?' he asked.

'That's your Gran,' Kevy said.

Dimly Johnny recognised someone he had only ever seen in a few photographs. But this was different. He felt that a third person had suddenly appeared in the workshop, although she had been standing there all the time. The carving wasn't life-size, he could see—just a bit taller than his own height. He could see also that bits of it weren't finished—details of the dress. The head and face and hands were complete, though. She seemed to be studying him in the same way he was looking at her.

'That's brilliant!' he said eventually. He didn't need to ask his Da if he had made the carving. No-one else could have.

'Yeh, well, maybe I'll finish it some time,' said Kevy. He took the cloth and arranged it over the carving again. He guided Johnny in cleaning up the mess they had made. Then he switched off the light they had needed to work, and they left together.

Half an hour later, when he knew that Kevy had left the house, Johnny approached his Ma in the kitchen and asked her if Eddy and Mary could come the following Saturday morning with Margaret.

'We're debating together in a few weeks. We could talk about how to do that.'

Anny considered for a moment, scratching her head. Mary was already known to her, Johnny knew.

'I suppose so. Make sure they ask their own parents, though, mind.'

'Yeh. And Ma, would you ask Da if he would show his carving of Gran to us on Saturday. It's great.'

Anny's face changed at that. She sat down.

'When did he show you that?' She was keyed up.

'Just now. When he was helping me with that box.'

'It's years since he's even looked at that himself!' she said in a wondering voice.

'He said he might finish it.'

'Did he now?' she said, surprised. 'It was after he stopped years ago that things got bad. As though he didn't think there was any point to anything any more.

'I'll see if I can get him at a good time,' she said then. 'If he tidied that workshop up your friends wouldn't be put off by it.'

'It's OK,' Johnny said. 'They'll know it's where he works.'

'I suppose,' she said doubtfully. Johnny knew she was anxious to make a good impression on Margaret and her mother, who would probably collect Margaret in the afternoon. She had already warned

Johnny he would have to make his room extra tidy if Margaret was to see it, and help clean the whole house too.

'Anyway, I'm glad you've made good friends in school,' she said then, standing up to leave.

'Yeh,' said Johnny. He already felt at home in Iona College, and was looking forward to showing Margaret and Eddy and Mary his room with all his posters and books.

That night Johnny was remembering his father holding him to make him stand properly behind the saw and the plane. And what Mary had done at the bus stop too—and how she had looked at him.

He felt happier. He wondered if Mary would write a bridgers' application, and what would happen if she did.

X

'Prefect elections everyone!' said Mrs Walsh, first thing in English class on Monday morning.

Margaret woke up suddenly from her focus on the upcoming debates—and on Mary McNevin beside her. Mary hadn't told her yet what had happened to her bridgers' application and seemed to be in a daze.

'There are three candidates for each post—three boys and three girls: Arona and Margaret and Bridget; Aidan and Johnny and Eamon. Just put two names on this slip of paper, for a boy and a girl, and hand it back. Yes, Aidan?'

'Can you vote for yourself if you like?'

'Yes, of course. That vote could make all the difference.'

Margaret didn't like the thought of Arona as a prefect. She was already inclined to be full of herself, and might use the role to throw her weight about. So Margaret decided to vote for Bridget and Johnny.

Soon the teacher had collected all the slips, and began counting them at her desk.

'Clear winners in both cases, both winning more than half the votes cast, even though all candidates received votes. Aidan will be the boys' prefect this term, and Arona the girls'. The others will get another chance next term when Aidan and Arona can't be elected.'

Gavan, sitting beside Aidan, was waving his fist in the air and looking exultantly over at Johnny. Aidan looked pleased. So did Arona, as Ann O'Kane patted her on the back.

Margaret was disappointed but knew she needed lots of thinking time anyway. Her Mum had already said she was getting absent- minded.

'Now, those debates,' said the teacher. 'Any decisions yet?' Margaret's hand was up at once—she wanted that debate to happen as soon as possible, and to make sure no other team in the year group would choose it before her own.

'That's great, you three' responded Mrs Walsh with some surprise.

'I'll let the other Year Eight teachers know straight away! I'm sure you'll know the proposing team soon enough.'

From the ranks of what Margaret was now inclined to call *The Insulters* there had been jeering looks at this exchange—but Margaret had expected that and didn't care.

'The Fame School TV people will be here in three weeks for auditions!' said Mrs Hayes at Music class after break. 'Tell me by this day two weeks from now at the latest if you want to perform for them.'

Straight away Ann O'Kane and Deirdre Hasson turned to Arona in excitement, who received this tribute in a manner that said 'I suppose … if I can find the time'.

Looking now at Mary beside her, Margaret could see that although she was not excited by the idea, she wasn't turning it down either, as she had been inclined to do the previous week. Any competition with Arona in it was likely to turn nasty, however, and Margaret wasn't sure it would be a good idea to encourage Mary to enter.

'Maybe your music is too quiet for that,' she said to her friend.

Mary gave a small look of appreciation, but didn't speak. That morning she had been almost completely silent, pondering something. Occasionally Margaret saw the faintest trace of a smile—as though her friend was recalling something that pleased her.

After lunch, on the boundary walk the story came as they sat facing the river.

'You know Gríanan—the fort?' Mary's mind was focused on something other than the scene in front of her.

Margaret knew Gríanan of Aileach well—a circular wall not many miles away, twenty feet thick, about fifteen feet high and surrounding an open space about fifty feet in diameter. She had often seen most of the two loughs by climbing that wall—Foyle and Swilly—and deep into Donegal and Derry. It had made her dizzy at first to see so far in all directions.

'My Mum loves that view. Last night, after I had written my bridgers' application, I was there again. When I went up on the wall as high as I could there was someone else. She was dressed in a grey cloak, with a hood—staring to the west. I couldn't see her face at first, until she turned and called my name.

'She was pale, and her hair was almost pure white. The bluest eyes I've ever seen. Not much older than us. "Mary," she called a second time as I drew near. "What bothers you?"'

'Not understanding,' I said.

'Your mother is in the darkest valley—the valley of winter. We never go there willingly, but sometimes we must—to find what has been lost.'

'How can I help?' I asked.

'By trusting in what you have been taught—and in your own deepest intention. She fears for you—for all of you. But you can quieten that fear by trusting the music that comes from your deepest heart—and in the music yet to come.'

'Nothing else?' I asked.

'Ask for the power of the bridge—as you have already done with other words. And seek its other name, a name that she will know—a precious name that also could be lost.

'I woke up then. I wasn't afraid. I felt … safe. And I still feel that way. As though I was in a fort that couldn't be ever broken down, as though it is coming with me wherever I go—guarding me, always.'

'Did she give a name?' Margaret asked.

'No. I didn't ask. I will next time. I'm sure I'll see her again. I want to go back to Gríanan, and find out more about it.'

They walked back to class. Margaret noticed Mary humming a new tune—and pausing, and then either nodding or shaking her head as she repeated it.

'Have you another song coming?' she asked as they approached the Geography room.

Mary nodded confidently. 'It began with something Mr Li told Eddy—from that old Chinese book. It was in my head this morning. I've got one whole verse, and half of another—and a good bit of a tune too.'

'What did you think of the story of Joseph then?' asked Miss Doherty in Religion class that afternoon.

She was about the same age as Mrs Walsh, and the two were often seen together on the terrace and elsewhere. She had dark unruly hair usually kept in some kind of order by a ribbon tied at the back, and wore rimless half-moon glasses for reading. She was often slightly scatty and tended to keep her desk piled high with books that often fell off as she moved things about. She had a habit of calling Jesus' heavenly father 'Abba'.

Margaret looked over at Johnny, and then at Eddy. She knew what she wanted to ask but didn't want a repeat of her experience the previous week. At last Johnny put up a hand.

'Johnny!'

'Are there other stories of people fighting in the Bible?'

'Yes, Johnny, lots—and often it was brothers who fell out.'

She then gave him three examples, all of which he noted, together with the keywords she gave to find them on the digital bible in the library.

'Why are you so interested, Johnny?'

'We want to understand why people fight, Miss—for our debates.'

'Don't mind him, Miss,' said Gavan. 'He's ... y'know.' He pointed to the side of his head and made a twisting motion. Miss Doherty wasn't impressed.

'What about sisters, Miss?' asked Margaret. 'Are there stories about them fighting in the Bible?'

'Not so much. Sisters were treated more equally. You didn't have them fighting over an inheritance, something their father left to just one of them. I can't think of any stories like that anyway. Apart from Martha who got annoyed with Mary, but that wasn't serious.

And that's interesting.' She paused thoughtfully.

'Girls don't fight as much as boys anyway, Miss, do they?' asked Catherine Canning.

'I'm not sure about that. In bible times women didn't often hold power, you see, so they had less to fight about. You do find women who aren't sisters quarrelling though. Often it has to do with babies or the lack of them. One example is the quarrel between two women over a baby, when one tried to steal it and King Solomon had to decide who the real mother was.'

'How would I look that up?' asked Margaret.

Miss Doherty stared at Margaret too then, as she made notes of the references given her.

'My goodness, you two are a pair! You've held up my lesson long enough, too.

'Now, listen up—this next question is the biggest question for this year. It will take you all the year to answer it properly, but you can begin thinking about it now. Coming up to Easter next you'll all write an essay on it.

She wrote on the board then: 'In what way is the story of Joseph like the story of Jesus?'

On the bus home that day Johnny let them know that his Mum had said OK to all three coming to his home on the following Saturday. Mary nodded and began her humming again.

'That debate on materialism will be in ten weeks time—Johnny, Margaret and Eddy.'

It was English class on Friday, second period. Mrs Walsh was reading from notes on a clipboard.

'Your opponents—to propose the motion, will be Maria Cunningham, Desmond Bradley and Peter Byrne from Eight A. Dr McGinnis has asked for that debate to go last for this term, as he believes it will be the most important debate of all, and will prepare everyone well for Advent.'

As Mrs Walsh went on to give details of the other debates Margaret felt pleased to be given so much time to make their speeches as good as they could be. She knew that Advent was preparation time for Christmas—a four week period beginning towards the end of November. Looking across at Johnny and Eddy she could see that they were pleased too. She looked forward to discussing the debate the following day, and to what she, Johnny and Mary had planned—to surprise Eddy.

'That'll be a walkover for Eight A. You losers will let us down!' jeered Gavan.

Johnny's home was always tidy, but that Saturday it had never been tidier. His Ma had made sure that every last rug and ornament was in its proper place, that the windows sparkled and that no dust showed anywhere. He could see she was anxious. He had told her about the antique vase in Margaret's home, and of its different rooms—and of the gardens at the back and front. His own home didn't compare in that way, so Anny might be worrying what Mrs Phillips would think of it, with its almost absent garden and five smaller rooms. He was sure she didn't need to, because Mrs Phillips wasn't snobby—but Anny mightn't know that.

'Is your room in proper order, Johnny?' she said, near to ten o'clock. This was the second time she had asked that in the past hour.

'Yes, Ma,' said Johnny, and it was too. Early in the week Kevy had set to making the bookshelves he needed—which meant his room smelt of varnish. He didn't mind that, because now on the wall he had all his books displayed, and the floor hoovered where those books had been. Everything was in place. There would just be room for his three friends and himself. For some reason his Da had excused himself from meeting Mrs Phillips when she came, but had said he would be back to meet Johnny's friends before they left.

'Don't worry, Ma,' Johnny said as Anny stared round her to find something out of place. 'Your scones smell lovely.'

They did too. Anny had woken early to make sure the bread would be freshly baked—golden wheaten scones, all now sitting in a bowl on the kitchen table covered by a crisp drying towel. She had home- made raspberry jam waiting as well, and whipped cream in a smaller bowl.

She smiled nervously—but at that moment Johnny heard another car come down the street, and looked out the front room window for the tenth time. It was Mrs Phillips's car.

'They're here!'

Margaret was first to the door, followed by Mary—with her guitar—then Eddy and Mrs Phillips. After greeting them Johnny knew to take them straight away into the kitchen, where his Ma had gone to put on the kettle.

'You're all very welcome!' Anny's cheeks showed embarrassment.

'Could you sit here, Mrs Phillips?' she said—gesturing to the chair nearest the door. 'Now, Margaret, Mary—and Eddy?' She shook his offered hand.

'Ah! That's what I could smell coming through the front door,' said Mrs Phillips as she took her seat. Anny had just lifted the cloth from the larger bowl, revealing what was underneath. 'Just what I need—those look delicious.'

They were too, Johnny knew. He could see Anny was pleased when Mrs Phillips 'mphed' with satisfaction as she ate, and even more pleased when she asked for the details of the recipe and the cooking time. Anny went to find a pen and paper straight away—and that passed nearly all of the time that Mrs Phillips stayed.

'I'll make a hash of them, I'm sure,' she said, taking the page and rising. 'I'm an awful cook.' Johnny knew that wasn't true, but guessed also why Mrs Phillips had said it. His Ma was clearly more than pleased as she led her guest to the front door.

'Now,' she said, breathing out and beaming when she came back to the kitchen. 'When you children are ready, Johnny will show you his room. If it gets too stuffy, come down to the front room.'

They needed no second prompt, as the three bridgers had already made a plan for the day. Johnny's heart was jumping with anticipation as he led them up the stairs and into his small room with all of its *Star Wars* posters. Margaret sat on his bed, nearest the window, with Mary next to her. She had brought her guitar with her.

'Here, Eddy,' said Johnny, pointing to his chair. He had placed it to face the bed, so that he and his two friends could face Eddy together.

Eddy meanwhile had been looking at the wall posters and the books. When he turned and sat facing them his face changed.

'What's up?' he said. Johnny guessed that was because his own face and those of Margaret and Mary were expressing excitement—and also a little anxiety. They had no idea how he would react to what they had decided to tell him.

'Do you remember that first day in Mrs Walsh's class, and what she asked us to do—to make up an organisation we would like to join?'

'Yeh—so?' said Eddy.

As agreed, Johnny began their story, telling Eddy of how he had come to write his bridgers' application. They watched then as his face reacted to Johnny's and then to Margaret's and Mary's accounts of what had happened to them afterwards, and of what they remembered of what they had been told of the bridgers. They kept back only what was personal to themselves.

Eddy didn't speak at all until they had almost finished. This time his face had been far from impassive. It had expressed total fascination—and, at times, disbelief. He didn't speak for seconds.

His face searched theirs carefully, more than once.

'Is this all a wind-up too?' he asked. 'Are you all getting back at me because of what I did last week?'

Johnny shook his head as hard as he could. 'No, it's all true,' said Margaret. Johnny knew she didn't make many jokes.

'Tell me that again,' Eddy said at last, to Margaret and Johnny.

'What Margaret was told about the greatest bridge—what Johnny hadn't told her.'

When they had done that they waited anxiously.

'It's what happened, Eddy. Honestly,' Margaret added. 'When you ask for the power of the bridge, even if you are in trouble, and remind yourself of what you have been told, something happens.

You think of what to say or to do, the very best thing. Sometimes what happens is not what you hoped, but things work out—better than they would have done.'

'And something has been happening to me all this week too,' said Mary. 'I wanted to write a song about copy wanting, and it's coming to me faster than anything I've ever written before. Here—give me your chair and sit here.'

Mary went for her guitar then, as Eddy took her place between Margaret and Johnny. He said nothing as she readied her instrument—just looked at the others and stared around him.

'OK,' she said at last. 'This comes from what you said, Eddy—something your Da told you about that book—the *Tao* ...?'

'The *Tao Te Ching*.'

'Why do we want what others want? Wasn't that it?'
He nodded.

'And your Da said to sit with the question too didn't he?'
'Yeh.'

'Well that's what I did, not just sitting but walking about. I said the question over and over to myself. A rhythm started to come as I walked, and then part of a tune—and then other words and questions too, and more of the tune. Here we go!'

Straight away Mary launched into the following—at times changing the speed and the rhythm to express different ways of feeling. She stopped between each verse to tap her instrument eight times.

Why do I want what others want?
Why copy others' wanting?
I do not need what I so crave,
Why this daily haunting?

Tap tap tap tap tap tap tap tap

When TV tells me what I need -
That is copy-wanting.
When you show off what I don't have –
Zap!—I'm copy-wanting.

Tap tap tap tap tap tap tap tap

Why can't I see what others need
When I'm copy-wanting?
Children cry but I don't heed -
When I'm copy-wanting.

Tap tap tap tap tap tap tap tap

If I must have what you must have,
We'll find we can't share it,
We must fight for all of it —
Wars come—who can bear it?

Tap tap tap tap tap tap tap tap

Why do we want what others want,
Why borrow their desiring?
Is it because we fear their jeers,
And long for their admiring?

Tap tap tap tap tap tap tap tap

If all must have what some can get,
Can Earth survive this getting?
Will wanting stop our Home's upset -
Or quicken its upsetting?

Tap tap tap tap tap tap tap tap

This is the chain that binds the Earth
Imprisoning us in sorrow.
It leaves us with no hope, no peace,
No beauty, no tomorrow.

Johnny was hearing this for the first ever time. Mary had slowed down the last verse to express what she was feeling. He didn't know what to say. Margaret wasn't speaking either.

'Mary wouldn't play it for me until we were all together,' she said at last. 'I've just never heard anything like that, ever!'

'I think there'll be more of it too,' said Mary, 'other verses. I have other words and questions but no complete verses yet. I think I'm supposed to wait. Maybe between each verse a violinist could improvise, or there could even be a dance.'

'What do you call it?' asked Eddy.

'I think *The Chain that Binds the Earth,*' said Mary. 'But if more comes maybe there'll be a better name.'

'Who wrote that book, Eddy?' Johnny asked.

'Lao Tsu is the name usually given, but my Da says that nobody knows for sure. That may be a made-up name.'

Johnny was wondering about 'the greatest bridger'—but was even more interested in how Eddy would react to all that he had heard.

'Where did the idea of the chain come from?' asked Margaret.

'I was thinking of how to say that we pass on our wanting to others—not just now, but down through time as well. And then the idea of a chain came, and then I remembered that a chain can be used to keep you locked up. And aren't we, in a way?'

Margaret nodded. Johnny could see she was feeling something deeply.

Eddy just sat there then for a while, as the others waited.

'I'll write my application when I get home,' he said at last. 'What harm could there be in that? Even though I'm not sure I'm fully awake now! Will you play that again, Mary?'

Mary produced the song typed on three sheets for them to read from as she sang, even to join in if they wanted. And so they did as best they could, though none could sing so well. Johnny knew he had trouble keeping a tune, but this one was simple enough. As he sang he found himself feeling what Mary was expressing.

There was a knock on the door then, and Anny stuck her head in.

'That's a funny way of debating. Are you going in for singing instead?'

They stared at one another. They had been so engrossed they hadn't realised they would be heard throughout the house.

'The song's about what we're debating, Ma,' said Johnny at last.

'It's Mary's song.'

'It's what?' said Anny, coming in the whole way.

'Here,' said Johnny, handing her the sheet.

Anny studied it to the end, her mouth slightly open.

'Where did you get words like 'admiring' and … 'crave' Mary?'

'Margaret told me about the thesaurus. It gives you lists of words that mean nearly the same thing. If you use that and a dictionary to find the exact meanings, rhymes come into your head.'

'But 'copy-wanting'—is that in that book too?'

'No—that's Johnny's and Margaret's word,' said Mary.

The room went still then. Anny was staring hard at the two last named.

'Where did that come from?'

So Johnny explained, not about the bridgers—but about the thinking that had gone into making up that word on his first day at Margaret's a fortnight before.

'Well!' she said. 'You *are* a pair.'

'Eddy gave me the line I started with,' said Mary. 'So all of us made it.'

She read through it again, nodding. 'Can I hold on to this for a while, Mary ... to show Johnny's Dad when he comes home?'

'Yes!'

'Come on downstairs now—it's time for your lunch!'

Anny had gone to a lot of trouble to entertain Johnny's friends. Johnny had asked her to make his favourite pizzas, and to bake some of her special cream doughnuts. She had everything ready and the small dining area had a different appetising smell. There was a choice of tea or lemonade to drink.

Just as they were finishing Johnny heard the front door open downstairs, and knew his Da had come in. Anny heard that too.

'I'll see if your Da would like to hear that,' she said. Johnny knew why she wasn't sure, and he feared the worst. However, she was back soon to say 'come on into the front room.'

Unusually for a Saturday, Kevy had bothered to shave and was wearing a clean shirt. Johnny knew he should introduce his friends. He could see his Da was uncomfortable and suddenly felt awkward himself.

'This is Eddy and Margaret, Da—and Mary—my friends from school. This is my Da.'

Eddy, Mary and Margaret shook hands with Kevy, who nodded and said 'H'lo' to both. He then sat on his usual front room chair. There was an awkward silence.

'They're getting ready for a debate,' said Anny. 'But you must hear what they have been up to.'

'Where do you live?' asked Kevy of Margaret.

'Out in Glencarn.'

'Glendermott,' said Eddy.

'Milltown,' said Mary.

'We're all on the same school bus,' said Johnny.

'Right,' said Kevy. 'That's handy.'

There was another silence then.

'How d'you like school then?' asked Kevy.

'It's great,' said Margaret. 'Interesting. There's lots to think about. Most of the teachers are interesting.'

'Who's your favourite teacher?' asked Anny.

'Mrs Walsh,' said Eddy. 'She treats everyone the same, and she makes you think.'

'So does Mr Foley,' said Margaret. 'He's funny. He asked Johnny if he was in a quiz, because he was asking so many questions.'

'Yes,' said Eddy. 'And when Gavan Maguire said Johnny was daft, Mr Foley made a joke at *him* for not asking any!'

Kevy's expression had changed.

'Gavan Maguire? Who's he then?'

'His Da's a builder,' said Eddy. 'They live out in Culmore.'

At this, Johnny saw Kevy look over at Anny. Anny had told Johnny that Kevy would sometime find out that Gavan was in the same class, and now it had happened. Kevy's face was stern, but he said nothing. Anny looked pale.

'Da,' said Johnny, after another pause. 'Eddy has to go soon.

Could you show us your carving?'

Without a word Kevy rose. 'C'mon then.' He led them into the kitchen and lifted the workshop key from its hook beside the door to the back yard. When he had opened the workshop door and let them in, Johnny could see that it had been tidied and vacuumed, and the windows had been cleaned. Also there was a new clean sheet over the carving.

Kevy switched on the light, walked to the back of the room and lifted off the sheet.

The two visitors looked at the carving of Johnny's Gran in silence.

'Wow!' said Eddy.

'That's beautiful,' said Margaret then. 'I didn't know you could carve wood in such detail. Do you need special tools for that?'

'Yeh,' said Kevy. 'I'll show you.'

He opened the cupboard and took out a canvas bundle tied in the centre. He untied this and spread out the bundle on the workbench.

About a dozen different tools were visible, each in its own pocket and each with a different glittering blade. He took out one of these then, and explained what it did.

'It must take a lot of time,' said Mary.

'Yeh,' said Kevy. 'You need to know exactly what each tool will do, so you don't make a mistake. I had to learn as I was going.'

'How long did it take you?'

'A few years, on and off,' said Kevy. 'I couldn't work at it full time, and I wanted to get it just right.'

'It's nearly finished, isn't it?'

'Yeh—just a few more weeks should finish it!'

'I love wood. And I feel it's a real person,' said Mary. Johnny didn't tell us you were an artist.'

'Yeh, well,' said Kevy. 'I'll show you again, maybe, when I've got it finished.'

He put the tools away then, and put the sheet back over the carving. Anny led them all out as Kevy turned off the light.

'Go and get your guitar, Mary,' said Anny as they were trooping back to the house. 'You must hear this, Da!' she insisted and led them all back into the front room. Kevy placed himself on his usual seat opposite the TV. Johnny, Margaret and Eddy sat on the couch while Anny took the other chair. When Mary appeared she was holding the three sheets as well as her guitar.

'Right,' she said and began their song.

As she played and sang, Johnny joined in each verse with the others, even though he was self-conscious. Watching his Da, Johnny saw he was wondering at them as he listened. At the last verse he was tapping to the same rhythm with his hand on the arm of the chair.

Then they had to go through much the same quiz as Anny had given them upstairs. He too then asked to see the words on the page, and studied them closely, nodding in a wondering way.

'That's a funny way of debating,' he said then—so Margaret told him about the Fame School competition—and that Mary might enter it.

'What's stopping you?' Kevy asked. 'You could win it with that, for sure. That's far better than most of drivel we have to listen to these days—especially in the supermarket.'

Mary coloured. 'Thanks, Mr Mullan. Maybe I will.' Kevy then looked at Anny, who turned to Johnny.

'You three stay here now, Johnny. That room of yours is all stuffy, and your Da and me need a cup of tea in the kitchen.'

As they left Kevy stopped suddenly at the door, and turned.

'Don't be strangers now, you three, d'you hear—Margaret, Mary and Eddy? You'll be welcome any time.'

'We have just half an hour before Mr Li comes for Eddy,' said Margaret then, when the door had closed. How are your speeches coming?'

'Mine's nearly ready,' said Eddy.

'Mine too,' said Johnny. He had to make a final draft, leaving out what he had crossed out, and making sure the handwriting was legible. Again he wished he had a computer to make all that easier.

He knew that if he had that he could get his speech printed at school.

'Great,' said Margaret. 'I'd like to give them to Patricia before the end of the week.'

'How would we find out if you have to believe in materialism?'

Johnny asked then. 'We'll be stuck if the other team say that and we can't answer.'

'Miss Doherty will know,' said Margaret.

'But if we ask that in class someone might tell the other team we did that. We need to make sure we don't tip them off—about anything.'

'I'll be seeing her for an interview next week,' said Margaret. 'She asked Mrs Walsh if I could get out of a class for that on Wednesday.

She won't give us away—I'll ask her. She'll know that Mrs Walsh said to do our own research—that's part of the test.'

'Right,' said Johnny, relieved. That question had been bothering him.

At that moment the doorbell rang.

'That'll be my Da,' said Eddy, and went out with Johnny to the front door.

Mr Li stood quietly as they opened it, and smiled. Dressed in smart casual clothes, he wasn't as tall as Kevy, and lighter in build.

'Ah, Eddy,' said Mr Li. 'I hope you have been behaving yourself.'

Johnny knew to invite him in to meet his own parents, who were waiting behind him. Again Anny and Kevy seemed slightly embarrassed as they shook hands.

'You must hear what these four have been up to, Mr Li. Do you have time to hear a song?'

'Yes,' he said, 'if it's not a whole opera.' He said this with a broad smile, so there was no offence in it.

Johnny made sure that Mr Li was seated—in the second chair of the suite, while he himself stood beside the TV to let Anny sit with Margaret and Eddy on the couch while Kevy took his own usual chair. Meanwhile Mary had made her guitar ready and handed the sheets with the words back to her friends.

'Eddy gave us the idea for this, Mr Li,' said Mary. 'Maybe you'll recognise it.'

And then she began *The Chain that Binds the World* again.

As they sang Johnny could see Mr Li was surprised—looking at each of them—and especially at Eddy with a puzzled expression.

When they had finished he remained quiet—but then said:

'Are you all becoming Taoists, then?' He was half joking, half in earnest.

'What do Taoists believe, Mr Li?' Margaret asked.

'In a source from which everything comes, and in a way of being and living that is respectful and compassionate. We can never know that source fully, but we can attend to that mystery, wonder at it, and find calm. *Tao* means way or principle of life.'

Johnny was struck by Mr Li's own calmness, and thought he should say something. 'We like that joke that Eddy played on us last week. And we like that song too. Thank you very much.'

Mr Li bowed his head in acknowledgement. 'Come and visit us in Glendermott soon. And now, Eddy …'

Everyone rose to see Eddy and his Dad to the door.

'I'll write my application tonight,' whispered Eddy to Johnny as he passed him at the front door.

XI

Soon the doorbell in Johnny's house rang again.

'That'll be Mrs Phillips to collect Margaret and Mary,' said Anny, and went out to the hall.

Johnny saw his Da stiffen. Then he stood up, looking towards the door.

'Come in and meet Johnny's Dad, Mrs Phillips,' said Anny then.

Johnny could hear anxiety in her voice.

Mrs Phillips entered. 'Mr Mullan! Glad to meet you.'

Kevy moved forward to shake her hand awkwardly. Johnny could see he wasn't sure what to say.

'Mr Mullan, would you show my Mum your carving?' Margaret asked.

Kevy looked surprised for a moment. 'Alright then,' he said.

'Wait till you see, Mum,' said Margaret, as Anny led them all into the hall and kitchen. This time she took the workshop key and led them all through the yard and opened the door.

'You'd better go first, Da,' she said.

So Kevy went into the workshop first, and Anny gestured to Mrs Phillips to follow. Johnny was last in—to total silence.

Mrs Phillips was looking at the carving without saying a word, for what seemed an endless time.

'I don't know what to say, Mr Mullan. That's remarkable. Do you have more work like that?'

'No,' said Kevy. 'I'm just learning.' Mrs Phillips shook her head.

'Can I change places with you so I can see from another angle?' Mrs Phillips turned to look at Kevy.

That happened.

'I'm not an expert, but I think you could exhibit work of that quality, if you had more.' She turned to look at Kevy.

'Thanks,' said Kevy, after a pause. 'It takes ages though.' He sounded surprised to Johnny. Mrs Phillips had not just been speaking politely—she had sounded genuinely impressed—and she had spoken to his Da with great respect.

'You must hear Mary's song now,' said Anny, as Kevy locked the workshop door behind them.

'What's that?' said Mrs Phillips

So they all trooped back to the front room as Margaret explained briefly to her Mum how Mary's song had come about. This time Kevy showed Mrs Phillips to his own chair. Johnny looked for the sheets with the words, and handed one to her. She was scanning it as everyone else arranged themselves in the room. Johnny waited till he found a seat beside Margaret on the couch.

'OK,' said Mary and began strumming.

As they sang Johnny began to lose his self-consciousness. Mrs Phillips was looking from the sheet to him and Mary and Margaret with the greatest surprise. She was silent for some moments when they finished—and then she put them all through an even longer quiz. Johnny could see that she wanted to be convinced that Mary hadn't just heard the song on the radio or TV and copied it. It was the word copy-wanting that convinced her. She understood what they meant, and said it had never occurred to her that this could be the meaning of 'coveting'. At last she shook her head.

'Definitely, Mary, definitely—enter that competition … do you hear! I'm not sure we adults should be filling children's heads with dreams of fame so early … but that song already deserves to be heard—and so do you. If more comes I want to hear it.'

Mary had coloured. Johnny could see she was greatly encouraged.

'Can I talk to your Mum and Dad alone for a few minutes now, Johnny' said Mrs Phillips.

'Go finish up, you three,' said Anny.

So they did, Mary taking her guitar to put it back in its case in Johnny's room.

'What do you think they want to talk about?' Mary asked.

'Us, I suppose,' said Margaret. 'But they're not mad at us anyway.'

Johnny felt sure that was true. He was feeling something else too.

He wanted to hug Mary for what she had given him—a belief that his own words and ideas could be put to music— music that thrilled and excited. He had given up hugging people his own age—but Mary had hugged him last Saturday and that had made him happy in a way that was strange. Could he risk it? He did what he was now used to doing before every big decision. 'Why not,' his head said.

'Mary, can I give you a hug? That song is just the most … super thing.'

Mary's face lit up and she put down the guitar. She hugged him just as tightly as he wanted, giving him a feeling of delight and wonder. It made his heart jump.

'Me too,' said Margaret, 'and Johnny as well.'

So they all did then. Johnny felt warm and glad to have such friends.

'What will happen to Eddy, do you think?' asked Mary.

'We'll soon find out,' said Margaret.

'Time to go,' called Johnny's Mum from the hallway. When they went down to the hallway Johnny could see that his Da had relaxed.

He was smiling—and looking at him in a different way. Mrs Phillips had already said goodbye and was waiting in the car outside.

'Here—I want to talk t'you!' said Kevy then, as the door closed. His voice was somewhere between angry and kind.

Feeling tense, Johnny followed him into the front room. Anny came too, looking slightly worried.

Johnny knew that Anny would want him to keep from Kevy many of the things that had happened since he had started at Iona. But if Kevy asked him tough questions how was he to answer?

'Tell me about Gavan Maguire,' said Kevy.

'What do you want to know?'

'Your friend Eddy said he called you 'daft'. What else has he called you?'

'He calls everyone names—anyone he doesn't like! He's always doin' it. He calls David 'slug' because he's a bit wide and slow on the pitch. He calls Eddy 'Chinky'. He calls me 'loopy' and stuff like that.'

'Why?'

'I think it's because I ask questions and I know stuff, and often he doesn't.'

'Has he ever hit you?'

'No,' said Johnny. That was true too, by a split second. Wrestling wasn't hitting exactly.

'Has he ever hit anyone else?'

'He pushes people sometimes, but not me.'

'Are you afraid of him?'

'No. I'm able for him!' That was true too, Johnny realised.

'Apart from those three—Margaret and Eddy and Mary—do you have any friends in school?'

'Yes—lots.' That was true too, Johnny realised. He felt that most people liked him.

'It's not a snobby place then?'

'No. A few people are that way, but that's all.'

'Do your friends stick up for you?'

'Yeh.'

Kevy said nothing then for a minute. He thought awhile, and looked over at Anny once. She gave a hopeful smile.

'Right then,' said Kevy. 'That's alright then. But if he gives you any trouble, let me know. Hear?'

Johnny nodded.

'Mrs Phillips is pleased with how you are all getting on,' his Mum said then. 'She says there's some kind of … chemistry between you all that she doesn't understand. But she wants it to continue, and so do we. So don't fall out.'

'We won't,' said Johnny, and went back up to his room, feeling sure they wouldn't.

—∘∘∘◉∘∘∘—

'I hadn't thought of that, Margaret. But why are you so sure that what you call copy wanting is what the commandments call coveting?'

Miss Doherty was asking this of Margaret over a desk in one of the interview rooms on the following Tuesday: Mrs Walsh had let her out of English class for this purpose. Her teacher was looking at her now intently over her half-moon lenses, with her arms folded—leaning back on the chair.

'Well, Miss, do you agree there is such a thing as people suddenly thinking they need something today that they didn't think about yesterday—just because they've seen somebody else with it?'

Miss Doherty considered for a moment. Suddenly she straightened up with a slight jolt, seemed to think about saying something, and then changed her mind. Then she had another think.

'Yes, that happens, definitely,' she said. 'Every time I see this year's model of my car, I wonder if I shouldn't change it. I can sometimes look for a good reason to do that, even though it's only five years old.'

'Shouldn't that have a sharp name then, Miss—a name that stands for just that kind of wanting, and no other?'

'I suppose …'

'And isn't it a *yearning*, a wanting that nags at you often, until you give in. And then often afterwards you can't understand why you did that?'

'Yes, that's true.'

'Well, Miss, if everyone does that, think of all the money spent on things we don't need—all around the world. Doesn't that help to explain why so many children don't get enough to eat, why the rain forests are shrinking—and climate change?'

'Well, yes, I suppose …'

'So don't you think that if the Bible is God's holy book he would have warned us about that? In those bible times wouldn't an ox have been like a car? If your neighbour's ox was a better one than yours, and if you were poor, wouldn't you have yearned for it? Mightn't you have said to yourself "if only I had that ox, I would be just as good as its owner—just look at this poor tired broken-down old ox that I've got instead"?'

Miss Doherty stared.

'And Miss, those two women who fought over that baby—the one that King Solomon had to decide about. What would the woman who rolled on her baby have thought would happen when everyone else woke and found she had done that?'

'She would have felt ashamed. Being able to have, and to look after, children was the most important thing for a woman back then.'

'Well, Miss, isn't that like the story of Joseph too. Didn't Joseph suffer in much the same way as the poor woman with the live baby, because someone wanted what he had?

Couldn't the bible be giving examples of why copy-wanting is wrong? And mightn't that be why coveting is warned about too—because it's the same thing? And mightn't that be why the apostles fell out too, because more than one of them wanted to be what only one of them could be—the greatest?

At this Margaret's teacher put her hand to her mouth and peered at her intently. She sat back and went on staring.

'Well … I … goodness me, I never thought of that. Could things be that simple? Let's go back to the beginning. Why did Cain kill Abel—what had Abel got that Cain could have wanted?'

Miss Doherty thought for a moment and sat up again. 'Yes, Abel's sacrifice had pleased God more—that's what the story says—and Cain could have wanted God's greater favour too, couldn't he?'

'Yes, Miss. That's it. That was God favouring one brother more than another—just as Jacob had favoured Joseph.'

'But if that's the case why wasn't I taught that? Why isn't it in my books?' Miss Doherty seemed to be asking this question not just of Margaret.

'I don't know, Miss. But that's what we'll be saying in the debate, Johnny and Eddy and I—that wanting the same thing is a better explanation for most of what's wrong. Not just buying what you don't need but bullying and wars and a lot of crime too. Anyone can understand that. Even we can. We're not sure we understand why materialism is supposed to be a bigger problem, but we're going to be opposing that anyway.'

'I see …'

'You'll keep that to yourself, won't you Miss—so that the other team won't get to hear what we'll be saying?'

'Can I tell just Mrs Walsh? She can keep a secret, and she's your form teacher. I'll not say a word to anyone else.'

Margaret agreed to that readily.

'And I'll be sure to be at that debate too, to see how it goes,' Miss Doherty went on.

'Miss, do we have to believe that materialism is a worse problem than copy-wanting or coveting? Does the church teach that?'

Miss Doherty stared again. 'The term is often used—even by bishops and the pope. It has just not been questioned, I think. I'll tell you what: I'll look into that and let you know. I can search the Catechism on the computer, for example. That'll be easy enough.'

'If materialism is a bad sin, wouldn't it be in that book? What does it say about coveting?'

'I'll look that up too. But Margaret, you'll be sure not to overdo it won't you? I'm concerned that you might give too much attention to all this over the whole term—maybe become exhausted with it.'

'We have ten weeks, Miss, and all of us have kept up with our work, honest. And then it'll be all over.'

Miss Doherty considered her for a moment and then smiled.

'Alright, then, that'll do us for today. Do you want me to say more about coveting in class now, since you asked me those questions?'

Margaret thought a moment, waited, and then shook her head with emphasis.

'No, Miss. Not yet. The proposing team might find out what we're thinking. Could you wait until the debate is over?'

Her teacher agreed. Margaret was about to get to her feet when another question occurred to her.

'Miss, what did Jesus want?'

Again her teacher paused before speaking.

'I suppose for us all to love Abba first, to love ourselves, to love one another, and to be at peace.'

That settled something in Margaret's mind. As she closed the door of the interview room she saw through the glass her teacher still sitting and staring at the desk without seeing it. Miss Doherty shook her head then, and climbed to her feet.

'How many of you will be at the first Year Eight debate this coming Wednesday? Hands up please!'

It was the Friday of that same week, second period. Mrs Walsh counted the raised hands, which included those of all three bridgers, as well as Mary McNevin.

'Just thirteen out of twenty-four? Have you others forgotten how much time and effort your teachers have put into arranging these four debates—and how valuable they will be for your education? And not just in this subject. I know some of you just can't stay late due to transport problems—but have you tried to arrange lifts?

'And are you forgetting who'll be debating for your own class—Aidan, Patrick and Gavan—opposing the motion that on balance the motor car was a bad idea? Don't you all want to see how they get on? Come now—we'll do that again. How many?'

Again she counted. 'That's better. Sixteen this time. I suppose that's two-thirds. All right then. Now, how is our other team getting on—Margaret?'

Margaret told her that her team's trial speeches would soon be passed to a senior debater for advice.

'That's good. I now understand that could also be an interesting event. All four debates this term seem to be on track.'

It seemed to Margaret that Mrs Walsh's gaze showed that she knew most of what she herself had told Miss Doherty on Wednesday, and had changed her mind on the difficulty of contesting the materialism motion. Margaret drew hope from that.

'Now, Eight B, why not give Aidan, Gavan and Patrick a round of applause for opening this year's debating season—to encourage them to do their best?'

That Friday, Margaret met Patricia Brolly, the Year Thirteen debater, as agreed in the library, and handed her the three draft speeches. Her own was neatly typed, as was Eddy's. Johnny's was handwritten but legible, with nothing crossed out.

'Good, good, good,' said Patricia as she glanced at them. 'I'll try to give you some feedback the week after next. OK?'

Margaret nodded excitedly. She couldn't wait to hear what Patricia would say.

'I was there in the middle of the square, Tiananmen, in Beijing.

Very early morning, I think—and smoggy. Many people were killed there in 1989, for protesting against the government, we don't know how many exactly. But now, for me in that dream last Saturday, there was almost no one about—just some police in the distance, in the haze.'

Eddy was telling Johnny, Margaret and Mary of his experience the previous Saturday night, following his application to be a bridger.

All four were sitting around the dining table in Margaret's home—the same table around which they had agreed to contest the 'materialism' motion a fortnight earlier. Spread on the table were photos of the demonstrations that had led to the Tiananmen atrocity—including one of a boy standing in front of a line of tanks

For all of the previous week Eddy had played inscrutable again—just shaking his head when he was asked what had happened and saying 'Saturday'. All he would say beyond that was yes, something had happened—and that his bridgers application had been accepted.

'I'll bet he's going to make another big production of it!' Margaret had said to Mary on Wednesday, confirming that they would meet in her home to hear. And that's just what Eddy was doing. Now he went on:

'Eddy, someone called from behind me. When I turned there was this bigger Chinese boy, dressed in a smart Chinese traditional suit I had never seen—grey-blueish with bluer buttons.

'Would you like to lock someone up for what happened here in 1989?' he asked.

'Yes, I said. Very much.

'It would take much effort and risk—and maybe most of your life—and you might fail in the end.'

'Yes, I said, but that I would like to try.

'Why do you think this happened?' he asked.

'My Dad says it was the government's fear of being overthrown.'

'Yes,he answered. And fear is a prison too. Fear of shame especially. What does the *Tao Te Ching* say about the biggest prison?'

'I told him I didn't know.'

'It says *care about what other people think and you will always be their prisoner*. People would have laughed at the government if it had been overthrown that way. It was the government's fear of what everyone would think that led it to behave as it did in 1989. So those strong men were already in the biggest prison in the world—the prison responsible for so many tyrannies. Much crime begins there too. Might it be better to be a crime-preventer?'

'I suppose, I said, and that I hadn't thought of that.'

'How might you go about that?'

'By teaching people not to be afraid of what others think?' I asked.

'Wisely said. And by being unafraid yourself. Every person has a precious value that no other person can take away. So could you think about how to teach that?'

'Yes, I said, but could I do some locking up as well?'

'He grinned and said: 'Maybe criminology—the study of crime—would suit you?'

'I said I would think about that—and then he said: 'Some detection may be required soon enough. Stay awake. Remember to ask for the power of the bridge—and to wait!'

'What's your name? I asked him.

'Li Po, he said.

'And that was it,' Eddy finished. 'When he turned and began to walk away I woke up, with all that clear in my head.

'Care about what other people think and you will always be their prisoner,' Margaret was repeating. 'Oh, I like that. And about that being the biggest prison in the world. Isn't that why people copy- want too? I'm always looking for some magical outfit that people will admire—to make them forget I'm a beanpole.

'When people insult you are they trying to put you in prison—to get you to be afraid of being ashamed, so that you will do what they want?'

'Yes, that's it, Johnny. And Mary, you mustn't let Arona do that. Remember what Li Po said: *every person has a precious value that no other person can take away.* If Arona has another go at you on Monday morning before music, just go inside yourself and ask for you know what. I'll be there anyway to back you up. Have you decided yet—what to tell Mrs Hayes about those *Fame School* auditions?'

'I think so,' said Mary 'but I'm inscrutable.' She made her face a blank wall. Eddy laughed.

'Why not try that on Arona too?'

'I'll practise it in the mirror when I get home and just deadpan her from now on. I'm no good at insults.'

'I'm better at it,' said Margaret. 'I have a few saved up just in case.'

'Tell us again what Miss Doherty said on Tuesday,' said Johnny to Margaret, and she did that.

'I wondered why Mrs Walsh was looking at us like that on Friday—as though she knew something,' said Eddy.

'She won't give us away though, will she?'

They all agreed on that. Then Margaret asked:

'Mary, is there any more of that song yet?'

'I think I've got the start of another verse.' She went for her guitar, tapped it eight times, and then sang:

'Did someone come to break this chain?…

'That came to me because the greatest bridger would have done something important—maybe made sure that together we could all break the chain if we tried.'

'Who *was* that?' Johnny asked.

Mary looked at Margaret, who nodded.

'We think it *could* be Jesus.

'Nnnggggg,' said Johnny, putting his head in his hands. 'I was afraid you would say that.'

'Why?'

'Because—well, often in those pictures he looks … just *cheesy*. And look at the fighting that went on here, in Derry. And what Eddy's

Da told him about the church handing over people to be tortured:

Too much blood in certainty: too many certain Christians.'

'Maybe Jesus didn't want that,' said Margaret. 'Maybe that isn't his fault. Maybe something went wrong.'

'What do you mean?' Eddy asked.

'Well, why *don't* Miss Doherty's books say that people fell out because they were just wanting the same thing in all those stories in the bible? Why *don't* they say that?

That's something else that's wrong. Something must have happened to stop people seeing that.'

'I'm sure Jesus didn't want fighting either,' Mary said. 'Didn't he say to turn the other cheek and love your enemies? He didn't fight the Romans either.'

'When did Christians *start* fighting and using force then?' asked Eddy,

'That's a good one, Eddy,' said Johnny. 'We could ask Mr Foley, couldn't we?' He was looking at Eddy, who nodded.

'But not in class. We could stay behind after last class on Monday.

That way no one would know what we're on about.'

Johnny agreed eagerly. 'Mr Foley told me to look up Hitler and Napoleon. And I'm sure he won't give us away either.'

Before they broke up that Saturday, Eddy told the others they were all invited to his own home in Glendermott the following week, for the Saturday morning. The four bridgers then sang the 'chain' song again. This time Mary showed them some riffs she was practising, to go between each verse—a slightly different one each time. She finished with:

'Did someone come to break this chain? …'

'Now, class, decision time!' Mrs Hayes was addressing Eight B on Monday in the music room. Sitting in their usual place, Margaret looked immediately to the person on her right, to Mary—who was still giving nothing away.

'Who will audition for the Fame School people when they arrive next Monday? Hands up now please!'

Instantly, sitting to their left and directly facing Mrs Hayes, Arona Gilsenan put her hand up. Deirdre Hasson clapped at that point, and Ann O'Kane joined in.

Eileen Daly's hand was up also, and Catherine Canning was clapping. 'That's great you two—anyone else?

Mary's eyes were closed as she sat with her head in her hands, both elbows on the desk. Then, without looking up, she put up her right hand.

'Hooray!' said Margaret, louder than she had meant to. She too clapped as hard as she could. When she looked to the front, Arona and her friends were staring around at them. Deirdre Hasson turned to Arona and said something that Margaret couldn't hear. Arona then shook her head as if to say 'it won't matter'.

'Good luck to all of you,' said Mrs Hayes, 'and make sure that your practising doesn't get in the way of your other subjects. I'll get into trouble with other teachers if it does. Not everyone is convinced that children should be encouraged to look for fame at all, you know.'

She then continued the class.

As they were leaving Arona approached, with her usual allies in tow.

'Mary, would you like the name of the best hair stylist in Derry?

He can work miracles!'

Mary's face was unreadable. She turned towards the door and walked on without speaking.

'The north wind doth blow, and we shall have snow— and what will the robin do then, poor thing?' said Margaret, trying to keep her own face inscrutable. She didn't wait to see the effect as Mary went through the door.

'That's *two* loopers,' said Arona behind her.

There was indeed a north wind—blowing heavy rain against the corridor windows. September was almost over, and the swallows had gone south.

'*Fighting?* Think for a moment, gentlemen!' Mr Foley was staring gravely at Eddy and Johnny in the history room. The bell had just gone, and the two had immediately made their way to their history teacher as he tidied his desk and the rest of the class made off. 'The word fighting could describe anything from strong disagreement to thermonuclear warfare. Could you be more precise?'

Johnny looked to Eddy—it had originally been his question.

'Serious stuff, Sir—with weapons, killing. When did Christians first do that, and start using force against people who disagreed with them?'

'Might my life depend on this? If I give you what I believe to be an approximately correct answer, will you be quoting me in the media or on the Internet?'

Most times it was impossible to tell if Mr Foley was being serious or pulling your leg. Johnny decided to take no chances.

'We won't do that, Sir. We know we would have to look for other evidence.'

'In that case then, Mr Mullan, I believe the serious fighting by Christians began when the Christian church was recognised by the Emperor Constantine in the fourth century. That began the centuries-long alliance between the church and the state. Until then, I believe, Christian men chose generally to refuse to serve in the legions.'

'What's the state, sir?' asked Eddy.

'Don't you two have buses to catch?'

'Yes, sir.'

'In that case, as you have asked me a question that requires a longer answer than you have time for now, you had better run along. If you haven't found the answer by yourselves by Wednesday tell me at lunchtime that day in the staffroom and we'll see what we can do.'

They thanked their teacher and headed speedily for the bus pick- up bays in front of the school. The rain blew hard in their faces as soon as they went outdoors, but they were soon seated together towards the front of the bus.

'Maybe the state is the government—whoever that is,' said Eddy.

'Fourth century,' said Johnny. 'That meant that Christians had refused to fight for three centuries. Until the 300s.'

'I wonder what changed their minds?' Eddy was staring at the rain.

'Could you look up 'the state' at home?'

Eddy nodded. 'Yeh—I could look up Constantine too.'

Johnny looked around, to see if he was likely to be overheard, and thought not.

'What do you think of what Margaret and Mary are saying—that the greatest bridger could be Jesus?' This had been on his mind since the previous Saturday. He wasn't sure if Eddy had felt able to be honest then.

'I don't know what to think about Jesus. Sometimes I think of him as just another person, but Christians say he was God too—and I don't know exactly what that means. For Taoists the Tao itself, the source, comes first—then there are many Gods, but they are less than the Tao and come from the Tao—which is unknowable.'

Eddy thought further for a moment. 'But you remember that when Julius Caesar was murdered, his friends said he was a God. So back then people sometimes made famous men into Gods. That had happened to Alexander too. Maybe that's what happened to Jesus too?'

'I'm not going to believe Jesus was the greatest bridger until I'm sure he didn't ever want to overpower anyone—to be a tyrant, like Caesar.' Johnny was saying this for his own sake, and not just for Eddy's. Mick had told him in the Bishop's Wood that bridgers could never overpower anyone—to do so would be to make a bad bridge. He reminded Eddy of this.

'I made a bad bridge once,' he said then. For the first time he told his friend of the episode with Patrick Andrews in the changing cubicles in the first week of term, when he had toppled their jibing classmate with a bar of soap. 'He hasn't forgotten that either. I know by his face. I was so mad at him, and the soap was saying 'go for it'—so I didn't stop to ask for the power of the bridge.'

'You should have done,' said Eddy. 'I'm used to that monkey stuff.'

He thought a moment and then went on: 'And if Jesus *was* the greatest bridger what bridge did he make? What obstacle did he overcome? We must ask Margaret and Mary that too.

'Yeh!' said Johnny.

—∘∘❦∘∘—

'The state *is* the government, Johnny. Any government. Only the state can lock people up without breaking the law. If I did that now—if I locked *you* up, the police would lock *me* up for doing it. Then I would be in court, in front of a judge. The police and the judges are both part of the state. So are the people who decide what the laws should be.'

'Right—the politicians who get elected to Stormont here in Northern Ireland. So the state can overpower people, but bridgers are not supposed to?'

Eddy nodded.

It was the following morning and they were again on the school bus, but this time heading again for the oldest Derry bridge and their school. The rain had cleared for the moment but it was colder, with a sharp northerly wind whipping up waves on the river Foyle. Eddy was going on:

'Mr Foley said that the state and the church became allies in the fourth century, and that from that time more Christians joined the Roman army and fought wars. So Christians did start overpowering other people then. They might have joined the Roman police too, and become judges.'

'And even executed people?'

'Will we ask Mr Foley that on Wednesday?'

'Why not!' said Johnny. He liked Mr Foley. History was already his second-favourite subject after English. Religion came next—because of the stories about copy-wanting. He struggled with Maths, but Kieran was helping him with that, and even in Science.

'Did Jesus want the state and the church to come together, I wonder?' Eddy was thinking ahead again.

'We could ask that too.'

Johnny looked round then, to where Margaret and Mary were sitting—three rows back and on the other side of the bus. He was glad Mary had decided to enter the *Fame School* competition, and wondered what would happen if she sang the chain song. Would anyone else understand it?

He put up a thumb, hoping especially to catch Mary's eye, and was glad again when she grinned and waved. She seemed much happier now than she had in that first week.

'Is this a cunning plan to arrange for my early retirement?'

Mr Foley was asking Johnny and Eddy this question— seated behind the table in an interview room near the staffroom at lunchtime on the following day, Wednesday. Again Johnny couldn't tell if Mr Foley was being serious, and again he decided not to take any risk.

'No, Sir. We like History, don't we Eddy?'

'Yes, Sir - 'specially that article you gave me on the assassination of Julius Caesar.'

'In that case, gentlemen, what you must not do is to quote me as an authority on these matters. Yes—as powerful people in the state, Christians did execute people they believed to have committed serious crimes for most of the centuries that followed. Even Popes did that, as rulers of territories in Italy. However, your last question takes us outside my domain as a History teacher—into the explosive domain of Theology. Remind me: who is your teacher of Religion?'

Eddy told him.

'In that case it is to Miss Doherty you must apply for a trustable answer to any question on what Jesus may have thought about anything—and in asking her you must not say anything like "Mr Foley says X, Y or Z". Look for other sources on questions of fact, and if you have an opinion of your own after that you must state it as such. Is that clear?'

Johnny looked to Eddy, and both assented readily.

'In that case I believe I am correct in telling you that some political scientists trace the origin of the modern separation of church and state to a saying of Jesus: *Give to Caesar what is Caesar's and to God what is God's.*

'But notice,' their teacher went on 'that I am *not* an authority on the history of political science either. You need to check that detail with, say, Mr Wesley, head of that subject in the school—if he could spare any time at all for junior pupils. But you must *not* say I sent you. If you do ask him that, let it be on your own behalf only. Is that clear too?'

Mr Foley looked at them then with particular seriousness, Johnny thought.

'Right, Sir—and sorry for taking up some of your lunch period.'

'My digestive system may tolerate rare and short tutorials of this kind,' said Mr Foley, rising. 'Fortunately I am free next period. I shall go back to the staffroom now, make myself a coffee, and prepare myself for whatever mines you two may now set off.'

Their teacher rose to leave them then, but turned at the door.

'Again, gentlemen, what mustn't you say if approaching any other teacher on this quest?'

'That Mister Foley says X, Y or Z!'

'Good, Mr Mullan, and Mr Li—but if I am ever told in the staffroom that you have forgotten that, there will be a reckoning.

Understood?'

They nodded and he left.

'Give to Caesar what is Caesar and to God what is God's— was that it?' Johnny turned to Eddy as the door closed.

'Yeh- maybe Jesus didn'twant the church to be an ally of the state, or to overpower anyone.'

'Why did it happen then?'

Eddy shrugged and shook his head.

XII

After school that same Wednesday, Margaret filed in with the other three bridgers to watch their first Year Eight debate. They sat together on a tier about half-way up the theatre. Just over half of the year group came to fill about a third of the large room. Again Mrs Walsh had written the motion up on the board: *'That this house believes the motor car was a bad idea'*.

This time Dr McGinnis didn't come, and there were just four seniors. One of them was Conor Maguire.

When Mrs Walsh invited the speakers to take their places, the proposition did so nervously. There was a gleaming new, and lower, lectern to suit the average height of the Year Eights. Mrs Walsh warned the audience not to put them off by making too much noise or by asking silly questions. Two of the proposing speakers were so anxious that their pages were quivering.

Even so they set out a good case against cars, Margaret thought. They caused not just accidents but health problems because people didn't take enough exercise. And they harmed the environment by causing air pollution and by needing too many roads and motorways through the countryside. The proposition also argued that far too many car journeys were unnecessary, and that if there were no private cars the buses and trains would be much cleaner, and more frequent—and people would be healthier by doing more walking. Also they were using up fossil fuels that couldn't be replaced. However, the opposition—Aidan, Gavan and Patrick— were far more confident. In responding they played to the gallery by asking how people would like it if their parents couldn't own cars. Everyone would have to get dirty buses and trains everywhere and how could people stay on at school late for debates and sport? Margaret noticed who went mostly with the opposition again, cheering when the third opposition speaker, Aidan, said: 'we need cars, because they tell people we have worked hard and been successful'. She made a mental note of that sentence, and of the fact that the environmental arguments didn't come first with some. Then, halfway through the last opposition speech a hand shot up.

'Yes, Paschal?' said Mrs Walsh, after asking the speaker to pause.

'Suppose you had an accident or got ill at home and had to get to hospital quick—before an ambulance could come. You might die if you had no car. Do you want people to die?'

The speaker seemed baffled for a minute, and looked around at her team. Then she thought of something.

'As we said, cars cause accidents and deaths too—maybe more than they save people.'

'That wouldn't do *you* any good!' Gavan Maguire shot back.

'Now Gavan—remember!' said Mrs Walsh. 'It's not your turn to speak. Finuala gave a good answer, and can carry on.'

She did too, when she had found her place, but she had been put off, Margaret thought. Meanwhile Patrick Andrews was patting Gavan on the back for all to see, a compliment he was receiving with satisfaction.

The opposition won the vote by a wide margin. Mrs Walsh then gave her own evaluation, complimenting the proposition on sticking to their guns. She gave marks for content and presentation for each speaker, and declared the debate a draw.

'A great start, from which you should all learn something. It's not at all easy to stand up here and speak to an unruly crowd for the first time, so give both teams a big round of applause!'

As she applauded Margaret could see that the three proposing speakers were all greatly relieved to have the ordeal over, while Aidan, Gavan and Patrick were celebrating. Her own stomach was already in a knot, and she still had eight weeks to wait. On the other hand she felt sure she could speak as well as the girls had done that day, and that Mrs Walsh wouldn't mind her team having their own ideas.

She was thinking that in her own class, in which people like Arona and Gavan and Aidan were confident and influential, most would probably go with the proposition in four weeks time. It might be the easier argument to make then too.

'Just wait!' said Eddy to her as they left.

Gavan went over to Johnny as they were leaving. She heard him say: 'That's the way to do it Mullan: listen and learn!' Johnny's face was a mask.

Then Conor Maguire went over to Johnny too—and whispered something Margaret couldn't hear. Johnny looked up at him quickly, and then made his face blank again, turning away.

'Hi dudes, what can I do for you?'

The person who asked this of Johnny and Eddy at the staffroom door after lunch on Thursday was about thirty-five, tanned and wearing a smart grey suit with a yellow tie. He spoke with an American accent. They had seen him about occasionally, but they knew that only seniors studied political science, so they had not been able to put a name to him until now. He was Mr Wesley, head of that subject.

'*Give to Caesar what is Caesar and to God's what is God's*—can you tell us what does your subject say about that?' Johnny had made this question as short as he could, practising saying it, so that he would not get confused.

Mr Wesley's eyes widened. 'Well, I—hold on a moment!' He stepped forward into the corridor, closing the door as they stood aside.

'Who am I talking to?' His eyes were still intent. When they had given their names he looked at his watch, said 'just ten minutes' then 'let's see here', and walked them back along the corridor to the interview room nearby. He peered through the glass, and then opened the door. 'In you go.'

'Now,' he said when they were seated, 'what makes you ask this question?'

'We're just interested, Sir—in what happened when the church and the state came together and Christians started overpowering people. We think maybe Jesus didn't want that.'

Again Mr Wesley seemed surprised, and didn't answer straight away. Eventually he said:

'That last question I can't speak to, not in my role as a political science teacher. Let's go back to the first question. Those who study the history of the relationship between church and state often say that, in speaking of giving different things to God and Caesar, Jesus was the first person of note to suggest that church and state could be separate and independent, as they tend to be in most western countries now.

'But of course,' he went on 'that is controversial—do you know what I mean by that?'

'Yes, Sir,' said Eddy, 'people argue about it. Do Catholics argue about it?'

'As it happens I am not a Catholic, Eddy, but I feel safe in saying that yes, they do argue about it—about whether church and state *should* be separate, and whether Jesus wanted that. Let's see—your Religion or History teachers, they would be better placed to comment on that too. But don't say I sent you, OK?'

They nodded and he rose, but Johnny was curious, and thought he could take another risk before he said goodbye.

'Can I ask you sir, if you're not a Catholic, are you a Christian?'

'Oh yes, Johnny' said Mr Wesley, closing the door to the interview room as they stepped outside. 'I'm a Mennonite. I'm here in exchange for your Mr Lennon, who's taking my place in my own school in Kansas, USA. I don't have time to tell you more now about my own tradition. You could look it up, and then, if you like, you can ask me about anything you don't understand—OK.'

'OK, Sir. Thanks, sir. Good bye.'

Mr Wesley turned to go, but then thought of something..

'If Mr Lennon was here he might be wanting you two to think about studying political science later, so I should say that to you myself. Do you hear?'

'Yes, Sir—I might do that, Sir,' said Eddy, as Mr Wesley turned to head back to the staffroom.

'So maybe we *can* believe that Jesus never wanted people to overpower or execute anybody.' Johnny turned to Eddy as they were heading for their next class—Information Science.

'*I* can believe it anyway,' said Eddy. '*You* might get into trouble for saying it.'

Johnny nodded. His mind was on all they had to tell Margaret and Mary on Saturday. And on who the Mennonites might be.

'Yes, Margaret. That word materialism does turn up in the Catholic Catechism, twice—but *only* as a way of thinking. There isn't ever a mention of a sin of materialism as such—and that's curious.'

Margaret had been called out of library class into the otherwise empty corridor by Miss Doherty during last period on that same day, Thursday. Her teacher went on:

'So it doesn't seem that a belief in the evils of materialism is actually required of us either, Margaret. It's not a dogma, a fixed teaching of the church'.

Relieved to hear this, Margaret thanked her teacher.

'What about coveting, Miss?'

'The catechism now uses a different word—'avarice'—instead of 'covetousness'. I used the word covetousness that day in class because it's the word I was taught when I was your age. But 'avarice' doesn't mean what you call copy-wanting—it means being greedy—not being able to stop hoarding money for example. Misers are avaricious, but we *all* copy-want—we all come to think we need something when we see someone else with it.'

She paused then and put her hand on Margaret's shoulder.

'Margaret, as far as I can tell, the Catechism doesn't have *any* word for what you call copy-wanting. It doesn't see it as a problem at all—and I'm puzzled about that. It doesn't seem to see that our desires can often begin when we see other people with something new.

That happens far more often nowadays—with so many people everywhere trying to make a fortune by making something different.

'That's where envy and jealousy begin too,' she went on 'if we just can't *get* what they have—and those *are* sins. And the worst things can happen then—feuds, wars and so on. Could the commandments be warning us of where those sins begin—with … copy-wanting?'

'Do *you* think copy-wanting is a sin then, Miss?'

'To commit a serious sin you must know you are doing that, so the beginning of copy-wanting cannot be wrong. It happens *before* you notice—but if you then settle into *yearning* for something you don't need—and if you ignore the needs of others, or fall out with someone, to get it—yes, *that* must be wrong. And we need to be aware all that can easily happen, don't we?'

'Yes, Miss. That's why we're speaking against that materialism motion—we mightn't ever get another chance to speak about this.

'Yes, I see that—and good for you too. That word 'materialism' doesn't account for people falling out with one another over, say, a job they are both in for, so you can certainly make a good argument.

Are you getting help from some seniors with your speeches?'

When Margaret spoke of Patricia Brolly's involvement her teacher told her she couldn't have made a better choice.

'Tell the others I'll be interested to see what happens, won't you?'

'Yes, Miss, thank you Miss—for looking all that up for us.'

'Right, then. Off we both go.'

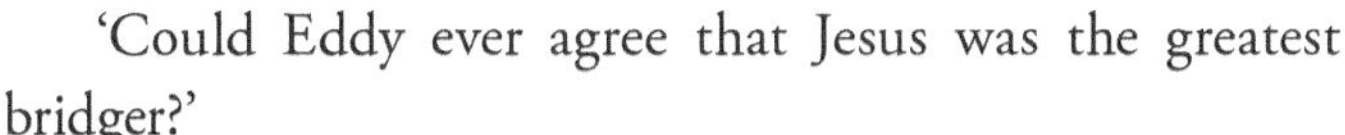

'Could Eddy ever agree that Jesus was the greatest bridger?'

Mary was asking this question of Margaret on the bus home that same day. She had been greatly encouraged by what Margaret had told her in the corridor of her chat with Miss Doherty, and was looking forward to meeting up with the boys the following day in Eddy's home in Glendermott—to hear what they had discovered.

'I've been thinking about that, Mary. You know how Miss Doherty always talks about Abba—Jesus' dad?'

Mary nodded.

'Well he's God the father too isn't he—the one who made everything in the beginning?'

'Yes.'

'Well isn't he the *source* then too—the start of everything?'

'Yes, I suppose—but he often got angry—those stories of the flood that killed everyone but Noah and his family, and the angel that killed the first sons of the Egyptians. Can those stories be true?'

'But didn't Miss Doherty say that Jesus is the final revealing of who Abba is—that when we think of Jesus we shouldn't think that Abba is different?'

'Yes, she did say that!'

'So if Abba, the one who made everything, is like Jesus, might Eddy see Jesus as a bridge to the source also—the mystery of the Tao?'

Mary considered for a moment.

'Should we ask Miss Doherty if we can think of Abba as a mysterious source?'

'We could—but it can't be me who does that this time. She has taken enough time with my questions. She needs a rest!'

'Mmm,' said Mary. 'We don't need to be in a hurry anyway.'

'Your Da's trying to stop drinking.' Anny was talking to Johnny on Friday evening in his room. His Da had gone out of the house—Johnny wasn't sure where.

'It's called recovery, because he's got an illness. It'll be tough for him, and he may be cranky. We'll have to put up with it. OK?'

Johnny had noticed a change in Kevy's way of talking to him since that day they had made the plywood box. His Da wasn't referring to him being a professor or a dictionary, or saying that he was 'too good for us now'.

And Kevy didn't talk any more about Iona College being a snobby school either. Johnny wondered if this was because he knew that Gavan Maguire was in his class.

'Your Da likes your friends—especially Margaret,' Anny continued. 'I think he expected her to be looking down her nose at him. But she didn't, and Eddy and his Da, and Mary, were the same. And Mrs Phillips too. He has never shown that carving before to anyone but me.

'And he said that Margaret wasn't just putting on a show. She was interested in the carving. He said she was sincere, and showed respect.

'So he has changed his mind about Iona, and about you being there. When he heard that Gavan was in your class he got a shock.

It brought everything back to him. I think he realises you will soon be the same age as he was when all that happened—and that you have your own battles to fight.

'Really he's proud of you now, Johnny, and he wants to help. He's seeing this man, Vincent, who's in AA—he's with him right now.

It's a self-help organisation for ... alcoholics. That's what he's got.

He admits it now, and I'm glad. He hasn't had a drink for a few days, and he's finding it tough. So put up with him, OK?'

Johnny nodded. He had noticed his Da looking pale and tired that week. He seemed to get irritated over small things—like when he couldn't find things in the kitchen, or the TV remote.

Johnny was still appreciating his new bookshelves—and the trouble his Da had taken to make them look better than anything he could have bought. Johnny had watched part of the making of them, even helped at times.

At first Johnny had thought Kevy should have said 'clamp' instead of 'cramp', when he had come to glue the finished shelves together.

Luckily Johnny had held his tongue, as 'cramp' turned out to be the right word when he had looked it up. Cramps were used to pull the sides and the shelves together, and hold them tightly overnight, while the glue set.

He had enjoyed what work on the shelves he himself had been able to help with. His Da had poked fun at him at times, but it hadn't made him feel bad as it did usually, because there had been no bitterness behind it. It had been the longest time he had spent with his father in a long while.

Kevy wasn't 'just' a joiner. He was a craftsman, and joiners' work was skilled and pleasant work. Wasn't he an artist also, for making that carving?

Suddenly Johnny realised that he should feel proud of his Da, for what he had put up with, and for what he could do. He thought he himself could put up with any grouchiness now, however bad it might get.

He could put out of his head what Conor Maguire had said on Wednesday in the lecture theatre: 'Iona is no place for touts, Mullan—you'll learn that soon enough'. He had memorised what Mick had told him five weeks earlier:

'nothing can destroy or harm the deepest part of you—the part that wants to be a bridger. No threat, no insult, no jeer can make nothing of your real self'.

—ooo◦❦◦ooo—

'First, about eighty-eight years before Jesus came, this man, Marius, wanted to be the first man in Rome. So did this man, Sulla, so war came to Rome—and Sulla won.'

Mary and her friends were in Eddy's house in Glendermott.

Johnny was turning over pages on the table, as Eddy had done in Margaret's house the previous week. Eddy had brought the pictures.

'Then about forty years later this man Pompey, and this man, Julius Caesar both wanted to be the first man in Rome—and war came again. Pompey was killed and Caesar soon became dictator of Rome.

'This man Brutus joined a plot against Caesar and he was murdered forty-four years before Jesus—and war came again to Rome. When the plotters were all dead, Caesar's nephew Octavian fought with Mark Anthony to be first man in Rome. Octavian won and became Augustus Caesar, the first Roman emperor.'

Johnny turned to Mary then. It seemed to her that he was asking if she had understood, so she nodded.

'Then Jesus was born in Palestine, in the time of Augustus, when Rome controlled that country. His followers came to believe he was the Messiah, the great leader promised by the Jewish holy books—and they let non-Jews join them. They called themselves Christians— and they spread that faith throughout the empire.

'About three hundred years later, around 312 in the Christian era, when there were a lot of Christians in Rome, this man, Constantine, and this man, Maxentius, both wanted to be first man in Rome.

Constantine killed Maxentius at the battle of the Milvian bridge, and became emperor. Here is a picture of that battle.

'But then a story was spread that before the battle Constantine had seen a Christian cross in the sky and beside it, in Latin, the words *In this sign you will conquer*. You can just make out this cross in the painting.'

'I just *don't* believe that!,' Margaret broke in indignantly. 'I *can't*.'

Mary, sitting opposite, was just as sure. 'Neither can I!'

'That painting is in the Vatican,' Johnny said.

Mary looked at Margaret in dismay. Margaret shook her head in disbelief.

Johnny went on: 'This story about the cross in the sky helped to bring Romans who were Christians onto the side of Constantine after the battle. Constantine then made it legal for Christians to practise their religion throughout the empire. From then on most Roman Emperors called themselves Christians, and the bishops of the church became closely connected to government, to the state.

'They seem to have believed the story of the cross in the sky.'

'Jesus stopped Peter from starting a war with the Romans,' Margaret insisted. 'That's why he was crucified. Why would he or Abba ever want anyone to see the cross as a sign of conquering?'

'That source also says that, before an earlier battle, Constantine had said he had seen a vision of Mars, the Roman God of war,' answered Johnny.

'That *proves* it,' Margaret insisted. 'Constantine couldn't tell the difference between Jesus and Mars. He made things up. He must have made that up about the cross to get the support of the bishops.' Mary agreed: 'Why did the bishops want to believe that anyway?'

'The encyclopedia says they probably wanted the protection of the Emperor—to put a stop to the persecution of Christians that had sometimes happened under earlier Emperors. From then on the Christian church had the government on its side most of the time, and it was the pagans, those who wouldn't convert, who sometimes got persecuted.'

'Do you two believe that Constantine saw that—*'In this sign you will conquer'*—beside the cross in the sky?' Margaret asked.

Johnny and Eddy shook their heads.

'I think that if Constantine told that story he made it up too,' said Eddy. 'Or else he was off his head before a battle—from worrying about it.'

Mary wanted to make sure of something: 'And that was the start of Christians fighting wars—is that what Mr Foley said?'

'Yes, and that's what the encyclopedia says too.'

Silence fell at that point in the room—a room set aside for study and contemplation in Eddy's home. It was plainly decorated, apart from three rectangular paintings of flowers on the white-painted wall facing the large south-facing window. In the centre of the table sat a square wooden block, and on every side of it appeared a symbol that Johnny had never seen before. It looked like two tadpoles facing one another in a circle, head to tail—one white with a black eye and one black with a white eye. Eddy had explained what these represented—Yin and Yang—opposites that somehow fitted together, such as light and darkness, or male and female, or life and death. There was no technology in the room, apart from some electric wall lights—turned off now because the window was large and was letting in enough light that October morning. At either end of the room stood two bookcases made of light-coloured wood, the same as the table. Each bookcase was divided into three sets of shelves.

Mary was feeling tense. There was something she wanted to know, but didn't quite know how to ask. So she did something that was now coming more easily to her—calming her mind, asking and waiting. A question formed, but first she had to explain why she wanted to ask it.

'My song came from that question in the *Tao Te Ching*—'why do we want what others want?' Whoever wrote that question—I'm going to call him *Lao Tsu* from now on—loved the Tao, the source of everything. And Jesus loved Abba, and taught us to love one another. Margaret and I have been thinking about this, and I am still thinking it after hearing about Constantine. The bishops didn't see that Constantine and Maxentius just wanted the same thing—to be emperor—so they couldn't see where their warring came from either. So could Abba and the Tao be the same person? Could all that warring that Christians did after Constantine have been the fault of the bishops, not of Jesus or Abba?'

There was silence. Johnny and Eddy looked at one another and hesitated, so Mary went on:

'Jesus to me is as strange as the Tao. He faced the Romans and Herod completely alone, without a friend—because he thought people were being misled and treated unjustly. And he forgave, too.

How could he have done that if he didn't have a friend in his heart, in Abba? And Jesus said that he and Abba were the same. So, mustn't Abba be the source of peace as well—the same peace there is in *this* house? And didn't Jesus escape from that biggest prison too - the prison made by fear of what others think?'

The silence that followed was broken eventually by Eddy.

'If Jesus wanted peace and nothing else, I could see him as a great teacher of the Tao, as a bridge to the Tao.'

At that Mary sensed the beginning of the ending of her tension.

'So could he not also be the greatest bridger, the one who can make a bridge between us four, and maybe everyone else too, if they can learn to see him as faithful always to the source of all peace—the one who didn't want anything but that, and who was ready to suffer with the poor to bring that about?'

There was silence again then, broken by the same voice.

'Maybe,' said Eddy, 'but are you—you Catholics—allowed to believe that?'

'We don't know,' said Margaret. 'But I want to find out.'

At that moment there was a knock on the door. Mr Li put his head in.

'If you are ready, you are all welcome in the kitchen.'

So in they went to where Eddy's Mum was waiting, smiling—and his younger brother and sister. On the table there were carrot sticks standing in clear glasses—and other drinking glasses filled with what looked to Mary like milk with water in it. The kitchen too had wall cupboards in threes, and bright red lanterns covering the light bulbs.

'Can we bless the food before we eat?' asked Mrs Li. When they nodded she said: 'We bless these gifts and the Source of all good things, and think of those who have nothing.' Without thinking, Mary had blessed herself also, and then wondered if anyone had noticed. She was soon reassured.

'That's rice milk,' said Eddy then, as they sat. 'And those are rice cakes. Try some with honey.'

So they did, enjoying the meal. To finish they had cooked pears in pear juice, with some plain yogurt.

'Do you like?' asked Mrs Li of Mary as she finished the pears.

'Mmm,' she said, nodding. 'Thank you—for the trouble you took.'

'No trouble, no trouble—is your talking making something?'

'Mmm. A lot. I love your home too. *And* the Tao.' That had come out without Mary thinking. She felt her face redden again then, as she realised what she had said. 'Eddy will explain,' she went on—because Mrs Li's kind face was asking the question.

'OK, Mary,' said Mrs Li. 'Make sure to come again— and all of you!' She turned to Margaret and Johnny.

'We will, thanks,' they agreed.

All helped then to tidy away, as Eddy was obviously expected to—but Mary's mind was racing ahead. Another line for her song was in her head, and as soon as they were seated again in the quiet room she came out with it.

'Jesus *didn't* want what Constantine wanted. That's coming to me in the song too.' She sang it then: *'He didn't copy anyone, or want what Caesars wanted.* I don't know what the rhyme could be yet—something to do with not being afraid, I hope.'

'Some teachers might not like you singing that,' said Johnny.

'Why not?' Margaret inquired.

Johnny explained then what both Mr Foley and Mr Li had warned against.

'They are both saying the same thing: not to come out with "Mr Foley says this", or "Mr Wesley says that". And then there's what Mr Foley said about us maybe causing an explosion—and what Mr Wesley says about some Catholics believing the church and the state should be together, and others saying no.'

Johnny paused, but soon went on: 'Eddy and I—we think our teachers may not all agree on things like that. Maybe they even argue about them—in the staffroom.'

As Eddy nodded, Mary's head had a question: 'How could we find out?'

'Best not to be asking *those* teachers anyway,' said Margaret. 'Miss Doherty needs a rest from me, and Mr Foley needs a rest from you two.' She looked at Eddy and Johnny. 'But I could ask my Mum.

She has a friend at work who knows Dr McGinnis. Maybe she knows other people who know things.'

'She'll maybe want to know why you are asking,' said Eddy. 'Have you told her yet what we'll be saying in the debate, and what it's about?'

'No,' said Margaret. 'I'm waiting to hear what Patricia Brolly will say about our speeches. She said she would maybe have word on Monday.'

That excited Mary greatly, and her head was racing to find another rhyme for *wanted*. Something within her was saying: 'You *will* sing that line, you *will*.'

'Is that OK, then,' asked Margaret. 'I'll ask my Mum, and if she wants to know why I'm asking I'll tell her we tried to find out why Christians started fighting, and some of our teachers gave us those hints—and Johnny and Eddy found out all that about Constantine and the cross in the sky, and what the bishops decided back then. I won't say who those teachers were, and I'll ask her to find out what she can.'

All readily agreed—and soon it was time to say goodbye to Mrs Li and Eddy, and to go with Margaret and Johnny with Mr Li to Margaret's, where Mary's Dad would be waiting.

She sat close to Johnny in the back of the car. She looked to catch his eye for a last time as she headed towards her Dad—and gave a wave. He seemed to be waiting for that, and waved back. That made her happy—almost as happy as she had felt that time in his own home when he had hugged her last, and thanked her for the song.

But then Margaret said to Johnny, just before he got in the car:

'Don't forget Mary will be singing at those auditions on Tuesday,' and Johnny turned and said 'I won't' and gave another wave. Mary waved back and hoped he could be there in the assembly hall for that, to give her support. Then her head turned again to finding rhymes.

XIII

'These have got me going!' said Patricia Brolly to Margaret at lunchtime the following Monday. The senior debater whom Margaret greatly admired was holding the pages that held the three bridgers' debating speeches. Patricia had met Margaret as she left the canteen, and the two had then sat on a bench on the corridor nearby, as the day was cold and wet.

'Do you mean they're no good?' Margaret asked anxiously.

'Oh, don't worry, it's not that! I'm impressed. You'll need to change some things, but I can see exactly how you'll be arguing against the motion. There are some things the proposition will probably say that you haven't thought of, and you need to leave more time to answer things that you can't predict. *And* you need to think about who will go first, and so on—but we can sort all that out later.'

Patricia paused then in a distracted way, as though she was trying to think about two things at once.

'Oh, by the way, Mrs Walsh is going to let you three Eight Bs out of English class on Wednesday next. There are two of us free that period after lunch. My friend Liz Wallace does Religion at senior level and she can tell you a few things to look out for. Mrs Walsh said to book one of the interview rooms off the front hall for the five of us. Is that OK?'

Margaret nodded excitedly. She remembered Mrs Walsh had talked about letting people out of class for coaching for the debates, so long as they made up whatever they missed in their own time.

'Good. No—the thing is that I'm doing English at senior level. I'm doing this essay on Shakespeare, comparing three plays. We have to look at something Shakespeare calls envy—the feeling one person has against another person because that second person has something they can't have. They can sometimes hate so badly they are ready even to kill, or betray, do you follow?'

Margaret nodded.

'Well one of those plays is *Julius Caesar.*'

'Oh!' said Margaret.

'Yes. Now your word 'copy-wanting' is used by Johnny when he talks about Julius Caesar wanting all the fame that Alexander had. I can see what you mean by copy-wanting— and I think it's connected to envy. When you copy-want something only one person can have, you envy the person who has got it, because they stop you from having it. Do you see?'

Margaret nodded.

'And you talk about copy-wanting being a kind of virus, something you can catch from someone else, right?'

Margaret nodded again.

'Well, listen. I think Shakespeare is saying that at least some of the plotters copy-wanted what Caesar had—for example, Cassius. And they couldn't get it without killing him. Do you see?

'Oops, I must go … but I think you're right about copy-wanting being a kind of virus! And I'm going to use that in my essay. I didn't know that about Caesar and Alexander, or maybe I had forgotten, but it's useful.

'And since Shakespeare wrote about the same thing in different plays, it's as though he's studying a virus by collecting examples of it. I'm going to say that too! That's why I'm in a bit of a dither. I'm sort of writing the essay in my head. I was even wondering if copy- wanting wasn't a good way of explaining envy, because it's so simple. It says exactly what is going on.'

Patricia paused then and smiled at Margaret.

'I didn't expect your speeches to get me thinking so much, do you see?'

Margaret nodded. She thought of something then.

'There's a source about Julius Caesar and Alexander in our history book. I could bring it on Wednesday.

'Could you? That would be great, thanks.' Patricia rose from the bench then.

'I've copied these speeches for Liz to read, so she can advise you—and you can have them back now. OK?'

Margaret nodded, took the pages and got up. She knew that what Patricia had told her about Shakespeare was important, but wasn't sure why.

'Bye then,' said Patricia with a smile. 'Until Wednesday.'

'*Project* yourselves!' said Keeva Trenney, the TV producer on Tuesday morning.

Dark, slim, dressed in a white shirt and black jeans and holding a clip-board, she was speaking from the brightly lit stage of the assembly hall at Iona College to about twenty hopeful pupils seated halfway down the darkened hall. Mary had found herself sitting beside Eileen Daly and Arona Gilsenan, whose eyes were riveted on the stage. To Mary's disappointment only those auditioning had been allowed out of class.

'Remember that the finals will be a TV event, with millions watching. To win and hold the attention of so many you will need to believe in what you are doing—that you can reach and hold those viewers. This could well be the most important showcase you will ever get.

'We need to capture the best of you on video.' She pointed to where two video cameras were positioned in the hall to right and left. 'These tapes will then be compared with all the others from the other schools. Just forty people will be called to a further elimination audition in January in London. The ten finalists will be selected then by well known celebrities.

'You'll be called in alphabetical order. Come up promptly. You're allowed to perform two items only. Introduce them yourselves, speaking into the mike and making sure to be clear. Look straight out as though there was a full audience here. Any questions?'

Five seconds of silence followed. Mary was too nervous to even think of a question.

'Right then! Imelda Brophy please.' Keeva then descended to sit on a chair placed centrally—just in front of where Mary was sitting Mary knew that Arona would be called before her. She began to wonder if she hadn't made a bad mistake in entering. Imelda's voice seemed far better trained than her own—even if she also seemed a bit overcome by the experience. She was backed by the musicians the producer had brought with her, placed just below the stage.

'Great, thanks Imelda. Eileen Daly!'

Eileen played some of her best piano pieces then, to applause from the keyboard player in the band. Soon it was Arona's turn. She performed *River Deep and Mountain High*, followed by *The Power of Love*. Her voice filled the hall. Mary could see that the musicians were impressed. They looked at one another as she hit the high notes, and one raised his eyebrows at the end. Again Arona bowed dramatically when she had finished.

'Wow!' said Keeva Trenney, seated immediately in front of the stage. 'We've certainly got a contender here!'

Three performers later it was Mary's turn. She had a tension headache and had never felt less inclined to project herself. As she climbed to the stage one of the musicians placed a stool and adjusted the microphone as she sat. Mary had decided to ask for no accompaniment as her music was all her own, and she couldn't yet write a score for other musicians. Quite terrified, and aware of Arona in the second row, she was barely able to remember to ask for the power of the bridge before she began.

'This is a song called *The Dark Switch*. It's about how I felt when I realised how many problems there are in the world.'

As soon as she had said this Mary suddenly lost her fearful awareness of where she was, and forgot Arona too. She felt as she had when she was writing the song about five months earlier, in her own room at home. At the same time she felt as though her own friends were there listening. She sang to them, knowing they at least would understand.

Keeva Trenney nodded approvingly and made a note, waiting for her second song.

'This is my latest song. It's about a big problem for young people today—our habit of wanting to copy others in what they own and wear and do. It's called *The Chain that Binds the World.*'

Mary knew that she had to sing this in a totally different style and mood, using the best of the riffs that she had practised. This time she felt as she had done when singing the song for the first time in Johnny's room, with the others singing along. She finished without using the line '*Will someone come to break this chain …*'

For a moment there was silence. Then she heard the drummer in the band below tap the rim of his drum four times.

'Singer/songwriter, Mary—both songs *genuinely* your own?' Keeva sounded surprised.

'I got the idea for copy-wanting from my friends, but wrote the words and music myself.

'That second song—I'm not sure how to describe it—protest song maybe?'

'Maybe …' said Mary after a pause. She hadn't expected the question.

'Both songs unusual, and different from one another. Versatility. You and Arona are in the same class too. Are you friends?'

Mary hesitated a moment.

'I suppose,' she said.

'Rivals, maybe?'

Mary was stumped by that and just shrugged. When Keeva turned to look at Arona she tossed her hair in a manner that said she didn't see Mary as competition. Keeva smiled and made a note on her clipboard.

'Right, Mary. Sean Quigley.'

Mary sat through the rest of the performances in a daze. She knew the audition had gone as well as she could have hoped. At least she hadn't let herself down.

'Dark switches and—what?—*copy*-wanting?' said Arona scornfully as they left the hall for lunch. 'Whatever next? Purple flying elephants?'

'Yes, Margaret—there are indeed deep divisions in our church.'

Margaret's Mum was regarding her thoughtfully at dinner time that same day. 'Some people think the church needs to update itself, to find a way of making our faith meaningful to twenty-first century people. Others say definitely not—we have to hold on to tradition. They mean the past. But what part of that past do they mean? Mostly they seem to mean the way the church was in the 1950s, just before the second Vatican Council in the early 1960s.'

Mrs Phillips paused then, to go to the salad bowl.

'I've heard Miss Doherty talk about Vatican II—is that the same?'

'Yes,' said her Mum. 'Pope John XXIII—now on the way to being made a saint—wanted to update the church. So he called all of the bishops together in 1962. "We're

tending a garden", he said, "not looking after a museum."
And many Catholics wanted to go with that idea. Others
were afraid that what was central to the faith could be
lost. When in 1968 Pope Paul VI repeated the teaching
that using contraceptives to plan families was wrong for
married people, most Catholics thought he had made a
mistake because they had expected updating on that as
well. The church split. The media talk about liberals and
conservatives—those who want to go forward and those
who want to go back—but it's not as simple as that.'

'Why not?' Margaret asked.

'Because, for example, for about the first thousand years
priests were allowed to marry. The conservatives don't want
to go back *that* far. The liberals mostly do—so it could
be argued that they are even more traditional than the
conservatives. Another thing—until the three hundreds
Christian bishops were generally expected to eat with the
poor every day, but that stopped about then. Many people
they call liberals would like to see that coming back too—
so aren't they traditional in that way also? Conservatives
generally want bishops to be ... up there,' she waved to the
ceiling ' you know—on thrones near the altar and dressed
in magnificent robes. That wasn't the way Jesus dressed, so
why do they call that traditional?'

Her Mum was getting indignant, Margaret could see—
and she had a question.

'When bishops stopped eating with the poor every day.
Would that have been about when Constantine became
emperor?'

'Yes, Margaret.' She sounded surprised. 'What do you
know about that?

So Margaret told her most of what Johnny and Eddy had discovered, without using their word copy-wanting.

'Are Catholics divided over Constantine too, Mum?'

'I should say so! Many are wondering if the bishops should ever have praised him the way they did—or if it was ever a good idea for popes and bishops to be close to emperors, kings and nobles—and even living like them. The reformers, the people who want change, say all that was a bad idea. The so-called traditionalists, or conservatives, often say the church has been going to pot ever since it lost all power over the state. That question too was debated at Vatican II, with the reformers winning in the end. The council passed what was maybe the most important of all the documents—the declaration on religious freedom.'

Margaret's ears pricked up at that. 'What did it say?'

'That the truth can never be imposed, forced, on anyone. As a loving truth, it can only be received, I mean taken hold of, if we become freely convinced of it. I'll find you the passage later. Here, time for dessert.'

As they finished the meal Margaret was excited. *There was a church teaching that everyone must make up their own mind!* She decided then and there that she was a reformer—but that she wanted to recover the copy-wanting meaning of *covet* also. So she was traditional too.

'Maybe one division in the church is between Constantinian Catholics and non-Constantinian Catholics.' Her mother broke in on her thoughts as they were finishing. 'That whole period, from about 300 to about 1600, is called Christendom—when rulers and bishops were in charge of everything together. Why would anyone want to go back to that? And we haven't even got started on how women are still being treated in the church! Fat chance of *you* ever being a bishop!'

Margaret was interested in that too, but riveted just now on something else.

'Mum, what do our teachers think—are they divided too, do you know? Might your friend in the university—the one who knows Dr McGinnis—might she know?'

Her Mum put down her coffee cup. 'I don't know myself. I could ask Naomi, as you suggest. She might—or know of someone who does. Why do you ask?'

'We've got this debate coming up, and we're not sure what some of our teachers will think about what we want to say—especially Dr McGinnis, who will be judging. Would you like to read my speech, the first draft?'

'Very much,' said Mrs Phillips. 'Go get it, dear, while I find you that passage from the Vatican II document on religious freedom.'

'Hi there,' said the senior boy with glasses, 'would you mind if I sat in? I'm free too this period. Liz and Patricia have told me what you're up to and I'm interested.'

Johnny had just arrived at the unglazed door of an interview room near the Iona principal's office—one he hadn't been in before. For a moment he couldn't think of this senior's name, but then it came to him—Peter Cullen, the debater who had made the opening speech in favour of banning advertising to children in the second week of term. Now he was waiting with Patricia Brolly and another senior girl whom Johnny supposed to be the Liz Wallace that Margaret had mentioned.

Johnny turned to Margaret and Eddy, who had arrived with him.

'I don't mind if you don't,' he said. Neither hesitated. 'OK, then,' said Peter, opening the door and ushering them all in.

A suitable plain table faced them. A landscape painting sat on each wall, and a large potted plant in one corner—and there were chairs enough for six people. Patricia Brolly took the centre chair at one side, with the other seniors to either side of her. Johnny took some file paper from his bag and sat opposite Patricia, with Margaret facing Peter and Eddy facing Liz.

'We've less than forty minutes now,' said Patricia. 'So quick intros first. Names only to save time.' That was soon done.

'Liz had better begin by talking about the debate,' Patricia went on, turning to her.

'I was impressed by these speeches,' Liz began. 'They've got me thinking again about materialism, I must say. First though, there are a few things you need to look out for.' Liz waited while Johnny's team readied themselves to make notes.

'For example, the proposition may well talk about the problem of world poverty. They could say that materialism in the rich world prevents people from being generous to the poor. People who spend a lot of money on luxury cars or bigger houses will donate less than they could to charities—do you see?'

The bridgers nodded, and Margaret took note.

'They will also probably argue that materialism stops people from being spiritual, or religious—and that this is the root of all problems—including the ones you mention. Another senior, Phil Forde, is advising the proposition, and she does Religion too. She's sharp. You'll need to look out for that.'

Johnny nodded, and was glad to see Eddy writing. He himself wanted to concentrate rather than write, so that he would miss nothing.

'But I was thinking about all that, and there's something you could maybe use. What people in the world buy most?'

The bridgers looked at one another.

'Americans?' asked Johnny.

'Right. The wealthier people of the USA, to be more precise. Now, what country in the richest part of the world has also the highest proportion of church-going people?'

'The USA again?' said Margaret.

'Right again! There's a puzzle there. If Americans are so religious, why are they also collecting all that stuff? Can you be materialistic and religious at the same time?'

The bridgers nodded as Liz went on:

'You should see if you can get some figures for all that. I could help, of course, but you need practice in digging out your own facts. If you get stuck, come back to me. OK?'

'Thanks,' said Margaret. 'We appreciate that.'

'But if you do all that, you can make a good case, I think. I wouldn't have taken this motion on myself! I think you're brave.'

'There's something else,' said Patricia Brolly. 'These speeches are all about the same length, but the first and last speakers for the opposition have different jobs to do. As the debate goes on, more time is taken up with rebuttal—with responding to what has been said before—and there is less time to present new information. Mrs Walsh has told us that she hasn't been stressing this too much as you're all beginners, but you could score points if you would spend more time on rebuttal. Your last speaker should rebut the opposition's last speaker, and tackle any other point that hasn't been answered. Who will that last speaker be?'

The bridgers looked at one another, shaking their heads.

'We don't know—we haven't decided.'

'Who thinks and answers quickest?'

'Johnny,' said Margaret.

Eddy nodded.

'Could you do it, Johnny?' asked Patricia.

Johnny knew it was a big responsibility, but he could see that neither of his friends wanted it. If he took notes on the day, and had answers thought out beforehand to likely questions, could he do it? He asked and waited.

'OK,' he said. 'I'll try.'

'Great!' said Margaret.

'Right. Now, which of you other two could outline best what your main argument is going to be—the best case you want to make against the motion? That person would have most time to get in the points you want to make.'

'Margaret,' said Eddy. 'She has thought more about copy- wanting and the environment.'

'OK, Margaret?' Patricia asked.

'Right,' she said.

'That's it then,' said Patricia. 'Margaret, Eddy, Johnny— that's your speaking order.'

'One last thing. You should all know what the others on your team are going to say, so you don't get in one another's way. That's most important for Johnny—he can make sure that all the main points have been made, just in case one of you others has to leave something out.'

The three nodded again.

'How did you three think up the word copy-wanting anyway?' asked Liz then, leaning back.

Again Margaret explained briefly about Aidan Maroney's computer, and her experiences in the shopping centre—and other examples she had seen since.

'But how did you notice that war and crime had to do with copy- wanting too?'

'I saw this source in our History book,' said Johnny. 'Margaret has brought hers to show you.'

Margaret meanwhile had been finding the page and now passed it over. The two seniors read through Plutarch's account of Julius Caesar weeping over the statue of Alexander. They looked at one another then, and nodded.

'Eddy's just mad about crime,' said Johnny. 'He notices things—like those American boys who thought Hitler was great and shot people in their school.'

'But I'm studying religion, and no-one has ever pointed all that out,' Liz went on. 'I'm stumped by that. Why doesn't the bible ever talk about copy-wanting if it's so important?'

'We think it does,' said Margaret. 'We think that's what coveting is, in older lists of the Ten Commandments.'

Patricia and Liz looked at one another. 'That's new to me too, Liz,' said Patricia.

'They say you're not to covet anything your neighbour has,' said Johnny. 'And you mostly will want something that's better than anything you have yourself—and every time the word coveting is used, a neighbour is mentioned also.'

'*Anything.* That doesn't have to be just an ... object or an animal, does it?' said Liz, looking at Patricia.

'No—it could be the power or fame someone has,' said Patricia.

'That's one more idea for that essay of mine!' She looked for her bag.

'Look at those stories in the Bible too,' said Margaret. 'Joseph and the dream coat—the two women fighting over the baby.'

The seniors quizzed her further on that then, Patricia taking notes.

'But why did you decide that, about copy-wanting being coveting?' asked Liz. Patricia nodded, indicating she wanted to understand that too.

'It was a coincidence, I suppose' said Margaret finally. 'I could see copy-wanting was a big problem, so I thought it might even be a sin.'

'And when Margaret looked up covet it said yearning to have what someone else has,' said Johnny.

'And Jesus didn't do that, did he?' asked Eddy.

The two seniors shook their heads, looking at one another again.

'That's so simple!' said Liz. 'It makes sense too. But why isn't it in our books? Maybe I should ask my teacher, Dr McGinnis!'

Johnny was aghast. *'No!'* he said. Margaret and Eddy were just as dismayed.

'Could you wait until after the debate?' asked Margaret. 'We want it all to be a surprise. In case the proposition gets to hear what we're going to say.'

'Are you going to say that about coveting in the debate?' asked Liz.

'Do you think we should?' asked Margaret.

'If you want to stump the proposition, that might do it!' said Patricia.

'You could do it, Johnny!' said Eddy. 'That would mean they had less time to think out how to answer.'

'Usually you're not allowed to bring in something completely new in the final speech,' said Patricia.

'I'll do it then,' said Margaret.

Johnny agreed, and Eddy. Patricia and Liz looked at one another then.

'Could be an interesting debate!' said Liz.

'Yes, indeed!' said Patricia. Then she turned to Peter Cullen.

'Now—Peter wants to talk about the school disco just before Christmas.'

The tall senior boy leaned forward, his hands clasped on the table.

'We want to run a campaign for everyone to dress down for that disco—to come in gear they already have, with no expensive logos—so everyone can give more to the Christmas refugee collection—for all the people in the world just now who have no homes at all. Not everyone up the school agrees with that, and we don't know yet what juniors will think. Could you three think about helping with that—by finding out how people in your year would react?'

Johnny looked to Margaret, whose face said 'definitely'— and Mary too. Peter made to get to his feet but Margaret had a question.

'Mrs Walsh has told us that Dr McGinnis will be judging the debate. Do you know, Liz, what he thinks about the environment? Does he think it's a big problem?'

'He doesn't ignore it, but he says that too many people are making a religion out of environmentalism when the problem is down to loss of Christian faith and to materialism. He's into what he calls *Catholic identity*—being proud of being Catholic and standing up to support the bishops. Too many Catholics are not thinking with the church, with our bishops, he says.'

'Does that mean he doesn't support Vatican II?' asked Margaret. Johnny didn't fully understand this question, and could see that Liz too was surprised by it.

'Not quite, Margaret,' Liz responded. 'But he says too many are misinterpreting what the council said, and taking it as a licence for disobedience. Relativism is infecting the church at every level, he says. You know what that means?'

Johnny shook his head, and could see that his friends were just as baffled.

'Relativism is the belief that there is no great big story that can be true for everyone—no fixed truth. So a relativist can't agree that even the Creed is true for example—because he or she will say it can't be true for everyone. The last pope, Benedict XVI, was strong against relativism, and Dr McGinnis is a big, big Benny fan.

'I once heard him say,' Liz continued, 'that if he had his way every subject in the school would be fighting relativism—Biology, English Lit, Geography—all of them!'

'Even History?' asked Johnny.

'Especially History. He says that those who are opposed to all religion—the strong secularists—have far too much influence over the way that History is written. He says they have an entirely wrong idea of the history of the church, and that if we don't do something about that we will forget that the church is the foundation of most of what is good in the world. He's strong on that.'

'Does he think that the church and the state should be close, the way they were in the past?' asked Eddy.

'Yes, that's interesting. He says the ideal situation is that politicians would be strong believers and supporters of the church, and we should all be striving to bring that back. He's often banging on about the period when rulers believed they had a duty to uphold the faith—and even fought wars to do that.'

'Mr Foley wouldn't agree with that,' said Peter Cullen at that point. 'I'm in his history class. He says that one reason so many people don't believe today is because the church, the clergy, had too much political power in the past and used it unjustly. For example by accusing people of heresy, false teaching, and then handing them over to the state to be tortured. He believes the close union of church and state was always a mistake.

'Mind you,' Peter went on, 'Mr Foley also says that's opinion not fact, ladies and gentlemen—and *you* must have *your own* opinions. Respect the facts, don't ignore the record of Christian persecution when you study the record of Christian achievement.' In quoting Mr Foley, Peter had managed a passable impression of his way of speaking.

'But why is Dr McGinnis so worried about relativism?' asked Margaret.

'I think it's because some seniors aren't sure what to believe, and some of the science people even say the creed is all bunk. Some even say: "Religion is being rammed down our throats in this school". I think he may know that.'

At that the bell jangled just outside in the hall. The three quickly thanked the seniors and gathered their belongings—to head to Mr Foley's history class. They didn't have time to discuss what they had just heard. Johnny was determined to forget none of it.

—•oo◦❦◦oo•—

'Johnny, could I sit with Eddy—I want to ask him something about the Tao. Would you go sit with Mary?'

Margaret was asking this on Thursday morning, on the bus—soon after Johnny had boarded it and found Eddy sitting by himself for once.

He got up immediately and turned to where Mary was sitting three rows behind, staring out of a window on the right hand side of the bus, with her bag on her lap. Her left hand was lying on the seat.

'*Could I?*' he asked himself as he sat down, placing his bag in the aisle. He waited then and a question came, a serious question. He looked toward Mary again, still facing out at the passing rows of houses, some cyclists—an old man walking a terrier. Her hair was as flyaway as ever and her shoulder was on a level just below his own. His heart and head together said '*yes!*'

So he lifted his right forearm from his lap and laid it down on Mary's left forearm. His heart thumping, he searched for her hand with his own, found it, and gripped it.

For a moment that seemed to last forever there was no reaction, but then he found his own hand clasped even tighter—and that didn't stop.

A few seconds later she turned her face toward him, looked at him, and went on looking—and he looked back. He saw her face close up as he had never seen it before—a snub nose and some freckles, and blue eyes. It was trusting him completely.

He knew then what he had hoped for, and didn't need to say anything. He could look away without moving his hand, knowing she would do the same. They sat like that, without speaking, for the rest of the journey to school.

'Will you do that then? Will you risk it?'

Mary was facing the three debaters on the Saturday, in Margaret's home, as they sat around the table. She had quizzed them on every detail of their meeting with the seniors, to make sure she understood. 'Relativism' had puzzled her until Margaret had explained it as the belief that there is 'no fixed, certain truth, no great story that could be true for everyone.'

'We don't believe that, do we?' she had asked—knowing who would answer 'No'.

He shook his head. 'The bridgers are true. They haven't let any of us down, have they? And I think the Creed could all be true too—what do you think, Eddy?'

'The earliest Taoists didn't believe in an afterlife,' said Eddy—referring to the story in the Creed of the coming-back of Jesus after his crucifixion. 'They believed in always living in the present. But they believed too that they themselves would live forever—that they would be immortal. So my Dad says that if we love as best we can, and do nothing seriously wrong, anything can happen. And I think Jesus loved better than anyone I've ever heard of.'

'So even if the worst happens, and Dr McGinnis calls us relativists, we can answer that,' said Margaret.

'Yes,' said Johnny. 'I think anyone could be a bridger—and if they knew Jesus never wanted to force anyone, they could believe in him too.'

'And I don't make a religion of the environment either,' said Margaret. 'I think Jesus is helping me to know what to do about it. I say the Creed too, all of it.'

'Me too,' said Johnny. 'Ma makes sure of that, every night, after homework, in the Rosary.'

'There's a difference between believing something strongly and wanting to force it on anyone,' Margaret said. 'Jesus believed in Abba, but let people go away who couldn't believe in *him*. And the church teaches that everyone must be free to make up their own minds. Look here.'

She then passed out four slips of paper, with the printed words her mother had copied for her from the Vatican II document on religious freedom:

Truth can impose itself on the mind of man only in virtue of its own truth, which wins over the mind with both gentleness and power.

'*In virtue of* just means *by,*' she said. 'It means *woman* too, of course,' Margaret went on. 'That can only mean the bishops know they were wrong ever to hand anyone over to the state to be tortured for their beliefs. We may not have to say that to Dr McGinnis, but we *can* say it if we have to.'

'Yeh,' said Johnny 'and *we* won't be forcing *him* to believe in copy- wanting either.'

'So why not say just what we want to say, as we have agreed?' asked Eddy. 'Even if he doesn't understand at first?'

The other debaters nodded.

'Will you do that then? Will you risk it?'

'Yes, Mary, yes we will—and stand by it together,' Margaret put out her hand, her elbow resting on the table. Johnny grasped it, and so did Eddy. And so then did Mary too.

'That's settled then. And now to find out all those things the seniors suggested, and revise our speeches.'

Margaret led them then to her computer, and they began looking hard.

XIV

Johnny had trouble later remembering all that happened between that day in mid October and their debate in late November. The bridgers had to be busy with ordinary schoolwork, to keep up. They also kept their promise to Peter Cullen to promote a dress-down 'no logo' code for the Christmas disco among people of their own year. Opposition had come to that from people disappointed not to be able to wear the latest styles—but they had support from their teachers.

They later found that the leader of the senior campaign against Peter's group was Conor Maguire. Gavan, Aidan and Patrick were leading opponents in their own class, and so were Arona Gilsenan and her friends. However, the worsening plight and growing number of homeless people around the world, from the Americas to Africa, the Mediterranean and even Ireland, swayed many to the 'no logo' side. By mid-November the bridgers felt that they would not be alone in dressing down when the disco came.

Then, as the time grew even closer for the debate, Mrs Hayes made an announcement one Monday in the Music Room.

'Great news everyone!' said Eight B's Music teacher. 'Both Arona and Mary have been selected for the *Fame School* semi-finals in London in January. All expenses paid, of course, for each of them and their parents. They are two of just forty young people selected from the two islands—and no other school has been given that honour. They'll both get personal letters soon confirming this. Show your appreciation.'

Margaret and Mary hugged as cheers rang out. Mary went over then to Arona to say how pleased she was, and Arona shook her hand and thanked her.

Mary later told the others it was in her mind to add a verse to *The Chain* to make the song more suitable for after Christmas.

In the changing room for swimming on the Wednesday of that same week Johnny and his friends had little sense of danger. Gavan, Patrick and Brendan had for some time seemed completely uninterested in them. So it was that Johnny's usual caution deserted him that day, and, during the ten minute free-swimming period, he became separated.

'Where's your fairy friend?'

This question came at Johnny as soon as he surfaced at one end of the pool. When he could see properly he found Patrick and Brendan on either side, grinning. He looked around quickly and saw Martin in the opposite corner—with Gavan Maguire and two Eight A boys hemming him in.

'Don't worry—we're just training him to hold his breath!' said Patrick.

Martin was then grabbed by Gavan and the others, and forced under the surface. Johnny launched himself towards the melee, but was immediately held by Patrick and Brendan.

'No point shouting here, Mullan—no-one's listening. Just watch what happens to freaks. Your turn will come!'

Struggling, Johnny, looked to see where the instructors were. Both were at the opposite end of the pool, concentrated on something else.

Desperately trying to escape, Johnny wrenched an arm free and struck out wildly. He felt his fist make contact.

'Ow!' said Patrick, letting go his arm. Johnny seized the advantage and pulled away from Brendan, diving under the water towards the corner where Martin was in difficulties. He swam straight into the jumble of bodies, hoping to surface in the centre. When he did so he found himself facing Gavan Maguire. Martin's head surfaced alongside, his face white. He had swallowed water and was gasping for breath.

'OK, Mullan, your turn!' said Gavan, putting his hand on Johnny's head. At the same moment Johnny found himself grabbed by at least four other hands. He took a deep breath as he felt himself forced under.

Knowing he mustn't breathe out, he felt for some kind of grip on the side of the pool, but the hands that held him pulled him away. He could sense that Martin was struggling with the group also. When would the others see what was happening?

He caught a glimpse of someone else joining the scrum then, and sensed the struggle becoming more fierce. Some of the hands that gripped him let go. He struck out again, and made contact. Kicking hard he found himself rising, and in a moment his head was clear of the surface. The first face he saw was Eddy's, grinning as usual, although one of his eyes was closed. He was striking back at Gavan. Martin too had his head above the surface.

Then David's bulky form came into view. He had his arm around Patrick Andrews' neck.

At that moment Johnny heard a piercing whistle blast.

'What's going on here?' an adult voice shouted from the poolside above. Mr Slaney's wide form loomed overhead. 'Stop that, all of you. Out of the pool!'

When Johnny had climbed out he saw that there were about ten other boys lined up with him, including all four of his own friends. Mr Slaney and the instructor were peering anxiously into the disturbed pool, to make sure no one was still under water.

'What happened here?' asked Mr Slaney then, scanning along the line as though he had no idea where to focus his attention.

'Just a bit of fun, Sir!' said Gavan Maguire.

'Was it indeed, Maguire. Some weren't finding it all that funny.' He was looking especially at Martin Cassidy, who was still gasping.

'Well, Martin, was it fun for you, then?' asked Mr Slaney.

'Yes, Sir,' said Martin, his chest heaving.

Mr Slaney gave him a hard stare, not convinced.

'You've been warned, all of you, not to fool around in the pool. Any more of that and you'll have me to answer to. Understood?'

They all nodded.

'Off to the shower now, the lot of you!'

In the shower, Johnny looked around again at his four close friends. Martin was still in some distress, but recovering. Eddy had his left eye closed still.

'What happened you?' Johnny asked.

'I saw Gavan stick your head under. I warned Kieran and David. They were a bit further away. When I got to where you were and grabbed Gavan, someone hit me in the eye. I didn't see much after that.'

'Can you open it?'

Eddy slowly opened his left eye. It was slightly bloodshot.

'Can you see alright?' Johnny asked, holding his hand over Eddy's other eye.

'Yeh,' said Eddy, blinking. 'It'll be OK, honest. It's not too bad.' Changing then with the others, Johnny reflected on what had happened. It seemed that Gavan and his allies had been organised and ready to take advantage of the distraction of the poolside teachers.

In any event, he had learned two lessons. The pool was still a slightly dangerous place, and Gavan Maguire had not forgotten what had happened to him in the wood in the first week of term.

Martin had been singled out again, and there had been an attempt to prevent any interference.

He guessed that the attack on Martin was probably a repeat of what had happened in the wood—an attempt to frighten him and get him to beg for mercy.

'They planned that!' said David to Johnny in a low voice then as he towelled his hair. 'I saw Gavan whispering to some of the Eight A fellas earlier. Then I saw the same Eight A crowd talking to the instructor and Mr Slaney down the other end. I think they were deliberately distracting them and getting them to look the other way—asking them questions about the lesson, I think.'

'Yeh, well—we'll know better next time,' said Johnny.

He looked enquiringly over at Martin then. He grinned back, a little shakily. He too had begun to relax a bit since the episode in the wood. From now on they would all need to remember that Gavan could plan ahead, and wouldn't give them any warning beforehand.

That evening, going home, Johnny wondered if he should tell Anny what had happened in the pool. No, he decided. He probably hadn't been in serious danger. Gavan just liked to try to dominate and humiliate people—he surely wouldn't go further than that. If Anny ever made a fuss with the school Gavan would call him a Mammy's boy—and Johnny hated to think of ever giving him that satisfaction.

On the Tuesday night before the debate Margaret's wall animals seemed restless, and their bright eyes seemed to stare more intently at her than usual. Worried that she mightn't be rested enough to remember everything for her speech Margaret eventually asked for the power of the bridge to overcome this obstacle too.

She fell asleep soon then, and found herself in a lonely forest. Its trees and plants were strange to her, but she put this down to her own ignorance of the rain forest. Then as she entered a brighter glade a large bird came fluttering to a branch above her head. It was more brightly feathered than any she had ever seen, with ivory, lilac and bottle green colours. It made a strange whistling noise that soared and swooped, dipping its long beak towards her. In all the TV programmes she had ever watched Margaret had never seen or heard anything so strange.

When her alarm woke her at half-past seven she felt well rested. As she dressed she practised her speech in a whisper. This was to be the most important day of her life so far, she decided. So she said the 'Glory' prayer to the ones she now called in her head the great bridgers.

'I'll do my absolute best!' she said to the animals and birds on her walls as she opened the door to leave.

—∞◦◦❄◦◦∞—

'This is where you freaks get annihilated, Mullan!'

These were Gavan Maguire's words to Johnny as he entered the lecture theatre for the debate on that Wednesday afternoon in late November. They left him in no doubt where the sympathies of some of his own class would lie over the next hour. They also tightened the knot in his stomach that he had noticed first at the bus stop that morning. It was worse than the one he had felt on his first day at Iona.

Knowing that he would soon be speaking from the front of the theatre, Johnny waited behind the door that opened into it. Eddy and Margaret soon joined him, both looking pale but determined. The tiers were filling with others from his year group in a way that had become customary, with Aidan Maroney taking his seat beside Gavan in the third tier. Arona and friends were in the row just behind.

Soon the three proposition speakers arrived, clutching their notes—two boys and one girl. Mrs Walsh followed, accompanied by Dr McGinnis, gowned and clipboarded. He took a chair at the opposite side of the room, facing the lectern that stood in the centre, four feet from the first row of seats.

'Proposition over here!' said Mrs Walsh then from her central chair behind the long desk. She gestured to her right.

'And opposition here.' She pointed to her left.

Margaret took the chair immediately to Mrs Walsh's left, and Eddy took the next. That left Johnny, heart thumping, on the outside chair, almost directly facing Dr McGinnis.

Already on the board behind them Mrs Walsh had handwritten the motion:

That materialism is Earth's biggest problem.

Again the lecture theatre was about half full, with more than half of the Year Eights present. Johnny could see that there was a big showing from Eight A to support the proposition.

As the trickle of latecomers dwindled, Mrs Walsh stood to introduce the debate. At that moment the door opened again and a large group of seniors trooped in. Leading it were Patricia Brolly and Liz Wallace, and Johnny recognised also some of the speakers from the exhibition debate at the start of term. Peter Cullen and Imelda Connolly had supported Patricia in proposing the motion on banning TV advertising.

Then, to Johnny's surprise, a group of five teachers entered the theatre—including Miss Doherty, Mr Foley and Mr Wesley. The other two he couldn't name. They climbed the steps and took seats in a row behind the Year Eight tiers.

Mrs Walsh waited while the seniors group took the highest unfilled tiers. Counting, Johnny saw that there were fourteen seniors altogether—far more than had yet attended a Year Eight debate.

'Welcome everyone!' said Mrs Walsh then. 'Especially you Year Thirteens. I know that some of you have helped to coach the teams for today's debate, so you are welcome. We didn't expect so many of you, but that will add to the occasion.

'Again Dr McGinnis has done us the honour to attend. He will comment when the vote has been taken at the end. These debates benefit greatly from his expertise, and this motion was suggested by his comments on the senior debate at the start of term. We will all be fascinated to hear his expert evaluations today.

'First, then, the motion: That materialism is Earth's biggest problem today. Speaking for the motion are Maria Cunningham, Desmond Bradley and Peter Byrne. Maria will begin. Absolute quiet please.'

A hush descended over the lecture theatre as the first speaker came to the lectern. Maria had straight blond hair tied in a ponytail. Wearing glasses, she brought her notes with her. Beginning in the usual way by addressing the members of staff who were present, she then launched confidently into her speech.

'Materialism is, first of all, the belief that only material things exist. Flowing from this error of the modern world there is also a tendency for people to collect material possessions and to live as though nothing else matters. We will argue that these two forms of materialism are the root cause of most of the biggest problems of the modern world.

'First, materialism is the root cause of the biggest environmental problems. The more possessions we collect the more factories are needed to make them—and all kinds of problems flow from this—including climate change. I will expand on this in a moment.

'Our second speaker will argue that this kind of materialism also creates injustice in the world, by soaking up wealth that could go to boost health and living standards in the Third World.

'Thirdly we will argue that materialism is the root cause of the falling away from religious faith that has happened in most of the world's wealthiest countries. This in turn has caused all sorts of other problems, such as addiction.'

Looking to his right Johnny could see that Margaret had carefully noted this order. She looked up and caught his eye, and nodded.

There was nothing there so far that they hadn't discussed, and Margaret was perfectly placed to respond to the first speech.

Eddy was also making a note. He would be responding to the 'injustice' argument—and he was prepared for that also.

And warfare hadn't been mentioned, not yet anyway. The word addiction also caught Johnny's attention—but should he use the idea he had only half formed? He decided to wait to hear the third proposition speech.

Maria again explained how the gathering of more and more possessions in people's homes increased factory production, and that this in turn had increased the use of fossil fuels to a level that changed the earth's atmosphere.

'We are still using up coal and oil and natural gas at a rate that is changing our climate. We have all heard our parents going on about how the seasons have changed since they were our age—storms in summer and warmer temperatures and more rain in winter, with flooding possible any time. Can anyone doubt our climate is changing, and causing famines also in warmer countries through drought? And can anyone doubt that materialism is the cause of all this?'

She went on to cover the well-known theory of climate change and its effects, suggesting that many allergies and asthma were linked with industrialisation also.

'Finally, species of plants and animals have already been made extinct by environmental change, and many more are threatened. Probably when our own children go to school in about twenty-five years time they will never be able to see in the wild many of the things we can see today. Ireland too may well be different then.

'So you can all see that, using this argument alone, the proposition can show that materialism is the biggest problem facing planet Earth. We are sure you will join with us in supporting this motion.'

Maria sat down to warm applause, especially from her own class. She had used her notes only occasionally, and this had made an impact.

'First speaker for the opposition, Margaret Phillips.'

Margaret rose immediately, taking her folder with her. She placed it in front of her on the lectern, but didn't at this stage take any sheets from it—and began in the usual way—'Madam Chairman, Members of staff, fellow pupils.

'The opposition has listed a number of big earth problems in that opening speech. We agree with that list, and will talk about it. We will also add some other big problems, however—problems the proposition hasn't yet mentioned.

'We accept also the proposition's definition of materialism. We accept that there is such a thing as a belief that only material things exists.

'What we are opposing is the argument that this belief is the main cause of Earth's biggest problems. People do indeed collect goods they don't need. But they do it for an entirely different reason. Our case is centred round that reason.

'That same reason explains the threat to the environment, and explains it far more fully. It also explains the injustice of the world, and the poverty of so many in it. And it explains two other enormous problems the proposition haven't even mentioned yet. Our second and third speakers will deal with those problems.

'What we want you to do is look closely at the reasons we all buy things we do not need. This is a Catholic school, so few of you will agree that you are materialistic. Yet I'll bet most people here have their own rooms at home. And I'll bet that in those rooms many of you have already collected things like computers, radios and even small TVs—even though there may well be large TVs, radios, computers and hi-fis elsewhere in your homes.

'We can explain why we all do that, and it has nothing to do with materialism. The reason is simply that we want to copy one another.

If some members of our class can afford all of these things, we all feel we should follow them.

'Look at this!' said Margaret, drawing a magazine page from her folder and holding it up.

'I'll bet most of you have seen this, as it's from a big teenage magazine. It's an ad for the latest in phones—the ones that give you fast live video of the person calling. They are expensive, but soon most of us will want one.

'Why is that? Is it because they are interested in the material from which the phone is made? If it was, this advertisement would tell you how much plastic, metal, silica and so on is in the phone. But there isn't a single mention of any of the materials in the phone.

'Why is that? It's because the firm that placed the advertisement knows why we buy such things—we want to copy or imitate one another, to feel we are equal. We want to imitate especially people we believe to be better or luckier or richer or more interesting than we are. And that's why most of this advertisement is a photograph of a person, not the phone itself. That person is a world-famous singer and actress—I don't need to mention her name. She is paid lots of money just to pose with this phone.

'And here's another ad of the same kind!'

Margaret drew next from her folder a magazine page of a movie actor wearing an expensive Swiss watch.

'Here again there isn't any mention of the metals and glass from which the watch is made. Instead we have an actor who plays the main role in the kind of action films that boys like.

'Men and boys want to copy this person—they must do, because this ad appears often in *Time* magazine, which is sold all over the world. Those ads cost thousands of pounds, and you can bet the watch maker will be sure his money has been well spent.

'Wanting-to-copy—that's the real problem. We copy people by buying material things, because they stand for success and fame.

'Materialism' cannot be the best name for that, because it makes us think that we are interested in material. We aren't. We are interested in items that appear magical because we think they will make others admire us.

'At first we couldn't find a word anywhere for wanting-to-copy, so we made one up. Copy-wanting. It says what is going on when people are influenced by all these advertisements. Later we found another word for this—a word found in the Bible. And it isn't materialism—a word that does not occur in the bible at all.'

At this point Johnny saw Dr McGinnis narrow his eyes, frown, and then make the first of many notes on his clipboard.

Margaret then held up in succession four more familiar magazine ads—for an expensive perfume, a digital TV recorder, a solid gold bracelet and a dining room suite. Three of them showed well- known media personalities owning or using these things.

'Now look at this last one. Here you see an expensive set of dining room furniture made from solid teak. Teak is one of the world's scarce and precious timbers. The ad says this is an exclusive offer—and that means that if you buy it you will become more important.

'This shows a direct link between copy-wanting and the threat to the environment. But in fact all copy-wanting is a threat to the environment, because it is the most important cause of over- consumption. If you doubt this, just start paying attention to the real message of the advertising you see all around you.

'We believe that the Gospels are telling us that we don't need to do that, because we are all equal. No-one can be more important than anyone else, no matter how hard we try. That is why Jesus scolded the apostles for wanting to be greater than one another. And that is also why he told us not to *covet*. We believe copy- wanting and coveting are the same thing.

'So far the proposition has not shown you one piece of evidence to prove that people are materialistic. We argue that these advertisements—and the hundreds of others we see every day—prove something else entirely. We ask you simply to see things as they are and reject this motion.'

Margaret turned then and walked back to her place. Clapping also, Johnny couldn't tell if the applause was any louder than for the first speech, but he could see that Margaret had made an impression. Her magazine ads had caught people's attention. Patricia Brolly was giving a thumbs up message from her seat and nodding at Margaret.

Looking to his right during the speech Johnny had also noticed that the proposition speakers seemed taken aback. Towards the end, Maria Cunningham had passed a note to her neighbouring team mate, who had read it quickly and nodded.

Meanwhile Dr McGinnis had also seemed more and more puzzled. He was still writing on his clipboard when Margaret finished, and did not put his pen or clipboard down to clap. He just patted the clipboard with his closed right hand three times, and started writing again. Now he was frowning still, and looking straight at Margaret as though seeing her for the first time. Then his gaze shifted to Eddy—and then to the person sitting on Eddy's left. For the first time Johnny found himself stared at directly by the head of Religion. It was a stare of disapproval, mixed with curiosity.

'Desmond Bradley for the proposition.'

Desmond was a tall boy with ginger hair and glasses. Johnny knew only that he was supposed to be one of the smartest in Eight D.

'Before I begin I would like to answer some of the points made by the last speaker. As she agrees that people do collect material goods we think she is supporting us. As we said, materialism is about collecting material things. People who do it are obviously materialistic. Anyone can understand that.

'She said we had no evidence for that, but the reason for that is simple. We don't need it. Materialism is all around us. Her own ads show that too.

'Now I will move on to another problem caused by materialism—all the injustice and poverty in the world. As you know, every day thousands of children die of hunger and disease in the third world—even though there is enough food and medicine in the world to stop all that. The reason that happens is that we in the richer part of the world spend too much of our money on things we don't need.'

Knowing that Eddy would be responding to this speech, Johnny quickly made a note and passed it to him. Eddy looked at it, nodded agreement and went back to listening to Desmond.

It was a good speech too, comparing things like the cost of the latest smartphone with an eye operation to cure blindness in Africa or India. Desmond also looked at the main centres of poverty in the world, most of them in the southern half of the globe.

'Materialism is the major cause of all these problems. It is well known that people who are religious tend to give more to charities. Look at our own country and the support it gives to organisations working in the poorest part of the world. Materialism is a threat to all that, and that is why we support this motion. We are sure that you will support it too.'

Although Desmond had been less confident than Maria, this speech too was well received, especially by his own class. Johnny noticed that this time Dr McGinnis put down his clipboard and pen to applaud.

'Edward Li for the opposition.'

'We want to ask the proposition a question,' Eddy began. 'Are they changing their definition of the motion?

'Their first speaker said that materialism was the *reason* people collect things. Their second speaker now says materialism is just a name for what people do. They should make up their minds.

'We believe it is far more important to understand *why* people do what they do. As our first speaker has said, the word materialism doesn't *explain* anything, and that is why we say it is not the *cause* of the world's greatest problems.

'The last speaker told us about the problems of poverty and injustice—the fact that the rich world has more than it needs while in the poor world people just cannot stay alive. We agree, but we are sure that the word materialism simply doesn't explain it.

'Why do people choose to spend more on themselves than they need to? For example, why will most people buy that most expensive smartphone the last speaker talked about—instead of sending the money to Africa?

'Isn't it because our friends have these things, and we then want them too? We want to imitate one another, because we think that unless we have lots of things other people will laugh at us for being different. That's copy-wanting.

'And copy-wanting is also a big reason for another huge Earth problem that the proposition haven't even mentioned yet. That problem is crime, especially violent crime.

'Take stealing. If one person has a flash car and shows it off, someone else is likely to steal it, if he can. And if the owner sees him doing it and tries to stop him, he can get run over. That has actually happened. Now we have another crime—a homicide. It started just with someone wanting something he couldn't buy.

'Do you think the man who stole the car said to himself "there's a lot of material things in that—glass and rubber and steel?" You know it's not.

'We think a lot of cars too, because they say things. A cheap car says we're not too rich or important. A big, expensive car says we're one of the top people. That's why people are willing to buy a luxury car they know has been stolen, and that's another crime. They want to copy high-up people.

'Many criminals want to steal something that they can hide easily, and then sell for a lot of money. Things like diamonds and other jewellery. Why do people pay so much for these things? Because they are the things that millionaires and kings and queens wear, and people want to copy them.'

At that point Eddy held up his picture.

'This is the Koh-i-Noor, one of the crown jewels. A diamond is made of carbon, just like coal. Why will people pay big money for the diamond? It can't be for the carbon in it, because they could get many tons of coal for the same price. A diamond says something—it says you're special. That's what people are looking for when they buy or steal a diamond—not the carbon, the material it's made from.

'Look at another crime—people stealing cars and wrecking them, just for fun. They do that often to show off to their friends, because they are poor and can't afford cars themselves. And that can lead to someone getting killed also. As you all know, that happened near here recently. One of the teenagers who did it said, "We saw this flash car with the keys in, so we took it to show off." Showing off is copying the owner of the car—copy-wanting again. He never said a word about wanting the material the car was made of.

'Another awful kind of crime: people taking guns to school and shooting people there. In Columbine High School in the USA in 1999 the two boys who shot fifteen people were Hitler fans. Hitler thought Germany was being picked on and that's why he was so violent. Those two boys thought they were being picked on too. They were copying him. They thought they would become famous, and that Steven Spielberg would make a film about them.

'Terrorism is the crime that frightens people most today. The biggest of all terrorist crimes was the attack on the USA on September 11th 2001. It was planned by a young Arab. The French ambassador to the UN said this in 2002 about young Arabs:

"When you have educated young people by the millions, with no future, that is the heart of the problem. They can't understand why they are deprived of what they hope for, which is an American way of life."

'In other words, many Muslim boys want to copy Americans but can't, because there are too few jobs in the Arab world, and they blame America for this.

'As our first speaker said, copy-wanting is the same as coveting. One of the greatest of all crimes in history was the murder of Julius Caesar. Shakespeare tells us his murderers envied his fame and power. In other words, they wanted to copy the biggest dictator that Rome ever had. They coveted his power, but couldn't get it without killing him.

'Materialism can't explain things like that either, because power and fame are not material things. But coveting can, because the bible tells us not to covet anything our neighbour owns—and that doesn't have to be a material thing.

'So—Earth's biggest problem by far is copy-wanting or coveting. It explains most crime as well as buying all that stuff we don't need. Materialism doesn't compare. It's a big red herring. We ask you to reject this motion.'

Eddy had become more excited as he went on, as he always did when talking about big crimes. And this had made an impact, Johnny could see. Johnny had also noticed most of the seniors clapping this speech. He remembered that Patricia Brolly had said she was going to tell some of her English Literature class about the debate.

But Johnny was now noticing also that Dr McGinnis was frowning even more deeply as he made notes on his clipboard. Especially towards the end when Eddy talked about coveting power and fame.

Maria had passed another note to the third speaker just before Eddy finished, and this speaker had then made a note of his own at the top of his pages.

Next it would be the turn of Peter Byrne—and then Johnny himself.

XV

'Peter Byrne—last speaker for the proposition,' Mrs Walsh announced. Margaret, her eyes riveted on the audience, couldn't tell how things were going.

Peter was smaller than Desmond, about Johnny's height and build, but with fair hair. His pages shook in his hands as he began.

'The last speaker said we hadn't mentioned crime as a big world problem. Well my speech is about that too. It's just one of a lot of big problems—caused also by materialism.

'You see materialists believe that only matter exists, things you can see and touch—like this lectern here.'

Here Peter paused and tapped the lectern hard with his knuckles.

'Now if only matter exists there isn't any God. And if there isn't any God then religion is all rubbish. That's what materialists believe. That's why so many people today don't believe in God, and don't pray.

'And that's why the Earth has so many problems today. Crime is just one of them. Drug addiction is another.

'When people become well off and can afford houses and cars they think they don't need God any more. They think that material things are all they need. That's what we mean by materialism too.

'If you look at the richest countries today, they have mostly stopped believing in God. And they have mostly big problems also.

Like crime, and mental illness, and drug addiction, and violence. That's what happens when people forget about God.

'There isn't any big problem in the world today that can't be explained by this.

'Look at our own country, and the problem of addiction. Back around 1900 there was a big drink problem in Ireland, and a priest, Fr Cullen set up the Pioneer Total Abstinence association. By 1959 it had over one hundred thousand members all over the country.

'Many of those were reformed alcoholics. The Pioneers got them away from alcohol, and helped their families.

'The Pioneers still exist, but not so many people want to join now. The reason is that the media are telling everyone that religion belongs in the past. And because people have more money now, they spend even more on alcohol. Ireland now has a bigger problem of alcoholism than it ever had.

'The reason is materialism. That is what is undermining the Church in Ireland, by telling people there is no God.

'And violence often happens then when people have had too much alcohol. People go wild and start fighting for no reason—only because they are drunk. And other kinds of addiction are a major cause of crime and violence also.

'The root cause of that is people turning away from religion—and they are doing that because they are being told by materialist thinkers that religion is all false.

'So we are sure you will agree that materialism is Earth's biggest problem, no matter what the opposition say. We are sure you will support the motion.'

Peter had made this short speech sincerely, despite his nerves, and that was why he too was now given a big round of applause. Without looking to see, Margaret knew that Dr McGinnis especially approved as there was loud clapping coming from that direction.

Looking hard at Johnny Margaret could see he had been surprised by this speech, maybe even worried.

'Johnny Mullan, final speaker for the opposition.'

Johnny lifted his folder and left his chair. Margaret could see that he was uncertain as he walked to the lectern. But when he got there and paused and closed his eyes for a moment she saw him relax. He too began in the usual way, by addressing the chair and all of the audience. She was glad he didn't forget to say, 'and teachers'.

'In the USA six people out of every ten say that religion is important to them. But the people of the USA also buy more things for themselves than any other people in the world. You can check this on the Internet, on the United Nations site.

'The USA is one of the most religious countries in the world. It is the most wasteful country too. As we all know, it is one of the most violent.

'So you can believe in God and still want to own lots of stuff. Doesn't that mean that materialism cannot be the reason?

'Christmas isn't far away, so think about what you yourselves want most for Christmas. I'll bet it's something you will be able to touch and see and feel.

'But I'll bet also that's not why you want it. I'll bet you've seen someone else owning or using it.

'I believe in God too. But I once wanted a pair of Benders football boots because I saw a famous player wearing them. And I wasn't a bit interested in what they were made of. I wanted to be better at football. Was that a material thing— being better at football?

'Why not just do this: ask yourselves why you want what you want for Christmas? If you want the plastic or metal—or whatever—in what you want, then you should vote for this motion.

'But if you have another kind of reason, what is it? I'll bet it often has to do with being like somebody else.

'I used to think that Jesus was soppy—too goody-goody to be real. But now I think he was smart. He didn't want to copy anybody else.

People thought he would copy David, who was a great fighter. But he didn't.

'That wasn't being goody-goody. That was being smart. I think Jesus knew how silly copying was.

'The most famous people in his time were Alexander the Great, and Julius Caesar, and King David. Alexander the Great copied his father and the fighting Gods that he believed in. He killed hundreds of thousands of people.

'And Julius Caesar copied Alexander, and killed even more. If Jesus had copied King David he would have killed lots of people too, because he had lots of enemies. The

Romans would have fought him too. And nothing would ever be different.

'The gospel tells us he was tempted to own all the kingdoms of the world, but didn't want that. That means he didn't copy-want what kings and emperors had.

'And that's why he didn't own anything either. He wanted to tell us that we don't have to own things to be important.

'The gospel says that Jesus didn't care what rank people were. That means he didn't believe that some people were better than others. If everyone realised that they were just as good as any person who lives in a palace, they wouldn't want to copy them. We think that's what Jesus was trying to teach.

'He never said: 'Don't be materialistic'. He said, 'Don't covet!' That means don't want what other people have—don't copy them.

'So when we are told to copy Jesus I think that means we should follow him and not copy other people. If we do that we will share what we have. And we won't want to own everything. We won't get jealous either if some people have more than us.

'And we won't fight wars over land or power, or oil. We'll just share everything.

'We all *need* material things—food, shelter, schools— even phones and computers nowadays. Are we being materialistic if we have these things? Of course not. So how are we to tell when we are collecting too much? I will not be able to tell just by saying to myself 'there's a lot of material in that'—but I can notice myself wanting what other people have—even when I don't need it.

'So, as we have said, we think that not copy-wanting is the answer to all the big problems of the world today—the environment, crime, violence and war.'

At this point, from the corner of his eye, Johnny saw a hand go up in the third row.

'Gavan?' said Mrs Walsh.

'What about alcoholics?'

Gavan was grinning maliciously. Johnny frowned darkly—and Margaret feared for a moment that he might forget everything else and go for him. Then he closed his eyes, and waited.

'Well, copy-wanting comes into addiction too, in two ways.

'First, people often start drinking or doing drugs because they want to copy people they think are cool.

'Second, alcoholism can happen if something bad happens to someone. For example, in the troubles in Derry some people were picked on for no reason—by people who wanted to copy war.'

Margaret saw Gavan's face change then. He went livid, and opened his mouth in anger.

'Wha...!

'That's enough, Gavan,' said Mrs Walsh sharply. 'Johnny, please continue.'

'So ask yourselves this. Does materialism say why we have so many problems on the Earth today? We think it doesn't. It just tells us what people do when they buy things, without saying why. And it doesn't explain crime and war either.

'We need a better answer—something we can all understand. We think that copy-wanting—coveting—is a far better explanation than materialism for the three biggest problems in the world today.

'We all copy others, even those of us who *do* believe in God. The proposing team never even noticed that, or tried to explain why. So we ask you to vote against this motion. Copy-wanting—coveting—is earth's biggest problem.'

As Johnny walked nervously back to his seat Margaret clapped as hard as she could and felt sure he had responded to every argument.

'Maria Cunningham to sum up for the proposition.'

Margaret had been watching Maria too while Johnny was speaking. She had been making notes. She seemed just a little flustered as she walked to the lectern.

'I've only a little bit to add to what we've already said.

'The last speaker said Jesus never used the word materialism, but that he did use the word covet. Well we think that coveting and materialism are the same thing. 'Copy-wanting' isn't even in the dictionary, I'll bet. They said it's their own made-up word, didn't they?

'We know what they mean by copy-wanting, though—so I'll bet there's some other big word for that. It's true we all do a lot of copying, but we all end up with material things don't we?

'And that's what we have said in all our speeches. Does it matter why we do things, if it all ends up in owning stuff? That's materialism, and it's a big problem.

'It's true too that people who are religious often own a lot of stuff. But probably they give a lot of it away too—more than people who don't believe in God.

'I'm sure most of you believe in God and so are against materialism. So I'm sure you'll vote for this motion: That materialism is Earth's biggest problem.'

Maria had bravely responded to Johnny's speech, so she got a big round of applause. Dr McGinnis clapped extra loud again, tucking his clip board under his arm to do so.

Mrs Walsh stood again.

'Congratulations to all concerned. Now, the vote. Miss Doherty and Mr Foley will count hands. First, the votes for the motion. If you believe that materialism is indeed Earth's biggest problem put up one hand.'

Miss Doherty and Mr Foley left their places at the back and came down the steps of the lecture theatre, one on either side, counting hands. Margaret could see that there were a lot of hands up among the Year Eights, but that some of the seniors, and all of the teachers, weren't voting.

Then the two teachers met near the lectern and put their heads together for a moment and nodded. Miss Doherty then turned and whispered the result to Mrs Walsh.

'Thirty-five votes for the motion.

'Now, votes against. Those who don't believe that materialism is Earth's biggest problem—put up one hand.'

Again the two teachers counted from either side of the room and conferred. This time Mr Foley gave the result to the chairman.

'Thirty-eight votes against.'

'The motion is defeated by three votes,' said Mrs Walsh, but she didn't need to. The winning voters, led by some seniors, were already cheering.

Eddy jumped up and made a victory gesture, waving his fists in exultation. Margaret was too amazed to do anything more than stare up at the tiers of seats where those who had voted against the motion were applauding. They included most of the seniors. Patricia Brolly and Liz Wallace were waving down at her team.

Turning to her right she saw that Johnny had both hands up to his face, quite unbelieving. He was staring at the seventh tier—where Mary sat, quite overcome also.

Johnny got up then and said 'C'mon' to Eddy. Margaret was already on her way to sympathise with Maria. The proposition were a bit downcast, Margaret could see.

'Your speech scared me,' said Johnny to Peter Byrne. Meanwhile Eddy seemed to be doing his best to suppress his feeling of triumph as he shook hands with all three opponents.

'Dr McGinnis will now give us his expert verdict on the debate. Please take your seats again.'

As Dr McGinnis rose and strode to the lectern, Margaret felt that he was anything but pleased. His eyebrows were drawn down into a straight line, and his mouth was a tight upside-down curve.

By the time the bridgers had returned to their seats, the head of Religion had been waiting at the lectern for several seconds. He had placed his clipboard in front of him deliberately and then looked upwards—towards the back of the theatre.

He waited then for a long moment—staring, it seemed, at the seniors—and the room went quiet.

'I must begin by congratulating the winning team,' Dr McGinnis began. The tall head of Religion then looked round at the bridgers' team for a moment, before turning his gaze again to the upper tiers where the seniors sat.

'But I must not forget those who coached them. Those coaches have worked extra hard, I believe, as we have heard today some very ingenious reasoning and some highly suspect ideas.

'It is the task of an opposition to oppose, of course—and they must have some freedom to present the most effective argument possible. So we cannot complain if sometimes they go beyond the bounds set by common sense.

'The opposition have worked hard on presentation, and they make a formidable team. All were outstanding under that heading—presentation. As to content, I shall have much more to say about that in a moment.

'Under the heading of content, the proposition were outstanding. They made so good a case that in ninety-nine cases out of a hundred they would have won the day. Unfortunately for themselves they came up against the hundredth case today and lost by the narrowest of margins. Perhaps if fewer seniors had been here they would still have won.

'For sincerity and Catholic wisdom I scored the proposition as clear winners, and was frankly amazed at the verdict of the house. Daring and originality—and perhaps our weak human preference for novelty over common sense—defeated them. They can take away with them the certainty that defeat on this occasion does not mean defeat for their cause.

'I must make it clear exactly why that was, as I have the highest responsibility for maintaining traditional Catholic truth in this school.'

Here the head of Religion paused for a long while, and then spoke slowly and solemnly.

'That truth is a precious deposit or treasure that we are all required to receive intact from those who teach us, and pass on intact to those we teach.

'By that I mean that nothing must be lost from that treasure ... and nothing ... must be ... added.'

Dr McGinnis raised his voice and put heavy emphasis upon the last five words, and then paused for the effect to sink in.

'To add anything that we may think up for the purposes of a debate would be to tamper with the deposit, to put counterfeit banknotes alongside the treasures of the faith.

'I fear that today we have been presented with a full wallet of counterfeit banknotes. First, coveting has been translated as wanting-to-copy or 'copy-wanting'. In the Catechism, however, coveting is perfectly well translated as avarice—greed—an inability to stop amassing wealth or property.

'Take away that corner-stone of the opposition argument, and it comes crashing to the ground. All of the remaining counterfeit banknotes will then show up as such under the searching light of truth. I feel sure that Mrs Walsh will agree with me that this idea—this counterfeit money—must now be taken completely out of circulation in this school. We must hear nothing more of coveting defined as 'copy-wanting' in any school forum such as this.

'I am sure the opposition will fall in with this decision, and never argue again as they have done today. We must not hear this dangerous—and, I have to say, childish, nonsense in any future debate in this school—or indeed in the classroom either.

'As the last proposition speaker, Peter Byrne, so wisely said, covetousness and materialism are indeed so closely related that it is impossible to separate them. And that means that Jesus did indeed condemn materialism—as he would today in this world that is almost wholly given over to it. He said—let us all remember—'man does not live on bread alone!' and bread is unquestionably a material thing.

'To their credit, the opposition also expressed faith of a kind in Our Lord—but it is not quite the true faith. It does not conform to Catholic tradition, and is therefore, I fear, faulty. Let them put these dangerous ideas aside, and study what the proposition have put before them. That should not be difficult, as I'm sure the case they put themselves was merely patched together for this occasion.'

Dr McGinnis turned then to the bridgers:

'So enjoy your victory, briefly, but burn then these counterfeit banknotes, beginning with that misunderstanding of covetousness as copy-wanting.'

He looked back up at the seniors then.

'I would caution especially the seniors to do the same. Some of you are studying senior religion, and must not become confused by the ill-thought-out theories you have heard today. Were you to respond to any examination question on the meaning of Christianity in terms such as these, you are certain to come to grief.

'Remember what I said about our greatest treasure, the deposit of faith. Receive it as it is presented to you by your teachers, change it not at all, and pass it on as you have received it. No other course is possible if this school is to remain a Catholic school.'

Dr McGinnis lifted his clipboard then and moved towards the door, still frowning. He did so in silence, as his annoyance had made itself felt by all in the theatre.

'Thank you, Dr McGinnis,' said Mrs Walsh, rising. 'I too would like to congratulate the proposition for their outstanding speeches. And the opposition too, for a startling victory. We must all obviously think hard indeed about what Dr McGinnis has said. Thanks again for the effective coaching of both teams from the seniors. We will see you all again next week.'

As the final, muted, applause rang out, Mrs Walsh turned then quietly to Margaret.

'Can I see you three before you go? If so, follow me to Interview Room One as soon as I have had a word with Dr McGinnis.'

She said this pleasantly, but Margaret sensed that her form teacher was troubled. Dr McGinnis was waiting behind the door, so Mrs Walsh went then to have a final word with him.

Meanwhile Patricia Brolly and Liz Wallace had come down the steps to congratulate their pupils. Patricia took Margaret's hand first.

'You were just brilliant! Dr McGinnis maybe thinks we gave you all that, but we didn't—we just helped you put it across!'

'What does that mean—what he said about counterfeit money?'

'Don't worry. He overreacted because he expected the motion to be carried. He has a thing about materialism. He doesn't know you believe all you said.'

'But we do! Can we never think or say so again?'

'How could he stop anyone saying what they believe? You didn't deny anything in the creeds. He has just gone a bit over the top, because he's annoyed. It'll work out, you'll see.'

'Mrs Walsh wants to see us now.'

'She will keep you right. She believes in people saying what they think.'

Patricia looked over then to the door, where the head of religion and Eight B's form teacher were still in serious conversation.

'Good luck anyway, and don't worry!' Patricia went then to shake Johnny's hand.

Eddy meanwhile was having his back slapped by Kieran Lowney and Martin Cassidy—and enjoying it.

'I've never seen a t..teacher so m..ad,' said Kieran, nodding towards the door where Dr McGinnis was still in conversation with Mrs Walsh.

'I know!' said Eddy, wide-eyed. 'Mrs Walsh wants to talk to us about what he said.

'I thought you were all great,' said Martin. That's the best debate we've had so far—and I thought it was going to be so boring!'

Margaret had told Eddy and Johnny of Mrs Walsh's request, so they followed through the doorway. She led them through the corridors to the interview room in the hall without a word, and ushered them in. They sat together on one side of the table while she closed the door.

'First, well done!' she said. 'That was an excellent performance for your first debate. You are a credit to me.'

She said this so warmly that the bridgers were in no doubt she meant it.

'Now, those ideas you were using—they *were* your own weren't they—not Liz's or Patricia's?'

'Yes,' said Johnny. 'Patricia and Liz just helped us to set them out.'

Margaret nodded and explained briefly how they had reached their earliest decisions.

'Hmm,' said Mrs Walsh when she had finished. 'Miss Doherty has explained that to me too. And there should be a word for that, shouldn't there? And if coveting isn't it, what is? That's a puzzle and no mistake!'

The three nodded.

'Dr McGinnis is sure you're wrong. But you believe all that you said?'

They nodded again, more vigorously.

'Well then, we've all got a problem, haven't we?'

'Yes, Miss,' said Margaret. 'Can we never say what we think again?'

'It's too early to answer that. You must understand that in our church there is a difference of opinion on how freely Catholics can think and express themselves. And now we in this school are faced with this question, in a way that hasn't happened in my time here. Can you understand that?'

They nodded.

'So I'm going to ask you something. Do you know what 'triumphalism' is, Eddy?'

'Is it what football players usually do after scoring a goal or winning a match? Running about and showing off?'

'That's it exactly. The worst thing that could happen is for you three to get notions about yourselves, just because you've won a debate in a clever way. That would make it easier for someone to argue that you weren't sincere, that you say clever things just to get noticed. Do you see?'

They nodded readily.

'So be modest, and don't think about all this as another competition—especially with Dr McGinnis. Do you hear?'

'We won't, Miss,' said Margaret, and the others nodded agreement.

'So if someone wants to make a big sensation out of all this, and urges you to be even more daring, what will you do?'

'Talk about something else?' Margaret asked. Mrs Walsh nodded.

'And if anyone speaks disrespectfully of Dr McGinnis to you?'

'Say that we respect him,' said Johnny, 'because he knows a lot and wants to make sure we all say what's true.'

'Good. All of that will help. Now—do you have copies of your speeches that I could read?'

They all nodded.

'Are there earlier drafts, showing how you started thinking about this when you first saw the motion—before you met with Liz and Patricia in October?'

'Eddy and I will have dated files of our first drafts on the computer—Johnny?'

'I'm almost certain I saved my first draft too—but that's on paper and won't have a date on it.'

'Get all of that for me then, and then have a good night's rest! I can see you've all been losing sleep.'

XVI

'*Moses!*' said Mrs Phillips in the car.

Margaret had taken the front passenger seat, while Eddy, Johnny and Mary sat in the back. She had given her mother a quick account of Dr McGinnis's reaction to their winning the debate, and then of Mrs Walsh's cautions.

'You lot will start another schism if you go on like this!' she said then with a half smile.

'What's a schism?' asked Margaret.

'It's a split in the Church. There have been two big ones. First, in the ten hundreds the eastern churches centred on Constantinople split from Rome. Then in the fifteen hundreds, Martin Luther started the Protestant Reformation. That's what separated Protestants from Catholics.'

'We don't want to do that!' said Margaret, looking anxiously at Johnny.

'I'm just pulling your leg, silly. People your age should be allowed to say what you like, unless it's obviously harmful to someone. Dr McGinnis is making a big fuss about nothing, if you ask me.'

'Mrs Walsh said you might want to see her,' said Johnny.

'Did she indeed! Well, if I do I'll be telling her you must not be silenced, even if you are all talking rubbish. I'll take it up with Mr Ferguson if necessary. I'm sure Johnny's and Eddy's parents would do the same.'

They were pulling in at Johnny's house at that point.

'I'll give your Mum a call later, Johnny, OK?' said Mrs Phillips, looking back as he opened the car door.

'Miss, can they never talk about copy-wanting again?' asked Catherine Canning first thing in Religion class the following morning.

Miss Doherty had begun the class by congratulating Johnny, Margaret and Eddy. Now she pursed her lips and hesitated.

'Well, what do you think, Catherine? Did you understand what they said?'

'Yes, Miss. It all made sense. That's true about Jesus. He didn't want what most other people want. I never thought of that before. And we all do copy-want.'

'Who agrees with that?' the teacher asked. 'Hands up.'

About a third of the class put their hands up straight away. More hands followed as others in the class looked round and realised they were not alone.

'What do you think copy-wanting means? Bridget?'

'Wanting something just because someone else has it,' said Bridget McSorley.

'Can you give me an example?'

'Yes, Miss. Last Christmas I wanted a mobile phone because my friend in primary school had one. I didn't need one, because we live near the primary school and my Mum teaches there.

'My Mum said that too, but I was annoyed because I didn't get one. And I don't think I was being ... materialistic. I just wanted to be like her.'

'Has anything like that ever happened to anyone else? Hands up.'

This time about a third of the class put their hands up. Some of these were people who hadn't been at the debate the previous day. They had picked up on the previous evening's events from the morning chatter in the corridors, and from what they had just heard.

'Does anyone disagree?'

'Yes, Miss,' said Gavan Maguire. 'Often you need things, and that's why you want them.'

'That's true too. Aidan?'

'If we stopped wanting things, factories would close, and there wouldn't be any work for people. The more people want things, the more jobs there are.'

'That's also true. Arona?'

'It would be boring if we couldn't ever buy just what we want.'

'That's true too, I suppose. All of that helps me to think more about all this. We must remember too what Dr McGinnis said—about the danger of adding new things to our faith. We'll not discuss this any further now, so. Thanks again to Margaret, Johnny and Eddy for getting us to think, anyway. That's exactly what a good debate is supposed to do. Let's move on now to that homework on the sacraments. Deirdre, tell us again what a sacrament is!'

As the class moved into another phase, Margaret realised that others in the class knew what they meant and were using their word.

She had noticed something else. Miss Doherty had not answered Catherine's question about Dr McGinnis's ban, and seemed to be testing the class's reactions to the debate. And she hadn't said copy- wanting was silly either. Margaret began to feel a bit less anxious.

'I suppose you think you're great now!' sneered Gavan Maguire to Johnny at break time. He had made a point of coming up to him in the tuck shop queue.

'No,' said Johnny. 'It was just a debate.'

'That's right, and you won just because the seniors were there.' Gavan looked around then, and said in a low voice.

'That crack about copying war and picking on people. Just what did you mean by that?'

'Just what I said,' said Johnny. 'What did you think I meant?'

'I think you're too smart for your own good, that's what. If I was you I would keep my big mouth closed.'

'That's funny. I was thinking of giving you the same advice.'

'Listen,' hissed Gavan. 'I've warned you before about that mouth. One of these days I'll close it for you, for good. Do you hear?'

'I hear, O Master of the Universe, but why should I obey?'

'Right, then! You've asked for it!'

Gavan turned on his heel then, and stalked off in a fury. Johnny felt better for answering exactly as he felt, but wondered if he might have gone too far for his own good.

—∘∘∘✦∘∘∘—

'He's mean!' said Mary to Margaret at lunchtime, seated in the central corridor in the main building.

Margaret had given Mary a brief account of what Mrs Walsh had said in the interview room the previous day, about the bridgers keeping a low profile to see if Dr McGinnis would think again about the debate and his ban on the bridgers talking about copy-wanting.

'If we're wrong, why can't Dr McGinnis show us, if he knows so much?' Mary asked.

'Yes,' said Margaret. 'But remember we're supposed to be bridgers. That means bringing people together, not starting a fight. But Mrs Walsh is on our side, I think.'

'And Miss Doherty is a friend of hers, isn't she?'

'Yes,' said Margaret. 'And she didn't stop the class talking about copy-wanting either, did you notice?'

At that moment Patricia Brolly and Peter Cullen came up. Patricia introduced Peter briefly to Mary.

'Peter's president of the Environmental Society in the school,' said Patricia. 'He wants to ask Margaret something.'

'Yes,' said Peter. 'I was impressed by your speech yesterday. I was wondering if you would like to join our society?'

'Thanks,' said Margaret, delighted. 'I'm not sure if I would have time. What do you do?'

Peter explained briefly, and said his group wanted to hear how her team had come up with the idea of copy-wanting

'But what about what Dr McGinnis said?' Margaret asked.

'How can you ban an idea?' Peter asked. 'It's like trying to put a genie back in a bottle. It's not just a religious idea, is it? It helps to explain over-consumption—people buying what they don't need—so it's a kind of Geography idea too. He can't say he owns it.'

'But if he heard?'

'We've told the head of Geography, Mr Swift, about the debate, and about what Dr McGinnis said,' said Peter. 'He looks after the society. He was surprised, rubbed his head as usual, and said: "Let me think about this!" He said he might have a word with Mrs Walsh about it.'

'But we'd better wait, hadn't we—just to see?'

'OK,' said Peter. 'I'll get back to you in a week or so. You lot have stirred things up, though.'

'It's an English Lit idea too, remember,' said Patricia. 'It's in my essay, and Mrs Walsh is my teacher. So you mustn't worry. OK?'

'OK,' said Margaret, nodding happily.

'Julius Caesar did want to copy Alexander, didn't he sir?' asked Michael Feeny in history class at the end of that day.

'Some of the most important sources do say that.'

'So he was copy-wanting power and fame, wasn't he?'

'Aha, yesterday's debate! For those who weren't there, three of your class—Margaret, Johnny and Eddy—won a debate yesterday, by coining a new word—copy-wanting. Catherine has just given you an example of its use. She's saying that Julius Caesar wanted just what Alexander had wanted, to be considered great.'

'Now why do people often want power do you think? Mr Lowney?'

'They get mmm...money as well that way.'

'They do indeed. As we have seen, people like Caesar were able simply to take the possessions of people they had defeated. And then they could apply taxes to make themselves even more wealthy. History is full of people who wanted everyone else to think they were great, and who fought for the privilege. You could say they all copy- wanted fame, power and wealth. Catherine?'

'Does that mean there is such a thing as copy-wanting?'

'Oh yes, there is indeed. It's interesting that I can't think of another word for just that idea. If that's what coveting means, that's interesting too. Even when the emperors recognised the church they continued to keep slaves—and the Church leadership did not finally and consistently oppose slavery for many centuries after that. Bridget?'

'When did it do that?'

'In the 1890s, long after Britain and some other countries had banned it. By then the Church was losing much of its power. It lost most of its lands in Italy by 1900. Now it only rules a small part of Rome, called Vatican City. Catherine?'

'Why can't Johnny and the others talk about copy-wanting, if it's something that exists?'

'Well, in my class they can if they wish—if it's relevant, of course. It's an idea that has meaning in this subject, and so it can be used here. Even the possibility that copy-wanting is covetousness can be discussed here, because we will discuss it merely as a possibility—something no-one is actually required to believe.

'In history we freely look into why things happen, so I'm not going to stop anyone speaking about that. History doesn't tell people what to believe, so people are also free to reject anything anyone says too. Mr Maguire?'

'Couldn't that get you into trouble, Sir?'

'Different subjects have different rules. History is not about the truths of the faith—it's a free investigation of the past, so our rules will be different from the rules relating to Religion. If saying that gets me into trouble, I can put up with that—but I don't think it will. Bridget?'

'Teachers don't agree about everything, do they?'

'No, they don't, Bridget. And if they did, life would be very dull. There wouldn't be anything to discuss.'

The whole class went quiet for a while then. Eventually Catherine Canning put up her hand.

'How are we to know what's right then?'

'On all sorts of questions we must all learn to reach our own conclusions. That's not always easy. There are big questions you will go on thinking about all your lives if you are wise. And it's always useful to have someone like the Pope to tell you what he thinks—that helps to keep us all together in the same discussion.

'But, to be grown-up, you must learn to put up with not being sure about everything. Don't always be looking for someone else to make up your mind for you.

'And now, as usual, Eight B has taken me away from the subject of this lesson—the Great Wall of China. So take this question for homework.'

Mr Foley turned to the board then and wrote: *Why was the Great Wall built, and was it effective?*

'You'll find the answer in your book, if you read carefully. You can start straight away now, as I am somewhat exhausted by all those questions.'

Mr Foley sat down in his chair then, and the class worked on till the bell. Johnny was last to leave the room. As he was about to reach the door he heard Mr Foley say: 'Mr Mullan!' He stopped and turned.

'Yes, Sir.'

'I'm keeping my eye on you!'

Johnny as usual wasn't sure how to take this, as Mr Foley's straight face gave him no clue.

'Thanks, Sir.'

'You and your friends have disturbed the waters here.'

'Sorry, sir.'

'Where now am I to get a quiet coffee?'

———∘∘∘❉∘∘∘———

'This is to keep you up to date with what's going on,' said Mrs Walsh.

It was Friday lunchtime, and the three debating bridgers were again in one of the interview rooms. In English class in second period, Mrs Walsh had quietly asked Johnny to take the others there.

'First, I've had good reports about all of you from your teachers. You've done what I asked, and no one has complained about any of you being cheeky or disobedient. And although some of the others in your class have taken your part you haven't been complaining yourselves.

'Patricia Brolly has also shown me her essay on Shakespeare. I'm impressed with her argument that your idea, copy-wanting, is closely connected to the word 'envy' that Shakespeare uses. That helped me to think out whether it applies in my subject, English.

'I've also been talking to Mr Swift, head of Geography, and to Mr Foley, your history teacher. They all think your idea is interesting, though it's far too soon to say how important it is. They can't see that it would be in any way harmful to discuss it in those classes either.

'All of that has helped me to think what to say to Dr McGinnis. We had a long chat yesterday afternoon, after school. I told him all this.

'I told him also that these ideas are your own—not something the seniors put you up to win the debate. He is surprised at that.

'However, he still thinks that your linking of the idea of copy- wanting to the Bible and Jesus is ... dangerous. He can't understand why you are so attached to it, and why you want to do that. He wants to ask you that—why you want to add that on to your own beliefs. He feels sure that he can persuade you that it is a ... an unnecessary idea, and that as good Catholic children you should simply accept what you are taught.

'So he wants to sit down and talk to you about it, tomorrow, to get the matter out of the way before December tests. Here, in this room.

'I said that as your form teacher I would need to be present also, and he has agreed to that. Miss Doherty also will be here, if you wish. Only if your parents approve, of course—you must ask them also. If they wanted to be present, we could arrange that too. Would you be willing to do that?'

The three bridgers looked at one another, trying to take in everything Mrs Walsh had said. Johnny found that Eddy and Margaret were looking at him to take a lead.

He remembered again Dr McGinnis's serious face, but then thought of Mick and felt certain he would want them all to talk to the head of Religion.

'It's OK with me,' he said.

'Margaret?'

'Yes, Miss. But I'd like Miss Doherty to be there.'

'Yes, Miss. Me too,' said Eddy. Johnny nodded.

'Very well. I've written notes for your parents explaining all this. I'm hoping they will send a note back, agreeing, tomorrow. Now, is there anything else you'd like to ask?'

'Is Dr McGinnis very annoyed, Miss?' asked Margaret.

'I would say concerned is a better word. But I think you will find that he is prepared to listen carefully to what you have to say. You must think out what that is, and say it as well as you can. You could maybe say a prayer about it all too.'

'If we still believe what we said, and Dr McGinnis does too, what will happen then?'

'We may need to ask the Principal, Mr Ferguson, to rule on the matter. But let's not think about that until we must—all right?'

The bridgers agreed.

Mrs Walsh reached into her briefcase then, and took out three white envelopes, handing one to each of them. The names had been typed. Johnny's read: *Mr K and Mrs A Mullan.*

'If that's all then, I'll simply say that I'm proud that three of my form class are doing so much thinking for themselves. And that they have set so many other people thinking too. That can't be bad for the school. Good luck on Wednesday—if your parents approve of the meeting, that is.'

Margaret was still feeling anxious, but thought that if Mrs Walsh and Miss Doherty were present on the Friday, nothing awful could happen.

'Well, now—would you like me to be there?'

Mrs Phillips asked Margaret this that afternoon in their living area at home, as they sipped cups of coffee.

She had just read Mrs Walsh's letter, saying 'Moses!' just twice.

Margaret was undecided. She wanted to be grown-up, but she was a little afraid of Dr McGinnis. He was so tall, and had such a deep voice. When he frowned he made you feel something awful was happening.

'I'm not sure. I'm a bit worried about what he said— about counterfeit money.'

'That's just rhetoric—something said just to impress. He knows how to frighten people, I think.

'Look, Margaret, I see it this way!' Mrs Phillips went on, sitting down at the dining table beside her.

'The world is full of different ways of thinking. There are many different kinds of Christians first of all. Then there are other beliefs altogether, like Buddhism and Islam and Hinduism, and Taoism—and they are all divided too.

And then there are people who think that all religion is bunk.

'Somehow we've all got to get along without coming to blows. And I think we can, if we just respect one another—if we all just let one another be.

'In the past Christians didn't believe that was possible. They thought that people with different ideas were dangerous. They were so convinced of that they murdered people whose ideas were different and made war on Islam and one another.

'But nobody won, and millions were killed. So gradually people got used to disagreeing with one another.

'But there are still some people who want a world where everyone thinks the same. They are afraid of difference. I think that's what's wrong with Dr McGinnis.

'There are still powerful people in the Church who think that way. They want everyone to think exactly what the Pope thinks, even on matters that are not that important. When any Catholic disagrees with anything he says they call that 'dissent' and go on as though that's awful—as though everyone will go to hell if they do that.

'I think that's where Dr McGinnis is coming from. He's just not ready to put up with people thinking differently, on anything.

'But Margaret—that's his problem, not yours! You have your own way of thinking, and you have a right to think that way. It doesn't matter who disagrees with it, or whether they think it's right.

It makes sense to you and Johnny and the others, and it makes sense to me too.

'And so does materialism and all that stuff. That was what I was taught, you see, and it makes a kind of sense to me still. So I can think in both ways, you see, and it doesn't bother me.

'He should be able to do that too, as a highly qualified teacher. He should be able to say: "You think coveting means copy-wanting? That's interesting!"—and then have a good-natured discussion about it. Instead he's making a big drama about it, and wanting to have his own way in his own school.

'So if you think that Dr McGinnis will try to frighten you, I'll sit in that room with you and quote him that sentence on religious liberty—and tell him *he* isn't the truth, do you hear?'

Margaret had never heard her mother speak in so determined and angry a way about anything. She pictured the scene in the interview room, with Dr McGinnis hearing her tall mother say that to him in that way—and suddenly lost her fear.

Margaret giggled suddenly. She then leaned over and pressed her mother's arm.

'It's OK, Mum! If he does try to frighten us, can't I tell him that myself?'

'Well now—here's a fuss!' said Anny to Johnny that same afternoon, after she had read Mrs Walsh's letter.

Johnny could tell that she wasn't mad at him. Already she knew what Mrs Phillips thought about the situation. Johnny had told her also what Mrs Walsh had said earlier.

'Do you want either of us to come?' she asked then. 'We will if you like.'

'No. There'll be the three of us, and Mrs Walsh will be there too. It'll be OK.'

Anny was a bit doubtful, but when Kevy came in later and read the letter he agreed with Johnny.

'Let him stand on his own two feet. He has the words for it, doesn't he? If they take it to the principal, then we can make a row, can't we?'

'I suppose. I just hope it works out, and they don't have to leave.'

'Well if the church just wants 'yes' people that's up to them. We Mullans make up our own mind. If they say he can't stay then Johnny's too good for them, isn't he? Any other school will be glad to have him.'

Although he was glad to have his parents' support, Johnny didn't want to think about leaving Iona College. All his best friends were there now. And what would happen to the bridgers if they were split up?

—ooo◆ooo—

On Friday at half-past three, Johnny, Eddy and Margaret stood waiting outside the largest of the school's three interview rooms off the front hall of the school.

All three were tense, Margaret especially so. She closed her eyes and asked.

At that moment three people came through the door at the back of the hall. Mrs Walsh was looking up and talking to Dr McGinnis alongside, and Miss Doherty followed behind. Margaret looked to see if Dr McGinnis was smiling, but wasn't able to tell. He wasn't frowning, but he seemed more serious than Mrs Walsh. He acknowledged the bridgers then.

'Ah, all punctual I see. That's good,' said Mrs Walsh to them. She was smiling, but seemed a bit distracted. She opened the door with a key and went in. The three debaters waited until the other two teachers had followed her before going in.

Already the furniture had been arranged. There were three chairs behind the table, where teachers usually sat. Mrs Walsh stood in front of the middle chair and waited while Dr McGinnis seated himself to her right. Miss Doherty took the seat to her left. She gave Margaret, standing opposite a brief encouraging smile.

'Now you three,' said Mrs Walsh. Margaret sat facing Miss Doherty, with Eddy on her left. Johnny was facing Dr McGinnis. To Margaret he looked even bigger than he had in the lecture theatre, because he was closer.

He was opening a black notebook. He laid this on the table in front of him. On the left hand page it had a list of numbered sentences, or maybe questions, as they ended in what could be either question marks or exclamation marks. It was difficult to tell as Margaret was looking at it upside down.

Mrs Walsh began with introductions. As she named the bridgers again for Dr McGinnis he nodded to them without smiling.

'Dr McGinnis has asked for this meeting, as he wishes to understand why you want to uphold the ideas you presented to us this day last week in the lecture theatre, and to explain his own reactions to that.

'Perhaps we could begin, then, by asking Johnny and Margaret to explain again how they came to make up the word 'copy-wanting'. Johnny could start.'

So once again Johnny gave an account of how they had come to use that word. Margaret joined in to give examples. She forgot where she was as she described how she had made the connection between copy-wanting and the environmental problems that so gripped her.

Dr McGinnis listened without any change of expression. Once or twice he made a note on the right hand page of his notebook.

'Good. Now Johnny, how did you come to connect copy-wanting and war?'

Johnny had soon explained that, without mentioning Mr Foley's help in finding out about Napoleon and Hitler 'Already Margaret wanted us to speak against the motion on materialism,' said Johnny. 'Because she thought we mightn't ever get another chance to talk about copy-wanting and the environment. And then Eddy said copy-wanting caused crimes as well.

'Tell us about that, Eddy,' said Mrs Walsh.

Eddy explained and gave some examples he hadn't used in the debate.

'But why did you connect all of this with the story of Jesus,' asked Dr McGinnis then, speaking for the first time.

'Well if copy-wanting was wrong I thought the Bible would say so,' said Margaret. 'I thought of the ten commandments, and when I looked up 'coveting' the dictionary said it was yearning for what someone else had. And Jesus didn't do that—so we thought that coveting and copy-wanting were probably the same thing.'

'That is not what the church teaches,' said Dr McGinnis. 'As I warned you, the Catechism uses the word avarice.'

'Sir, none of your books are thousands of years old, are they?' asked Johnny.

'No, young man, they are not, but why is that relevant?'

'Well coveting is a very old word, sir. And people don't use it much now. Maybe it did mean copy-wanting back when Jesus and Moses used it, and people have just forgotten that.'

'You are, I think, just eleven years old. How can you question hundreds of years of thinking otherwise?'

'Well, Sir, I'm nearly twelve. And if coveting isn't copy-wanting, and the Bible and Jesus don't say copy-wanting is wrong, do *you* think it's wrong?'

Dr McGinnis paused for a moment, and then sighed impatiently.

'You are asking me to comment on a word that isn't even in the dictionary!'

'But Sir, copy-wanting is real, isn't it? People do it all the time, so there should be a word for it, shouldn't there?'

Dr McGinnis sighed again impatiently, leaned back and brushed back his dark hair.

'Mrs Walsh, these children are presuming to teach me my own subject. Could you kindly please explain to them the difference between the role of the teacher and the role of the pupil.'

Mrs Walsh paused for a long moment then, looking at Johnny. To Margaret it seemed she wasn't sure what she should say next. Then she made up her mind.

'I'm sorry, Dr McGinnis, but it seems to me that Johnny, as a pupil, has politely asked a fair question of a teacher. He and Eddy and Margaret have described clearly something they see happening around them. I have taught them that everything that is clearly seen and described can have a word attached to it, so it is reasonable for them to ask what that word is in this case. I can find no exact match in my own sources, but 'coveting' comes closer than anything else.' Margaret saw the first flash of anger pass over Dr McGinnis's face at this point. She had half expected this would happen, but she knew also that none of the bridgers had provoked it.

'Mrs Walsh, you must understand that the language in which the church chooses to discuss matters such as this must be defined by the church's own experts. We can't allow new words to be added at a whim by children.'

'But surely young people's questions are important, Dr McGinnis. Is it not our responsibility to answer them as best we can? These pupils have clearly described a phenomenon—something that does often happen—a phenomenon that is, if you are correct, without a name. Don't you find that interesting?'

'No, Mrs Walsh,' said Dr McGinnis. 'I find it ... tiresome. The unknown words in which these children think do not interest me. They are effectively trying to alter the terminology of an entire subject. Where they see, hm ... 'copy-wanting' I see other things that travel under other names, such as materialism, aggression and theft.'

Mrs Walsh paused then for the longest time before continuing.

'Nevertheless, Dr McGinnis, Johnny has asked a question that relates to what is right and wrong, and to what our Lord would say about something they see happening all around them in their own world. If the Religion department cannot answer it, should we be surprised if he and his friends propose their own answers?'

Mrs Walsh was speaking calmly, but Margaret sensed from his grimace that Dr McGinnis was becoming more and more annoyed.

'Mrs Walsh, the church's teachings have had centuries of development. Together they make up an elaborate and complex system of ideas which takes years to master. These children then come along and propose an entirely different and childishly simple solution for problems that theologians and philosophers have explained in other ways. How *can* we take them seriously? Are first- year pupils to take the place of teachers in this school? Why must they insist on thinking and speaking as they do?'

'Well, perhaps we should ask them,' said Mrs Walsh, turning towards the three debaters. 'Eddy, why do you want to go on believing and saying that Jesus was against copy-wanting?'

'Because copy-wanting is wrong, isn't it? That's the way I think now, about the reasons for all sorts of crime. For example, some boys in my class don't like Mr Slaney when he sends us out running in the wind and hailstones. Suppose some of them wanted to copy those boys in Germany and America who shot their teachers—I wouldn't be able to warn Mr Slaney, would I?'

Margaret thought he saw the briefest of smiles flicker across the face of Mrs Walsh. Miss Doherty put her hand in front of her mouth at the same moment. Dr McGinnis just stared.

'Johnny? Why do you want to say Jesus was against copy- wanting?'

'People always wanting to be great and powerful, Miss. That's what I don't like. I think that's why Jesus didn't want all the kingdoms of the world, Miss. If someone has too much power, then other people have no ... freedom. We're all equal, Miss, so no-one can be greater than anyone else. I think that's what Jesus was trying to say. If I'm not allowed to say that, I won't be able to say why I like him so much, will I?'

Dr McGinnis leaned across the table towards Johnny.

'Equality—hah! That dangerous illusion of the modern mind. Listen carefully to me young man!'

At this point Dr McGinnis drew himself up on his seat.

'Are you equal to me in height?'

'No, Sir.'

'Are you equal to me in years, in experience?'

'No, Sir.'

'Are you equal to me in knowledge and education?'

'No, Sir.'

'Then in what possible way would the Lord Jesus say you were equal to me?'

'In *value*, Sir.'

Dr McGinnis immediately pulled backward. He looked then towards Johnny's form teacher.

'Mrs Walsh, are you not going to reprimand this child for his impertinence?'

'Dr McGinnis, Johnny was not being impertinent. He said 'in value ... Sir,' showing due respect. And are we not all equal in value, in dignity—male and female, adult and child? Is that not what our church teaches, in *Pacem in Terris*, for example?'

Dr McGinnis began to redden. He folded his arms, and looked to the ceiling, saying to no one in particular:

'These children are impossible! And yet they are allowed to speak!'

'Let's hear them all out, Dr McGinnis. Margaret—why do you want so much to be free to speak out?'

'Miss, before we found out about copy-wanting I didn't know Jesus said anything that would help us to save all the forests and the animals. I found that strange. If coveting isn't copy-wanting, then what would he say about all the ways people buy things they don't need? If every priest and clergyman and teacher could warn people about copy-wanting, and the Pope said that too, things would change, Miss, I'm sure they would. And people would see that living simply is the way to save the world.

'If I can't say that, Miss—if all I can say is that he was against materialism, then I'll have to give a big complicated explanation of what that means, and people will be bored. They won't listen. They're not listening now, are they? That's because they think that materialism doesn't have anything to do with them—they think it's just what other people do.

'But everyone understands copy-wanting, Miss, because almost everyone does it. People in our class understand it, Miss, after just one debate, and some of the seniors too. If I can't say Jesus was against copy-wanting, then I can't say what I believe, deep down. I'll have to give up what's deep inside me, in here, and in my mind too, my own faith, my own ... conscience—my very own—in my own school.'

Margaret stopped at that point, almost tearful. Miss Doherty spoke then.

'Dr McGinnis!' she murmured urgently. 'Jeremiah 31:31.'

'Thank you, Miss Doherty' said Dr McGinnis. 'I'm familiar with the text. And that's what worries me. What we are dealing with here is far more serious than you realise.'

He folded his notebook and stood to address the room from his full height.

XVII

'On Wednesday last I thought we were dealing with nothing more than ignorance. Now I see that the situation is far, far more serious.' The gowned head of religion stared at the bridgers then and turned to Mrs Walsh and Miss Doherty—now also standing.

'Does nothing strike you about all three of these children? This obstinacy, this lack of compliance, this ... headstrong conviction? This modern fixation about liberty and equality? This sureness that they can interpret scripture without reference to the church's tradition? What does this bring to mind?'

He waited then, as the two other teachers looked at one another, and shook their heads.

'Isn't it the *Protestant* tradition? The tradition of protest and dissent?'

'Dr McGinnis, that's go ...,' Mrs Walsh tried to speak but the head of religion swept on.

'These children have grown up in a largely Protestant culture, remember. They all live to the east of this city—the more Protestant part. The media they watch are tinged with Protestant and secular influences. Subtly, they have been separated from the culture of obedience and docility that is so much a part of our own true Catholic tradition—especially in children of their age.

'Everything I've heard today has confirmed my worst fears. We are dealing here with the demon of dissent—the same demon that is at work in the Church throughout the west, undermining the discipline it must have to survive.

'I have heard quite enough. I must ask you now, Mrs Walsh, to instruct these children, as their form teacher, on no account to repeat these semi-heretical theories to anyone else in the school. They must either agree to be silent, or look for another school.'

There was total silence for many moments. Margaret wondered if it would ever end.

'I won't do that, Dr McGinnis,' said Mrs Walsh then calmly. 'I am satisfied they are sincere, and that they have denied no essential Catholic teaching. I am proud to have them in my class. We have far too few pupils with a vital, thinking faith as it is.'

'I agree with Mrs Walsh,' said Miss Doherty, looking steadily at her superior.

'So,' said Dr McGinnis, pale, stiffening. 'Dissent is spreading even as we speak, even among colleagues. I must take this matter to the principal immediately. There is no more to be said.'

The head of religion turned away then and swept out of the room.

'Miss,' said Margaret after a moment. 'That wasn't fair.'

'I know,' said Mrs Walsh. 'I'm sorry. No teacher should ever speak like that to you, or about you.'

'What will happen now?'

'We will appeal to Mr Ferguson on your behalf. Today you were all respectful and sincere. Nothing you said has justified Dr McGinnis's reaction. We will give Mr Ferguson a full account of what happened here.'

'I'll tell him the same,' said Miss Doherty. 'That was awful!'

'What did he mean by ... 'semi-heret ... ical theories'?'

'I don't think it meant anything,' said Mrs Walsh. 'A teaching is either heretical—contrary to essential Catholic teaching—or it's not.

It's not for any one of *us* to pronounce on that either. As far as I am concerned you Margaret, and you, Johnny are good Catholics still.

And Eddy has been true to his own good conscience.'

'I agree,' said Miss Doherty.

'Will we be allowed to stay, and to say what we believe?' asked Johnny.

'That will be up to Mr Ferguson, and to the school governors. I certainly will impose no such ban. I'll be writing to your parents, confirming my own support for you. They may wish to see me, and Mr Ferguson—and the governors too, if it comes to that. This matter won't be resolved until after Christmas now—because tests begin shortly for everyone. But if you can't stay at Iona, I'm not sure I'll want to stay here either.'

'Nor I,' said Miss Doherty. She seemed quite shocked by what had occurred.

'Please keep everything that happened today to yourselves, for your own sake ... and the school's sake. Will you promise not to talk about it to your class?'

The three were ready to do so.

'Miss, my Mum is picking us up now. Could you explain to her...'

'Of course. Get your bags now, and meet back in the hall.'

The three bridgers went to the lockers then.

'We know what he's like when he gets mad now, don't we,' said Eddy, wide-eyed.

'Yes, but it wasn't just us that did it, was it?' asked Johnny.

'Wait till my Mum hears!' said Margaret.

Going back through the hall she met Miss Doherty, carrying her briefcase.

'Are you all right, Margaret?'

'Yes, Miss—or I will be soon. But can I ask you something?'

'Of course!'

'After I said why I want to go on thinking the way I do, you said something to Dr McGinnis—something about Jer ... Jeremiah?'

'Yes—the Book of Jeremiah, chapter thirty-one, verse thirty-one.

It's the start of a famous passage in the Bible. You know how to look that up don't you?'

'Yes, Miss.'

'Read it when you get home, and the next few verses, especially verse thirty-three.'

'Thanks, Miss.'

'It's more than a pleasure,' said Miss Doherty.

She smiled and put her hand on Margaret's shoulder.

—•००◦००•—

'Methuselah!' said Mrs Phillips, looking over at Margaret as she drove home. 'The man's bonkers! Semi-heretical indeed! I wonder what a solicitor would have to say about that!'

Margaret had never heard her mother calling a teacher 'bonkers' before—or anyone else either. She was still quaking, but also felt strangely inclined to laugh.

'I wonder what Mr Ferguson will say,' said Johnny.

'Will he want to see us too?' asked Margaret.

'Maybe,' said Mrs Phillips. 'But this time I'll be there— and you two boys' parents should be also. I think I'll have a chat with all of them, to see where we go from here. Tell them I'll give them a call.'

'Give us that again!' said Kevy. 'When you told McGinnis everyone was equal!'

Kevy was sitting at the dinner table that same Friday evening.

Anny and Kevy had listened in complete silence to Johnny. Kevy had even stopped eating at times, so that he could concentrate.

Johnny again described how Dr McGinnis had asked him in what way they were equal, and how he had answered.

'Humph!' said Kevy in wonder, turning to Anny. 'In our day if I talked like that I would have got a clatterin'! And when I got home me Da would maybe have given me another one!'

'But Johnny's right, Da,' said Anny. 'That man was just trying to bully him. Johnny wasn't being cheeky, just telling the truth. Good for him, I say!'

Kevy nodded.

'He's got the words right enough, hasn't he! And McGinnis got into a bate then, and went to see the Principal? Teachers not backin' one another up! That's a new one too!'

'Will we go to see the Principal, if Mrs Phillips says we should?' asked Anny.

Kevy pondered for a moment, sucking on a tooth and staring at Johnny.

'Why not?' he said. 'Just to back him up. But maybe we'd better let him do the talkin'!'

Anny smiled at Johnny and shook her head.

'Dignity!' said Kevy again in a thoughtful way. He started thinking about something else then. His eyes were staring at the water jug, but weren't seeing it.

On Saturday morning Margaret learned from her mother that Mr Ferguson had decided to refer the whole matter to the bishop's representative on the school's board of governors.

'He says you went through enough on Friday and shouldn't face another ordeal like that so soon,' Mrs Phillips said. 'And I agree.

Mrs Walsh and Miss Doherty made a strong case in your favour, he says. He agrees that the matter raises serious questions for the school.

'We'll be telling him we may well be taking legal advice,' she went on. 'I'm not sure the school is entitled to act as Dr McGinnis wants it to.'

'But will we not get a chance to tell Mr Ferguson, or the governors, what we think?'

'We will insist you are heard by whoever makes the final decision, don't worry!'

Later, when the others arrived with the same news, Mary had to hear in detail what had happened, and had become thoughtful.

'What does it say?' she asked. Margaret had finished by telling her of Miss Doherty's reference to the prophet Jeremiah.

'I've got it here,' said Margaret, reaching into a pocket in her blouse. 'I'm learning it off.' She found a slip of paper and read:

'Behold, the days are coming,' says the Lord, 'when I will make a new covenant with the house of Israel and with the house of Judah -- I will put my law in their minds, and write it on their hearts; and I will be their God, and they shall be my people.'

'Let me see,' said Mary.

She read the passage to herself then slowly.

'A covenant is an important agreement, isn't it?' she asked.

Margaret nodded.

'That's what's happened to us then, isn't it?' Mary asked. 'Being a bridger and knowing Jesus is the greatest bridger?'

'Yes.'

Mary was silent then for a while, as though in two minds about something. Then she suddenly decided.

'Whatever happens to you, I want it to happen to me too! You're the best friends I've ever had, and I'm a bridger too. I'm going to tell my Da that I think the same way you three do—and that I won't stay if Mr Ferguson says you must go to another school!'

Margaret was silent for a moment.

'What will your Dad say, do you think?'

'I'm not sure. But he knows your Mum now, and he knows what good friends we are. If I tell him what's happening, would your Mum explain everything to him?'

'I'm sure she would!'

'Then he could ring Mr Ferguson, and tell him I'd be leaving too, if you go.'

'Are you sure, Mary?'

'Yes,' said Mary. 'I like Iona but I definitely don't want to be here if you're not here. Especially if that ... Dr McGinnis ever becomes principal.'

At that moment Mrs Phillips came back to the room, having made another phone call.

'The bishop's representative—yes, it's a Monsignor Murphy. He was a teacher himself for years. Then he became a principal. He spent some time in America too, studying for a degree in Catechetics—that's about how to teach the faith. He's also got a degree in English literature, because he likes reading.'

'What does monsignor mean?' asked Eddy.

'It's from the Italian for my lord. It means he's more important than a parish priest, but less important than a bishop.'

There was silence then for a bit. Johnny didn't seem to like the sound of Monsignor Murphy.

'How old is he?' asked Margaret. Monsignor Murphy must be old, she thought, if he had done all that.

'About seventy-five. He's semi-retired now, and helping out in a parish in Donegal, near where he was brought up.

They say he's orthodox—that means he believes the whole creed—but a bit of a character also.'

'What does that mean?' asked Johnny.

'I suppose it means that you can't easily describe him—and that he's a bit unpredictable ... that he makes up his own mind, I suppose.'

'Does he know Dr McGinnis well?' asked Eddy.

'No-one knows that for certain. They have met of course, but maybe not much. Dr McGinnis is only in Iona for about six years.

Before that he was teaching in a college in England. The two would have met occasionally when Monsignor Murphy came to the school for meetings of the board of governors. They may know one another in other ways of course—no one's sure.'

'Does Monsignor Murphy want Dr McGinnis to be the next principal of Iona?' asked Mary.

'No one knows,' said Mrs Phillips. 'That's a good question too, Mary. If it's true that the bishop wants that, then the monsignor will know that. But that doesn't mean he would necessarily make a decision against you. In a way Dr McGinnis is on trial in this whole business too.'

'What do you mean by 'on trial'?' asked Margaret.

'Well, he has made an enormous fuss about three, and now four, first-year pupils speaking their own minds. And that's all liable to end up on the TV news. There's a big question about how wise he is to do that just now. I'm hoping that Monsignor Murphy will understand that better than Dr McGinnis does, as he knows Ireland better.'

'What would happen to Dr McGinnis if Monsignor Murphy said he was wrong?' asked Mary.

'No-one knows that, but it could be serious. It could mean he wouldn't be offered the principal's job.'

'Wow!' said Eddy. 'That would be great, wouldn't it?'

'Who would get it then?' asked Johnny.

'Well, it would have to be advertised anyway, of course, so it could go to an outsider. Or it could go to another teacher in the school.

Mr Foley is popular with everyone and maybe deserves it, but he's not too far from retirement age, so they might look for someone younger.

'I've also heard Mrs Walsh's name mentioned,' Mrs Phillips said then. 'She is gifted with children, and well qualified also. She's younger than principals usually are, but they say the job needs younger people now, with so many changes taking place in education.'

The four bridgers looked at one another.

'Wow!' said Eddy again. 'That would be even better!'

'Mrs Walsh said she might leave Iona if it decided against us,' said Margaret.

'Did she now!' said Mrs Phillips, sounding surprised. She thought about that for a few seconds.

'Well if she said that to you, she may well have said it to Mr Ferguson too. And if she did, he would certainly pass that on to Monsignor Murphy. That would be serious for the school, as her senior pupils get some of the top marks in English in the whole country. That's one of the main reasons I wanted Margaret to go there.'

'Does that mean everything depends on what we say to Monsignor Murphy?' asked Johnny. 'Even who is to be the next principal of Iona?'

'Don't you worry your heads about that!' said Mrs Phillips. 'You four should forget about the whole matter for a bit, and just get on with your work as if everything was normal.'

Margaret agreed with her mother, but she knew it would be even harder now to forget about Monsignor Murphy, and what he might ask them.

'Let's go for a walk!' she said. 'The sun's come out.'

At the end of English class on Tuesday morning Mrs Walsh asked the bridgers to stay on after the class had left.

'Monsignor Murphy wants to talk to you all on Thursday, after school. I have notes here for your parents telling them this. They could be present too if they wish. Or if they prefer, I could sit in with you.'

'I'd like you to be there, Miss,' said Margaret. 'It's not easy for my mum to get off—I think she's teaching that afternoon.'

'Same here,' said Mary. 'I'm sure my Da will say it's all right for you to be there too.'

Johnny and Eddy nodded also.

'Thank you for that vote of confidence,' said Mrs Walsh. 'You mustn't worry about this, you know. Monsignor Murphy is a nice person, I've heard. He just wants to get to know you all.'

'But it's important, isn't it Miss?' asked Mary.

'Yes—I suppose it is. But I'm sure if you four are just able to be yourselves, and answer as you have done up to now, the monsignor will see there is nothing to be concerned about.'

'How are *you*, Miss?' Margaret asked then. Now that she was up close she could see that her form teacher looked tired behind her glasses, with darker patches under her eyes.

'I'm well thank you, Margaret. Life is ... interesting for me just now, that's all.'

'We hope we can stay, and you can too, Miss,' said Johnny. 'You're the best teacher we've all ever had, by a mile!'

'Why thank you, Johnny!' said Mrs Walsh as the others nodded.

'And the rest of you too. You are rewarding pupils. Now take these notes and off you go quickly, to your next class.'

Looking back at the door, Margaret saw that her form teacher had her hand to her mouth and was blinking behind her glasses.

'Bye, Miss,' she said softly.

Mrs Walsh just dipped her head slightly, and blinked again.

Later that day a rumour of something serious began to circulate at the college—and that all would hear of it the following day at assembly. When the bridgers arrived there and took their places with their class the following morning they saw both Mr Ferguson and Miss Considine, the vice principal, on the stage, conferring with another teacher whose name they didn't know.

Johnny half-expected some revelation to do with what had been happening to themselves, but after prayers Mr Ferguson soon showed that he had something else on his mind.

'You will all remember the school rules and a warning I myself gave from this stage at the start of the year—about the consequences for any pupil of being found in possession of illegal substances.

Tragically, our worst fears have been realised.

'A senior pupil who should have been listening that day did not take heed. Last week it came to our attention that he might be an offender in this most serious matter. A search of his belongings in the school confirmed the worst. He has been suspended, pending a meeting of the school governors. I cannot see how he can avoid the penalty he was warned about—summary expulsion. Prosecution and a criminal record may well follow, a complete disruption of the expectations his poor parents and he himself have had.

'We tell you this for your own sakes. Avoid all contact or dealings with these dreadful substances. We cannot overlook their dangers for all pupils. We will pray for this pupil and his family, now—led by Mr Swift, the form teacher of the boy concerned. You should all be deeply conscious of the tragedy for any pupil who has stood in this hall never to be able to stand among us again. Pray for yourselves also, at this beginning of Advent, that this will not ever happen to you.'

The third teacher stepped forward then and read solemn prayers, without naming the pupil concerned. All in the hall responded with Amen, the juniors' voices drowned by the seniors.

Johnny could feel depression in the hall. He could see that none of the bridgers doubted the seriousness of what had happened. Mary especially seemed troubled. She was saying a line over to herself. He knew this habit well now, and asked her as soon as he could what it could be.

'*Will someone come to break this chain,*' she said.

———◦◦◦❖◦◦◦———

'None of us have heard anything then?' Margaret asked. Johnny too shook his head.

The four were in the same interview room alone on the Morning of the Thursday of their meeting with Monsignor Murphy. Miss Doherty's and Mrs Walsh's classes followed one another on that day of the week, and their teachers knew they wanted a last chance for a conference.

'The bridgers must think we're ready, then,' said Johnny.

'But what if we're asked something tricky?' asked Mary.

'Yes—Monsignor Murphy might do that,' said Margaret. 'Dr McGinnis is saying some of our ideas are Protestant, remember.'

'But some Protestants say the same creeds too, Miss Doherty says,' Johnny reminded them.

It was a gloomy November day. A drizzle had stopped momentarily, and through the window they could see wisps of fog over the river.

'So we can say we do believe in the creeds then, can't we?' said Johnny.

The others nodded.

'We three *are* Catholics, aren't we?' asked Mary. 'And Eddy has never tried to make us Taoists.'

'Protestants are Christians too,' Johnny said. They stand up for what they believe. I like that. I wonder if there are Protestant bridgers—like us I mean.'

He turned to them questioningly.

'That would be cool!' said Eddy. 'Maybe it wouldn't be awful if we all had to go to a Protestant school.'

The others were silent for a while, thinking about that.

'Come on,' said Margaret then. 'We *are* ready. We all know what to do if we get stuck.'

—∘∘∘⦁◈⦁∘∘∘—

As the bridgers entered the main hall that afternoon for their meeting with Monsignor Murphy, they met Dr McGinnis leaving it. He saw them, but then turned his head in another direction.

Most pupils had headed home already, so the hall was almost empty. There was a small group of seniors near the door, however, and Margaret recognised Liz, who gave a wave.

She saw Mrs Walsh then, standing outside the interview room.

'Let's go in,' her teacher said, pushing the door open. 'The Monsignor is with Mr Ferguson, and will be along in a moment.'

Again they found the furniture had been arranged for them, with four chairs on one side of the table, and one on the other. Mrs Walsh took another chair that had been placed to the side.

'Sit down,' she said, 'and relax for a moment.'

Margaret found that difficult to do. She had a picture in her head of a tall, stern priest who would have a fat notebook like Dr McGinnis, and she expected that image to come through the door at any moment.

'Have you met him yet, Miss?' asked Mary.

'We've met, of course, about other matters—but not about this as yet. He's not someone you should be afraid of.'

Mrs Walsh was trying to reassure them, Margaret could see, but their form teacher wasn't her usual bright and relaxed self either.

They heard men's voices then approaching the door, and two people came in. One was Mr Ferguson. The other was a grey- haired and quite small priest wearing rimless glasses. He was dressed in the black suit that priests often wore, but Margaret noticed a purple trimming. He had a bald patch on top of his head.

Mrs Walsh stood immediately, and the bridgers followed her example.

'These are the children, Monsignor Murphy,' said Mr Ferguson—'and Mrs Walsh, their form teacher.'

'Mrs Walsh!' he said, and shook hands.

'And these are the children with all the original ideas, are they?' he asked, turning to the bridgers for the first time. His expression was friendly, but searching also. He held Margaret's gaze for a long moment before looking with equal attention at the other three.

'John Mullan, Edward Li, Margaret Phillips and Mary McNevin,' Mrs Walsh announced, running along the line that the Monsignor saw, from right to left. 'This is Monsignor Murphy.'

'I'll leave you all to it then,' said Mr Ferguson, withdrawing and closing the door.

'Well, now,' said the Monsignor, sitting down. 'Sit down everyone. This is a get-to-know-you session. When I'm thinking about people I like to have a clear picture in my head of who I'm thinking about.

'The same is true for you, I suppose. Until you saw me you might think that a Monsignor would be some kind of giant who's about to gobble you up. So now you can see I'm not, can't you?'

The old priest paused then and peered at them as they nodded.

'Don't call me Monsignor either,' he went on. 'It makes me feel strange. The Church keeps titles from the past that might be better forgotten, in my view. So 'Father', or 'Sir' will do. I'm not entirely happy with 'Father', either but if you started calling me by my Christian name, which is Martin, the bishop might object, so 'Father' or 'sir' will have to do for the moment. All right?'

Again he paused.

Margaret suddenly began to feel less tense. If the monsignor could tell them his first name, then maybe he wasn't someone to be afraid of.

'We could call you 'Father Martin', couldn't we?' Johnny asked.

The monsignor peered at him for a moment, and then gave a half smile.

'Yes, John. That will do just fine. Is John what they call you?'

'Johnny.'

'I'll call you Johnny then too, all right? Well, Johnny, I've read your speech too, and I've read Mrs Walsh's and Miss Doherty's reports about you all, and interesting they are too. You thought up the word 'copy-want' didn't you?'

'Yes—but it was Margaret who said we needed a word for it. We did it together.'

'Ah, Margaret.' He peered at Margaret again then. 'You're the environmentalist, aren't you?'

'Yes, Father. But I agree with Johnny about power too. I don't think Jesus wanted it.'

'Why didn't he then?'

'He wants to change us inside, I think—not force us to do what he wants.'

'Johnny—how would he do that?'

'By not copy-wanting anything, not even power. That meant that he couldn't start a war when they came to kill him.'

'I see. So how does that make you feel about him?'

'I like him, Father. More than anyone else I've read about. I think he was smart, and brave too.'

'More than Spiderman or Batman or Captain Kirk or anyone like that?'

'Yes—because he was a real person, and he was smarter than they were.'

'Why do you say he was smarter?'

'Because he knew about copy-wanting, and how it starts wars.'

'How does it do that exactly?'

'Well if two people want the same thing, and it can't be shared—like a crown or a country, or something valuable that's running out, like oil—then they will probably fight over it, won't they? Or if a few people want to be the top person, like Julius Caesar and Pompey, or Octavian and Mark Antony. There can only be one top person too, so copy-wanting is likely to start a war too.'

'I see. So you think Jesus wanted to stop all that, do you?'

'Yes, Father.'

'Hmm,' said the monsignor. 'That's interesting. But what do you think about what you have been taught. What do you think communion is all about then, the Eucharist that we receive at Mass?'

'I'm not sure, but everyone can take it, can't they? It's not just for high-up people, is it?'

'No—so?'

'So maybe it means we're all equal too, and special as well. He doesn't make just one person special. He makes everyone special, because he comes inside them. Everyone has the same value then, don't they?'

'Humph—value—that's a strange word for someone your age. Where did you learn it?'

'It's in the *Tao-te-Ching*, Sir—and it means the same as dignity.'

'I see,' said the monsignor thoughtfully. 'We'll come to that book in a moment. So you think that if everyone knows they are special...?'

'Then they won't need to fight over who's the greatest, will they?'

'I see.'

The old priest pondered for a few moments, and then turned to Margaret.'

'I've read your speech too, and Mr Ferguson has showed me the advertisements you used. So I think I understand what you are saying. Is that idea, equality, important to you too?'

'Yes,' said Margaret. 'The reason people buy more than they need is to be greater than one another too. They're competing with one another.'

'Do you agree with what Johnny said about the Eucharist?'

'I didn't hear him say that before, but that makes sense.

Communion makes me feel special too, so if everyone feels that way, we shouldn't need to buy things to compete with one another, should we?'

'You think people compete?'

'Yes, mostly they do. That's why houses in America are getting bigger all the time. That's happening in Ireland now too, isn't it?'

'So how are we to stop all that then?'

'By thinking about Jesus, and how he lived, and how he died—and by praying to him too.'

'Do you pray then?'

'Yes—all the time.'

'Can I ask you how—what do you say?'

'I ask him to help us save all the forests and the animals, by teaching everyone not to copy-want.'

'Do you pray, Johnny?'

'Not so much. I used to think it was soppy, but now I do it more, because I think Jesus is real.'

'What do you mean by real?'

'A real person, not just someone cheesy that people make up. He's in history, like Julius Caesar.'

'But he's dead, isn't he, like Julius Caesar?'

'No—he came alive again, because he was the only one ever not to copy-want anything.'

'Do you all think that?'

Margaret, Mary and Eddy all nodded.

'So what do you think he wants you four to do?'

'Make bridges between people,' said Mary.

He looked closely at her then.

'Mary, isn't it? What do you mean by that exactly?'

'Well, as Margaret says, people wouldn't want to compete so much if they all knew they were special, would they?'

'No—so?'

'If you make them feel that, then you are doing what Jesus would do, aren't you?'

'So?'

'You're a bridge then, aren't you—between him and them?'

Monsignor Martin thought about that for a long while, looking at each of the four in turn.

'Do you all agree with that?'

They all nodded.

'Edward—do they call you Eddy?'

Eddy nodded.

'Well, Eddy, you give examples of copy-wanting causing crime, and that's why you think it's wrong, is it?'

Eddy nodded again.

'Why are you so interested in crime?'

'I'm going to be a detective. I hope so anyway.'

'Why is that?'

'I like the idea of solving puzzles, and locking up bad guys.'

'But you'll need power to do that, won't you—you can't do it if you're just equal to them, can you?'

'No,' said Eddy. 'But I'll have to keep the rules. I won't just be able to beat someone up if I don't like them.'

'Do criminals have value, dignity too then?'

'Yes. I've even read that policemen and bad guys often get quite friendly.'

'But doesn't it take away a person's dignity to lock them up?'

'Yes, in a way—but you do it to stop them doing something worse—killing someone maybe.'

'So it's not a complete solution then, locking them up?'

'No—you hope that they'll change when they think about what they have done.'

'I see. Would hearing about Jesus help them change?'

'Yes—because he didn't ever even lock anyone up. He just asked people to change.'

'Would you be able to say things like that, if you were a policeman, do you think?'

'Yes, I think so.'

'So even as a policeman you could do what Mary says— be a bridge for someone who had broken the law?'

'Yes.'

'I see. I see.'

The monsignor thought awhile then, looking at all four of them in turn. He was sitting back in his chair, with his hands folded.

'Mary—you didn't make a speech about copy-wanting like the others. How do you fit into all this?'

'Margaret's my best friend, and I agree with what all the others said. I've written a song about copy-wanting, and if they couldn't say what they think in Iona I wouldn't be able to play that song here either, would I?'

'No—I suppose not. Mr Ferguson told me about that song—I'd like to hear it. Could you play it for me?'

As Mary left the room to fetch her guitar the Monsignor turned to Johnny again.

'What do you want to be, Johnny?'

'I'm not sure, Father. A writer maybe, or a teacher.'

'What would you like to teach?'

'English, or maybe History—I haven't made up my mind.'

'I see—and would you write, or teach, about copy-wanting?'

'Yes, I think so. It definitely comes into history, and Mrs Walsh says it maybe comes into English too—Shakespeare.'

'Does she now—we could maybe have a talk about that!'

The monsignor turned to Mrs Walsh, who nodded.

'Margaret—what do you want to be?'

'I'm not sure—something to do with explaining to people why copy-wanting is so big a problem for the Earth, and helping to stop it. Teaching maybe too, or writing.'

'What would you teach, if that was what you decided?'

'Religion, maybe, or Geography, or English too.'

'And could you bring Jesus into Geography too?'

'Yes, Father. I'm told Mr Swift says it could be important if copy- wanting and coveting are the same thing. He thinks it might change the way the books talk about Christianity and the environment.'

'Mr Swift is ...?' The monsignor turned to Mrs Walsh.

'The head of Geography, Monsignor.'

'Is he your Geography teacher?' he asked Margaret.

'No,' said Margaret. 'The school's environmental society wants us to talk to them next term, and he will be there.'

'Did it now? Maybe I should have a word with him as well then. So, let's suppose you were a Geography teacher, and you were talking about the environment—what could you say about Jesus?'

'That he was someone who wants to save the Earth, as well as all of us. He lived simply, and everyone should do that too, and he told us not to covet.'

''To save the Earth.' That's interesting. You know how people say 'Jesus saves'?'

'Yes.'

'Another way of saying that is that he brings salvation. Would 'salvation' for you include saving the earth then?'

'Oh yes!'

'Anything else?'

'Saving us from ruining it too. He wants us to save it ourselves, I think, by following him.'

'I see. Hmm. You say, 'living simply'. Would that mean no mobile phones or computers or other gadgets?'

'There's nothing wrong with having one or two of them, but we shouldn't all want all of them—just the ones we need. It's better to do without things, if you can, so that others can have what they need.'

'Right. Right. I see.'

The monsignor pondered for another moment then. Mary returned at that moment and began tuning her guitar in the corner, but the monsignor didn't seem to notice.

'Let's see: You say copy-wanting comes into History, Johnny—and maybe English—and Margaret says it comes into Geography.

And of course, if that is what coveting is, it would come into Religion too. Do you like Religion class too—Johnny?'

'Yes. The bible has great examples of copy-wanting.'

'Tell me one.'

'Joseph's brothers wanted his coat, because it meant Jacob preferred him. They knew they couldn't have it so they hated him for it. That's why they gave him away as a slave.'

'And the woman who stole the other woman's baby, in King Solomon's time,' said Margaret.

'I see. I see. Any others?'

'Cain wanted to be God's favourite, but God preferred Abel,' said Johnny. 'So Cain copy-wanted what God gave Abel, but couldn't have it.'

'So the first murder in the Bible was a copy-wanting crime too!' said Eddy.

'Well now, I never thought of that,' said the Monsignor. 'So you like the Bible, Eddy?'

'Yes—I think it's like the *Tao te Ching*—because it's warning us not to copy-want. So it must come from the Tao too—the source of everything. Abba and the Tao are the same, I think.'

'Is the Tao a person then too? I thought that Taoists see the Tao as *not* being a person.'

'Well if the Tao is the source of everything, it has to be a person too, I think—because we all come from the Tao. Jesus helps me to see that—to see the Tao as kind and gentle, like the Prodigal Son's Dad, like Abba, and like my own Dad.'

The monsignor went quiet then, and nodded to himself twice.

Then he turned towards Mrs Walsh and nodded again.

'I think maybe that will do us for today,' he said then. 'I've got to know you all, and you've given me something to think about, haven't you?'

'Can we stay at Iona?' Mary asked.

The monsignor looked at her seriously.

'Iona is a Catholic school, Mary. You know that, don't you?'

'Yes.'

'Well, what does that mean to you exactly? What makes Iona a Catholic school?'

Mary thought a moment.

'Fr Phil's Mass at the start of term—he said the most important meaning of Catholic was *welcome*. He made us feel welcome too.

He said we should feel able to be ourselves here, saying just what we think, even though we are all different.'

'I see? And what did you think about that Mass?'

'It was special too. It was just for us. It made me feel special. I felt as if Iona was my home too. I hadn't felt that before.'

'I see. What about the rest of you? Was that Mass important to you?'

They all nodded.

'What would you say if I said you four were *too* different, that you were trying to change the Catholic character of the school—by bringing in something that wasn't there before—especially this copy-wanting idea?'

XVIII

There was silence then. Johnny knew the monsignor was asking an important question. He remembered suddenly a conversation they had all had about this. He wasn't sure he should speak of it, so he asked the usual question inside himself, and waited. Then he said:

'We think we're maybe bringing back something that got lost somehow—something important that fits with everything else.'

'How could it have got lost?'

'Well you know the way the church in the beginning was for poor people and didn't have any power?'

'Yes.'

'And then it got powerful, when Constantine made it legal?'

'Yes.'

'And from then on a lot of powerful and rich people joined it?'

The monsignor nodded again.

'Well maybe then priests and bishops didn't want to talk about copy-wanting things like big houses and power, in case they annoyed those people.'

'Why would that be exactly?' the monsignor asked.

'Well, you copy-want things that rich people have, but, if a priest says that, won't he annoy the people who are already rich—those who give a lot of money to the church? Won't they think he is getting at them? So maybe bishops and priests just stopped doing that, so that the rich people would stay in it.'

Monsignor Murphy pondered for another long moment.

'Hmm..' he said. He looked to Mrs Walsh. 'That comes close to home, I suppose.'

She gave a slight smile.

'But now when everyone's trying to be rich we've got to bring it back, haven't we—the way Pope Francis says?' asked Margaret.

The old priest studied Johnny and Margaret for a long moment.

'You've all thought a lot about this, I can see. That's definitely enough for now,' he said then, half-smiling. 'Mary—that song. Let's hear it now.'

As Mary played, the monsignor nodded occasionally to the rhythm, and seemed to listen closely to the words. Again she stopped at the 'Chain' verse.

'Do you have the words of that, Mary?' he asked. 'I'd like to study them too.'

She had a copy ready. He folded it carefully and placed it in the inside pocket of his suit.

'It's not finished yet, I think,' she said.

'Well if other verses come to you, give them to Mrs Walsh also—to pass on to me. You're talented, Mary. I suppose you want to be a famous singer?'

'No. I think I want to be a counsellor.'

'Humph,' he said. 'That's interesting too.' He studied her for a moment, and she didn't look away.

'Well, thank you all. I think I can find my way back to Mr Ferguson's room. Thank you, Mrs Walsh, also. You have four bright pupils here, haven't you?'

Mrs Walsh nodded and smiled. She moved towards the door, and opened it for the monsignor, who turned to the bridgers finally:

'I know you want to know as soon as possible if you can stay at Iona. I'm impressed by the fact that you all want to. I have some reading and thinking to do—and I must talk with some others. I should have reached a decision well before the end of next term—and I'll tell Mr Ferguson then. All right?'

He gave them a last nod then, and left.

'How did we do, Miss?' whispered Margaret when she was sure the monsignor was out of earshot.

'As well as you could have!' she said. She seemed relieved.

'He listened to us anyway, didn't he?' said Margaret. 'Not like Dr McGinnis!'

'Yes,' said Mrs Walsh. 'And that could make all the difference.

'I must go now,' she said then. 'The monsignor wants a word with me before leaving. You head off home now. Focus on the tests from now on, and try not to worry.'

'He was all right, wasn't he?' Johnny asked the others, when their form teacher had left. 'He asked us hard questions, but he didn't get mad when we told him what we thought—even when I said that about the bishops.'

'It's hard to know what he thinks, though,' said Mary. 'He could still side with Dr McGinnis.'

'Yes,' said Margaret. 'If he had decided to let us stay he would have been much friendlier, wouldn't he?'

The others nodded. They were all glad there hadn't been another row, but their future was still uncertain.

'You're all gettin' expelled, aren't you!'

Gavan Maguire said this exultantly to Johnny in the front hall in Iona the following morning.

'Where did you hear that?' asked Johnny, startled.

'My Da's on the board of governors, isn't he?' said Gavan. 'He says that Dr McGinnis has decided you four don't belong here, and he's going to be the next principal, isn't he?'

'Mr Ferguson will decide about us,' said Johnny. 'And he hasn't made up his mind yet.'

'Is that so?' said Gavan. 'Well maybe there's something about you he doesn't know—something he might find out!'

He left Johnny standing looking after him, thinking. Johnny knew Gavan hated him, but couldn't think what he might mean by his parting sentence. Unless it had something to do with Kevy—but why would anything to do with his Da be of interest to Mr Ferguson?

Johnny had a sense of hidden danger. There was something about Gavan's gloating tone that made him shiver.

In that week all pupils in the school had been sitting Christmas tests. These were especially important for Year Eights, to enable their teachers to give progress reports to their parents in the new year. They were not yet over by the weekend so the bridgers agreed that they would not meet that Saturday. They would use the time to revise, and try to put the future out of mind for the sake of the upcoming holiday. 'There's more verses coming too,' said Mary to Margaret on the bus home on Friday. 'About Christmas, I think.'

And soon came the last week of term.

Johnny had always looked forward to Christmas, and to his birthday early in January. His Mum had always made sure that he would not be disappointed by his Christmas gifts, and he knew now that his Da was getting more work. He knew what he wanted, but that would be impossible again. Maybe it would be discs of the latest *Star Wars* films?

He loved when it got colder around Christmas—especially if there might be snow. That hadn't happened in a while—but now the weather was indeed turning wintry, with sleet sometimes.

He wondered also if Mick would come again, or any of the other night-time bridgers.

The school disco was to happen soon, on the Friday before Christmas. The hall had been decorated by the seniors during the final week, with glittery hangings and balloons and a Christmas tree. His Mum had been glad she didn't have to kit him out to match what wealthier familes could afford—just a new pair of jeans and new trainers from the least expensive store in the city. He was sure he wouldn't feel out of place.

When Mrs Phillips arrived with Mary, Eddy and Margaret at seven o'clock he was more than ready. He got to sit beside Mary, who looked different in a light blue dress, with a matching band to keep her hair in order. Eddy was dressed much as he was, while Margaret wore smart navy trousers and a yellow top.

He hadn't ever danced at a disco, or with Mary, so he looked forward to that. He knew that he would feel awkward at first—but hoped the hall would have low light.

Thumping disco music was already audible as they approached the assembly hall. Just outside in the foyer, decked with balloons and glitter, stood a barrel with a slot in the top, for donations for the refugees. Mrs Walsh and Miss Doherty were already there, more brightly dressed than usual. Mr Slaney and Mr Foley were talking to a senior pupil who seemed out of it, propped up against the wall.

'Around the rugged rocks the ragged rascal ran—say it Mr Logan,' Mr Foley was reciting.

'I couln't say that if I was s.s.sober, Sir,' said Mr Logan.

'Right,' said Mr Slaney. 'Another candidate for the sin bin, the breathalyser and a quick trip home.' He led the precarious senior pupil away in the direction of the Music Room.

'I do hope *you* will be able to boogie without falling over, Mr Mullan,' said Mr Foley.

'He will, Sir,' said Eddy. 'I took the bottles from him in the car. Are you enjoying yourself, Sir.'

'As well as that night the roof fell in,' said Mr Foley. 'But Advent will soon be over. In with you now, to that hellish din. Please ask them all to get it over with as soon as possible.'

He had gestured towards the doors of the hall. The heavy thumping of the amplifiers came louder as they opened one of these, and wreathes of artificial fog crept out.

Mary took Johnny by the hand, and drew him into the most exciting and noisiest place he had ever experienced. Already it was well peopled with couples and groups dancing in the flickering, colour-changing light. They went towards the windows where there seemed to be more room—and began moving to the beat. Mr Wesley came by, in a party hat, and waved. Soon Johnny forgot to be self-conscious in the dimmed light and let the music tell him how to move. Mary seemed magical to him, as her hair band flickered. They could hold hands at times when they could jive. He found that just as exciting as when they had first held hands in the bus to school.

Throughout the evening other teachers circled the hall to make sure of proper order. This included prising apart dancers who came too close during the slower numbers. Persistent offenders were also led away to the sin bins. No one he could see was wearing showy new gear Johnny had never been happier. He knew that he and Mary would be talked about if they stayed together throughout the evening—so he wasn't annoyed when she waved at him after the first set and headed off to another group. He went to look for anyone he knew, and found Kieran Lowney in a corner, watching.

'Come on, ' he said. 'I'm thirsty.'

Out in the hall a stall for soft drinks and crisps had been set up, so they went there and enjoyed themselves. Kieran was trying to say something then, but between the racket and his stammer Johnny couldn't make him out. So he drew him towards the doors to the corridor and took him into the relative quiet beyond.

'Gavan says you'll be exp…pelled. Is that true?'

Johnny shook his head, and leaned back against the wall. He sucked on the straw awhile and said: 'It's being decided.'

Noticing his friend's raised eyebrows then, he said. 'It's about that debate. Dr McGinnis wants us to shut up about what we think, but other teachers don't want that. So the school has to make up its mind—by Easter. In the meantime we can have fun, so come on.'

They went back to the hall then and found other members of their class. Johnny pushed Kieran out from the wall, and wouldn't let him back until he had danced too—with Catherine Canning. Then he went looking for Mary again. After that dance he went out to the foyer to see how Mr Foley was holding up. Already he looked as though he hoped the roof *would* fall in.

Johnny went back into the cacophonous hall again, to see if he could find Margaret. He found her eventually near the stage with her hands over her ears trying to talk to Bridget McAlonan. Eddy was nearby, dancing with Mary.

'C'mere,' Johnny shouted. 'Come outside and see Mr Foley's face.' Eddy didn't properly understand, so Johnny grabbed him by the arm and headed towards the doors.

When they eventually made it to the foyer, Mr Foley and Mrs Walsh were dealing with another couple removed from the hall. Eddy gestured to Johnny that they should sidle over to hear—and so they did, supposedly by accident.

'Miss Wilson and Mr Hill again! You have a problem—would you agree?'

'Yes, Sir.'

'It has to do with those mysterious entities called hormones, I fear. At your age you both need to think of hormones as Daleks. Thousands of them are shouting at you those fatal words—*'resistance is futile'*—but that's not the only problem. In there, drowned by that din, and in semi-darkness, you are inclined to believe them, am I right?'

'Yes, Sir'

'So why not take a leaf out of the book of the good people of Derry during the siege. What did they all say back then, when faced with that other Dalek, King James?'

'No surrender, Sir.'

'One last chance to fight the Daleks then, you two,' said Mr Foley, pointing to the doors.

'C'mon,' said Eddy, giggling. 'Let's tell the girls!'

Eddy found Margaret first, and, not far away, Johnny found Mary dancing with Kieran. The set ended just then, so Johnny drew Mary as far from the speakers as he could and managed eventually to relay Mr Foley's advice to the clinging couple in the foyer. She broke up, and had to hold on to the window frame, to prevent herself from falling.

Then she cupped her hand over Johnny's ear and shouted: 'Are they getting at you too—the Daleks?'

Johnny shouted back 'I suppose—a little!'

She laughed again. Then she looked around for a moment and said:

'When the music starts again kiss me—without grabbing me! Then shout No surrender!'

He couldn't believe she was serious, and made his face into a question. She looked around again. Then, as the beat began again, she nodded, leaned forward, closed her eyes, tilted her head and pursed her lips.

When she had stayed in that position for a second Johnny knew he couldn't miss this chance. He kissed her then, for the first time. When his right hand touched her shoulder she jumped back, raised her right index finger and yelled:

'1…2…3!'

'*No surrender!*' they shouted together.

After goodbyes for the holiday, Christmas came soon, in a cold hush. It was dry but overcast in the days just before, and then—on Christmas Eve—the temperature fell further and it snowed the lightest, driest flakes. Three inches lay on the ground by evening, and Johnny enjoyed snowballing and a slide that he and some neighbouring boys had made by pouring cold water on the pavement hours earlier, when it had started to freeze.

Then he was called in by Anny, to make sure he went to bed early enough to be well asleep by midnight. He had to read himself into a doze before that happened. When he woke at six o'clock he knew that something would be waiting for him under the tree in the front room. In dressing gown and slippers he went down. As soon as he switched on the light in the front room he got a shock. There in the corner opposite the window stood the carving of his Gran that his Da had made, on a low stand. It almost made him forget what he had come for. He turned then to the Christmas tree—to find three parcels for himself: in one a DVD of the latest *Star Trek* movie, in another a new pen and in a third, from his Auntie Kath, a track suit.

Anny and Kevy were also watching him by then, and, when he had opened and appreciated all of his gifts, Kevy said: 'run up and put that DVD on your shelf before you lose it'. It seemed an unnecessary thing to say, but when Johnny went up anyway, and opened the door to his room, there on his table, ready and glowing, was a new laptop computer— the thing he had wanted most of all but thought he couldn't have! The screen showed text crisply, and the keys gave a soft click. There was a separate mouse too, far better than just a track-pad. Even the speakers seemed loud and clear. When he looked, there was the good free set of programmes for word-processing and other school tasks that Mrs Walsh had recommended. Elsewhere there were games.

'Sorry—no Internet for now. But there's an encyclopedia installed. Much love, Mam and Dad,' read the card sitting on the keyboard.

They had followed him up to see his face. He turned to them and thanked them from his heart. For two years he had wanted this, believing his writing would magically improve if he ever got one. He knew his Da had tried to get well for him, and work more often—and Kevy was truly better. Occasional bad temper had never gone to hitting for months now.

'There's a thumb drive in the drawer,' said his Da. 'You can use it to get your work printed out in school for a while, can't you—until we get a printer?'

'Yeh,' he said. 'Easy.' And then, turning to them from his key- pressing, mouse-clicking and menu-hopping: 'This is the best Christmas ever.'

'You won't mind if there's nothing much for your birthday, will you?' said Anny.

'Naw,' he said, still wondering at and exploring what he already had.

———∘∘○❂○∘∘———

They all went back to school the day after Johnny's birthday, January sixth. The passing back of tests and marks came then. None of the bridgers had suffered disaster—and Margaret had come first in her year group in Geography, as well as winning excellent marks in science. That was Johnny's weakest suit, but he had still managed to pass comfortably, thanks to Kieran's help. His best marks were in English and History and, surprisingly, in Technology. Eddy had also come in the top tier of achievement in science, technology and maths, while Mary's best subject had, as expected, been Music.

'No—I've heard nothing from Monsignor Murphy,' said Mrs Walsh to them in an interview room on the Thursday of the first week. 'It could be weeks yet—remember that there are eleven weeks to go until Easter! Nothing might happen till towards the end of March. That's what I wanted to say to you: I'm pleased you've all done well and not let last term's ... trouble affect you. But will you all be able to put your heads down this term and stay positive, hoping that you will all be back next year? Good—but remember to come to me if you start feeling any pressure.'

She seemed less tired, they agreed. Mr Foley too seemed to have recovered from the disco night. And there was something else they learned about Mr Wesley and the Iona staffroom.

'The Mennonites are sort of Protestants—but they are different too,' Margaret told them at their first Saturday meeting together in her house in the second term. 'Like Baptists and the Amish and the Quakers they don't believe in baptising babies. They think you need to be grown up—when you can know more about Jesus and be sure you want that. But listen: they mostly don't believe that Christians should take jobs in the government, like policeman or judge. They think that any use of force is wrong, except in self-defence. And they mostly think the church was wrong to accept what Constantine said about seeing that cross.

'Also the Mennonites were sometimes killed by other Protestants way back for their beliefs. They are into peace-making, and some of them helped to end the Troubles here.

'My Mum says too that she has heard that Dr McGinnis did not like the exchange of teachers that brought Mr Wesley here from Kansas. He doesn't like any teachers who aren't obedient Catholics being on the staff at all. She thinks that this has annoyed many on the staff, because Mrs Hayes, for example, is Church of Ireland. Those teachers are well liked.

'But then other teachers, like Miss Considine, think that the school needs to go with what Dr McGinnis wants. "We're losing our Catholic identity", she told someone, "and that's why so many senior pupils stop practising—they don't know what it means to be Catholic anymore."'

'But if people like Mr Wesley won't be welcomed any more, what's Catholic about that?' asked Johnny.

'For Dr McGinnis Catholic means everyone thinking the same things, my Mum says—but she doesn't agree.'

'What does the bishop think?' asked Mary.

'My Mum says no one knows that yet.'

'Does Dr McGinnis want people like me in the school?' asked Eddy.

'Yes,' said Margaret. 'But only if they don't ever question anything the church teaches, and keep all the rules.'

'It won't be any fun if I can't question stuff,' said Eddy, 'And if I can't talk about copy-wanting either.'

—∞∘◦◈◦∘∞—

'I'm glad I got to go there—I learned a lot,' said Mary to the others the following Saturday in Johnny's house, having returned from London with her Dad the previous day from the *Fame School* semi-finals. 'And I'm glad that Arona has made it to the TV finals, even if I haven't.

'More verses for *The Chain* have been coming to me, to be sung for Easter—and I sang those for the judges in the second semi-final. They were kind, but they explained that many people are against all religion these days because they think it leads to violence. They asked if I had anything else that was new, to go with the *Dark Switch* song—and I didn't. Not yet anyway.

'I'm thinking about that word *'Fame'*. There's something about it I don't like, what it does to people who want it badly. Those photos of Michael Jackson—how he changed: they scare me.

'The other performers were kind to me too, though some seemed anxious—but I must tell you about Hester

McCauley. She's from Carson College on this side of the river—our age too. She was there when I sang, and she was staying in the same hotel. She came to our room that evening, with her Mum. She had her violin with her.

'"Could you play that chain song again?" she said, and when I did she came in between each verse with her violin. She understood the way I feel, with a different tempo each time. She asked me for the words and if it would be all right for her play it for her minister where she goes to church. I couldn't think why not—even though she's Church of Ireland, Anglican. And we swapped email addresses and phone numbers too.

'I think that's why I was there,' Mary continued, 'to see everyone compete, and how they were in themselves—and especially to meet Hester. That day last term in school, when we had to decide if we wanted to audition. The whole thing scared me, so I shut my eyes and asked for the power of the bridge, and I felt then that it would be alright so long as I didn't get too excited and expect to win. I think I went there to learn more about all that celebrity stuff that people are mad about these days. Nearly everyone our age is wanting to be famous.'

She played then the new verses that had come to her since they had last met.

'I'm going to ask Hester if she could come with me to visit my Mum, to play together and try to cheer her up,' said Mary.

Johnny felt glad that things had turned out that way for Mary in London—but couldn't think why.

'Someone's pinched it—I know they have!'

Aidan Maroney said this in great annoyance at lunchtime two weeks later, on a Wednesday. He said it to Eddy, the only other person there at the time. Aidan's locker was just beside Johnny Mullan's, and Aidan had been searching frantically.

'It's a mini directional microphone—the very latest,' he answered.

'For detecting and boosting distant sound anywhere. You just point it anywhere you want to listen and bingo, you can hear! Even in the bus. My Dad gets that stuff from people he knows. It was a Christmas present too—and that's the second thing I've lost from my locker this year.'

'Are you sure you left it there?' asked Eddy. Mrs Walsh had warned them all about leaving valuables in their lockers for any length of time. He knew also that the school did not accept responsibility for anything stolen.

'I'm certain! Just yesterday too.'

'Was the door of your locker broken open?'

'No—there isn't a mark on it—look! And I'm certain I locked it.'

'But I thought only the caretaker and Mr Ferguson have master keys that will open any locker.'

'I've heard that sometimes ordinary keys will open more than one lock, especially when they get worn a bit,' Aidan replied. 'A senior told me that some people go around trying locks when it's quiet. Sometimes people even take a file to keys they find, to try to make a master key.'

'Was that gadget valuable?'

'Yes—it was an early sample. My dad will have a fit. I'd better not leave anything else in there. The person with that key could come back. Maybe I should ask to have the lock changed, or make a row at the office, or even get my Dad to do that.'

Eddy suddenly thought he had a far better idea.

'Let's catch the thief ourselves, Aidan! Only the two of us know about this, right? And if you don't tell anyone—and I keep quiet too—the thief might try again. He or she may think you don't care—and come back with that key. Especially if you flash around some other stuff like that—without risking it in the locker.'

'What if he does come back? He won't do that when anyone's here.'

Eddy explained what he had in mind, and the two agreed to keep the idea entirely to themselves.

—∞◦❁◦∞—

January passed into February, the weather getting slightly less harsh. As the weeks passed the bridgers knew that a decision on their fate could not be long delayed.

On the Monday of the last week of February the Year Eight boys dressed in the changing rooms for another circuit of the wood in their games period. Delayed by a broken shoelace, Johnny was almost the last to head out into the cold.

'Hey—are you Johnny Mullan?'

The call came from a senior pupil standing against the wall just outside the exit to the grounds. He was coughing and wrapped in a grey scarf that concealed the lower half of his face.

'You're wanted at the office,' he said when Johnny answered. 'It's urgent. Go right away.' And then he turned away, still coughing.

Keyed up as he was for just this kind of urgent summons Johnny didn't hesitate. It took him less than a minute to make his way, without running, back through the changing room and the linking corridors to the front hall and the office hatch.

'No message for *you*, sorry Johnny,' said the school secretary, Mrs Grant. 'That's the second stupid hoax we've had today too. Better get off quickly to your class.'

Annoyed, Johnny set off by the quickest route to the running track, knowing he would be lucky to catch the rest of the group.

'Maybe I'll catch David at least,' he thought, heading out of sight of the built-up part of the school and into the wood.

There was no sign of anyone by the time he saw the tree with the strange lopped branch that marked the path into the wood that he had taken so long ago in search of Martin Cassidy and Gavan's group.

Then suddenly out from the wood in front of him stepped Colin Woodside from Year Thirteen, a boy he knew as part of the group that had supported Conor Maguire in the campaign to block the No Logo push by other seniors in preparation for the Christmas disco.

Colin was grinning, and when Johnny looked back over his shoulder the track behind him was blocked by another of the same group, Sean Anderson.

'Boo!' said a voice. When he turned again Conor Maguire was tapping him lightly on the shoulder with a long stick.

'No help possible this time, Mullan. What do you think I will do with you now?'

As the three seniors closed all possible escape routes around him, Johnny knew that the less he said the better.

'Now,' said Conor, standing over him, with his stick held behind his back. 'Just who do *you* think you are?'

There was such bitterness in the words that at first Johnny was startled. But there was also such arrogance in the question that Johnny suddenly remembered everything that had happened to his own family at the hands of the Maguires and felt deeply angry.

'Johnny Mullan,' he answered defiantly.

'Johnny Mullan, Johnny Mullan, Johnny Mullan,' echoed Conor sarcastically. 'Can either of you two tell me what a Johnny Mullan is exactly?'

His supporters shook their heads. Johnny found himself being pushed by Sean against Colin and back again.

'Gently, gently, lads,' said Conor. 'We need to find another Johnny Mullan somewhere about here, to get a real grip of this problem.'

He then began turning over leaf debris at the side of the track with his stick, peering closely. 'Aha,' he said at last, and lifted a withered leaf. He carried this carefully over towards Johnny until it touched him on the nose.

'Look, Mullan—here's another member of your family—and a distinguished one at that.'

When Johnny could focus he saw a beetle smaller than the nail of his little finger making its bewildered way across the leaf. It had a greenish-red iridescence.

'Now, Johnny Mullan—watch carefully. This is what happens in the end to all Johnny Mullans.'

He placed the leaf on the ground, and then stamped on it sharply with his right foot.

'That Johnny Mullan hadn't annoyed me at all,' Conor went on.

'But that's what happened to it anyway.' Then he laid the stick on Johnny's shoulder.

'This Johnny Mullan has been mucking up my windscreen since September—without ever saying sorry. It makes jokes. It backs up weirdos. It tells lies in debates. It plots with its green welly friends to turn the Christmas disco into a ragamuffin's dance. It even answers back when warned.'

He thrust his face right at Johnny. 'It might even answer back now, mightn't it?'

Johnny did indeed feel like saying something.

'No person can ever take away the value of another person.'

He had an impression of a fist being raised to his right.

'No, Colin. That's exactly what this Johnny Mullan wants—so it can go whining to the office about victimisation, with all the evidence on its face. Instead it needs to get what that other Johnny Mullan got—a sudden blow from nowhere that it cannot even understand. It has set me a challenge too—to see if I can't take away the *value* it thinks it has. I need to think hard about that.

'So for now this Johnny Mullan can run about among the leaves. That other Johnny Mullan had far more value to me than this one. But your day will come soon enough. And when it does no one will remember Johnny Mullan ever again.'

He kicked at the leaves again, gestured to the others and headed back towards the school.

Johnny watched them to the turn and then bent to see what had happened to the beetle. He could find no trace of it among the leaves.

'Maybe he missed it,' he said to himself—but he couldn't be sure.

'Now comes the dangerous time!'

This was Mick's sombre warning to Johnny on a Friday night, two weeks later. Asleep and dreaming Johnny had found himself following Greeta to the place where he had first met the bridger in the Bishop's Wood at Downhill. And there was Mick, waiting on the rustic seat.

'Has it something to do with the Maguires?' asked Johnny.

'Yes. You have made serious enemies there,' said Mick. 'That's not your fault, of course. You have been a banana skin under Gavan's foot once too often—and what you said at the debate has especially annoyed him and his brother Conor. The 'No Logo' campaign hasn't helped. You all wanted to run the risks involved in being bridgers, didn't you?'

'Yes,' said Johnny.

'The risks this time include physical danger, which is bad enough. Worse, though, are shame and disgrace. Are you still willing to run those risks, for the sake of the bridge?'

'Is there any way out?' Johnny asked.

'Perhaps. You could apologise to Gavan, in front of others in the class, for what you said at the debate, and tell him you will never get in his way again.'

'I can't do that!' said Johnny immediately. 'He has tried to bully everyone he thinks won't fight back. I would have to be like Patrick Andrews, backing him up in whatever he does.'

Mick nodded.

'Then I just won't,' said Johnny. 'I'll take the risks.'

'Even the risk of disgrace?'

'That's what happened to my Da—and he has put up with that for ages. I'll put up with that too, if it will help him.'

'It may do that. But prepare yourself for a double blow,' Mick went on. 'The biggest obstacle to the plot being hatched is that you Iona bridgers trust one another, and that you are all worthy of trust. None of you has done anything to be ashamed of. Margaret, Mary and Eddy are being spoken to also just now. Trust us, and keep faith with one another. Will you remember that?'

'Yes,' said Johnny. 'I will—whatever happens.'

'Don't accuse anyone,' Mick continued. 'Let them accuse themselves. There will be a calm then after the storm—and some important bridges will be complete.'

The following day in Margaret's the bridgers shared much the same news—of a crisis that could not be long delayed—affecting Johnny especially, but all of them to some degree.

'How can you be so calm?' Mary asked Johnny anxiously.

He told them about the trick that had been played to make sure he would be met when alone by Conor Maguire in the wood some weeks before.

'I was afraid, so I did what we all do now. I felt sure then that none of this was my fault, and that I wasn't alone at all. It was like watching a TV show—about Conor. I remembered what Mick had said on that first day, that nothing that happened could destroy the most important part of me, and I believed it. I believe it now too.'

By now Mary had all the verses she needed to sing The Chain that Binds the Earth from start to finish at Easter— just four weeks away. They sang it together and parted to face whatever would come.

XIX

It usually took Johnny about five minutes to walk home from his bus stop, along Inishowen Avenue and into Inishowen Park. Both were lined with terraced houses, each with a small garden in front. Some gardens were well kept, with small patches of grass and flower beds with rose bushes or small shrubs. However, a few had over-large bushes and grass that had become unkempt. In some cases hedges had expanded up and out over the low walls that separated the gardens from the pavement.

This meant that the pavement itself was obstructed in places, so that if you met someone you had to step out onto the narrow road. This too was obstructed at intervals by parked cars.

As Johnny made his way home that Thursday afternoon in Lent nothing seemed unusual at first. It was a gloomy day, about ten to four, with a light drizzle. There was almost no-one else about.

Then ahead of him he noticed someone coming towards him on the same pavement. He had a scruffy baseball cap pulled low over his eyes. He was wearing jeans and a dark jacket, with the collar pulled up over the lower half of his face.

Johnny stepped out onto the road to let him pass. As the man was about to do so he stopped and said roughly:

'Hi—you're Johnny Mullan, aren't you?'

'Yes, why?' Johnny replied. He didn't recognise this person, and couldn't properly see his face.

'Nothin',' the man said. 'I just thought it was you.'

He walked on then. Johnny was puzzled, but walked on also. Then, on an impulse, he turned and looked after the man. He expected to see his departing back, but instead the man had turned also, to face back in Johnny's direction. He had his hand raised. When he saw that he was observed he quickly turned again to walk away towards the main road.

Sensing danger Johnny immediately turned to hurry home. In the same moment he saw a car door swing open across the narrow pavement ahead. Someone got out whose face he couldn't see—because he was wearing a black hood covering all of his head. The hood had only three small openings for its wearer to see and breathe.

'Here, ye wee tout!' this person shouted menacingly, and came towards Johnny, running.

Johnny was trapped. He knew that the man who had asked him his name—the man who now stood between him and the main road—was as big a danger as this hooded man who had cut him off from the safety of home.

'Help!' he shouted as loud as he could, dropping his school bag. He dodged out onto the road between two parked cars, to get past the hooded man who was only feet away. He had almost passed the car from which this man had emerged when another hooded figure loomed up ahead of him on the road, with arms held wide.

Desperately Johnny veered to the right, towards the opposite pavement, trying to find a gap between the third man and the garden wall. He sensed that he was closely followed, and knew he had only a slim chance of escape.

'Help!' he shouted again. At that moment his left arm was gripped in a vice and he was pulled off his feet.

'Gotcha, ye wee divil!'

Johnny felt himself falling backward onto the pavement, with only the overhead telephone wires visible. The shock of the impact made him gasp. Then he doubled up as he was kicked. He had a close up view of the bricks on the wall to his right before he closed his eyes tight.

Instinctively he drew his knees up further and put his hands up to protect his head. He felt further kicks to his back and legs.

'Steal from us, would ye?' someone shouted. 'You ... double- crossing ... wee ... pest!'

Next moment he felt a thumping blow to the side of his head, which then made hard contact with the wall. A bright light flashed for an instant in the darkness he was seeing ... and then he lost all interest in what was happening. He was somewhere else, in a place where nothing mattered much.

True, he could hear things vaguely in the distance. A shout or two, and running feet. Car doors slamming and an engine firing and revving hard. Tyres squealing then, further off. But all of that had nothing much to do with him.

There were other voices then, one especially close, asking gently and anxiously:

'Are you all right, son?'

What a silly question. He had never felt better. He was on another planet somewhere, a planet called Nothing Matters. It was time to fall asleep there, as he felt tired enough. He had been running, after all, and felt warm.

He relaxed then, and let the planet take him wherever it might want to go. He pulled the blankets closer over his head and fell asleep.

An hour later Margaret was at home in her room when she heard the telephone ring. Her mother answered it, as she was closer.

As usual Margaret couldn't hear exactly what was being said, but the tone of her mother's voice quickly changed. She was asking short, urgent questions—but mostly listening to the person at the other end.

Suddenly alarmed, Margaret rose from her desk and opened the door into the hall. When she saw her mother's face—concentrated to hear every word from the caller—she knew something awful had happened. Mrs Phillips looked up and saw her, and her face immediately sent a message that Margaret understood.

'She's here beside me,' Mrs Phillips said. 'I'll tell her now. If there's anything we can do, let us know. We'll pray for good news.' She put the phone down then, and looked hard at Margaret.

Then she put her hands on her daughter's shoulders.

'That was Johnny's Mum. Johnny's been attacked—on his way home from school. He's in the hospital, unconscious.'

Margaret had been expecting a blow, but still felt overwhelmed.

'How bad is it?' she asked, weeping.

'They don't know yet. He's in intensive care. He's got a broken arm, and some cracked ribs. But ... it's his head they're worried about. They're taking more x-rays. He's stable, but they're waiting for him to regain consciousness.

'He was lucky, it seems,' she went on. 'His dad was coming early from work and heard him yell. He ran at them—the thugs beating him up—and they made off. And someone else with a phone saw what was happening and called the hospital immediately. It's not far away, and an ambulance was already on its way down the main road. It was there almost immediately. They had him in casualty in less than twenty minutes.'

Had Mick allowed for that, Margaret wondered—such danger and pain? He had talked of risks, and there wouldn't be a real risk unless there was a real danger. Somehow, yes, Mick had foreseen this. He must have. And things would work out somehow. Johnny would wake up, and be all right.

'I'd better tell the others,' she said.

'Yes—his Mum wants you to do that. She has already contacted the school, and Mr Ferguson knows. He'll tell Mrs Walsh. Mrs Mullan says not to think of going to the hospital just yet, as there wouldn't be any point. She'll let us know if there's any change.'

Margaret nodded. She phoned Eddy first. He pumped her for every detail, sounding angry but calm. Mary was different, as Margaret knew she would be. She broke down, and Margaret had to assure her there had to be a reason that Johnny had not escaped without injury.

But she remembered also that Mick had warned them that physical danger was not the worst kind. Something

even worse could—would—happen yet. But what could
possibly be worse?

Johnny, meanwhile, was exploring the planet called
Nothing Matters.

The sun was shining from a cloudless sky, but the sky
was an unusual light blue. He was walking along by a river
that tumbled in the same direction over a rocky bed. The
bank he walked on felt spongy. There were thick trees on
both banks, coming quite close to the edge. In one place a
tree had fallen across the river, its top just nestling among
the other trees on the far bank.

They were like pine trees he had seen, and they had
needles too—and it was these fallen needles that made the
riverbank soft.

Johnny could see that the trees became much thicker
ahead, where a stream entered the river from his right.

There was no sign of any human presence anywhere he
looked, and no human sound either. He felt lonely, but safe.
And he didn't need to hurry. He was just supposed to explore.

The stream blocked his way along the bank now. He
could wade across, but why not simply follow the stream
until he found a place to cross without getting wet?

He turned up along the stream. The going was easy at
first, but the trees soon became thicker. When he found a
place to cross, on large, spaced stones, he did so.

There was a natural path through the trees there—
leading roughly, Johnny thought, back to where the river
might be found again, further downstream. So he followed it.

Soon, though, it began to curve away to the right. The trees began to change, becoming leafy, and much taller. After a good long while he was in a quiet forest. Unusual sounds came to him. Of animals or birds in the distance.

The plants and trees and noises were all strange. He couldn't be sure he had ever seen or heard them before, even on one of those TV nature programmes, the kind that Margaret liked.

He found himself then in a small clearing. There was a fluttering of large wings, and a big bird appeared suddenly and perched on a branch. It had a large hooked bill, and feathers of gold and lilac among mostly dark blue ones. It looked at Johnny for a moment, and then dipped its bill towards him and whistled in the strangest way. The sound was more like a flute than a whistle. It made him feel lonely again in the stillness of the forest, but didn't seem to be in any way a threat. The bird flew off then, on down the natural path through the trees.

The path grew mostly dark as trees met overhead, but Johnny thought he could see in the far distance a small patch of brightness. He made his way on down, and the patch became gradually brighter. Although he walked and walked he never seemed to get any nearer. The patch had a vague, fuzzy shape. There was no identifiable object—just a hazy oblong of light. Surely if he got closer he would be able to see what it was.

Then it occurred to Johnny that he was maybe trying to see something with his eyes closed. So he tried opening them.

He found himself looking at a bright bar of light set into a cream- coloured ceiling. The forest had disappeared.

When he tried to look to the side he found he could move his head only slightly. All he could see was the top of some kind of machine, with lights blinking. It was hard to turn his head to see much more.

'Johnny?'

The voice was Anny's. Her face came into view then—anxious and a bit puffy.

'Hi Ma,' he said.

'Oh, thank God!' she said, her eyes filling.

Another face appeared then—Kevy's. He looked hard at Johnny.

'Do you know me, son?'

'Why wouldn't I, Da?'

Anny started sobbing then. There was a rustling sound and another woman's face appeared—one he didn't recognise. She shone a bright light into his eyes, one at a time, and stared.

'What do they call you?' she asked.

'Johnny. Johnny Mullan.'

'How many fingers do you see?' she asked, holding up three. He said so.

'What day is it, do you know?'

That was a puzzle. In the forest there hadn't been any day in particular, because that didn't matter either.

'I'm not sure.'

It came to him then that he was in a hospital—and that you went to hospital if something was wrong with you. What could be wrong though?

In an instant Johnny came fully away from the planet called Nothing Matters, back to Inishowen Avenue—where the last thing he had seen was bricks in a wall, up close. He had been on his way home from school and…

'I remember now. I think it's Thursday—is it?'

'Humph,' said the doctor. 'That's good, Johnny. Don't try to remember any more just now. You've been injured, but you're all right now. You're in hospital, not far from home. You've got a bump on your head, two broken ribs and a broken right forearm, but that's been set. OK?'

'What time is it?'

'It's half-past-eight on Thursday evening. You were injured around four o'clock, so you've been dozing away for about four hours. A good idea that was too—it made you a good patient.'

She smiled at him then.

'Try to sleep now. Do you feel sore anywhere?'

Johnny considered that question carefully for a few moments.

'My head hurts. I feel kind of … heavy and my arm's sort of … tight and hot.'

'That's the plaster. If you feel sore, there's a button in your left hand. There. Can you feel that?'

'Yes,' said Johnny as he felt his thumb being moved to make contact with a smooth round surface.

'Press that then, if you need to. Now get some rest. OK?'

'OK,' said Johnny.

The doctor went away then. Johnny could hear voices whispering in the distance for a while, and then Anny and Kevy came into view. Anny wasn't crying any more, just looking happy.

'You're a tough one then, aren't you?' said Kevy. He was talking in a different way. More gently.

'Did they catch those men?' Johnny asked.

'No. They got away, the ... sc! The police will be asking you some questions—but that will wait till the morning, OK?'

'Yes,' said Johnny. He remembered vaguely what Mick had said about something else happening—something worse—but didn't want to think about that now. He was feeling drowsy again. Maybe he could go back to that planet for a while, the one with the river, the forest and the strange bird.

He slept again then. He didn't see Anny and Kevy watching him for a while, or the whispered argument over which of them should keep vigil through the night. Kevy won, and Anny reluctantly left.

First she stopped for a long moment, with her head to one side, looking at Johnny, before going out through the door. She could see what Johnny could not—the seven stitches in his scalp, just over his right ear. There were other smaller cuts on his face, and some bruising, but nothing that wouldn't heal.

Anny had promised to ring Mrs Phillips with news, no matter how late it came—so Margaret knew by nine o'clock that Johnny was out of danger. He was still under close observation, the normal procedure with a head injury. But he knew who and where he was, and was sleeping soundly. She wept with relief and rang Mary and Eddy immediately. 'He'll be all right,' said Mary. 'I know he will.'

Margaret's mum sent her to bed then. She didn't think she would sleep, but dozed off soon enough. The worry of the night before had exhausted her.

When she woke at the usual time she took a few moments to recall the previous day's events. Johnny was in hospital. He was lucky, by all accounts, to be alive. She might be able to see him later in the day. In the meantime she could stay at home, if she liked, as her mother had said she would need more rest.

But she began to feel something other than tiredness, something that made her determined to go to school.

'I'll be all right,' she told her mother. 'I want to see the others.'

'All right then,' her mother said, after looking at her closely. 'Tell them I'll pick you all up after school for a short visit to Johnny, and drop them home afterwards.'

Usually on a Friday morning Eight B began the day with a form period with Mrs Walsh, but when Margaret reached the lockers she found her form teacher waiting there—something that had never happened before.

'Margaret,' said Mrs Walsh in a low voice, coming towards her, 'something awful has happened!'

'I know, Miss—Johnny's been hurt, but he's out of danger.'

'There's something else, Margaret!'

Margaret had never seen Mrs Walsh this way before. She was pale. She seemed not to know what to say—as though she had news that she didn't know how to give.

'What is it, Miss?'

'Not here. Let's go to an interview room.'

It wasn't far away, but that journey along the corridors of Iona, on the heels of her form teacher, was one of the longest Margaret ever took. She knew from the way Mrs Walsh had spoken that the second blow had fallen, and that somehow she herself was directly involved.

They used the smallest interview room this time. Mrs Walsh sat Margaret down and then faced her across the small table.

'Johnny was attacked around four o'clock yesterday—am I right?'

'Yes, Miss.'

'Soon after that, around half-past-four, an anonymous call was made to the school office. The voice, a youngish man's voice, said: "Johnny Mullan and his friends are dealing drugs in Iona College. He got what he deserved. You'll know where to look." That was all.

'Mr Ferguson hadn't heard yet about the attack on Johnny. He didn't want to believe the accusation, but he had to check it out. He went with the caretaker to the lockers, and opened Johnny's locker.

'He found a small plastic bag with a lot of money in notes—and twenty yellow tablets. Then he opened Eddy's locker. There was nothing there. But then he opened yours.'

Mrs Walsh paused then, stricken. Margaret was ahead of her.

'He found something there too, didn't he Miss?'

'Yes, Margaret—do you know what it was?'

'I don't know, Miss—but I think I can guess. More money and tablets.'

'Tablets only. Ten this time. In a plastic bag again. The same shape and colour. Mr Ferguson has seen tablets like these before. He says they look like what's called ecstasy, or a substitute. He's having them all analysed by the police.'

That was it, then, Margaret knew. This was the worst possible—the shame and the disgrace.

'It wasn't us, Miss. Someone wants to make sure we're expelled!'

Margaret had another thought then.

'And they probably want to make out that Johnny was attacked because he was dealing in drugs, Miss. So that the police will think that too. And not try to find the ones who beat him up.'

'You're giving me your solemn word, then, that you know nothing about these drugs—if that's what they are?'

'Yes, Miss. You know me. You know I wouldn't ever do that, don't you?'

Mrs Walsh's face became less clear as Margaret's burning eyes filled up.

'Yes, Margaret, I believe you. I do—but who would do such an awful thing?'

'It's hard to understand, Miss! But the truth will come out, I'm sure it will!'

'There's something else, Margaret. There's someone who claims to be a witness. The mother of a Year Nine boy rang Mr Ferguson just after he had heard of the attack on Johnny. This boy had just told her that last term Johnny offered to get him an ecstasy tablet for the school disco.'

'That's not true either, Miss. I know it's not.'

'I know that too, Margaret. There are too many things happening too quickly there—all in the space of an hour. Think about it.'

Margaret knew then from her tone that Mrs Walsh was truly a friend, and not just interrogating her for Mr Ferguson. She instantly felt a renewal of hope.

'Yes, Miss. It was all planned, wasn't it?'

'I think so. But how are we to prove that? If this boy keeps to his story—and of course I can't tell you who he is—and if we can't prove who put those tablets in your locker, then what are we to do?'

'Something will happen, Miss. I'm sure of it.'

'I hope it happens soon, Margaret. Mr Ferguson wants to see you now, and will probably ask you the same questions. He has already phoned your mother, and she's on her way. Is there anything you want me to do?'

Margaret thought desperately. Who might know what to do next?

'Tell Eddy, Miss. There's nothing against him yet, is there?'

'No—not yet. I'll do that then. Now, chin up. You've got to walk with me to Mr Ferguson's room, past all the people in the hall. Can you do that?'

Already Margaret was asking for the bridger's power. She felt a sudden calmness sweep over her. She took off her glasses and wiped her eyes with a hanky.

'Yes, Miss. I'm all right. It will all work out, you'll see.'

As soon as she was out the door Margaret could see that no one was yet aware of what had happened. Everyone had other business to attend to. No one was looking at her especially. Mrs Walsh went ahead in the direction of Mr Ferguson's room, and Margaret fell into step behind. They were halfway across the hall when she felt a hand on her shoulder.

'Margaret, what's wrong?'

When she turned, there was Mary McNevin, pale as a ghost.

'Catherine saw Mrs Walsh take you to the interview room. She said Mrs Walsh was looking for you early on, and was worried about something. Has something worse happened?'

'The second blow, Mary. Mrs Walsh will tell Eddy, and he will tell you. I can't stop now. Mr Ferguson wants to see me. Please don't worry. You know why you mustn't, don't you?'

Mary, eyes wide and filling, bit her lip and nodded.

'Yes. OK. See you later then.'

She put her hand down then, as Margaret turned and followed their form teacher across the hall.

—∘∘—❁—∘∘—

Minutes later Eddy was searching urgently for Aidan Maroney.

—∘∘—❁—∘∘—

Johnny had woken again at half-past-eight on Friday morning, feeling much stiffer and sorer. Kevy was still there, and Anny soon arrived. They watched him eat a breakfast of cereal, boiled egg and toast, with Anny doing for him what his right arm couldn't.

Another doctor examined him then, and was apparently satisfied.

'You're a medical miracle!' he said.

'Margaret and the others will be coming to see you later, after school,' said Anny after he had left.

She sent Kevy away to work then, and settled down to watch him. She didn't seem to want to do anything else.

At nine o'clock a policewoman came to question him on the attack. He gave her the best description he could of the three men, but it was vague.

'Can you think why they might have attacked you?'

Johnny remembered what Mick had said about accusations. All he had was a deep suspicion anyway.

'No. But they knew who I was.'

'How d'you know that?'

'The first one asked me my name.'

'Why would anyone pick on you in particular?'

Johnny shrugged. The policewoman looked at him especially hard.

'Someone heard one of the men say you had stolen something. What was that about?'

'I don't know, and I don't steal!'

'You were wearing your school uniform, weren't you?'

'Yes.'

'Did any of the men say anything about your religion?'

'No.'

'No names—you know the kind bigots call Catholics?'

'No, but one of them said 'wee tout'.'

'Right,' said the policewoman, closing her notebook. 'We've taken other statements, of course. The car they used had been stolen. It was found burning on the other side of the city—the usual thing. There's not much to go on. We'll let you know if we find out more.'

She put on her cap then and left.

Soon after, a nurse came into the room and told Anny there was a phone call for her. When Anny came back her face had changed again. It was bitterly angry, but her eyes told Johnny she wasn't mad at him.

'That was Mrs Phillips. Something's happened at the school. There was an anonymous call yesterday after school, naming you. It said to look in your locker, and the others.'

'They found something, didn't they?' said Johnny.

'Yes. Some money. And drugs. And Margaret's locker had drugs in it too. That's ridiculous. What's going on, Johnny?'

Johnny wasn't sure what to say next either, but he knew he had to find some way of preparing Anny for what would surely follow.

'Do you remember what I told you I said at the debate, to Gavan?'

'Yes—it was clever, and it made him angry.'

'Not just him. His brother Conor too. And Conor was annoyed when we supported the school's No Logo campaign last term too.'

As Johnny explained Anny's face began to set into an expression that Johnny remembered. Behind the anger there was weariness, even hopelessness.

'They're doing to you what they did to your Da, aren't they?'

'I think so—and to Margaret too.'

'Poor Margaret—and Mrs Phillips. They're not used to this sort of thing, are they?'

Johnny shook his head.

'But Ma, this time they've made some kind of mistake—I know they have.'

'I hope so, Johnny. I hope so.'

Johnny knew that Anny was thinking that the three of them would go on living forever with disgrace—the way they had since Kevy had been accused so many years ago. And maybe she was worrying about what he himself would do if he was shamed as Kevy had been. And what Kevy might do now too.

'Even so, Ma. It'll be different this time. You'll see.'

Anny just nodded. Johnny knew she didn't want to take away from him the hope she didn't have herself.

She did something then that she often did when she was feeling that way. She reached into her handbag and took out a small black purse. From this she pulled a string of dark blue rosary beads and began praying to herself, slipping the beads silently through the fingers of her right hand. This lay on her lap, with her left hand folded across it. Her eyes meanwhile did an unseeing tour of everything in the room, coming alive only when they looked at him.

XX

Mary and Margaret usually had Home Science for two periods after break on Fridays, but Margaret had not rejoined the class after Mary had last seen her in the hall before first bell. Mary was therefore on her own at a cookery station near the end of the double period. She was constantly forgetting where exactly she was in an everlasting journey towards the perfect lasagne. Eddy had given her a quick thumbs up in the corridor before first class, but then rushed off somewhere, so she had no idea what was going on.

Suddenly the door of the Home Science room opened and Mrs Walsh entered. She looked for Miss O'Boyle, Mary's teacher. When she caught sight of her over at the sinks she went over and whispered. Miss O'Boyle raised her head, and her voice.

'Mary McNevin?'

'Here, Miss.'

'Can you finish up quickly? Mrs Walsh needs you to go with her now.'

'Yes, Miss.'

Hurriedly Mary binned the ill-fated lasagne, lifted her bag, and followed Mrs Walsh out the door. Her heart was thumping like a bass drum.

Eddy was waiting for them in the corridor, excited but saying nothing. Her form teacher quickly turned to face her. She had a strange expression—the kind that people have when too many unusual things occur too quickly.

'Something else has happened, Mary—something that completely exonerates Johnny and Margaret. It's shocking for the school. Everyone will know the main details by Monday, probably, but you and Margaret and Johnny need to be told today. Eddy here already knows most of it. I'm taking you both to the hospital now. Margaret is on her way there too. It's best if you all hear together. Cheer up and be patient for half an hour, can you?'

'Exoner ... Does that mean...?'

'We know—*we know for sure*—that you four are all completely innocent. And we know who isn't. That's the shocking part. Can you wait now till we get to the hospital?'

'Oh yes, Miss.'

'Off we go then!'

As she followed her teacher to the car park, Mary knew only that somehow her agony had been ended quickly, and that everything would be all right. She was interested in the details, surely, but far more anxious to see Johnny and Margaret, and watch their faces as they heard those details too.

Not long after Anny had put her rosary beads away, the same nurse came back with the same message: a phone call. When Anny came back to Johnny's room she was different—excited.

'That was the school, Johnny. Mrs Walsh is on her way here. With good news, they say. And with Eddy and Mary—and Margaret is coming too, with her Mum. What could it be?'

'It's what I said, Ma. The Maguires have made a mistake this time. You'll see.'

Anny just looked at him. She was still apparently afraid to hope. Fifteen minutes later the nurse came back, all bustle.

'You shouldn't be having so many visitors all at once so soon. The doctor says it's all right this once, but only for half an hour. And keep the noise down.'

Then the door opened again, and in came Mrs Walsh, beaming. Behind her, each carrying a plastic chair, came Margaret, Eddy and Mary. Their eyes were wide as saucers and they were trying to make no noise. Mrs Walsh sat beside Anny at the foot of the bed and the others came round the side, with Mary sitting closest.

'Does it hurt much, Johnny?' Mary asked.

'A bit,' said Johnny. 'I just can't move much yet. But what's happened at school?'

'Eddy—you start,' said Mrs Walsh. 'And remember what I said about keeping calm.'

'It was Aidan Maroney, Johnny,' Eddy began. 'He and I set up something no one else knew about. Do you remember where exactly my locker is?'

Johnny thought a moment.

'Just across from mine.'

'Right—and just across from Aidan's too. He had something expensive pinched from his locker in January, but didn't tell anyone. I was there when he found it gone—a small gadget for listening to any sound too far away to hear with your own ears. He didn't tell anyone except me. You know the way Aidan is about those things, don't you?'

Johnny nodded.

'At first he wanted to make a big fuss, but I told him we could catch the thief ourselves. His Da has this technician in his factory who knows all about security stuff—tiny video cameras and so on. They use them in the firm. Aidan and I thought the thief might come back if we kept quiet, so he asked this technician to let him have a small battery-powered video camera, connected to a storage system for the pictures. They're tiny, those things, now. They look just like a black radio.

'We stuck that box to the inside top of my locker—it's self-stick, push-on. You won't see it unless you know it's there. The lens is on the end of a bendy wire, so we set that just behind one of those air holes—you know the ones above the door of the locker?'

Again Johnny nodded. Despite Mrs Walsh's warning he was getting excited himself.

'The technician put a program on Aidan's computer that let him look anytime at what the box was storing, from anywhere in the school. I made him swear that he wouldn't tell anyone else—not even his closest friends—so he made me swear the same. Aidan soon got bored with it, because nothing was happening. He decided he would only look at the pictures if something got stolen. And nothing did. But I went on changing the batteries anyway, just in case.

'When I told Aidan this morning what had happened to you yesterday, and to your locker, he got his computer out straight away. Every frame is stamped with the date and time, so we soon got to the pictures for half-three yesterday, when we all left.

'Aidan fast-forwarded it then. A few people came past soon after that, but no-one stopped at your locker. Then there was a long time with nothing—until five minutes to four.'

Eddy paused then.

'Someone came then. When we rolled the pictures back and slowed them down you could see someone come just opposite the camera, with his back to it. Someone taller than us. In an Iona blazer.

'He opened your locker, and bent down. You couldn't see who it was or what he was doing—just the back of his head. Then he stood up and closed the locker door and locked it. If he had turned to the left then and gone back out he might never have been caught—he would have walked back out of the frame.

'But he turned right round—because he wanted to put something in Margaret's locker too. And Margaret's locker is right beside mine. The camera got him full on then. And now the police have a copy too.'

Johnny felt sure he knew what was coming, but even so it came as a shock.

'It was Conor Maguire, Johnny.'

Anny gasped. She put her hands to her face and began to shake. Mrs Walsh thought she understood, and began to comfort her, as did Mary—her face the strangest combination of tears and smiles. But only one other person in that room knew fully what those four words had meant to her. And he wasn't able to see anything clearly himself at that moment.

'Maybe that's enough for now,' said Mrs Walsh anxiously, looking at both of them.

'No,' said Johnny. 'I'm all right. Tell us the rest. My Da will want to know it all too.'

Mrs Walsh took a moment to be reassured by Anny. She nodded to Eddy then.

'You can see the bag with the tablets in his hand, Johnny, before he put it in Margaret's locker. You can see it clearly. That's on the record now—and no one can wipe it off. Aidan has witnessed it.'

Mrs Walsh added something then.

'And Mr Maroney has told Mr Ferguson his technician will swear the date and time are accurate.'

'What does Conor say?' asked Margaret. She was weeping tears of relief too. They hadn't been dammed up nearly as long as Johnny's Mum's but they were made of the same stuff.

Eddy shook his head and looked over to Mrs Walsh.

'Nothing, Margaret,' said Mrs Walsh indignantly. 'Absolutely nothing. When he was shown that piece of video in Mr Ferguson's office he wouldn't answer a single question. He wouldn't even confirm or deny he was at Johnny's and Margaret's lockers at that time, or give himself an alibi. He just sat there with a set face—and then said: "I want to phone my Dad."

'So Mr Ferguson phoned Mr Maguire. *He* said Conor shouldn't be asked any more questions—he would come to the school immediately to collect him. He asked that Gavan be told he would be collected also. Then he asked to talk to Conor.

'Conor just said 'right' a few times. Then he put the phone down and said: "I'm not to say anything else. You're to leave me alone until my Dad comes. I'll get my things and wait in the hall for Gavan."

'He just stood up then, and walked out! No apology to anyone for anything. As if nothing had happened.'

'What'll happen to him?' Johnny asked.

'He'll be suspended immediately, of course. Then the board of governors will decide. Mr Maguire will not have any voice or vote in that decision either, of course. I can't see how Conor could be allowed to stay at the school.

'But that's the least of it, Johnny,' Mrs Walsh went on. 'The police now know that you were being falsely incriminated—framed—in the school, at almost the same moment you were being beaten up on your way home. They must be looking hard for a connection. I'm not a lawyer, but words like conspiracy, assault, and maybe even worse, come to mind.

'It'll be a big scandal,' she continued. 'The biggest Derry has had in a while. Conor Maguire could go to prison over this, and there will be consequences for Gavan too.'

'Why Gavan?' asked Eddy.

'It was Gavan who put that Year Nine boy up to telling that story about Johnny. The boy has admitted it. He said he was threatened and bribed to do it on Wednesday. He was even told exactly when to tell the story to his mother. He's a bit of a loner, it seems. Gavan has been calling him vicious names all term, and he just couldn't take it any longer. He's sorry.'

Johnny nodded as best he could. 'It's not his fault,' he said.

'Mr Ferguson says it's the worst thing to happen in his time as principal of Iona,' Mrs Walsh went on. 'Conor Maguire might have become head boy next year if it hadn't been for this. Mr Ferguson wants to know why all this happened, so he'll be asking—and I'm sure the police will too.

'That's enough for now, everyone,' Mrs Walsh finished. 'You can all come back tomorrow. Johnny needs rest, and Margaret also. You all do.'

'I've got to tell my Mum, too,' said Margaret. 'She's waiting outside.'

'Say goodbye then,' said Mrs Walsh.

Before she left Mary made sure to find Johnny's free hand—to give it a tight squeeze. She was about to go, but then turned back and put her head down to his, and touched his forehead gently with her own, with her eyes closed.

Margaret went to Johnny's mother, and gave her a close hug. Anny returned this fully, and kissed her on the cheek.

Eddy took Johnny's free hand then. 'I'm a real detective after all, amn't I?'

'You're the best one I know,' said Johnny. 'You can catch criminals even before they do anything. Thanks!'

His Mum came then and hugged Eddy as hard as she could.

Anny sat looking at Johnny then awhile. Johnny could see she was trying to take in everything that had just happened.

'Your Da will need to know everything, Johnny,' she said eventually. 'I'll have to tell him that you know what Hugh Maguire did to him. And I'd better tell him now, before the police start asking more questions.'

Johnny gave the smallest possible nod.

'It'll be OK, Ma. He's better now, isn't he?'

'He's better than he was, but he's still going to be ... upset. Will you be all right on your own for a while?'

'Yeh.'

'You mustn't answer any questions from the police, mind, until we're back!'

'OK.'

She left, but put her head in again straight away.

'You and Mary—you're fond of one another, aren't you?'

'Yes, Ma.'

'I thought so. I'm glad. You make me think back.'

Johnny was on his own then, for over an hour. Most of the time he was remembering exactly how Mary had been looking at him, and how it had felt to have her forehead resting gently on his own, with her hair falling around him.

Then his parents came back, together. Kevy was white. He sat looking at Johnny for almost a half minute before deciding what to say.

'That day I asked you about Gavan Maguire—why didn't you tell me?'

'You didn't ask me the right question. He was annoying me—but you just asked me if he had hit me. And he hadn't then.'

'But how could you think of facing him on your own, with that thug of a brother standing behind him?'

'I wasn't on my own. My friends stuck up for me—I told you that.'

'And that's why they had to get you on your own, isn't it?' Kevy said.

'I suppose.'

Kevy was silent then for a while.

'Why did you stick up for me, when I was ... giving you a bad time?'

'You're my Da. I knew Ma was telling me the truth about you, why you were ... not well.'

Kevy looked at him a long while then, and at Anny.

'I thought I had nothing!' he said then. 'I didn't know how much

I had!'

He bent over to Johnny then, and did something he hadn't done in ages. He mussed his hair.

Two other policemen arrived soon after, in plain clothes. One was much older than the other. They questioned Johnny for half- an-hour, and would have gone on longer if his parents had let them. Kevy and Anny had told Johnny to answer truthfully any question he was asked, but not to go beyond that. When the detectives left they knew the main events concerning himself and Gavan and Conor Maguire since the start of term in Iona, but nothing yet about the story of Kevy and Hugh Maguire.

'They're interested anyway,' said Kevy then. 'I suppose there's still history between the police and Hugh Maguire, even though the war is supposed to be over.'

'And we're stuck in the middle, as usual,' said Anny.

The last visitor Johnny received that day, in the afternoon, was the principal of Iona College, Mr Ferguson—looking serious and upset.

'We nearly made a bad mistake about you, young man,' he said.

'I must make sure not to make another, mustn't I?'

'Does that mean we can all stay?' asked Johnny immediately.

'One thing at a time, Johnny,' said Mr Ferguson. 'First we need much better security in school. And I need to find out the whole story of what happened this year between yourself and Gavan and Conor Maguire. The board of governors will want a full report.

'On the other matter I can tell you, though, that I've heard from Monsignor Murphy. He says he has made an important discovery. He said it would take too long to explain on the 'phone. He has some more reading to do, he says. It'll take about a week. Then he'll want to see you all again. You should be well enough for that by then, I hope.'

He was looking questioningly at Anny, who nodded.

'Mrs Walsh will be back to talk to you then—about all the bullying that has gone on. No holding back, mind. This is far too serious a matter for you to have any reason to protect anyone who has broken the law. Martin Cassidy's parents have come to see me too. Martin told them how you stood up for him months ago and he wanted to do the same for you. No holding back on any of that now, understood?"

Johnny nodded. There was no point in keeping from Mr Ferguson what he had already told the police, not now.

'If it's the last thing I do as principal, I'll put a stop to organised bullying at Iona College! That's a promise.'

The principal looked at all three of them, then, in a determined way, and left.

'I suppose he's afraid we'll think he wasn't doing his job,' said Anny then.

'Aye,' said Kevy. 'That he is. He's maybe even afraid of a lawsuit.'

Johnny found that strange. He didn't blame the school at all for what had happened.

'It's not his fault,' he said. 'I like Mr Ferguson. How could anyone be up to the Maguires?'

At the end of the following week, with his right arm still in plaster, Johnny was allowed to go home. His arm and ribs still hurt, but he was bored with hospital, especially the food, and wanted to be in his own room again.

When he booted his laptop he found he was online, with welcoming email from his friends waiting.

Already a letter had arrived in Johnny's home from a well known firm of Derry solicitors. Acting on behalf of the two Maguire boys the lawyers asked for the address of Johnny's solicitor.

Kevy and Anny had already talked about getting legal representation over the issue of freedom of speech in Iona College. Now, after a brief discussion they went ahead with this plan.

'What do you think the Maguires want?' asked Johnny of his parents.

'Maybe they want us to go easy—to see if we would go for a lesser charge than the worst one,' said Anny.

'Some hope!' said Kevy.

From that moment an idea began to take shape in Johnny's mind. It grew when they heard from the solicitors that the police had caught one of the three men who had beaten him up. This man had then given evidence about the other two, and about the Maguires' organisation of the assault.

By then, however, something even more momentous had happened. Mr Ferguson asked all four bridgers to prepare for a meeting with Monsignor Murphy just ten days before Easter.

※

'I've asked you all to come to hear Monsignor Murphy summarise his report. We'll all have a discussion then on how to proceed.'

It was the Tuesday afternoon of the second-last week of term. Mr Ferguson was speaking—in the large imposing room in Iona College used by the board of governors. He sat at the top of a long gleaming antique mahogany table. Large mirrors and oil paintings—mostly of former principals—decorated the walls. There was a strong smell of furniture polish. On the wall behind the principal loomed a large version of the school crest.

To Mr Ferguson's right, along the side of the table, sat Johnny with his parents, and then Eddy and Margaret with their parents. Opposite Margaret sat Mary McNevin and her dad. Next sat Mrs Walsh, with the Monsignor alongside, and Miss Doherty. Lastly, on Mr Ferguson's left, came Dr McGinnis. Dressed in a smart grey suit, but without his academic gown, he sat with his arms folded and his face downcast—a different person from the one Johnny had seen storming out of that interview before Christmas.

Johnny now felt almost completely better after the experience that had put him in hospital. His arm was still in a cast, however, and he found that he was more nervous when he had to walk along the road past the place where the assault had happened—even though Kevy would never let him do so alone.

Monsignor Murphy had placed on the table in front of him three hardbound books. In his hand he held some sheets of paper, to which he referred occasionally as he spoke.

'To begin with I must say how impressed I was by the sincerity of all of you young people, and of Dr McGinnis also, of course. There is no question that all of you are concerned for the truth. Dr McGinnis especially has a heavy responsibility for maintaining the wholeness of Catholic truth in the school.

'I was at first puzzled by the novelty of what the young people were saying. They had apparently invented a completely new term to describe something they saw in the Bible. They have a different way of looking at the bible world—a way that allows them to interpret their own world, putting Jesus at the centre of some of its most critical problems.

'At the same time I was impressed by the fact their term 'copy- wanting' did indeed describe accurately many of the behaviours of modern culture—such as over-consumption and violence. I could see straight away that if copy-wanting was indeed what the bible calls coveting, then it is an even more important book than we had all realised.

'So I went looking for any evidence that might support that viewpoint. Among theologians I found almost nothing at first, but a younger acquaintance suggested I take a look at the writings of someone who is not a theologian—a Frenchman called René Girard.

'Professor Girard has many qualifications. First, he is a historian. Next, he is a learned literary academic—that is, someone who taught world literature at university level in the United States for many years. Third, he is a philosopher.

Fourth, he is a cultural anthropologist—someone who tries to understand why we humans organise ourselves the way we do. In particular he has put forward a theory of the origins of religion and violence, a theory that is now widely discussed by other academics in the same fields. He uses his exceptional knowledge of the world's literatures to support this theory.

'His most important ideas centre on what he calls *mimetic desire*—desire that unconsciously mimics the desire of someone else. You will see straight away that 'mimetic desire' describes exactly the same thing as the young people's term, 'copy-wanting'. It sounds grander, more impressive—but 'copy-wanting' arises out of simpler language, and may therefore be easier to understand.

'Professor Girard is equally convinced that mimetic desire and covetousness, are exactly the same thing. As a Catholic he is convinced that the Bible is the central text of all world literature, revealing the power of covetousness to cause problems for everyone.

'He goes on to argue that covetousness was always the root source of human violence—and that the gospels especially reveal this. Jesus was accused because he stood out against injustice—and powerful people copied that accusation also, because by killing him they could avoid the kind of confused violence that often broke out in those times, with unpredictable consequences. All were covetous, but by pointing the finger of accusation at Jesus they could avoid the consequences of their own sins.

'I should say at this point that I found Professor Girard's work not always easy to read so I would not recommend it for you four students just yet. However, there are able accounts written by others that will be accessible to your teachers.'

Looking across the table, Johnny could see that Dr McGinnis was unusually troubled. He unfolded and refolded his arms, sometimes gripping the table with both hands. His notebook was nowhere in sight.

'I have discovered that already some teachers of Religion in Catholic schools have experimented with some of these ideas—as a means of explaining profound problems such as the crucifixion, and the idea of original sin. I have spoken with a few of them, and they say the results are promising.

'This development in our understanding of covetousness does not, I believe, amount to a rejection of anything the Church holds to be central to faith. There may be room for a difference of opinion about that, but it is my recommendation that since these ideas are being discussed in the wider church by theologians, philosophers and others, the novelty of these ideas does not justify their suppression in this school.

'So, I believe, these young people—and the others they have influenced—should not be prevented from discussing and advancing their ideas, provided they do so in a way that is duly respectful to those who differ.'

Dr McGinnis seemed about to say something at this point, when the principal, Mr Ferguson, intervened.

'I have decided to accept this recommendation…'

'*Yay—we can stay*,' shouted Eddy, 'and we can say what we think—isn't that it?'

Next moment, when Mr Ferguson nodded, Margaret and Mary were laughing, weeping and hugging all at once, having met at one end of the table—and Eddy had left his seat to meet Johnny and celebrate by joining his fist to Johnny's good one. It took many seconds before the principal could proceed.

'I have invited you all here to see if we can restore good relationships—accepting the expression of different points of view. I am impressed with the fact that other heads of department in the school, especially languages, Geography, History and English, would prefer this solution to the problem. And that some able senior pupils have also petitioned for freedom of thought and expression on the issue.'

The silence that followed was broken at last by Dr McGinnis.

'I am grateful to Monsignor Murphy for accepting that I was sincere in regarding the ideas of these young people as likely to be confusing, and therefore potentially dangerous. However, I was seriously at fault in declaring Johnny and Margaret to be outside the Catholic tradition, without investigating as thoroughly as the Monsignor has done— and in accusing them, Mrs Walsh and Miss Doherty, of dissent. I apologise to all of them for that, and to the parents of the young people too.'

There were murmurs of acceptance from all to whom the teacher had spoken so penitently. But the head of Religion hadn't finished.

'There's something else. On the day after Monsignor Murphy had explained to me the results of his research I happened to be reading again the story of how Saint Columba had come to exile himself on the island of Iona so long ago. Historians generally agree that the most likely explanation was that he blamed himself for a dispute that had led to a war in which many had died.

'That dispute was over the ownership of a handwritten copy of the Psalms—a copy that Columba himself had made, after borrowing an earlier manuscript from its owner, St Finnian. Those two saints both claimed ownership of that same copy. They both came from powerful families—and, according to this account, the most serious violence followed.

'I cannot now think of a better word to describe their problem than Johnny's and Margaret's word, copy-wanting. I also find it now impossible to think of that problem under the heading of 'materialism'—as those two saints were both convinced they had a claim on something that was in essence spiritual, the written word of scripture.

'It seems that my own education was not complete when I adopted a fixed, immovable position on this matter too quickly. Overwork may be part of my excuse, so I now feel that I need to take at least one year out to put my head fully around this entirely different way of approaching scripture. What I will do then I cannot say. Mr Ferguson has given me a year's leave to do that, after which it may well prove advisable for me to take up a different post in a different institution. This school may well deserve a permanent rest from my fixed ideas.'

'Thank you for that, Dr McGinnis,' the principal went on.

'Monsignor Murphy had a few other proposals to make, but perhaps these must wait now?'

'There is one that might still proceed, Principal,' said Monsignor Murphy. He turned towards Mrs Walsh.

'One of Professor Girard's most important works deals with the theme of mimetic desire in Shakespeare. I should like Mrs Walsh to read it and to write an assessment of its significance for the teaching of Shakespeare, and indeed English literature generally, in Catholic schools.'

'Mrs Walsh?' Mr Ferguson looked towards the head of English.

'Of course, principal,' said the bridgers' form teacher. 'I should be only too delighted!' She took the book the monsignor passed to her.

'Other heads of department, for instance Geography, could perhaps do similar studies of the importance of covetousness, understood as copy-wanting, as a theme in those subjects,' the monsignor continued. 'These children and their friends in the senior years would be glad to help, I'm sure?'

The four bridgers agreed immediately.

'All of this may also lead to Iona College joining with other Catholic schools to seek changes to Northern Ireland courses of study and the examinations systems. This would mean that no-one at Iona need suffer in any way from adopting and expressing ideas unknown to the present system.'

'I will pass on that suggestion,' said Mr Ferguson. 'Is there anything left to discuss before we take refreshments?'

He looked around the table, but found only smiles and shaking heads.

'Very well, then,' said Mr Ferguson. 'My congratulations to you four. Your first year here has been in every way exceptional. In particular it has helped us to get to grips with a problem of bullying that had become more serious than we had realised. We will hope for even greater things in the future.'

—∘∘⊰❉⊱∘∘—

Kevy wouldn't let Johnny go out anywhere on his own in the days that followed. He went with him and Anny even to the Easter reconciliation service on the Monday before the feast—and to one of the confessing priests for the same blessing. Then on Good Friday he strictly observed the fast also. At the vigil Mass on Easter Saturday evening he came up to communion with them both, with his hands resting on Johnny's shoulders.

That night all four bridgers were visited by their bridging guides and told they had passed their apprenticeships.

'There will always be more to learn, of course,' said Mick to Johnny. 'But now, on this night, it's time to rejoice that all will forever be well.'

In due course Mrs Cliona Walsh became principal of Iona College. Arona Gilsenan came third in the *Fame School* competition and got her recording contract. Conor Maguire faced a trial that sentenced him to a year in prison—with only six months of that suspended. Gavan received a severe reprimand from a different judge, and chose to change school. The boy he had set out to intimidate, Martin Cassidy, ended the year by winning the Top Eight award, the shield for all-round academic excellence.

Also, in the summer, a bold-printed two-column apology appeared in Derry newspapers from Hugh Maguire— for injustices committed under his command during the

Troubles, with specific mention of false accusations against Kevin Gerard Mullan in a specific year.

And already, in the second week of April, Mary McNevin's Mum had fallen into non-stop tears and begun to come out of the worst of her depression. She came home finally in early May.

Long before all that happened, however, the bridgers had celebrated Easter together—as well as Mary's birthday, which fell on the same day.

———∞∞❧❦❧∞∞———

'Meet Hester McCauley everyone. Hester—these are my friends in Iona.' Mary introduced the other bridgers, and Catherine Canning, Kieran Lowney, and Martin Cassidy.

All eight were in Margaret's home on the Saturday after Easter. Kieran and Martin had been peppering Eddy with questions in the last days of the term before Easter—especially how it had come about that the Maguires were no longer at the school and how he, Johnny and Margaret had survived the ban by the head of religion. So, while Eddy played inscrutable, the bridgers had agreed a plan.

Hester was blond and willowy, with a ready smile—and she had brought her violin.

'First, here we go everyone,' said Mary, passing out sheets.

And off they went with the complete words for *The Chain that Binds the Earth*. Between each verse Hester came in with different violin solos.

Why do I want what others want?
Why copy others' wanting?
I don't need what I so crave,
Why this daily haunting?

When TV tells me what I need -
That is copy-wanting.
When you show off what I don't have —
Zap! – I'm copy-wanting.

Why can't I see what others need
When I'm copy-wanting?
Children cry but I don't heed -
When I'm copy-wanting.

If I must have what you must have,
We'll find we can't share it,
We must fight for all of it —
Wars come – who can bear it?

Why do we want what others want,
Why borrow their desiring?
Is it because we fear their jeers,
And long for their admiring?

If all must have what some can get,
Can Earth survive this getting?
Will wanting stop our Home's upset -
Or quicken its upsetting?

This is the chain that binds the Earth
Imprisoning us in sorrow.

It leaves us with no hope, no peace,
No beauty, no tomorrow.

Did someone come to break this chain?
Whose love is not desiring?
Oh yes he came – we killed him, yet
He lives – us all inspiring.

Kieran and Martin appeared to enjoy the singing and playing too, Johnny thought. Even so they were getting restless, in the absence of answers to all their questions.

'You promised to tell me how you came to write that, Mary' said Hester. 'Can you please do that now?'

'It didn't come just from me, Hester,' said Mary. 'That's why we all needed to be here. Johnny?'

'Kieran, and Martin and Cathy, do you remember that first day in September last?' Johnny began, turning first to the boy he had befriended on his first day—the same boy who had sat with him in class after that, and helped him with his maths and science homework. 'The Friday, when Mrs Walsh asked us to make up an organisation and then write an application to join?'

'Yes,' said Kieran. 'And you thought up something called the b…bridgers.'

'Yes,' said Johnny. 'Well, today the four of us want to tell you three, and Hester too—all about the bridgers …'

- End -

ABOUT THE AUTHOR

Sean O'Conaill taught History and Current Affairs to young adults in Northern Ireland during three decades of civil conflict ('The Troubles'). He retired in 1996 to write on the developing wider world crises of violence and the ecosystem—using insights gained from the courses he had taught and from young people impatient for answers.

Convinced that the world's worst problems have always stemmed from a mistaken human search for personal prestige—the pursuit of admiration—and that the Christian Gospel story is above all a revelation of this, he defended this position in Scattering the Proud (1999) and in over one hundred articles in major Irish periodicals.

The Chain that Binds the Earth draws these themes together in a work of fiction for young adults.

All author royalties for this edition of
The Chain That Binds the Earth will be
devoted to the mental health of young people
in Northern Ireland, sorely tested in the
aftermath of conflict.

9 798893 566963